A.J. MACKENZIE

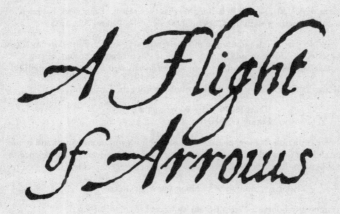

A Flight of Arrows

D1464527

CANELO

First published in the United Kingdom in 2021 by

Canelo
31 Helen Road
Oxford OX2 0DF
United Kingdom

A CIP catalogue record for this book is available from the British Library.

Print ISBN 978 1 80032 279 0
Ebook ISBN 978 1 80032 278 3

Look for more great books at www.canelo.co

Printed and bound in Great Britain by Clays Ltd, Elcograf S.p.A.

3

To John, Richard, Jenny, Mary, and Armand – it all began with you

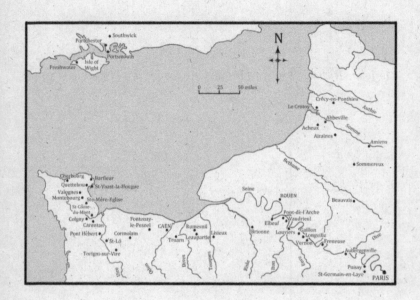

Prologue

Freshwater, 6th of July, 1346
Evening

The king and his court demanded fresh butter for their bread, so in the end they had to bring two of the cows ashore. Garnet and Marigold were brought up on deck and hoisted over the side of the cog into a smaller boat. They looked so funny, Nell thought, hanging in the slings with their legs dangling, mooing with distress, and when Garnet finally landed in the boat, she kicked one of the sailors so hard he fell overboard. The other men cheered her for a stout lass who didn't take nonsense from anyone.

The chief herdsman should have gone with the cows, but he was heaving his guts out with seasickness, so Nell went instead. The sailors handed her down into the boat and she held the cows firmly by their halters as they were rowed ashore. Once on dry land, she herded them to the nearby manor of Freshwater, right at the western end of the Isle of Wight. Every so often she turned to look out through the rain at the English ships, riding at anchor with their sails furled, unable to make headway against the strong west wind. She thought about the thousands of soldiers packed inside them like saltfish in a barrel, many of them being just as sick as the chief herdsman.

They were expecting her at Freshwater, and the yeoman of the kitchen, Master Coloyne, showed her a byre where she could stable the cows and do the evening milking. Most of the royal household was there, although the king had taken himself off to Carisbrooke Castle a few miles away. Master Clerebaud the sauce-maker reckoned it was because the beds were softer there. After milking, she warmed herself by the hearth, and then sat down with the scullery lads and maids to eat hot pottage with beans and onions and some bacon thrown in. The pottage warmed them all and kept out the cold. 'You'd never believe it was July,' someone said.

'Never mind,' said Master Coloyne. 'It'll be warm enough when we get to France.'

'Why will it be warm in France?' Nell asked.

'Further south,' said Master Clerebaud. 'Stands to reason.'

It was growing late by the time they finished eating. They offered her a blanket in the kitchen to sleep on, but Nell wanted to keep an eye on Marigold, who hadn't given as much milk as usual and might be suffering from the long confinement aboard ship. She accepted the blanket and went back to the byre to check on the cows, then lay down in a pile of straw, pulling the blanket over her and falling asleep. After a while, she slipped into a dream, in which she could hear voices, quiet like they were coming from a long way away.

Curse this weather. If the wind stays against us, the king could abandon the entire expedition and go home. All that preparation and expense, and nothing to show for it.

Calm yourself. The king's heart is set on this venture. He won't turn back, not now.

Something in the straw tickled her nose and she woke up. She heard again the two voices from the dream, only it wasn't a dream and the men were right outside the byre, speaking softly.

'This delay could ruin everything.'

'The weather won't last forever,' the second voice said. 'The wind will change, and as soon as it does we will cross over to France. Trust me, I know the king as well as anyone. He'll not turn back now.'

'And Bertrand? If the army doesn't arrive when expected, he and the other Norman loyalists will think we have played him false. What do we do about him?'

Nell lay still, listening hard. Their English was accented, and she had to concentrate to understand what they were saying. The worried man sounded like he came from the West Country; she thought the other might be from somewhere in the north.

'We need to get word to him,' the second man said. 'Get a messenger across to Normandy and tell him the king still intends to land at Saint-Vaast but it will be later than planned. He needs to hold his men together and wait.'

'And how am I meant to get a message to France? My ships cannot sail into a headwind, any more than the king's can.'

'You have money,' the northerner said. 'And as you keep telling me, with the right amount of money, anything is possible. Make it happen.'

The West Country man growled under his breath. 'Oh aye, very well. I'll see what I can do. What about Harcourt?'

'If Bertrand succeeds, then Harcourt will be discredited. Do you see now why this is so important? You must get that message to Bertrand.'

'I will. Christ, now it's raining again. A pox on this bloody weather!'

The voices faded as the two men walked away. Silence fell. Nell lay for a moment in the darkness, trying to work out the meaning of what she had heard. They needed to send a message across to Normandy, to warn someone called Bertrand. But who was Bertrand? An enemy? Or one of the king's Norman friends?

She wondered if she should tell someone what she had overheard. But she was a fourteen-year-old cowherd from Hampshire, and she had no idea who to approach or whether they would listen to her. She couldn't tell her own master, the chief herdsman, because he was still sick aboard the transport. She would tell Master Coloyne tomorrow, she decided, and let him decide the matter.

Pleased at having reached a decision, she fell back into sleep.

1

As the northern man had predicted, the bad weather did not last forever. On the 11ᵗʰ of July, the clouds rolled away and the wind changed. The invasion force unfurled its sails, swept down the Solent and out into the open sea, turning its bows south towards Normandy.

At dawn on the 12ᵗʰ, the first ships arrived in the Bay of Saint-Vaast and the leading companies of the army came ashore. Archers and men-at-arms jumped out of their boats into the shallow water, alert and looking for the enemy. Some climbed up the steep escarpment overlooking the bay, taking up defensive positions around the village of Quettehou. Others ran towards a row of ships drawn up on the sand near the little fishing port of Saint-Vaast. Within a few minutes, these were burning fiercely.

King Edward III of England came ashore mid morning, landing on the beach beneath a sky stained with smoke. Clad in armour and a surcoat bearing the royal arms, three snarling gold leopards on a field of red, he stepped out of the boat and stood for a moment, hand resting on his sword hilt, while he gazed at the scene around him.

'I have come to claim what is mine,' he said. He took a long stride up the beach, tripped, and fell flat on his face.

His courtiers paused in horror, then rushed to help him to his feet. Thomas Beauchamp, Earl of Warwick and Marshal of England, coughed behind his hand. 'It seems your land is eager to embrace you, sire.'

'Don't be sarcastic, Thomas,' the king said curtly, brushing sand off his surcoat and wiping blood from his nose. 'What is our position?'

'We have met with no resistance, sire. Both Saint-Vaast and Quettehou are abandoned.'

'Any sign of the enemy?'

'Not yet.' Warwick paused. 'But they were here, and quite recently too. And what is more, they were expecting us.'

The king stared at him. 'How do you know?'

'We found the remains of campfires near Saint-Vaast.' Warwick pointed to the smouldering remains of the ships. 'And those vessels were fitted out for war. They had castles fore and aft, and some were armed with mangonels. There is no doubt about it, sire. Robert Bertrand and his men intended to mount a strong defence of this place.'

Blood continued to drip down into the king's moustache. His secretary handed him a square of linen. Irritably he wiped the blood away. 'But how did they know we were landing *here*?' he demanded. 'How did they know about Saint-Vaast?'

Warwick shrugged his shoulders, not an easy thing to do when wearing a mail coat with plate armour over top. 'We have spies in Paris. We must assume the adversary also has spies in London.'

The king looked dissatisfied. 'So where are they now? Why did they not stay and fight?'

'We don't know.' Warwick paused again. 'The first element of the plan is complete, sire. Lord Cobham, Sir Thomas Holland and the Red Company have established a defensive line to protect the beach. Shall we proceed with the landing?'

The king nodded, wiping his nose again. 'Make it so. Where is my son?'

Edmund Bray, esquire to the Prince of Wales, stepped forward. 'His Highness has just come ashore, sire. He sent me to ask what your orders might be.'

More ships were moving into the bay, dark red sails glowing in the strong sunlight. 'Now that the prince is here, I think we should hold the ceremony without delay,' the king said. 'I shall first confer the accolade of knighthood on my son and heir. After that, as a demonstration that I am king of France, Godefroi d'Harcourt will do homage to me for his lands in Normandy. That will hearten the troops and put the fear of God into the rest of the Norman nobles. It will make good reading back home, too.'

Warwick raised his eyebrows. 'I am certain it will, sire. But is this the right time? We need to get the rest of the army ashore first, find the enemy and learn what strength they have. Robert Bertrand and his troops might still be in the area. With respect, sire, I think we have better things to do.'

Another man, stocky and dark-haired in a blue surcoat with white trefoils over his gleaming armour, shook his head. 'The purpose of this campaign is to take and hold Normandy,' he said. 'If we can wrest our adversary's richest and most important province from his control, his power will begin to crumble. His nobles will turn against him and he will be forced to make peace, on terms advantageous to us.'

'Get to the point, Eustace,' the king said impatiently.

'We cannot hold Normandy without the support of the Norman nobility, sire. You said it yourself. My lord of Harcourt's pledge of fealty to you, especially with fifteen thousand troops at your back, will concentrate their minds. Once they learn that one of the most important Norman barons has publicly backed you, others will follow his example.'

'Yes,' said the king, dabbing at his nose again. 'Yes, I am persuaded, Eustace. Where shall we do this?'

Eustace Maninghem, the lord of Rowton, pointed towards Quettehou up on the escarpment. 'What about the church up there? I believe it is dedicated to Saint-Vigor, one of the patron saints of Normandy. Perfect symbolism, sire, don't you think?'

'Quettehou is on the perimeter of our position,' Warwick said. 'We have sent out scouts to the west, but have yet to hear reports from them. If Bertrand attacks during the ceremony, you and the prince will be vulnerable, sire. If we are going to do this, do it down here, on the beach.'

Rowton shook his head. 'We should hold the ceremony in a sacred place, to show the people that God is on our side. God himself will be witness to the oaths that are sworn there. I am sure the king's house-hold knights will be able to protect him and the prince.' He looked at Warwick. 'And you said it yourself, my friend. The enemy have departed. For the moment, at least, I think the danger is hypothetical.'

The king rubbed his chin. 'What do you say, Thomas?'

Warwick knew when he was beaten. He smiled. 'I defer to the sage advice of my friend Lord Rowton.'

'Good,' said the king. 'It is settled. Send word to all the captains, and instruct them to join us as soon as they land. God is welcome to attend this ceremony, but I want plenty of mortal witnesses as well. Master Bray, tell the Prince of Wales to attend on me at the church in Quettehou at midday.'

Bray bowed his head. 'Yes, sire.'

The king waved a hand in dismissal. 'Thomas,' he said to the marshal, as Bray turned away, 'I want to know how the devil Robert Bertrand knew we were landing at Saint-Vaast. Find out for me, will you?'

—

Bray hurried back along the beach through curtains of drifting smoke. More men were coming ashore, men-at-arms in glittering mail and plate, archers with their longbows slung across their backs, Welsh and Cornish spearmen shouting to each other in their own tongue. Skittish horses, released from confinement aboard ship, pranced and galloped on the beach while grooms tried to round them up. Further on, men were dragging wagon boxes up onto the sand and jacking them up to fit them with axles and wheels.

Sniffing the smoke in the air and quivering like a hunting dog waiting to be let off the lead, the sixteen-year-old Prince of Wales stood waiting by the boats. His esquires and attendants gathered around him, the golden dragon standard of Wales floating overhead in the wind. 'Well?' he demanded. 'Did you find him?'

'Yes, Highness,' said Bray. 'We are summoned to join the king at midday, at the church in Quettehou.'

'Oh yes, the ceremony,' the prince said carelessly. 'My father is going to claim the throne of France. Again. Where are the enemy, Edmund?' he demanded. 'When do we get to do some fighting?'

'Patience, Highness,' Bray said, smiling. 'As part of the ceremony, his Grace will also confer on you the honour of knighthood.'

'He's going to make me a knight?'

'That is what he said, Highness.'

'Yes!' With a clash of armour, the prince raised one clenched fist in the air. 'At last I shall have my spurs! Now everyone will see that I am no longer a child!'

The young Earl of Salisbury, the prince's closest friend, clapped him on the back with delight. Fitz-Simon, the standard-bearer, waved the gold dragon with enthusiasm. The others cheered, some more dutifully than others. Roger Mortimer, a tall young man in a blue and gold surcoat, folded his arms across his chest. The prince's herald, wearing a tabard in the royal colours stiff with gold embroidery over a plain tunic and hose, cleared his throat.

'With the greatest of respect, Highness, may I remind you that it is customary to reward the bearer of good news.'

'What? Oh, yes, of course!' The prince turned to Bray. Slipping off one gauntlet, he pulled a ring from his finger and pressed it into Bray's hand. 'Take this, Edmund, as a token of thanks for all the good services you have done me. Not just today, but in the past too.' He smiled, his face vivid with excitement. 'And also in the future, of course.'

'It is I who must thank you, Highness, for allowing me to serve.' The gift was a generous one; the ring was solid gold with a cabochon ruby. Selling it would recoup a fair amount of the money Bray and his father had spent on equipping him for this campaign.

The herald cleared his throat again.

'What is it now?' asked the prince.

'It is also customary that when the king's eldest son is knighted, he in turn knights some of his followers. Those he deems worthy of the honour, that is.'

All the other young men stopped and stared at the prince. 'I see,' he said. 'Well, of course, why not? Will,' he said, turning to Salisbury, 'you must be the first, my friend.'

Salisbury bowed his head. 'Highness, you do me great honour.'

'Nonsense. It is no more than you deserve. Now, who else… why, Roger, of course! Knighting you would really bury the past, wouldn't it? People will finally stop talking about your grandfather, and how he was executed for high treason and all that.'

Mortimer bowed stiffly. 'Thank you, Highness. Like my lord of Salisbury, I am sensible of the honour you do me.'

'And my valiant esquires, of course, Edmund Bray and William Ros. And...' The prince looked around at the circle of eager young faces. 'Oh, hang it. My friends are gallant fellows, each and every one. I shall knight them all. I can do that, can't I?'

'Of course, Highness,' replied the herald. 'It is a very generous gesture.'

The prince looked pleased. 'What about you, Merrivale? I could knight you too, if you wish.'

The herald smiled and bowed. Unlike the men around him, he wore no armour and there was no sword at his belt. 'Thank you, Highness. But it would not be appropriate.'

'No, I suppose not.' The prince looked up, catching sight of a familiar figure further along the beach. 'Oh look, there is Sir Bartholomew! I must go and tell him the news.'

He galloped away down the beach with a clatter of metal, all gawky arms and legs. Salisbury followed him like an attentive lapdog. The others watched them go.

'Now they will see that I am no longer a child,' someone mimicked.

'There's certainly one advantage to being a knight,' Mortimer said. 'We won't have to wipe his snotty little nose any more. Or his arse.'

'Careful,' Bray cautioned. 'We are still in his retinue. And he is the king's son.'

The corpse of Mortimer's grandfather had hung from a gibbet at Tyburn for two days, dangling in the wind until his lover, the king's mother, received permission to take it down. 'Damn that,' Mortimer said darkly. 'I am a better man than that *boy* will ever be. Mark my words, my friends. The day will come when I bow the knee to no one.'

Sunlight flowed golden through the windows of the church of Saint-Vigor. The king, standing with his back to the altar, was haloed with light. His polished armour shone dazzling silver, and the leopards on his surcoat were a golden blaze. His nose had stopped bleeding.

More than a hundred men were gathered inside the church. Looking around, Bray saw the king's friend Lord Rowton standing with Warwick and the Earl of Northampton, the Constable of England. A couple of younger knights were with them, Sir John Grey and Sir Richard Percy, the captains of the Red Company. Both men were high in Warwick's favour, but Bray's nose wrinkled a little. He had met the pair back at Portchester before the army embarked. Percy was good company, but he thought Grey was superior and smug.

The king raised one hand. Silence fell inside the church. From outside they could hear a gentle murmur, the bustle of the army coming ashore on the beach below, and nearer at hand, the tread of restless feet, archers from Sir Thomas Holland's retinue guarding the church.

'Kneel, my son,' King Edward said.

The Prince of Wales knelt before his father, hands clasped in front of him. The king drew his sword and held it up, a ribbon of steel shining in the sunlight, and then lowered the blade until it rested on the young man's shoulder. His voice rang out, echoing a little off the stone walls.

'Will you swear an oath, by the love of Jesus Christ and His Mother the Blessed Virgin Mary, to uphold the laws and customs of the ancient and honourable order of knighthood? Will you swear to defy anyone who does reproach to God, to your sovereign lord the king, to any woman or orphan or helpless person of any estate, or to any of the aforesaid laws and customs of knighthood?'

The prince's voice was low and quiet. 'I do so swear, before Jesus and the Virgin Mary.'

'Knighthood is an honourable estate, the true occupation of a man of noble blood. For a knight to be true to his faith, he must be a lover of the common weal and the common good, for these things are greater and more necessary than his own good or need. Edward of Woodstock, will you devote yourself to this estate, humbly and truly in the eyes of your king and the Lord?'

'So help me God.'

'He is actually doing this rather well,' Bray whispered to Mortimer. The latter looked sour and said nothing.

'Then be a good and faithful knight, honouring God, your liege lord and your vows just taken.' The king lifted his sword and laid the flat of the blade against the side of his son's neck, holding it there for a moment before withdrawing. 'You may now rise, Sir Edward of Woodstock.'

The prince rose to his feet. Father and son embraced, breastplates and armguards clanking together. 'As a mark of my favour, I now permit you to knight those of your followers whom you deem worthy,' the king said. 'You may summon them now.'

Red-faced with pride, the prince turned to Simon Merrivale. 'Call their names, herald.'

Salisbury was first, of course; Salisbury would always be first. Mortimer followed, reciting his oath in a voice so quiet that people strained to hear. William Ros was next, and then came Bray's turn. He knelt, listening to the prince's young voice as it stumbled a little with excitement. He recited the oath, pleased at how calm his own voice sounded, and felt the cold steel blade against his neck and heard the prince's voice again: 'You may rise now, Sir Edmund Bray.'

He stood waiting while the others were knighted, the words repeating themselves in his mind. *Sir Edmund Bray. Sir Edmund Bray.* Ah, he thought, it does have a nice sound to it. I understand how the prince feels. I am a man of consequence now, deserving of respect.

The ceremony ended and the new knights stepped back. Godefroi d'Harcourt, the Norman exile, a battle-scarred older man in a surcoat decorated with red and gold horizontal bars, limped forward and knelt before the king. 'I, Godefroi d'Harcourt, Vicomte de Saint-Sauveur, renounce my allegiance to the false king and usurper Philippe de Valois, and declare King Edward III to be the rightful king of France and my own liege lord. I will remain faithful to you, sire, even unto death.'

'So be it,' said the king, and he took Harcourt by the hand and drew him to his feet. Harcourt stepped back to join his own Norman retainers. One of them was missing, Bray saw. Well, that was no surprise, given what he had learned back in Portchester.

Absolute silence fell once more. Everyone knew what was coming.

'Hear now my words,' the king said. 'We did not wish for this war. As all men know, I am the rightful king of France; my lady mother is the only surviving child of the old king, Philip IV, and by rights the throne should have passed through her to me. But I was content to forgo my claim, so long as my own lands and those of my lady mother should be left to us in peace. That is all I asked.'

A gentle murmur ran around the church. 'But Philip would not have it so,' the king continued. 'He has chosen war, and resisted all our offers of peace. Very well. By choosing war, he has also chosen his own doom.'

A chorus of agreement echoed off the stone walls. The king's voice grew stronger. 'Before you all, I make this solemn vow. I swear to you by the blood of Christ that we shall prosecute this war to the end. We shall break the usurper's power. We shall do such damage to the might of France that it will wither and blow like dust before the wind of England!'

The crowd shouted, men clashing their gauntleted hands against their breastplates and yelling their approval; and then, cutting through the noise, they heard the sound of a trumpet blowing the alarm.

–

Outside the church, Holland's archers were alert and ready, bows strung and arrows resting in the nock. A company of spearmen from Carmarthenshire came hurrying up from the beach to reinforce them; another band of archers, Tracey's men from Devon, were also moving up the hill, with Hugh Despenser's company close behind them. Men-at-arms crowded around the church door, calling for their horses. Bray spotted his own horse and ran to it, stepping into the saddle and taking the reins from his groom just as Roger Mortimer rode up alongside him. 'Where are the French?' Mortimer asked.

'I don't know.' Bray shaded his eyes against the sun, watching the fields and hedgerows stretching away to the west of the village. 'I can't see anything. Do you suppose it's a false alarm?'

'I hope not. I'd like to do some fighting.'

Bray grinned at him. 'You sound just like the prince.'

'Be very careful,' Mortimer warned.

A scout, another of the Norman exiles, dismounted and knelt before the king. 'I spotted horsemen coming up the road from Valognes, about two miles away, sire. They're riding under a banner, green lion rampant on gold. Bertrand's colours,' he added.

The king turned to Northampton and Warwick, the constable and marshal. 'What do you advise?'

'For your own safety, sire, we should retreat to the beach,' Northampton said.

'Retreat?' The king stared at him. 'Did you not hear what I said just now? We came to seize this country and hold it. How will we do that if we fall back now, without even striking a blow?'

Warwick cleared his throat.

'Take that look off your face,' the king snapped at him. 'I know you advised delay, but what's done is done. Can we hold this position?'

Northampton frowned. He was quite calm, Bray thought. If there was danger, he did not seem very worried about it. Come to that, neither did the king or Warwick. 'How many men does Bertrand have?' the constable asked the scout.

'I am not certain, my lord. At least two or three hundred, possibly more. They had outriders and flank guards, and I was unable to get close.'

Northampton looked at the marshal. 'Further reconnaissance is needed, I think.'

Warwick nodded. 'I will go myself.'

'Take a strong escort,' Northampton said.

'I'll take the Red Company. That should be enough.' Warwick turned his horse.

Mortimer raised a hand, intending to volunteer to go with him, but Bray grabbed his arm and pulled it down. There was something he needed to do, and he was not going to let his friend get in his way. 'My lord of Warwick, may I accompany you?' he asked.

'And me,' Mortimer said quickly.

Other voices joined in. Warwick frowned. 'This is a reconnaissance, not a hunting party. Very well, one of you may join us. Sir Edmund, as you were first to speak, let it be you. We'll give you a chance to win those new spurs of yours.'

'Bastard,' Mortimer hissed at Bray. The latter grinned back at him.

'All is fair in love and war,' he said. 'I'll bring you back a Frenchman's head.'

–

Inland from Quettehou the landscape was a patchwork of fields and forests, bisected by lanes and thick hedgerows. The Norman scout led the way down the road towards Valognes; he was a local man, he said, and knew this area well. The Red Company, a polyglot mix of archers, crossbowmen and spearmen identifiable by their dark red steel caps, fanned out across the surrounding fields. Ordinarily the Red Company was mounted, but most of its horses had not yet come ashore. Its commanders, John Grey and Richard Percy, rode beside Warwick, scanning the landscape and talking about the enemy.

None of them paid any attention to Bray. He did not mind; he was where he wanted to be. Everything was working out just as he had hoped.

'Bertrand is uncertain of our intentions,' Grey said. 'He garrisoned Saint-Vaast and brought in warships, and then for some reason withdrew. Of course, we arrived about a week later than planned. Perhaps he decided we weren't coming after all and pulled his troops back. It is likely that he received reports of the landing, and has come to investigate.'

Percy agreed. 'Bertrand and my father served together in the Scots wars, twenty years ago. He is a canny old soldier, and a hard fighter, too. He knows all the tricks.'

'I wish to God we had more men ashore,' Warwick said. 'If Bertrand finds out how weak we are, even three hundred men-at-arms and crossbowmen could do a great deal of damage.'

Grey looked around at the woods and hedges. 'Especially in close country like this. Lines of sight are limited, and there are plenty of places for an ambush.'

'I agree,' Warwick said. 'Halt your men.'

A horn sounded and the Red Company stopped, archers nocking arrows and crossbowmen kneeling down and presenting their weapons.

'We need a vantage point,' Warwick said to the scout. 'Somewhere we can spy out the country.'

'There is the chapel of La Pernelle,' the Norman said. 'It is on a hill a little way north of here. From there, you can see for miles.'

'Take me there. John, Richard, hold your company here and wait for further orders. Sir Edmund, stay with them. Watch how Sir John and Sir Richard handle their men. You could learn from them.'

Warwick and his esquire rode away across the fields, following the Norman. Bray waited, fidgeting on horseback. His dislike of John Grey had increased. Learn? he thought. Learn what? Arrogance? Grey had spent the entire ride out from Quettehou trying to show Warwick how clever he was. And earlier, at the church, during that powerful speech when the king had proclaimed his lordship of France, he had caught a glimpse of Grey's face. He could have sworn that the other man was trying not to laugh.

He was looking for someone, another of the Norman knights, but there was no sign of him. Irritable, restless and just young enough to be foolish, he pointed down the road towards Valognes. 'I'm going to ride on ahead. I might be able to catch sight of the enemy.'

'Warwick told you to wait here,' Percy said.

'I am a retainer of the Prince of Wales, not the Earl of Warwick,' Bray said sharply. 'He does not command me.'

'Strictly speaking, as marshal of the army he commands all of us,' Grey said. 'Didn't you hear? You could be walking into a trap.'

'I'm not afraid,' Bray said sharply. 'Are you?'

The men around him murmured, and he realised he had over-stepped the mark. John Grey gazed at him for a few moments, brown eyes level and cold, until Bray began to squirm inside his armour.

'No,' Grey said. 'I am not afraid. I am realistic, and I don't take risks unless I need to. You should read your Vegetius. He who hopes for success should fight on the basis of principle, not chance.'

'I don't care what some dead Roman said,' Bray snapped. 'I am going to scout. I will report back if I find anything.'

He pulled the visor of his helmet down and urged his horse to a canter, riding away down the track to the west. Behind him, Grey and Percy looked at each other. Percy shrugged. 'You heard Warwick. Let him win his spurs.'

'Robert Bertrand may well have crossbowmen. If he runs into those, he won't be winning his spurs, he'll be coming back on his shield.' Grey called to two of the red-capped archers. 'Matt, Pip, go after him. If he gets into trouble, try to get him out of it.'

–

Riding hard and fast, Bray rounded a bend in the road. Ahead he saw two horsemen, men-at-arms in armour and bright surcoats, halted in the middle of the road and talking together. They had heard him coming; one was already hauling his horse around spurring hard and galloping away down the road towards Valognes. The other turned towards Bray, drawing his sword.

Bray pulled his horse to a halt. He was suddenly acutely aware that he was alone, with no one to rescue him if things went wrong. 'What the devil are you doing out here?' the other man demanded.

'I could ask you the same question,' Bray said. 'Who was that man?'

'That is none of your business! Why did you come here? Who else knows you are here?'

Bray's eyes narrowed. 'He was a French man-at-arms, wasn't he? What did you tell him?'

'Nothing that concerns you. Stay out of this, Bray!'

'You bloody traitor,' Bray said, and he reached for his sword.

Something whispered in the air behind him, and a hammer blow struck him in the back. Pain stabbed across his body and forward into his chest. He drew his sword, but his hand seemed to go numb and the weapon fell from his grasp and clattered to the ground. His breath caught in his throat; he leaned forward over his horse's neck, gasping and trying to suck in air. Another heavy blow hit him in the back, and this time all the strength went from his limbs and he fell heavily to the ground, landing on his side. From the corner of his eye he could see the other man looking down at him, silhouetted against a sky that seemed strangely pale and light, and then the light faded and the world went black.

2

The English did not find Robert Bertrand; instead, he found them, announcing his presence with a savage attack on their position at Quettehou. Holland's archers and the Welsh spearmen blunted the first attack, but Bertrand gathered his three hundred men and struck again. This time the Red Company moved across and took the French in the flank, driving them back. More English men-at-arms hurried up from the beach to join the fighting, but despite being heavily outnumbered, the French continued to resist for several hours. Only when most of his men were dead or wounded did Bertrand finally retreat.

Simon Merrivale, the Prince of Wales's herald, watched the Earl of Warwick dismount outside the church in Quettehou. The marshal was covered in dust, and there was blood on his surcoat. 'Has Sir Edmund Bray returned?' Warwick asked.

The herald shook his head. 'We assumed he was with you, my lord.'

'The young fool left his position and went off scouting alone. He has probably got himself captured by the French.'

'Let us hope that is the worst that has befallen him, my lord.'

Warwick turned away to talk to his officers. Roger Mortimer came up to Merrivale. 'Is it true? Edmund is missing?'

'Yes, but don't worry. In the morning I will send a message to the French and ask if he has been taken. If he has, you can help arrange his ransom.'

Mortimer nodded, but Merrivale thought he looked anxious. The traitor's grandson had few close friends, and Bray had been one of them.

As the fighting died down, the king and prince and their retinues went down to the camp, a sprawling collection of wagons, tents and pavilions that had been set up near Saint-Vaast. Along the beach, a steady stream of boats brought men, horses and supplies ashore. The unloading of the ships would continue for several days.

More smoke rose in the distance. The troops had begun to loot the countryside, carrying away everything they could and burning what they could not. Merrivale had seen this on other campaigns, but it still depressed him.

He heard the beat of hooves behind him, and turned to see two horsemen riding into the camp, leading a third horse by the reins. A body clad in armour was tied across its saddle. Oh God, Merrivale thought, and he closed his eyes and uttered a short prayer. He knew the arms on the surcoat all too well.

The two men lowered the body gently to the ground and stepped back, bowing their heads respectfully. They were men-at-arms but clearly rather impoverished ones, in scuffed leather jerkins rather than mail and armour. One wore heavy boots, the uppers of which were badly cracked. A battered shield hung from the pommel of his saddle, bearing three red eagles on a white field.

The Prince of Wales ran forward and knelt beside the body. The other young men gathered around, their eyes wide. 'What happened?' the prince asked.

The broken stumps of two arrows protruded from Bray's backplate. The shafts were black with dried blood, and more blood stained his surcoat and armour. 'He was shot, Highness,' the herald said.

'In the back? By God, the French really are cowards. An honourable man faces his opponent.' The prince rose to his feet. 'Poor Edmund,' he said. 'He was an excellent fellow, and would have made a good knight.' He started to say something else, but checked. Instead, he swallowed suddenly and turned on his heel. 'Such are the fortunes of war,' he said abruptly, and walked away leaving his retinue staring after him.

Mortimer knelt by the body, looking down at the dead face framed by the open bascinet. After a moment, he reached out and closed Bray's eyes with gentle fingers. His own face was covered in tears. Merrivale rested a hand on his shoulder.

'Take him up to Saint-Vigor,' the herald said gently. 'Let his body rest by the altar tonight, so that his soul will be close to God. Tomorrow we shall bury him.'

Mortimer nodded. Merrivale looked for the two men-at-arms, but both had disappeared. He turned and walked away, frowning.

–

More tents were going up, some with banners or pennons in the colours of their owners. Merrivale spotted the yellow chevron of Cobham, the red pile of Chandos, the red and gold stripes of one of the Bassets; the lord of Drayton, his herald's memory told him. Further along were the familiar ermine and red chevrons of Sully. He looked at these for a moment and then walked towards the tent. A groom stood outside, combing a bay horse.

'Is Sir John within?' Merrivale asked.

'Aye, he is,' said a voice inside the tent. 'Come in, herald, and take the weight off your feet. Baker, pour Master Simon a glass of wine.'

Merrivale smiled and entered the tent. Sir John Sully of Iddesleigh sat in a folding wooden chair, one leg stretched out stiffly before him. An ebony stick rested against the side of the chair. He had discarded his armour, though he still wore an ancient sweat-stained arming doublet. White hair flowed down over his shoulders, but his blue eyes were bright with youth.

'Sit, lad, sit.' Sully pointed to another chair. 'Are you well?'

'All the better for being back on dry land,' said Merrivale. He sat, his heavy embroidered tabard lying in folds over his lap, and took the glass of wine the esquire held out to him. A dog lying in a corner of the tent raised its head and looked at him; recognising the herald, it settled back to sleep once more.

Sully chuckled. 'Not seasick, were you? You're a Devon lad like myself, Simon. The sea should be in your blood.'

'I was born and reared on Dartmoor, remember. It's rain I have in my blood, not the sea.'

The humour faded from Sully's voice. 'Aye, I remember.'

The herald's childhood memories were full of rain, endless days of rain that saturated the ground and turned the streams and leats of Dartmoor into rushing brown torrents. For three long summers there had been no sign of the sun, only leaden skies and steady downpours and wind. The sheep died first; he could still remember their rotting carcasses in the fields, legs sticking upright out of the mud. Then, when the last one had perished, famine crept in. They had buried his two sisters ten days apart; a month later, his mother followed them into the ground. He remembered their deaths, the cramp of hunger that fastened itself like a vice on his bowels and never let go, and the final terrible journey from a homeland that had become a charnel house, down to poverty and exile in the lowlands around the moor.

He shrugged off the memories. 'It was a long time ago,' he said.

'It's an odd thing, old age,' Sully said. 'Everything seems like a long time ago, and yet at the same time it feels like yesterday.' He smiled. 'But you have done well for yourself, lad. King's messenger for ten years, then herald to the Earl of Lancaster and now to the Prince of Wales.'

'All of which I owe to you, Sir John. It was you who plucked me from obscurity after our family's lands were confiscated, and obtained a post for me in the king's household.'

'I gave you a leg-up at the beginning of your career, no more. Your own hard work and integrity have done the rest. The gossip says you'll get the top job one day, when Andrew Clarenceux hangs up his tabard. How would that suit you? Herald to the king himself.'

Merrivale smiled a little. 'I am content with my present post.'

He looked at the wine in his glass and his smiled faded. Sully watched him. 'You don't look content. What troubles you?'

'We lost a man today. Young Edmund Bray, formerly one of the prince's esquires. The prince knighted him a few hours ago. They brought his body in just now.'

Sully watched him with sympathy. 'Poor fellow. How old was he?'

'Eighteen.'

The older man clicked his tongue. 'All his life before him. What a waste. The prince must be grieving his loss.'

'If he is, you would never know it. Bray was his friend, and yet he was quite offhand, almost callous. All he said was "Such are the fortunes of war."'

'He thinks this is how a real man behaves.'

'Perhaps.'

Silence followed. Sully drained his cup and held it out to his esquire to be refilled. 'You still haven't told me what is really troubling you.'

'I think Bray was killed by one of our own men,' the herald said.

Sully's eyes opened a little wider. 'Ah. Now what makes you think that?'

'The arrows that killed him are still embedded in the body. The shafts have been broken off, but they are definitely not crossbow bolts. They are longbow arrows.'

'The French have bows,' Sully suggested.

'Little hunting bows for sport, yes, but in war? They rely on crossbows, and always have done.'

Sully watched the herald's face. 'What do you want to do, lad?'

'I want to discover who killed him,' Merrivale said. 'And why.'

Sully continued to study him. 'We are at the beginning of a long, hard campaign. Many more men will die before this is over. Why care so much about this one?'

'It is one thing to die in battle,' Merrivale said. 'It is another to be murdered by one's own people. If this had happened back in England, there would be a commission of oyer and terminer. A suspect would be identified and brought to trial before the courts. Bray was serving his king and his liege lord the prince. Why should he be denied the justice he would have received at home?'

'Others will see the matter differently,' Sully said. 'He is a casualty of war, they will say. Bury him, say a mass for his soul and move on.'

'Do you believe that?'

Sully smiled, his weathered old face creasing into wrinkles. 'What I believe doesn't matter. It's what *you* believe that counts.'

'So what should I do?'

'Follow your heart. Do what your conscience tells you, and damn the rest. That's the only thing a man can do.'

Merrivale smiled too. 'I wish I had your wisdom,' he said.

'You will, when you have my years. But then, like me, you'll be too old to do anything about it.'

Merrivale drained his glass. 'Too old. You weren't even the oldest man in the field today. You're sixty-two. Robert Bertrand is ten years older.'

'And that why he failed today. He tried too hard to be clever and canny. A younger man wouldn't have stopped to think. He would have charged straight in and not stopped until he had pushed us into the sea.'

'He came close enough,' Merrivale said, rising to his feet. 'Thank you. As always, you have helped me see things more clearly.'

'Then I wish you good fortune in your quest,' said Sully.

Saint-Vaast, 12ᵗʰ of July, 1346
Evening

The sun had gone down behind the escarpment, though the sea still glowed with light and the sails of the ships waiting to debark flamed like lanterns against the darkening east. Men were lighting torches around the camp, and more torches flickered on the beach where the unloading of ships and boats continued. Further along the coast, fires flickered into life as houses and barns were set alight. Smoke rose in clouds, lit from beneath by flames and sparks.

Merrivale found Warwick still in full armour, talking with Sir Thomas Ughtred, the under-marshal. 'We will not advance inland until all the troops are ashore,' Warwick was saying. 'That is Northampton's view, and I agree. We have seen off Bertrand for the moment, but we have no idea what resistance awaits us at Carentan, or Caen.'

'I am worried about those French warships,' Ughtred said. 'There might be more of them in other ports; Barfleur or Cherbourg. They could do a good deal of mischief.'

'Huntingdon is preparing to attack Barfleur,' said Warwick. 'Cherbourg will follow. Very well, Tom, that is all for the moment.'

Ughtred departed. 'What is it, herald?' Warwick asked.

'Sir Edmund Bray, my lord. Did you know he was dead?'

'Yes. Damned fool. He should have obeyed orders, instead of walking into a French ambush.'

Merrivale shook his head. 'Sir Edmund was killed by one of our own men, my lord. I am quite certain of it. He was shot by an archer, not a crossbowman.'

Warwick paused. 'You are certain of this?'

'I am, my lord. I saw the arrows still embedded in his back.'

'Perhaps it was an accident.'

'Perhaps. But there should be an inquisition all the same.'

'For God's sake, herald. You are right, of course, but think of the practicalities.' Warwick gestured at the torchlit chaos around him. 'Do you think we have nothing better to do?'

'Certainly,' Merrivale said. 'I have no intention of adding to your burdens or those of the other officers. I propose to conduct the investigation myself. My office gives me certain powers.'

Warwick snorted. 'The power to adjudicate in disputes over coats of arms, yes. Not to investigate a death.'

'That power can be extended, surely. Murder is a crime, on the campaign trail just as anywhere else. You are right, my lord, it may well have been an accident. But if Bray *was* murdered, then his killer should be brought to justice.'

Warwick seemed amused by this. 'Have you any idea how many convicted murderers we have in the ranks of this army? The king offered pardons to all who would agree to serve, as an alternative to the hangman's noose. Suppose we do arrest this man and convict him of murder. Shall we then pardon him and send him back to his post?'

'What happens after he is convicted is not up to me,' the herald said. 'If the principle of justice does not sway you, my lord, then consider this. Bray was a friend of the prince. Whoever killed him may well intend to kill again. Others of the prince's companions might also be at risk.' He paused for effect. 'Or even the prince himself.'

'Body of Christ.' Warwick looked up at the sky, cloudy with smoke, and then back at the herald. 'Very well. Come with me.'

The royal kitchens were sited in and around tents not far from the beach, and as they passed, Merrivale smelled the tang of coal smoke and the more pleasing scents of mustard and garlic. He followed Warwick to the king's pavilion, its canvas covered with royal leopards on red silk. Guards bowed their heads and moved aside to let them enter.

The king was closeted with his secretary and two advisers, Lord Rowton and Thomas Hatfield, the Bishop of Durham. He had removed his armour and was clad in a long red robe. 'Who is setting all these damned fires, Warwick?' he demanded as the marshal entered.

'Looters, sire,' said Warwick. 'I am afraid there is nothing we can do to stop them.'

'Nothing we can do? God damn it, Thomas, I am the king! Northburgh,' he said to the secretary, 'draw up a proclamation. Remind the troops that arson and looting are strictly forbidden. Anyone caught plundering or fire-raising will be hanged immediately. Is that clear?'

'Yes, sire,' said the secretary.

Rowton shook his head. 'There is an old rule in warfare, sire, that goes back to the Romans and beyond. Never give an order unless you know it will be obeyed. I fear this particular order will not.'

'The men want plunder,' Warwick agreed. 'Many joined the army to enrich themselves, both men-at-arms and ordinary soldiers. If you hang every looter, sire, you will soon have no army left.'

'This is my country!' the king protested. 'For Christ's sake, I laid claim to it again only this afternoon. The Normans are my subjects. Are you telling me I can't protect them?'

'Perhaps you could make an award of compensation, after the fighting is over,' Rowton suggested.

The king looked at him. 'Don't be ridiculous, Eustace. What would I compensate them with? We have already drained the exchequer to pay for this campaign.' He sighed heavily. 'Very well. If we can't protect the countryside, at least we can preserve the towns from harm, and the churches and monasteries. See it done, Northburgh.'

'Yes, sire,' the secretary repeated.

Warwick cleared his throat. 'A rather delicate matter has arisen, sire,' he said. He turned to Merrivale. 'Repeat to the king what you told me.'

The herald did so. The king listened intently. At the end he said, 'Do you think there is a threat to my son?'

'I do not know,' Merrivale said. 'But it is possible. To make certain, we need to find out who killed Sir Edmund Bray, and why.'

The king nodded. 'Then we shall take no chances. Warwick, see that my son's bodyguard is doubled. And we need someone to carry out an inquisition into Bray's death.'

Merrivale bowed. 'I have already asked my lord of Warwick for permission to do so, sire.'

'You? You are a herald, a messenger and ambassador and a scholar of armorial bearings. Not a sheriff.'

'I am familiar with the principles of conducting an inquisition, sire. I respectfully request that you place me in charge of this one.'

'Why?' the king demanded. 'Why you in particular?'

'Because if I am in charge, sire, the inquisition will be carried out thoroughly and competently,' Merrivale said. 'I will see to it that justice is done.'

'Are you implying that my other officials are not thorough and competent?'

'No, sire. But they are likely to be busy carrying out your orders and conducting this campaign. My duties, as you have rightly pointed out, are largely ceremonial. I have the time to devote to this matter where other men might not.' He paused for a moment. 'I have served your Grace well in the past. Have I ever failed you?'

'No,' the king said. 'You have not. Very well, herald, I am placing this matter in your hands. You have my authority to investigate Bray's death. Report developments to my secretary, Master Northburgh.'

Merrivale bowed. 'Yes, sire.'

The king raised a finger. 'One more thing, herald. Whatever romantic notions about justice you may cherish, your principal task is to protect the Prince of Wales. If any harm comes to him, you will suffer for it. Is that clear?'

'Yes, sire,' Merrivale said steadily.

'Good. Find your man, and find him quickly. Very well, herald, that will be all.'

—

Merrivale's official duties were few at present: acting as messenger and ambassador when needed, keeping record of which armorial bearings belonged to which knights, and adjudicating disputes over who had the right to bear arms. His unofficial duties were sometimes rather different.

His status brought with it his own tent and a staff of two, a manservant and a groom. Warin, the groom, was a Devon man like himself; short and stocky, with a shock of red hair, he hailed from Hexworthy on Dartmoor, where his family were tin miners. Mauro, the servant, was, as his name suggested, a Moor, or at least part Moorish; he himself was vague about his parentage. He had come into Merrivale's service when the latter was herald to the Earl of Lancaster on the embassy to Castile in 1343. Both men were discreet and utterly reliable.

Entering his tent, Merrivale lifted his tabard over his head and laid it aside. Mauro poured a glass of wine, adding water to his master's taste. 'The prince's steward bids me tell you that dinner is about to be served, *señor*.'

'Thank God for that.' Merrivale rubbed his stomach. It had been a long day, and he was ravenous; dinner was always late when the army was in the field, served after they had made camp for the day. He drank some of his wine and set his cup down. 'I need to speak to both of you,' he said.

They faced him, all attention. 'A man was killed today,' he said. 'A young knight in the prince's service. I believe the killer was someone on our side, and I intend to find him. I have the king's authority to do so.'

He paused for a moment, collecting his thoughts, rehearsing what he knew about the case and realising it was not very much.

'The dead man is Sir Edmund Bray,' he said. 'He accompanied the Earl of Warwick and the Red Company on a reconnaissance party.

Sir Edmund disobeyed orders and rode out into the field alone. Some men-at-arms found him later, shot in the back, and recovered his body. That is all we know.'

'Perhaps it was a *venganza*,' Mauro suggested. 'Did he have any enemies, *señor*?'

Merrivale shook his head. 'None that I know of. He comes from Cheshire. Since he arrived at court he has had his share of young men's quarrels, mostly over dice and girls, but nothing serious.' He pondered. 'But you may be right, Mauro. It is possible there was some family feud back in Cheshire. Someone may have followed him to Normandy and set a trap for him.'

'There's a lot of Cheshire men in the army, sir,' Warin said. The prince was also Earl of Chester, and his officers had recruited heavily in his domain lands.

'Lord Rowton knows Bray's family. It was he who recommended the lad for a post in the prince's household. I shall have a word with his lordship and ask if he knows of anything in Bray's past.'

'Begging your pardon, sir,' Warin said. 'What if it turns out there was no feud?'

'Then I must consider other possibilities.' Merrivale thought for a moment. 'Perhaps he ran across a party of looters and confronted them, and they killed him. Perhaps my lord of Warwick is right, and it was an accident. Or perhaps it really was the French. Someone in their force had a longbow, an English or Welsh deserter, perhaps.'

'Forgive my presumption, *señor*,' Mauro said. 'But you are using the word "perhaps" in a way that suggests you do not believe what you are saying.'

Merrivale smiled a little. 'Correct. None of these explanations rings true, although for the life of me I cannot tell you why. And that is what bothers me. Nothing about this seems right.'

The two servants watched him, waiting. 'I need your help,' Merrivale said. 'Keep your eyes and ears open, both of you. Listen to servants' gossip. If you learn anything, tell me.'

Both men bowed. 'Now I must go and dine with the prince,' Merrivale said, picking up his tabard. 'Make sure you get fed as well, and then you can retire. Despite Bray's death, the young men will want to celebrate. I may return quite late.'

He drained his wine cup and looked through the doorway of the tent at the shimmering sea dotted with ships. 'Cheshire,' he said quietly. 'He came a long way to die, didn't he? I don't know who killed you, Edmund Bray, but with God's aid I will find out.'

Saint-Vaast, 12th of July, 1346
Night

Lit from within by lamps and candles, the coloured silk pavilions glowed like jewels in the warm night. Two men stood on the beach not far from the smoking embers of the burned warships, gazing at the king's red pavilion. They were far from the camp, away from any eavesdropping ears; this time there was no young cowherd to overhear them.

'What do you suppose they are doing in there?' the West Country man asked.

'Holding a council of war,' said the man from the north. 'They are deciding the plan for the rest of the campaign.'

'Shouldn't you be in there with them?'

'Oh, I will rejoin them in a moment. I merely stepped out for some fresh air. In any case, I already know the plan. Once the army has landed, we will march west to Valognes, then south to take the bridges at Carentan. After that, we will move east to Caen. If Philip still won't yield, at least we have a base for launching further raids into France, until he capitulates or his nobles overthrow him and sue for peace.'

'Ambitious,' the other man said mockingly.

'One cannot accuse Edward of lacking ambition on this campaign. What happened to Bertrand? He was supposed to attack with all the force he could muster, not three hundred poxy men-at-arms.'

'That *was* all the force he could muster. He received our message about the delay, but by then he had run out of money.'

The man from the north stared at him. 'Out of *money*? In God's name, how did that happen?'

'The French royal finances are in a state of chaos. Bertrand's crossbowmen and the sailors demanded their pay, and when they didn't get it, they deserted their posts. All Bertrand could gather was his own retinue and some local gentry.'

'Suffering Christ. We had a golden opportunity today, and it slipped through our hands. We need to get Doria on board with this venture.'

'I have talked to him, several times. He won't budge. His loyalty is to France, he says.'

'God preserve us from honest mercenaries.' A sudden note of humour entered the northern man's voice. 'If only they were all like you, my friend. The world would be a much simpler place. Although not necessarily a better one.'

From the Prince of Wales's pavilion they could hear music playing and voices uplifted in song, punctuated by bursts of laughter and cheering. 'Celebrating their first day of war,' the northern man said. 'There will be sore heads in the morning. Very well, our first plan failed. Now we need another one, and quickly.'

'What do you want to do?'

'I shall leave the details to your fertile imagination. I don't think we should meet again, at least not until after Carentan. I know I can trust you to do whatever is necessary.'

'Indeed you can,' said the West Country man. 'Then I wish you good night. Sleep well, and dream of the riches and power we shall soon acquire.'

'I dream of nothing else,' said the man from the north.

3

They buried Sir Edmund Bray in Quettehou church, his comrades standing around the grave with uncovered heads while Brother Geoffrey of Maldon, the Augustinian canon who served the king's household, recited prayers. The prince stood silent throughout the ceremony, biting his lip. When it was over, he strode out of the church, mounted his horse and rode back down to Saint-Vaast.

Merrivale thanked Brother Geoffrey, whom he had known for many years, and walked out of the church into the morning sunlight. To his surprise, Lord Rowton was waiting for him. 'A sad day,' his lordship said quietly. 'Bray was a fine young man. I know his family well, and his loss will hit them hard. I grieve for them as well as for Edmund himself.'

Generous words, Merrivale thought. Perhaps you could teach them to the Prince of Wales. 'We all feel the same, my lord. He was so young, with so much before him. There is a sense of waste, as well as loss.'

'Indeed there is.' Rowton paused. 'I assumed you would want to speak to me.'

'Thank you, my lord. What do you know of his family? Were they involved in any quarrels with their neighbours, perhaps, or their overlord?'

'No, absolutely not. The Brays are well regarded by all, including myself. John Bray has lands next to mine in Lancashire, and I bought one of his manors in Cheshire when he was short of money. He's a decent and honourable man. Is your theory that Edmund was killed as part of some family feud?'

'It is one of several,' Merrivale said cautiously.

'Then allow me to point out a flaw. Edmund's decision to ride out was taken on the spur of the moment. How could a killer have known when and where to find him?'

'Perhaps it was not really the spur of the moment,' Merrivale said. 'He may have been going to a prearranged meeting, which turned into a trap.'

'Have you any evidence to support this notion?'

'No.'

Rowton nodded. 'You should go through his baggage. See if he received any letters inviting him to a rendezvous.'

'Thank you, my lord. I shall do so.'

'May I ask a question of my own? Why did you insist on being appointed as inquisitor?'

Merrivale considered this for a moment. 'You said it yourself,' he said finally. 'He was a young man, full of promise, and he deserves justice. If I do not take up his cause, then who will?'

Rowton grimaced. 'No one, of course. As you said to the king, everyone else is busy, and most of his erstwhile friends agree that he was a casualty of war. By the time this campaign is over, they will have forgotten him.'

'Then, my lord, you have answered your own question,' Merrivale said.

–

Rowton departed. Roger Mortimer was standing by the door of the church, staring out across the bay and the rippling sea beyond. There is one who will not forget, Merrivale thought.

On impulse, he walked over to the young man and put a hand on his arm. 'You have suffered a great loss, Sir Roger, but do not let your sorrow overwhelm you. Remember that your friend has gone to a better place.'

'Do you believe that priest's cant?' Mortimer asked. 'I am not sure I do.'

'That is grief talking,' Merrivale said gently. 'Grief, and perhaps remorse also. You feel partly responsible for his death.'

Mortimer looked at him. 'What do you mean?'

'You tried to volunteer for the reconnaissance, but Sir Edmund forestalled you. Now you believe that if you had gone in his place, he would still be alive.'

'I should have insisted,' Mortimer said. 'I should have pushed him out of the way. I should have knocked him off his damned horse and stood on his head, done whatever I had to do to prevent him from going.'

'He knew the risks,' Merrivale said, although he was not entirely certain this was true.

'He was my friend, herald, my only real friend. All the others whisper behind my back, even the prince. But not Edmund, not ever. His friendship was honest and true. God, how I miss him... and that little shit just stood there by the grave in silence, and then walked away.' There were tears in Mortimer's eyes.

'Sir Roger, I must ask you this,' the herald said. 'Did Sir Edmund have any enemies in the army? Did he ever speak of feuds concerning him, or his family?'

'No,' said Mortimer. He thought for a moment. 'He did quarrel with Sir Thomas Holland, back in Portchester before we embarked.'

This was news to Merrivale. 'Do you remember what it was about?'

'The Countess of Salisbury,' Mortimer said. 'Holland made some slighting reference to the earl, her husband. Edmund then said something coarse about the countess. We had to pull them apart. So far as I know, they never spoke to each other again.'

The herald considered this. Salisbury, the prince's close friend, was married to the king's first cousin, the lady Joan of Kent. Only after the marriage vows had been exchanged did it emerge that a year or so earlier she had secretly married Sir Thomas Holland. When Holland returned from service overseas and learned of the marriage to Salisbury, he tried to assert his rights but was firmly rebuffed: he had

married a ward of the king without the king's consent, which meant –
according to one interpretation of the law, at least – that the marriage
was invalid. Angry and humiliated, Holland seldom missed a chance
to denigrate his rival.

The feud between Holland and Salisbury was a bitter one, and Bray
had been a fool to get caught up in it. But was it sufficient justification
for murder? Holland could be an unpleasant man, even a dangerous
one, but would he order an assassination at the start of an important
campaign? Surely he would meet his enemy face-to-face; as the prince
had said, that was what men of honour did.

The question, of course, was whether someone who entered into
a secret marriage with the king's cousin could be considered a man of
honour.

—

Bray's servant was sitting inside his master's tent, staring at nothing,
probably wondering what would happen to him now that his master
was dead. 'I wish to see Sir Edmund's baggage,' Merrivale said.
'Unpack it for me, please.'

The baggage consisted of two painted wooden chests. The first
contained Bray's armour, including his blood-stained arming doublet;
the second held several suits of clothes, fashionably cut, and personal
effects including a razor and a comb. The ruby ring the prince had
given him was there too; the friars must have removed it when they
washed the body last night. Merrivale thought about returning it to the
prince, but put it back in the chest. Let Bray's family have something
to remember him by.

All around them the camp murmured with the tramp of marching
feet and the rumble of wagon wheels as the army continued to flow
ashore.

'Did your master receive any letters? Between the time the household left London and the embarkation at Portchester?'

The servant shook his head, mute. Merrivale walked out of the tent
and stood for a moment, thinking.

Why did Bray leave his post and ride out to meet his death? The last people to see him alive, apart from the killer, were Sir John Grey and Sir Richard Percy and the men of their company. Perhaps they could shed some light.

Quettehou, 13ᵗʰ of July, 1346
Midday

From the escarpment they could see a massive column of smoke rising five or six miles to the north, boiling into the sky and dispersing slowly on the wind. 'Barfleur,' Sir Richard Percy said sombrely. 'Huntingdon's men were ordered to burn enemy ships, but it looks like they've set light to the town as well.'

More fires flickered nearer at hand along the coast. The sun glowered red out of a sky dark with smoke and ash. 'What has the king to say about this?' Sir John Grey asked. 'According to him, the Normans are his subjects now. They're going to be damned unhappy subjects if his troops keep burning their houses down.'

'He is issuing a proclamation banning arson and looting,' Merrivale said. 'But only in the towns.'

'Only in the towns?' Grey stared at him. 'Do the lives of country people have less value? No, don't bother to answer that.'

'Nor has he managed to save Barfleur. But then I've never known soldiers to take much notice of proclamations,' Percy said. 'Have you, herald?'

'No.' Merrivale looked at the men of the Red Company, standing guard or sitting and cleaning their weapons. 'You manage to keep your men under control. How do you do it?'

'We pay them well,' Grey said. 'In return, we expect obedience. And, they don't like it when I get angry. How may we serve you, herald?'

'I have been charged by the king to enquire into the death of Sir Edmund Bray,' Merrivale said.

'So we heard. What do you want from us?'

'You were in the thick of the fighting yesterday afternoon. Did the enemy have archers?'

'No, and that surprised us. Usually when you run across French men-at-arms, they have a few crossbowmen in support.'

That ended any notion that Bray might have been killed by the enemy, Merrivale thought. He nodded. 'That has been my experience also. But Bray was shot by a longbow.'

He waited for a reaction. Neither Grey nor Percy said anything.

'Bray was with you yesterday afternoon,' the herald continued. 'My lord of Warwick ordered him to stay with you, but he disobeyed orders. Do you know why?'

'He wanted to prove that he was better than me,' Grey said. 'He didn't like me. I don't know why.'

Percy grinned. 'Plenty of people don't like you, and you never understand why,' he said.

'Could his departure have been premeditated?' Merrivale asked. 'Is it possible that he was actually riding out to meet someone?'

Grey thought. 'Anything is possible, but somehow I doubt it. Nothing in his demeanour said he was anxious, or in a hurry. He was a young, rather vain man who badly needed to show off how clever he was.'

'Which is exactly what he thought of you,' Percy said, 'and he didn't trouble to conceal it. I agree with John. Bray was in a bilious mood, and he wanted to prove himself.'

'We tried to talk him out of it, but he wouldn't listen,' Grey said. 'After he rode away, we sent two archers after him in case he ran into trouble. But they never caught up with him.'

Two archers. Bray had been killed by two longbow arrows. 'May I speak with these men?'

'Of course.' Grey turned to another archer standing nearby. 'Rob, fetch Matt and Pip, will you?'

The two archers arrived a moment later, touching their foreheads in salute. They were both in their late teens, Merrivale guessed, slender, with fine features; they looked like brothers. They wore plain jerkins and hose and rough boots, with quivers full of arrows strapped across their backs and knives tucked into their belts.

'You wished to see us, sir,' said Matt, the taller of the two.

'Sir John tells me you were instructed to follow Sir Edmund Bray yesterday afternoon. Did you do so?'

'Yes, sir,' said Matt. He had a light, pleasant voice and spoke with a strong Midlands accent. 'That is to say, we tried, sir. But he was riding hard when he set out. We ran after him, but was he still faster than us.'

'Which direction did he go?'

'Down the road towards Valognes, sir. Straight towards the enemy, as it happens.'

'Did you find his body?'

Pip shook his head. 'No, sir. We didn't get very far, not more than half a mile from the rest of the company.'

'Oh? What happened?'

'As we were following Sir Edmund, sir, another horseman came down the road towards us. Man-at-arms, he was, and riding like the wind. When he saw us, he turned his horse and rode back the way he had come. We thought he might be an enemy scout, so we followed on carefully.'

'If you thought he was an enemy, why didn't you shoot?'

'We thought he *might* be,' Matt corrected. 'But we weren't certain. Things were a bit fluid out there. We didn't know for certain who we might be shooting at.'

'Very well. What happened next?'

'Well, sir, it wasn't more than a few minutes later that we spotted the enemy. There was one company coming down the road towards us, and more over the fields towards Quettehou. We didn't know what had happened to Sir Edmund, but there was nothing we two could do against so many, so we legged it back to report to Sir John and Sir Richard.'

'The company on the road was a flank guard,' Grey said. 'We saw them off, and moved across the fields to join the fighting at Quettehou. The rest you know.'

'The first man-at-arms you spotted. Did he have a coat?'

'He did, sir,' said Matt. 'A red lion upright, with his paws like so. On white.'

A red lion rampant on white. Merrivale searched his herald's memory, trying to think who might bear this device. It was no English coat that he knew. He studied the two men. For ordinary archers, they are very confident, he thought. All of the Red Company bore themselves like professionals, but these two were different, in a way he could not quite put his finger on.

'Are you quite certain you never saw Sir Edmund again after he left your position?'

'Quite certain, sir,' said Pip.

Matt looked at the herald, searching his face. 'Pardon me for being presumptuous, sir,' the archer said. 'But are you thinking we might have killed him?'

'The thought crossed my mind,' Merrivale said.

Pip shook his head. 'No, sir. We didn't know Sir Edmund, and we had no score to settle with him.' He looked at Merrivale with clear brown eyes. 'And if we had, sir, we wouldn't have wasted a second arrow. One would have been enough.'

'Don't be impertinent,' said Sir John Grey, but he sounded amused rather than angry. 'All right, both of you, dismissed.'

'How well do you know those men?' Merrivale asked when Matt and Pip had gone.

'They joined our company last winter,' Percy said. 'Our master archer recruited them in Warwickshire. They're good archers, among the most reliable we have.'

Warwickshire, the herald thought. A long way from Cheshire. Bray had not been killed by the enemy, and the idea that he had died as a result of some family feud was looking weaker and weaker. Like the smoke that boiled up from the ruins of Barfleur, his suspicions were growing steadily darker.

Quettehou, 13th of July, 1346
Afternoon

The looters had become bolder. The houses of Saint-Vaast had so far been spared, thanks to the fact that the king was camped nearby, but as Merrivale rode back down the hill, he saw the first flames spurting from the roofs of the town. By the time he reached the beach, clouds of smoke and ash were rolling through the camp. Around him, men were already striking tents and packing wagons. The livestock the royal kitchens had brought with them, cattle and sheep and pigs, were all clamouring with fright, and as Merrivale passed one wagon he heard chickens clucking frantically in their crates.

'The household is moving to Morsalines on the other side of the bay,' said Andrew Clarenceux, the royal herald. He was a serious man, with tufts of grey hair fringing a bald head. People sometimes asked if he had taken holy orders. He did not find this amusing. Around him his staff were packing up, flinging parchment rolls into chests and carrying them outside. 'The king is furious, as you can imagine. He keeps calling for the looters to be hanged, but every time the serjeants go out to arrest them, they disappear.'

'Andrew, I am looking for two men-at-arms. I know their devices, but I don't recognise them, and I am hoping you might know who they are. The first is a red lion rampant on white.'

Clarenceux considered. 'How was the head positioned? Guardant or combatant?'

'I fear I do not know.'

'If it was guardant, it might be one of the Lestranges... but no, none of them are serving with the army. If it was combatant, I have no idea.'

'Could it be a French device?'

'That is entirely possible. I know the coats of all the important French nobles, of course, but there are thousands of provincial knights. I haven't yet managed to memorise all their devices.'

'The other is three red eagles displayed on white, with elevated wings. It was his men who brought Bray's body into camp yesterday afternoon. I wondered if that might be an Irish device.'

Clarenceux nodded. 'Sir Nicholas Courcy, from Kingsale. He is in Northampton's retinue. Is this about Bray, then? Do you really think you can find out who shot him?'

'Yes,' said Merrivale.

The first wagons were already rolling away. A man and a girl herded the cattle behind them, the girl calling to the cows and waving a long stick. She looked barely more than a child, Merrivale thought.

The town was burning hard now. Smoke blew across the bay in clouds, and the sails of the fleet shimmered through haze and heat waves. Still the landing went on, boats grounding in the shallows and men coming ashore. Some of them laboured around a boat, dragging a portable blacksmith's forge up onto the beach; others carried hurdles and bundles of faggots and coils of rope. Further on, another group were unloading wooden barrels and heavy stone spheres, piling them up at the head of the beach next to four long hollow wrought-iron cylinders. The barrels were marked with black arrowhead brands, signifying that they were the property of the royal armoury.

More smoke blew around them. 'Jesus, cover those powder kegs!' a man shouted. 'One spark on those and we'll all be seeing paradise a damned sight sooner than we'd like. Quickly now!'

Men rushed to drag a tarpaulin over the barrels. Merrivale looked at the shouting man and noticed with surprise that he was one of those who had brought in Bray's body, wearing the same scuffed leather jerkin and cracked boots. He saw the herald, and grinned. 'Serpentine,' he explained. 'It's the very devil to handle. Too wet and it won't burn at all, too hot and it burns when you don't want it to. Have you heard of gunpowder, herald?'

Merrivale nodded. 'Master Mildenhall the armourer told me about the new guns the king has ordered. Do you work with him?'

'From time to time, when needed. I dabble in alchemy, so I know a wee bit about powder.'

'I am looking for your master,' Merrivale said. 'Can you tell me where to find him?'

The other man smiled. 'Sir Nicholas Courcy knows no master but God,' he said.

'You are Sir Nicholas?'

Grey eyes twinkled in a broad, handsome face. 'The devil himself.'

'Do you mind if I ask you a few questions?'

Courcy waved a negligent hand. 'At your service, sir.'

40

'Thank you for recovering Sir Edmund Bray's body. Where did you find it?'

'Out on the Valognes road, perhaps two miles from here. One of my fellows, Donnchad, spotted him and realised he was a man of worth. I recognised his coat and knew he was the Prince of Wales's man, so we brought him in.'

'Then you disappeared before anyone could talk to you.'

'Aye, well, we weren't interested in hanging around. To tell you the truth, we were hoping there might be a reward. But when the prince walked off, we realised nothing was coming our way, so we got back to work.'

'You are of course due some recompense for your services,' Merrivale said. 'I will speak to the prince's steward. What were you doing out there? Were you involved in the fighting?'

Courcy grinned again. 'Indeed we were. Afterwards, once old Bertrand had retreated, we decided to take a look around. You know. In case someone had left something behind.'

'Looting,' Merrivale said.

'Don't be too hard on us poor fellows, herald. My father's family are richer than Midas, but I was born on the wrong side of the sheets. I must make a living however I can.'

'Then you missed a chance,' Merrivale said. 'Bray had quite a valuable ring on his finger. Did you not notice?'

'I still have some pride, herald. I haven't taken to robbing corpses. Yet.'

'I have a theory that he may have run across a party of looters and confronted them, and they killed him.' He looked Courcy in the eye. 'What do you think?'

Most men would have been offended at the insinuation; some would have exploded with rage. Courcy just grinned again. 'I think that's unlikely now, don't you? Me and Donnchad and the boys were the first ones into that area after old Bertrand and his lads cleared out. And Bray was already dead when we got there.'

Merrivale waited. 'Ah, I see now. You think *we* might have killed him. But why would we go to the trouble of bringing in the body with all that nice expensive armour still on it, and that grand big ruby on his finger? That wouldn't be good commerce, herald.'

'You were involved in the fighting, you say. Did you see any archers among the enemy?'

'Not a one. A pother of men-at-arms, no more.'

'And do you have any archers in your own retinue?'

Their eyes met. 'No, herald. My gallowglasses don't approve of killing at a distance. They like to get in close and see the whites of their enemy's eyes before they ram a spear through his guts.'

The gallowglasses were Courcy's Irish followers, professional soldiers. 'During your travels, did you happen to see a man-at-arms bearing a device of a red lion rampant on white?'

'No.' It was said quickly and definitely.

'One more question, if I may. The shafts of the arrows had been broken off. Were they like that when you found the body?'

Courcy nodded. 'I reckon someone tried to pull the arrows out, but the shafts snapped. The heads were lodged very deep in the body.' He paused. 'That must have been some powerful bow. Either that, or the archer was standing almost within touching distance. The poor fellow was wearing an iron backplate over a mail coat, and the arrows drove straight through both of them.'

'Yes.' That also ruled out Warwick's idea that it had been an accident. Bray had been killed deliberately. 'Thank you,' Merrivale said. 'I hope my questions did not give offence.'

'Not in the least. If you're trying to catch the fellow who shot him, good luck to you.' Courcy eyed him for a moment. 'Do you not carry a weapon, herald?'

Nearly every other man in the army wore a sword or a knife at his belt, but the herald was unarmed. 'The laws of war forbid it,' he said.

'Do they now? I seem to recall that a herald is permitted to wear a blunted sword.'

Merrivale shook his head. 'A sword that has no edge is not a sword, just a useless encumbrance. I prefer to do without.'

'But surely you are allowed armour.'

'My status as herald gives me all the protection I need.'

'Sure, now. To attack you would be an offence against God, and a breach of the laws of war. All the same, herald, let me give you a piece of advice. If you intend to investigate this matter, watch your back. That tabard won't keep out a longbow arrow any more than Sir Edmund Bray's armour did.'

Morsalines, 13th of July, 1346
Evening

The smoke hung thick, obscuring the view across the bay. Ships and boats moved slowly through drifting clouds full of sparks and ash. Merrivale could taste the smoke in his mouth, and his clothing and hair stank of it. At his tent he called for water and washed his face and hands thoroughly, but could not rid himself of the smell.

He dined with the prince's household in a pavilion outside Morsalines. The young men talked eagerly about how well Saint-Vaast had burned, and Barfleur. A minstrel came in and sang some old verses by the troubadour Bertran de Born about the joys of war and plunder.

Love wants a chivalrous lover,
Skilled at arms and generous in serving,
Who speaks boldly and gives generously
And knows what he should say and do
In his hall or outside it, as befits his power.
A lady who lies with a lover such as that
Will be cleansed of all her sins.

The prince and his companions cheered raucously and began to play a drinking game, shouting and laughing. Lord Rowton was right, the herald thought. Edmund Bray will soon be forgotten.

After the prince withdrew, unsteady with wine, Merrivale rose and went out into the hot evening, where the crimson bars of sunset competed with the glow of fires. The prince's bodyguards bowed as he passed. Further on, a man stepped out of the shadows with a jingle of mail, inclining his head.

'Good evening, Sir Edward,' said Merrivale.

'And a fine evening to yourself, herald,' said Sir Edward de Tracey of Dunkeswell. He smiled a little. 'I enjoyed the singing.'

'Did you?' said Merrivale. 'I remember that Dante consigned Bertran de Born to the eighth circle of hell. He appears naked, carrying his severed head in front of him glowing like a lantern.'

The other man chuckled. 'Dante had quite an imagination, didn't he? To be fair, I believe the punishment was for Bertran's role as a sower of discord rather than for his *sirventes*.'

'That may be so,' said Merrivale. 'Your memory is better than mine. Were you waiting for me?'

'I was hoping to have a word with you, yes. Rumour has it you are looking for a man with a particular device. A red lion rampant, head combatant, on white.'

Merrivale became alert. 'Yes. Do you know him?'

'As it happens, I do. His name is Jean de Fierville. He comes from the Cotentin.' Tracey hesitated. 'I've known him for a good few years. His family and mine have... done business together for some time now.'

'May I ask what sort of business?'

The pause this time was longer. 'The Fiervilles are shipowners. That is to say, they are involved in all sorts of trade. Some legitimate, some not. Not dissimilar to my own family, come to that.'

The Traceys had gone through some dark times during the troubled years of the king's father's reign and emerged with a rather dubious reputation. Sir Edward's father, Sir John de Tracey, had been accused of piracy and other crimes, for which he was eventually pardoned. Times had changed: Tracey's brother was the king's banker, and Tracey himself had married the sister of the Earl of Arundel.

'So, the Fiervilles,' Merrivale said. 'Are they pirates?'

'Frankly, it's hard to tell the difference between trading, smuggling and piracy. You're likely to find the same ship doing all three things, sometimes even at the same time.'

'That doesn't answer my question.'

'Yes,' Tracey said finally. 'Fierville was involved in the attack on Southampton back in '38.'

The French attack on Southampton in 1338 was notorious. Hundreds of people had been slaughtered, and many others were still missing; it was widely believed that they had been sold into slavery by the pirates. The herald struggled to keep the distaste out of his voice. 'Whose side is Fierville on now? Is he one of Bertrand's men? Or one of ours?'

'One of ours, definitely. I saw him in Portchester, and he told me was in Harcourt's retinue. I have to say, I was surprised.'

'Why?'

'The Fiervilles always look out for their own interests. What would possess a man like Jean de Fierville to risk everything by taking up with a rebel like Lord Godefroi?'

'Do you know where he is now?'

'No idea, I'm afraid. In all the confusion of embarkation and landing, I haven't seen him since Portchester.'

'I want to talk to him,' Merrivale said. 'If you see him, will you be so good as to let me know?'

'Of course.' Tracey paused again. 'It's certain, is it? Bray was killed by one of our folk?'

'Yes,' Merrivale said.

Tracey nodded. 'Then I hope you find him.'

-

Returning to his own tent, Merrivale removed his tabard and called for his writing case. Mauro set the box on his folding desk, laying out pen and ink, parchment and shaving knife in an orderly fashion just as he knew his master liked it. Sitting down on a wooden stool, Merrivale stared at the smooth sheet of parchment for a moment, marshalling his thoughts. Then he picked up the pen, dipped it in the inkwell and began to write.

Inquisition into the death of Edmund Bray, knight, near the village of Quettehou in Normandy on the XIIth day of July, in the nineteenth year of the reign of King Edward III.

Following an action against the French, Sir Edmund's body was found by the miles Sir Nicholas Courcy of Kingsale and his men and returned to the camp. Sir Edmund had been shot in the back at close range by two arrows. It can be assumed that the first arrow did not kill him immediately, so he was shot a second time to administer a coup de grâce.

Item, as to whether Sir Edmund was killed by enemy action. This can be discounted, as there were no archers with the enemy force.

Item, as to whether he was killed by accident. His decision to go scouting alone seems to have been a spontaneous action. He was shot at close range, and two arrows, as indicated above, is consistent with hostile action.

Item, as to whether he was killed as a result of a feud or quarrel. This cannot be discounted entirely, but it seems unlikely. Apart from a public quarrel with the miles Sir Thomas Holland at Portchester, there is nothing to suggest that Bray had any enemies.

Item, as to whether he was killed by troops whom he encountered looting. Bray's body had not been robbed. The corpse was discovered by men of the retinue of Sir Nicholas Courcy of Kingsale, who had no archers of his own.

The herald paused, thinking about Courcy's final words. *That tabard won't keep out a longbow arrow.* A warning? Or a threat?

Item, a Norman miles, Jean de Fierville, was allegedly spotted near the scene where Bray was killed. I am told he is in the retinue of the lord of Harcourt.

He paused again, thinking. Two archers had been sent after Bray; two longbow arrows had killed him. That in itself was not evidence. But there was something false about Matt and Pip, he was quite certain of it. To tell the truth, until Tracey had identified Fierville, he had wondered whether that entire scene on the road might have been their invention.

And indeed, it still might be. Jean de Fierville was with the army, but that did not mean he had been on that road that afternoon.

He dipped his pen in the ink and wrote *Item*, but then stopped. Sir John Grey and Sir Richard Percy would not take kindly to an accusation against their men unless there was very strong evidence, and this the herald did not have.

No, he thought. Better to find Fierville and get his version of events first. He picked up the little shaving knife and sliced away the top layer of parchment to erase the word, then dipped the pen in the inkwell again and signed his name: *Simon Merrivale*, heraldus.

–

The king had taken over the manor house at Morsalines for his personal use. His secretary, Michael Northburgh, had set up his office in the great hall, and even though the hour was late he was still hard at work. 'I thought it wise to provide a written report,' Merrivale said, handing over the parchment. 'However, the fewer eyes that see this, other than yours and the king's, the better.'

'Of course.' The secretary scanned the report quickly. 'Jean de Fierville? The name does not spring immediately to mind, but let me check the muster rolls.'

He turned to a wooden pigeonhole beside the desk and began pulling out rolls of parchment. 'Here we are, the retinue of the lord of Harcourt.' Untying the red tape that bound it, he spread the parchment out flat. 'Fierville, Fierville... ah, there it is. *Miles* Ioannes de Fierville, joined the army at Portchester, fifteenth of June. Indenture signed by said Ioannes de Fierville and Godefroi d'Harcourt, *vicecomes* de Saint-Sauveur. Yes, that's your man all right. He joined the army late, hence me not recognising the name.'

'So he is not one of the original exiles who came over with Harcourt last year.'

'It doesn't look like it, no.'

The herald rubbed his chin. 'I must talk to this man.'

'You will need to ask Harcourt's permission first,' Northburgh warned. 'And you know how touchy he can be.'

'Yes,' said Merrivale. 'Do you know where I can find him?'

'He is closeted with the king now, but they won't be long. They are discussing how to persuade the Norman lords to join us.' Northburgh held up a sheet of parchment. 'Have you heard the latest? Letters are going out to all the important barons and knights, urging them to pledge fealty to the king. Harcourt's men are carrying the letters under flags of truce.'

Merrivale looked doubtful. 'Will this work?'

'Unlikely, I'd say. Harcourt's own brother has already pledged his fealty to France. Do you really think the rest of Normandy will rise up and proclaim his Grace as their king? I reckon we'll see the king's herd of pigs sprouting wings and flying off over the Bay of Saint-Vaast before that happens.'

Northburgh gathered his papers and rose. 'I'm off. Wait here if you like. His lordship will be down soon.'

The herald waited, listening to the sound of voices coming from the solar above the hall. After a while, the door opened and Godefroi d'Harcourt came down the broad stone stair, followed by several of his men. Merrivale bowed.

'My lord. May I speak with you?'

Harcourt halted. 'What is it?'

'I wish to interview one of your men-at-arms, Jean de Fierville. Will you grant me permission to do so?'

The other Normans stared at him. 'What do you want with this man?' Harcourt asked.

'He may have been present when Sir Edmund Bray was killed yesterday afternoon.'

'Are you accusing him of involvement in the killing?'

'No, my lord, but he may have seen the culprit. Do I have your consent?'

'No,' said Harcourt. 'You will not question members of my retinue, or meddle with them in any way.'

'My lord, I am investigating on the king's orders.'

'Then take it up with the king,' Harcourt said, and limped past Merrivale towards the door.

'My lord!' the herald called after him. 'I must speak with Jean de Fierville!'

One of the Norman men-at-arms spun around, hand on the hilt of his sword. 'You heard my lord,' he snarled. 'Stay out of this, herald.'

'Are you threatening me?' Merrivale asked.

'No, of course he isn't,' said another Norman, pulling the first man's hand away from his sword. 'All the same, herald, I would take his advice if I were you.'

4

'Gracious king, we humbly beseech you to spare our poor worthless lives. Our homes, our possessions, everything we own, we give to you. We ask only that you spare us and our families. In the name of the Blessed Virgin and her son Jesus Christ, we ask for mercy.'

The burgesses of Valognes, dressed in their richest clothes and some wearing chains of office, knelt in the dust of the road with their hands clasped in supplication. Behind them lay the houses, mills and priories of the unwalled and undefended town, its cobbled streets shimmering in the heat. Two dogs stood watching the scene, stiff-legged and ears pricked, ready to bolt.

Seated on the back of his massive black horse, the king raised his visor and smiled down at the kneeling men. 'Do not fear, good people,' he said, raising one mailed gauntlet in benediction. 'You are my subjects, and thus under my protection. By my order, you and your possessions and chattels will be safe, and all the rights, privileges and customs of your town will be respected. Arise now, and go in peace.'

The burgesses scrambled to their feet, straightening their gowns and bowing low. 'Sire, you are wise and merciful,' stammered one. 'God save your Grace for his clemency.'

'Yes, yes,' said the king, waving his hand. 'Oh, and we require billets for myself and my captains. Make it so.'

The burgesses hurried back into the town. The king watched them go, and turned to the men around him. 'Did you see that?' he asked. 'My subjects ask for royal mercy, I grant them clemency, and they are grateful and praise me accordingly. Northburgh, make sure word of this gets back to England. I want people to know how magnanimous I have been. Northampton, Warwick, take note. Every time we conquer a new town, I want a reception like this.'

'Yes, sire,' said Northampton.

The king lifted the reins of his horse. 'Now. Let us go and inspect our new possession and greet our loyal subjects.'

–

The army had remained another four days at Saint-Vaast while the last troops and stores came ashore. Looters continued to burn and pillage the countryside, and Merrivale waited for Jean de Fierville to appear. He had asked Mauro and Warin to keep watch, and he felt certain that Edward de Tracey would be looking out too, but there was no sign of the Norman. Northburgh reminded him that several of Harcourt's men were carrying letters around the countryside urging people to defect to the English. 'Fierville might be one of them. If so, he may not return for several days.'

'That would be a pity. At the moment, he is my only remaining lead.'

Well, not quite. He thought about interviewing Matt and Pip again, and decided against it. Let us hear what Fierville has to say, he thought. Then, if he can prove he was somewhere else when Bray was killed, I shall be having a strong word with those two archers.

Before marching from Saint-Vaast to Valognes, the army was organised into three divisions. The Prince of Wales, to his loud and enthusiastic delight, was appointed to command the vanguard, although everyone knew that real command was vested in Warwick, the marshal.

'And what a sack of cats he will be marshalling,' said Sir John Sully. Returning from delivering a message to the king, Merrivale had encountered Sully as the last of the army was moving up off the beach. 'Have you seen who his captains are?'

Merrivale raised his eyebrows.

'Oh, they have given him some good men, no doubt,' Sully said. 'But whose idea was it to order Thomas Holland to serve alongside the Earl of Salisbury?'

Merrivale blinked. 'Perhaps they will learn to get along,' he said.

'Holland? That man is so full of choler, it is a wonder he doesn't boil over. Lock him up in an empty church and he'll pick a fight with the gargoyles. And that's not all.'

'Oh?'

'Hugh Despenser was originally ordered to serve in the rearguard, but at the last moment those orders were changed and he was assigned to the van. He will be rubbing shoulders with young Mortimer. And to crown it all, Matthew Gurney has been assigned to the same division as well.'

'For God's sake!' the herald said sharply. 'Why?'

'There are two possible explanations,' said Sully. 'One is that our good marshal has taken leave of his senses. But I've known Tom Beauchamp since he was a wet-nosed pageboy, and I've never seen any sign of mental aberration. The other explanation is that someone is deliberately meddling in the dispositions of the army.'

'What do you mean?'

'The army that fights well, fights together. The men put aside personal quarrels and rivalries and become brothers in arms. They are united in one task, defeating the enemy. If you want to break an army's fighting spirit, the fastest way to do so is to sow discord, particularly among the captains. Once they start fighting each other, the army quickly falls apart. I've seen it before, lad. At Bannockburn, and elsewhere too.'

'Do you really think these men will start fighting each other?'

'They'll be at each other's throats before midnight,' Sully predicted.

'You think someone is meddling. Who?'

'Now then, boy, wouldn't that be useful to know?' said Sully.

–

And so the army marched, through pomegranate-red sunlight along the dusty roads and tracks of Normandy. Men-at-arms jingled with harness and spurs, bright-polished armour dazzling in the light, brilliant surcoats and shields and banners a kaleidoscope of moving colour; light horsemen, hobelars from the north country and the Welsh marches, fanned out across the fields in little companies, with lances upraised like the quills of a hedgehog; long columns of archers in green and russet slouched down the road with their bows over their shoulders and quivers strapped across their backs; Welsh and Cornish spearmen sweated in their quilted gambesons and heavy leather skullcaps, daggers and axes tucked through their belts. The prince's division passed, then the centreguard under the king, with Northampton and Harcourt at his right hand, then the long rumbling column of baggage wagons, among which could be found a young English girl driving a small herd of recalcitrant milk cows, and finally the rearguard, commanded by the Bishop of Durham and the Earl of Arundel. As the dust settled behind them, the smoke of burning farms began to rise once more.

In Valognes, the citizens hid indoors while armoured men-at-arms rode through the streets looking for their billets. To the south, an enormous column of smoke billowed into the sky, obscuring the sun. By the time Merrivale reached the Duke of Normandy's house, where the king had taken up residence, the wind had changed and smoke was blowing across the town, dropping ash and sparks onto the thatched roofs below. An archer stood in the courtyard of the house with the carcass of a deer over his shoulders, haggling with one of the cooks. 'Come on, man! Look at her, she's a prime red deer hind! That's worth ten pence of the king's money any day!'

'Ten pence! Do you think we are made of money? Sixpence and not a farthing more.'

Northburgh came out to meet the herald. 'Chaos,' he said, motioning towards the hall. 'Not content with that piece of mummery outside the town, the king has invited the burgesses to join him for dinner, so that they can make further speeches praising his generosity. Any news?'

Merrivale shook his head. 'I am afraid not. There's still no sign of Fierville.'

Northburgh paused for a moment. 'Simon, my friend,' he said. 'Please do not take this the wrong way. But is it possible that you are mistaken? Is the prince's life really in danger?'

'I can only give you the same answer I gave the king,' Merrivale said. 'I do not know. The problem is that all the more commonplace explanations, such as accident or enemy action, do not stand up to scrutiny. I am convinced that Bray was killed deliberately.'

'And what is the link to Fierville?'

'He was spotted on the Valognes road at about the same time.'

'He might well have been on reconnaissance,' Northburgh said. 'Several Normans were sent to spy out the country soon after we landed. Fierville may have been one of them.'

'Yes. According to witnesses, he was seen riding hard down the road from Valognes, away from the enemy. But as soon as he saw our men, he wheeled and rode away again, back *towards* the enemy. Why?'

Northburgh did not answer. The cook and the archer struck a bargain at eight pence and the latter ran out of the courtyard whooping with delight, clutching the equivalent of nearly three days' pay in his hand. In an hour's time, Merrivale thought, he and his friends will be roaring drunk.

'There is something you should know,' Northburgh said finally. 'Our arrival at Saint-Vaast was expected by the enemy. They had a strong force ready in wait for us, on both land and sea.'

'Why did they withdraw?'

'We don't know. More worryingly, we also don't know how they knew when and where to expect us.'

⌐

–

Northburgh went back inside. Merrivale turned to find the cook standing in front of him, bowing. 'Sir Herald. Might I have a word with you?'

'Of course. You're Coloyne, aren't you? The king's head cook.'

'I am the *yeoman* of the kitchen, sir,' the man said stiffly.

Which meant, head cook. 'What is it?'

'I must apologise, sir, but after that impertinent archer departed, I fear I overheard some of your conversation with Master Northburgh. Concerning the landing at Saint-Vaast, that is.'

Behind him, two more cooks were hard at work skinning and butchering the deer. 'Go on.'

'While the court was ashore at Freshwater, one of my junior staff overheard something. She reported it to me, as was right, but I am afraid I dismissed the matter as being of no importance. But after hearing what Master Northburgh said, I fear I may have been wrong.'

'What did she overhear?'

'Perhaps it would be best, sir, if I summoned the girl and she told the story in her own words.' Coloyne turned to one of the men behind him. 'Fetch the cowherd, if you please.'

She came into the courtyard a few minutes later. Merrivale recognised her at once as the girl he had seen herding the cattle away from the fires at Saint-Vaast. She wore a pair of scuffed leather turnshoes with laces around her ankles, and an unbleached kirtle in an indeterminate shade of grey. Seen close up, she was not quite so young as he had thought; thirteen or fourteen, but small for her age. Her eyes widened a little at the stiff, glittering embroidery of his tabard, but she curtseyed and then stood straight with her hands at her sides, meeting his gaze. She was not short of confidence, he thought.

'What is your name, girl?' he asked.

'Nell Driver, sir.'

'Where are you from?'

'Southwick, sir. It is hard by Portchester.'

'How do you happen to be with the army, Mistress Driver?'

She blinked at the formality, but he wanted to show her she had nothing to fear. 'The herdsman was looking for someone to help with the cows, sir. The pay was good, a penny a day, so I said I would go.'

'Did your parents make no objection?'

'There's only my ma, sir, and she didn't mind. I'm one less mouth to feed. I wanted to see what the rest of the world looked like, sir,' she added.

Ash fell like black snow in the courtyard, and the men butchering the deer had to cover the carcass. This is what the world looks like, thought the herald. 'I understand you overheard something at Freshwater. Tell me what happened.'

'I went to sleep in the byre, sir, so I could keep an eye on the cows. One of them had been poorly. When I woke up, I heard two men outside. They were talking of the wind, and the delay it had caused, and how it could ruin all their plans. One man told the other he must get a message to France, to someone called Bertrand.'

Despite the summer heat and smoke, a cold finger ran down the herald's spine. 'Did they say what the message was?'

'Yes, sir. The first man said the king would still land at Saint-Vaast as planned, and Bertrand should hold his men together and wait. He said it was important, because if Bertrand succeeded, then my lord of Harcourt would be discredited.'

Merrivale kept his voice calm. 'Was there anything more?'

Nell thought. 'It was mostly just more of the same, sir. The one man kept repeating how important this all was. Then it started to rain and they went away.'

'Did they call each other by name?'

Nell shook her head. 'No, sir.'

'Would you recognise their voices if you heard them again?'

She paused. 'I don't know, sir. I might. They had powerful strong accents, both of them.'

'Where were the accents from, would you say?'

'The one man's was a bit like yours, sir, from out west somewhere. The other was from the north, I think.'

'Can you be more specific, mistress? Was it a hard accent like Northumberland or Cumberland? Or rounder, like you would find in Lancashire or Cheshire?'

For the first time, some of her confidence deserted her. 'I really don't know, sir. I'm not even sure where them places are. Until I joined the army, I'd never been further than Portsmouth.'

Merrivale smiled. 'Of course. It was a foolish question on my part. Just one more thing, mistress, if I may. During your travels with the army, have you seen a man-at-arms with a red lion in white on his coat and shield? His name is Jean de Fierville, and I wish very much to talk to him.'

'I have seen no such man, sir. I am sorry.'

'There is no need to be sorry, mistress. You have done very well.' Reaching into his purse, he took out a groat and handed it to her. 'Thank you,' he said.

A groat, four pence, was worth several days' wages. To his surprise, she smiled and shook her head. 'I'm well provided for, sir. Send it to my ma in Southwick, if you please. She needs the money more than me.'

—

The Prince of Wales had taken up residence in the second largest house in Valognes, a big town house belonging to the Bishop of Coutances, hanging his banner over the gate. Here too the courtyard was full of servants preparing dinner; ovens were roaring in the kitchens, and the smell of the prince's favourite spiced beef pies filled the air.

In the great hall, men milled about, some still in part armour or mail, others changed into tunics and hose and soft shoes, talking, drinking, shouting, laughing, celebrating the first day of the march. The prince sat at the high table playing dice with his friends, banging his fist on the table when he won, shouting with laughter when he lost, which was often. His tutor, Sir Bartholomew Burghersh, sat behind his shoulder, watching the play with a faint smile on his lips.

Most of the vanguard captains were there; Merrivale saw John Sully talking with John Grey and Richard Percy and the latter's older brother, Harry. Nicholas Courcy was there too, and their eyes met briefly before Courcy smiled and raised his glass. Thomas Holland was on the far side of the room next to a big brick fireplace, standing pointedly with his back to the Earl of Salisbury. He was a square-built man, dark-haired and deep-voiced, with a Lancashire accent; there were scars on his neck and cheek, and he wore a black patch over one eye. That sense of restless, barely suppressed anger that Sully had spoken of was palpable. Holland shifted on the balls of his feet, fingers sometimes tapping on his sword hilt.

Spotting Holland reminded the herald of the quarrel Mortimer had mentioned back at Portchester. Bracing himself for a difficult interview, he began to make his way across the room towards him.

He was halfway there when someone stamped into the hall and slammed the door shut. 'Holland!' a man shouted. 'I want a word with you!'

Holland stiffened but did not turn around. The man by the door was still in full armour, stained with dust and smoke, his face bathed in sweat. Merrivale did not need to see his surcoat – white quartered with gold frets on red and a black ribbon – to know that the newcomer was Sir Hugh Despenser. Twenty years might have passed, he thought, and yet for some in the room it still felt like no time at all.

'Holland!' Despenser shouted again. 'God damn you, look at me!'

Slowly, so slowly that the movement was an insult in itself, Holland turned to face him. 'What do you want, Despenser?'

Sir Hugh walked forward, people hurrying to get out of his way. 'Did you not hear the king's proclamation? No towns are to be burned or looted!'

'I heard it.'

'Do you see that smoke out there? That is Montebourg, the next town to the south. Those thieves you call your retinue have burned the place to the ground! Looted everything they could carry and put torches to everything they couldn't. Churches, priories, everything gone. What do you think the king will do when he hears this?'

Holland shrugged one shoulder. 'I have no idea. Why don't you run and tell him?'

'You stupid bastard! We are supposed to protect these people! How can we persuade them to join us when your brigands are burning them out of house and home?'

Matthew Gurney started to laugh. 'Well, well,' he said. 'A Despenser showing respect for the law! Whatever next? A horse that can play the bagpipes? A fish that can walk on land? Or just another obnoxious donkey braying in our midst?'

Laughter exploded around the room. The prince watched the scene, dice forgotten in his hand. Despenser looked at the circle of laughing, jeering faces, and his own face reddened. He reached out to the nearest man and ripped the goblet of wine from his hand, raising it in the air.

'I'm told you children like to play drinking games,' he said. 'Shall we play one now? It's called Happy Families. I'll show you how it works.'

He stabbed one finger at Holland. 'Did your father burn my father's lands, Sir Thomas? He did? Good! Take a drink! Are you a bigamist?' he asked, rounding suddenly on Salisbury. 'Why, of course you are! Take a drink! Ah, Sir Roger Mortimer, our newest knight. Did your grandfather hang my grandfather? Yes, by God, he did! Go on, take a drink!' Shouting over the rising tide of noise, he turned on Gurney. 'And you, Sir Matthew, did your father by any chance shove a red-hot poker up the old king's arse? Why, yes, he did! *Take a drink!*'

Holland, Salisbury, Mortimer and Gurney were all moving towards him. Despenser threw his goblet on the floor, wine spraying across the rushes. 'Do you want to fight me, girls? Come on outside, then. We'll see who can hold their claret, by Christ we will!'

A fist banged on the high table. '*Enough!*'

Every head turned. To Merrivale's surprise, it was the Prince of Wales who had spoken. He had risen to his feet, and now he banged the table again. 'The only fighting to be done here is with the enemy! That is my order, do you hear? Sir Hugh, do you hear me?'

'I hear you,' Despenser said stonily. 'Lord Prince, if you will not let me fight, then will you grant me another favour?'

The prince straightened. 'What is it?'

'My original post was with my lord of Arundel in the rearguard. Grant me permission to return there.'

Having briefly sounded like a leader of men, the prince now reverted to being a sixteen-year-old boy. 'Return to the rearguard? The vanguard is the post of honour, Sir Hugh, though perhaps the term *post of honour* means nothing to you?'

Hugh Despenser reached for his sword. Had he drawn it, the act would have cost him his life, but before his hand could touch the hilt, Merrivale ripped the weapon out of its scabbard. 'Outside! Now!' he snapped. 'My lord of Salisbury, I advise you to return to your seat immediately. Sir Roger, Sir Thomas, Sir Matthew, you will kindly accompany me. *Now!*'

He was not certain they would obey, but they did. Merrivale looked once at Burghersh, who should have intervened himself to stop this – who should have ensured that the scene had never happened in the first place – and the older knight gazed back at him with a face as blank as stone.

The herald followed the others out into the courtyard and presented Despenser with his sword, hilt first. Despenser slammed it back into the scabbard with a clash of metal.

'I presume, Sir Hugh, that you already appreciate your folly in attempting to draw your sword in the royal presence,' Merrivale said. 'I will say no more on that matter. As for the rest, you all heard the prince. We are in the presence of the enemy. Fighting each other is foolish and dangerous, and will draw the king's anger down on your heads.'

'I don't care,' Mortimer snapped. 'I will not stand idly by while this man insults my family.'

Despenser sneered. 'I merely stated some historical facts.'

'Lies,' spat Gurney. 'That is not how the old king died, and you know it!'

'Do I? Ask any alewife between Canterbury and Carlisle and she will give you a different story.'

'Then perhaps you should stick to keeping company with alewives, Despenser. You are clearly at home among them.'

'Indeed I am. Give me an honest alewife over a thief or a murderer any day.'

'Enough!' barked the herald. 'Sir Hugh, I will inform his Highness that you are unwell, and you will retire to your quarters. You will make your apology in the morning. Sir Matthew, Sir Roger, return to the hall, and let there be no further breaches of the peace. Sir Thomas, a moment of your time, if you please.'

–

The others departed. Holland shifted. 'You take a great deal upon yourself, herald.'

'If you dispute my actions, you may raise the matter with the king.'

'What do you want with me?'

'I am told that you had a dispute with Sir Edmund Bray at Portchester, not long before the fleet sailed. May I ask what that was about?'

Holland's good eye glared at him. 'How do you know this?'

Merrivale said nothing.

'He insulted my wife,' Holland said. 'That is all I am prepared to say.'

'Not everyone would agree that she is your wife.'

'I don't give a damn. In the eyes of God, she is mine!'

'You have no idea what God sees, and neither do I,' the herald said. 'Did the quarrel persist? Did you exchange words with him again?'

'No. The little turd avoided my company after that. He knew what I would do to him if I caught him alone. Then we embarked and I didn't see him again until the ceremony at the church.' Holland snorted. 'Bray, a knight. Christ in heaven. The prince will be knighting his grooms next, or his tailor.'

'Bray came from a good family, my lord.'

'He had Eustace Rowton for a sponsor. Otherwise he'd still be slopping out pigs back in Cheshire.'

'Did you kill him?' Merrivale asked.

'Did I— Jesus! You speak very boldly, herald!'

'And I am waiting for an answer,' Merrivale said. 'Your attempt to lay claim to the lady Joan very nearly cost you your head, Sir Thomas. You were reprieved because the king respects you as a captain. Show him, and me, that you are worthy of that respect. Tell me the truth about what happened between you and Bray.'

'He spoke badly of my wife and I punched him in the face. His friends dragged him away. That was all. I never spoke to him again, and I certainly never killed the little shit. Nor would I. He was beneath contempt.'

They looked at each other for a long time in the dull smoky sunlight. 'Go in peace, Sir Thomas,' the herald said.

It was nearly sunset when Warwick returned to Valognes. Along with Harcourt, Reginald Cobham and the Red Company, he had scouted far down the Cotentin, and he returned to headquarters dusty and tired and stinking of smoke. Dismounting, he handed over the reins of his horse, took a long draught from the glass of wine his esquire handed him and turned to Merrivale, who awaited him.

'Well? Any news?'

'Some,' the herald said, and he related what the cowherd had told him. Warwick listened intently, wiping the sweat from his grimy face.

'The fact that there are French spies in the army is hardly news. Is Fierville one of them?'

'That is a possibility. On another note, we had an unpleasant incident this evening at the prince's court.'

Again Warwick listened while Merrivale recounted what had happened. 'My lord, was it a good idea to put those men to serve cheek by jowl in the same division?'

'It was nothing to do with me,' Warwick said briefly. 'The order came from the king. I will speak to Despenser in the morning. As for the rest, let's hope the prospect of some real fighting will give them a distraction.'

'Oh?'

'Robert Bertrand is in Carentan, and he intends to make a stand there. The town is surrounded by marshes and water, and it won't be easy to take. We must try to keep those quarrelsome children under control until we get there, at least. And let me know as soon as you find Fierville.'

5

The long road south from Valognes was choked with traffic, wagons, carts and marching men pushing on through the shimmering heat. The air was full of dust and smoke. Earlier, they had passed Montebourg, piles of rubble and ash with scavengers picking through the ruins. Up ahead, the next town on the road, Sainte-Mère-Église, was already burning.

A hobelar, a light cavalryman armed with a long iron-tipped lance, reined in alongside Mauro's cart. He was sweating profusely under his quilted jack. 'Can you spare us a drink, brother?'

He caught the waterskin Mauro threw him and drank thirstily, then tossed it back. 'Where are you from?'

'Spain. And you?'

'Westmorland. Both a damned long way from home, aren't we?'

Up ahead, the traffic had jammed, for the dozenth time that day, and the long line of wagons rolled to a halt. Mauro engaged the brake on the cart, which contained his master's tent, baggage, portable furniture and records, and sat waiting for something to happen. A file of archers, dusty in green and russet, prowled past with their bows over their shoulders. They looked eagerly at the waterskin, and Mauro smiled and handed it down.

'Who are you with, brother?' the hobelar asked their leader.

'Sir Thomas Holland,' the man said. He was a big man, bald as an egg in the sunlight, with the tanned naked skin of his head split by a livid scar running from forehead to crown. His neck was thick with muscle and his face was seamed with wrinkles. Small, vivid blue eyes watched the world with a mixture of cunning and calculation. A veteran, Mauro thought. God knows how many battlefields he has seen, or how many atrocities.

'Holland? You lot are all Lankies, then?' the hobelar asked.

Heads nodded. 'Wigan and thereabouts,' one man said.

'Been out foraging? Any luck?'

The leader winked and lifted the flap of his haversack. Sunlight gleamed briefly off a pair of silver cups. The hobelar stared at them enviously. 'Where'd you get those? Sainte-Mère-Église?' The archers nodded. 'That's a lot of silver to be carrying around,' Mauro observed. 'Aren't you worried someone will steal it?'

The leader smiled, showing broken yellow teeth. 'No,' he said. 'I'm not worried. Anyone who wants to try is welcome.'

'We won't be carrying it around for long,' another man said. 'The bank will take care of it for us. Then we'll go out looking for another load, and another after that.' He grinned. 'This is a sweet little war, boys. Come summer's end, we are all going to be very rich.'

The hobelar looked at him, his envy growing. 'Bloody archers,' he said. 'We hobelars do the scouting, the men-at-arms do the close work once it gets sticky, but what do you lot do? Not much, I reckon.'

The leader turned to face him, caressing the riser of his longbow with a grimy hand. 'We do the killing, mate,' he said. 'We're hell's gatekeepers. Never mind your precious men-at-arms, we're the real butchers.' He nodded. 'Wait until the bastards show themselves. Then you'll see what we do.'

'Brag,' said the hobelar in disgust. He turned his horse and rode away down the column. The archers stared after him, and one lifted his bow and sighted on the hobelar's back. 'Shall I give him a shaft up the arse? He'll know we're not bragging then.'

'Don't waste an arrow on that shit,' the big man said. 'We'll get him alone one day. Then we'll shove something else up his arse. Something he won't forget.'

The others chuckled. The leader looked back at Mauro. 'Thanks for the drink, mate. Who's your master?'

'Herald to the Prince of Wales,' Mauro said.

'Soft billet,' commented one of the archers.

'You're a well-set-up lad,' the leader said. 'Why not throw in with us?' He tapped his haversack with a metallic clink. 'You could do well. Like Jannekin said, we're all going to be rich by summer's end.' He winked. 'And there's plenty of chances to raise hell on the side. If you know what I mean.'

Mauro looked at the fires raging in Sainte-Mère-Église. The church roof was beginning to burn, the tower already half obscured by smoke. 'Thanks. But I'll stick where I am.'

'Please yourself,' said the leader. He took another long drink of water. Mauro watched him, thinking.

'Holland's retinue,' he said after a moment. 'You must have been one of the first companies ashore, back at Saint-Vaast.'

'Us, Cobham's men and the Red Company.'

Mauro nodded. 'Once you were ashore, did you get a chance to do any foraging? Around Quettehou, maybe?'

The other man lowered the waterskin. 'What of it? I thought you weren't interested.'

'While you were out in the field, did you happen to see a Norman man-at-arms? Red lion on a white coat?' Was it his imagination, or had the little group of archers gone rather still?

'Why do you want to know?' the leader asked.

'My master would like a word with him, that's all.' Mauro hesitated for a moment. 'He did say there might be a reward.'

'A reward, now.' The leader scratched his scarred head. 'How much?'

Careful, Mauro thought. Offer too much and he'll grow suspicious and demand to know more; too little and he'll lose interest. 'I think I heard my master mention two shillings.'

The leader held out his hand. 'Do you have the money?'

Mauro didn't move. 'Did you see him?'

After a moment, the leader lowered his hand. 'Aye. At least, we saw a man wearing that coat. He was out on the Valognes road, talking to another fellow.'

'Any idea who the other fellow might have been?'

'Oh, we knew *him* all right. He's an old friend of the master. His name is Chauffin. Macio Chauffin.'

'And who might he be? We could make it three shillings.'

Suspicion and greed struggled in the leader's small blue eyes. Greed won. 'He's a French man-at-arms. In the service of the Count of Eu, the Constable of France.'

Mauro rubbed his jaw. 'How does your master know him?'

'Four years ago, there was a truce between England and France, so we all went off to Prussia together, Sir Thomas and his men, and the Count of Eu and his. We served together under the Teutonic Knights, campaigning against the heathen. Chauffin was with the count.'

'And he and your master became friendly?'

'Aye, and the count too. Like brothers they were.' The leader tilted up the waterskin again.

'Curious, that,' said Mauro. 'Bosom friends one year, trying to carve each other's guts out the next.'

'That's war,' said the big man. He threw the empty waterskin back, and Mauro caught it one-handed. 'In the end, mate, your only friend is yourself. Thanks for the water. And tell your master we want that reward. If we don't get it, we'll come looking for him, and you.'

Up ahead, the column was moving again. Thomas Ughtred, the under-marshal, galloped down the line on a lathered horse, shouting at the drivers. 'You men!' he snapped at the archers. 'What are you doing here? Get back to your company at once!'

The leader touched his bald head and the file of archers moved away across the fields through the drifting smoke. Mauro whipped up the carthorse and then sat back holding the reins, frowning.

Saint-Côme-du-Mont, 19ᵗʰ of July, 1346
Evening

The bells of Carentan were ringing vespers when Mauro finally drove the cart into the English camp on the heights at Saint-Côme-du-Mont, two miles from the town. The tide was in and the marshes that surrounded Carentan were flooded, a broad sheet of water stretching away to the south and east broken here and there by little islands and stands of trees. A long, narrow causeway ran across the marshes towards the town.

Mauro found his master with the Prince of Wales and his knights, standing and staring across the flooded marshes towards Carentan and listening to the distant bells. They could see the walls enclosing church towers and the ramparts of a distant castle. This was where Bertrand had chosen to make his stand.

'*Señor*,' Mauro said quietly, 'I have news about Jean de Fierville.'

'Come with me.' They walked away from the group until the others were out of earshot. 'What is it?' Merrivale asked.

Mauro related what he had learned from Holland's men. 'I promised them a reward,' he said. 'I hope I did the right thing, *señor*.'

'You did very well, Mauro. Thank you. I shall see that the money reaches them.'

Before joining the herald's little household, Mauro had experienced many years of slavery and hard servitude. Never before had he had a master who thanked him and praised him. Now he glowed a little with inward warmth. 'Fierville was meeting with a French knight in the service of the Constable of France,' he said. 'That does not sound good, *señor*.'

'No. Particularly when that knight is also a personal friend of Sir Thomas Holland. I wonder if Bray also witnessed this meeting.'

'Perhaps that was why he was killed,' Mauro said.

'Perhaps… one other thing bothers me. Sir Nicholas Courcy claimed he and his men were the first to go foraging in that sector. Now Holland's men are saying they were there too, perhaps even earlier.'

'Maybe Sir Nicholas was mistaken, *señor*,' Mauro suggested.

'Or he was lying.'

'Yes, *señor*. That is also possible.'

Merrivale looked out across the rippling flood towards Carentan. 'We need to find Fierville'.

It was Nell the cowherd who spotted him first, and came running through the camp to the place where the prince and his household were dining in the open air. Stopping and drawing breath, she spoke to one of the guards. He gave her a suspicious look, but when she repeated her request, pleading a little, he relented and came to find Merrivale.

'Sir Herald? Sorry to intrude on your dinner, sir, but there is a girl who wishes to speak to you. Nell Driver, her name is.'

'I will come at once.' Dinner that night was a simple affair, salt cod with pickles, pease porridge and onions, and chunks of white Somerset cheese with bread; the men were still under arms, ready for an assault on Carentan as soon as the orders came through. Carrying his wine cup and a piece of cheese, Merrivale followed the guard to where Nell stood waiting.

'He's here, sir,' she said. 'The man with the red lion. I know where he is.'

'Good lass.' He reached for his purse, but saw that her eyes were fixed on the piece of cheese. Smiling, he gave it to her and watched it vanish into the pocket of her kirtle. He drained his wine cup and handed it to the guard. 'Take me to him,' he said.

The king had established his headquarters at the manor house in Saint-Côme-du-Mont, not far from the little church. The man with the red lion on his surcoat was standing outside the gatehouse, arguing with the guards in the descending dusk. He was a tall man in a mail hauberk with a cuirass and arm guards strapped over the top of it, all covered in dust. 'I tell you, I have urgent business with the lord of Harcourt. I demand you admit me at once.'

'And I am telling you, *messire*, the lord of Harcourt is not here,' the captain of the guard said. 'And you will not interrupt the king at his dinner. Move along.'

'Do not give orders to me, villein! My lord is here, I tell you. He is the king's close companion. Now open the gate and let me enter.'

'The captain is telling the truth,' Merrivale said. 'My lord of Harcourt was dispatched with a flanking column this morning to cover the army's advance.'

Fierville turned. 'Then where is he now? I must see him. It is urgent.'

'Favour me with a few moments of conversation first.' Merrivale motioned with his hand and walked away from the gate, and after a moment, reluctantly, the knight followed him. Nell stood watching from a distance, taking a quick bite from the piece of cheese before putting it back in her pocket.

'Messire de Fierville,' the herald said. 'I wish to ask you about the events of the day we arrived at Saint-Vaast. Where did you go once you had landed, and what did you do?'

The question was purposefully vague, and he could almost see the wheels of Fierville's mind turning as he tried to work out what answer was required. 'I was sent out to scout the Valognes road,' he said.

'Who gave the order?'

'My lord of Harcourt, of course.'

'Did you know Sir Edmund Bray?'

He saw Fierville consider several possible answers and finally settle on the truth. 'Yes, I knew him.'

'When did you first meet him?'

'At Portchester, shortly after I joined the army. We met several times after that. I did not know him well.'

Merrivale paused for a moment, trying to decide how far he could go. Harcourt had directly forbidden him to question the Norman men-at-arms. Now he was breaking that order. He did not fear the consequences for himself, but there was always the concern that as a favour to Harcourt, the king would hand the inquisition over to someone else. 'Sir Edmund was killed on the Valognes road, in the same sector where you were scouting. Did you see him?'

'Yes,' Fierville said. 'That is to say, I saw his body.'

'Tell me.' His voice sounded more peremptory than he had intended, but Fierville seemed not to notice.

'I had spotted the French advance, and was riding back to report to his lordship. I found Bray's body lying in the road. He was already dead. There was nothing I could do for him. The French were coming on fast, and I had to fall back and leave him there.'

You are a bad liar, Merrivale thought. 'You did not see who killed him?'

'No.'

The herald nodded. 'And when did all this happen, *messire*? Before or after your meeting with the French knight Macio Chauffin?'

Fierville said nothing, but Merrivale saw his eyes widen.

'I have witnesses,' the herald said. 'They saw you talking to Chauffin just before Bertrand launched his attack.'

'Of course I was talking to him,' the Norman said. The impatience in his voice had a false ring to it, Merrivale thought. 'I was trying to open negotiations with him on behalf of my lord of Harcourt. Chauffin is in the service of the Count of Eu, but he is also friendly with my lord's brother, the Count of Harcourt. My lord is trying to persuade them both to defect to our cause.'

That was possible, Merrivale thought. Harcourt was desperate to bring the Norman lords to the English side. His own credibility, and the favour of the king, depended on his ability to do so. 'You met Chauffin by prior arrangement? When did you contact him?'

'That is none of your business.' The Norman raised a threatening finger. 'Keep quiet about this, herald. Not a word of this matter to anyone. Do you hear me?'

'My profession depends on discretion,' Merrivale said. 'You may rely on me.'

'Good. Now, I think we are finished here, no? Kindly tell me where my lord is, and I will be on my way.'

'He is at Coigny, five miles to the west,' Merrivale said. 'If you ride hard, you can reach him before dark.'

—

Mauro walked up behind him as Fierville rode away. 'Did you hear all that?' the herald asked.

—

'Yes, *señor*.' One of the things that made Mauro valuable as a herald's servant was his extraordinary hearing. Warin claimed he could hear a bat squeak at a hundred paces. 'Do you think he was telling the truth?'

'About some of it, perhaps. But he was lying when he said he found Bray already dead, and he lied again about his meeting with this man Chauffin. What is he hiding, I wonder?'

Nell the cowherd stood watching them with wide eyes. 'You could have arrested him, *señor*, and put him to the question,' Mauro said.

The herald shook his head. 'I cannot touch him. I shall need to speak to the Earl of Warwick.'

He paused for a moment, staring out over the marsh towards Carentan. 'And I fear he may not be very happy with me,' he said.

Saint-Côme-du-Mont, 19th of July, 1346
Night

'The causeway across the marshes is intact, so far as we can tell,' Warwick said. 'But Bertrand's men have broken down the bridge over the River Douve, halfway between here and the town. We must repair it before we can advance.'

The day's heat had gone and a chilly wind swept across the marshes. Men stood around them holding up torches that flickered in the blast. 'The tide is ebbing,' Edward de Tracey reported. 'By midnight the marshes will be uncovered. That should give our carpenters access to the foundations of the bridge.'

John Grey nodded. 'But they will have to work quickly,' he said. 'The tide will be at full flood again by morning.'

'John, Richard, find some boats and take your company across the Douve,' Warwick said. 'Protect the far end of the bridge, and sound the alarm if the enemy approaches. Edward, Hugh,' he said to Tracey and Despenser, 'cover the near end, but send every man you can spare to help the carpenters. I want that bridge repaired by first light. As soon as it is ready, we advance on Carentan.'

'What opposition can we expect?' asked Despenser. He did not look at Merrivale, and was clearly doing his best to pretend the herald did not exist.

'We don't know for certain how many men Bertrand has, but he has been calling up the local men-at-arms and seems determined to resist. When we advance, the main force goes straight for the gate. At the same time, Harcourt's column will move up from Coigny and attack from the west. By assaulting from two directions, we hope to overwhelm the defence.'

'How will we break down the gate?' Tracey asked.

'Cannon,' said Warwick. 'Courcy, I want those four gunildas up at the front of the column, ready to advance with the rest. Tracey's company will protect you and the gunners.'

Nicholas Courcy scratched his chin. Unusually for him, he looked worried. 'Well now. There might be a slight problem with the cannon, my lord.'

'What is it?'

The torches fluttered and roared in the wind. Merrivale noticed Roger Mortimer standing in the circle of men, watching.

'The gunpowder has gone missing,' Courcy said.

'*What?* All of it?'

'I fear so, my lord.'

'Body of Christ!' said Warwick. Angrily he smacked one gauntleted hand against his thigh. 'What happened to it?'

'I don't know, my lord. I suspect it has been stolen by looters.'

'Well, have you searched for it?' the marshal demanded.

'Not yet, my lord.'

'Why in hell's name not?'

'With respect, my lord, because I have not had time. You called on my services as an engineer to help repair the bridge, remember? In any case, I doubt we'll find it again. The looters will have hidden it by now, or sold it on.'

'We can break down the gates with mangonels,' John Grey said.

'Which means diverting some of the carpenters from work on the bridge to build them. Yes, yes, I know it must be done, but Christ's wounds! It is bad enough that these thieving bastards are pillaging the countryside, but if they have started robbing army stores as well, then we have a serious problem.' He looked at the men around him. 'Captains, control your men. And Courcy, I want that gunpowder replaced as soon as possible.'

The captains and knights dispersed. Warwick turned to the herald. 'Well? Have you found Fierville?'

'He has returned, my lord. I spoke to him earlier.'

'Spoke to him?' Warwick was still angry. 'I told you to let me know when you found him, not to interrogate him yourself.'

'Yes, my lord. I fear I was in error. But it seemed like a good opportunity to ask him what he knew about Bray.'

'God damn it, herald, I am not interested in Bray. I want to know whether this man is a French spy!'

'He is, my lord, I have no doubt of that. Fierville admitted to me that he was out on the Valognes road the morning we landed. There he met a French knight named Macio Chauffin, from the retinue of the Count of Eu. He claims he did so on behalf of my lord of Harcourt, who is negotiating with Eu, but I do not believe it.'

'Why not?'

'I was a king's messenger for ten years, my lord. Being able to judge a man's character quickly often meant the difference between life and death. Fierville does not dissemble well. I read his thoughts without difficulty.'

Warwick calmed a little. 'Where is he now?'

'Gone to join his master at Coigny. My lord, you may not care about the fate of Sir Edmund Bray, but I do. Fierville knows what happened to Bray, I am quite certain of it. At the very least, he is a witness to the killing.'

'Very well. I will speak to Harcourt as soon as he rejoins us, and then summon Fierville and question him myself. You can be present.' Warwick looked at him. 'You are wondering why his lordship is so protective of his men.'

'I am, my lord.'

'They are aliens in a strange land, herald. They have given up everything to follow him. Some of his supporters have already been executed, and the men who serve him now face the gallows if they are captured. Harcourt protects them out of loyalty.'

'Indeed, my lord. But permit me to wonder if that loyalty is misplaced. The lord of Harcourt cleaves to the English cause. But eight years ago, Fierville was one of the French leaders at the sack of Southampton.'

'I am aware of that,' Warwick said. 'But if you are right, herald, and he really is a spy, then he can expect no mercy.'

'No more than was shown to Sir Edmund Bray,' Merrivale said quietly.

–

From further along the causeway came a loud splash, the sound of something heavy hitting the water, followed by men shouting. Warwick and Merrivale ran towards the scene to find Nicholas Courcy climbing out of the river below the broken bridge, dragging with him the heavily armoured semi-conscious body of Roger Mortimer. There was a pause while Courcy heaved the younger man onto his side, then unlaced his backplate, peeled it off and thumped him on the back. After a few hard blows, Mortimer gagged and then rolled over and began to spew river water.

'What happened?' Merrivale asked.

'He fell into the river,' Courcy said. 'Luckily he landed in the shallows and I was able to pull him out. If he had gone into the deep stream, that would have been the end of him.' Weighed down by eighty pounds of mail and plate, Mortimer would have drowned before anyone could rescue him.

Hugh Despenser walked up to Mortimer and looked down at him. 'Are you all right?'

Mortimer retched again, and sat up, dragging air into his lungs. He nodded. Despenser turned on his heel and walked away. Mortimer started to say something, but choked and vomited again. The herald waited.

'I did not fall,' Mortimer gasped finally. 'Someone pushed me. They hit me from behind and shoved me into the river.'

'Did you see who it was?' Merrivale asked.

'It was that bastard Despenser! Or one of his men. By God, they should have hanged the whole bloody family and made an end to them.'

'Easy,' said the herald, placing a hand on his shoulder. 'You have had a narrow escape, Sir Roger. Go back to camp and get some rest. Let the carpenters get on with the job. There will be work for us all in the morning.'

Slowly, his clothes and armour streaming water, Mortimer rose to his feet and walked with as much dignity as he could muster back along the torchlit causeway towards the camp.

Men hurried past, carpenters shouldering heavy wooden beams. The thump of hammers and rasp of saws echoed through the night air across the dark marshes. Warwick went down to the water's edge to check on progress. Merrivale turned to Courcy. 'Did you see what happened?'

'The devil I did,' said Courcy. 'One moment he was standing beside me, the next he was down in the river. I didn't see anyone push him, if that is what you mean.'

Merrivale studied him. 'Alchemist, now engineer,' he said. 'You've many strings to your bow, Sir Nicholas.'

Courcy grinned. 'I've been a shipmaster, too, and I worked for a while as a coiner at the mint. I studied the liberal arts at Balliol College for a year, until the master threw me out. Yes, I've turned my hand to plenty of things in my time.' He paused for a moment. 'None of them, I would say, with any conspicuous success.'

'What do you think happened to the gunpowder?'

'Like I said, it's these cursed looters. There's nothing they won't steal.' Merrivale could not see Courcy's face in the flickering shadows, but he could hear the humour in his voice.

'I have another question for you. When you found Bray's body, you claimed you were the first ones into that sector after the fighting. But some of Holland's men say they were there before you. Did you see them?'

'Ah, the Lanky boys.' Courcy's voice held a mixture of admiration and despair. 'No, I didn't see them, but it wouldn't surprise me, Sir

Herald. It wouldn't surprise me at all. I count myself a pretty fair forager, but those fellows make light-fingeredness into an art. Blink and they'll steal the eyebrows off your face. Yes, there's a fair chance they were there before us. That could explain why we found nothing worth stealing,' he added wryly.

He looked at Merrivale. 'Do you think they might have killed young Bray? Perhaps he caught them in the act of looting and threatened to report them.'

'Would they really kill an English man-at-arms? One of their own side?'

'The only side those vultures are on is their own. They'd do it, herald, if it suited them, and they wouldn't think twice about it. They're not like the rest of us, you see. They're not the usual plough-boys and herdsmen and apprentices who took the bounty so they could see the world and make a little money on the side. Holland's men have been with him for every campaign for the past five years, France and Prussia and Spain. They've been at war too long. They're not just good at inflicting misery; they enjoy it. But they would not have left that great ruby ring behind.'

The vehemence in his voice was quite out of character. 'You sound angry,' Merrivale said.

There was a short pause, and then Courcy laughed. 'Angry?' he said in his usual light tone. 'Bless you, herald, but no. Life is a beautiful thing, and I don't propose to waste a minute of it on something so futile as anger. All the same, I wish someone would do something about those bastards. They give good honest pillagers like myself a bad name.'

-

Back at the camp, Merrivale made his way to Roger Mortimer's tent. He found the young knight lying on his cot; he had removed his armour, but was still in his wet arming doublet and hose, staring up at the wind-ruffled canvas. A single candle burned on a wooden chest beside the cot.

'How do you feel?' the herald asked.

'Like I have swallowed half the river. I still have a gutful of water.'

'You said someone pushed you. Are you quite certain of that?'

'Yes,' said Mortimer without moving. 'I am quite certain.'

'Why would anyone wish to do such a thing?'

'To settle old scores, of course. Everyone hates the Mortimers.'

'That is not true,' Merrivale said quietly. 'The prince, for example, does not hate you. I think he is actually rather fond of you.'

Mortimer gave a snort of disgust. 'That little shit is fond of no one but himself. He is just as arrogant as his father, perhaps even more so.'

'You do remember I am his herald,' Merrivale said, his voice still quiet. 'And I should be careful also not to bite the hand that feeds you. Service in this army is a chance for redemption, for you and your family. Your knighthood is a symbol of that.'

'Redemption? Why in hell do I need redeeming? *I* have done nothing wrong.' Mortimer finally turned his head to look at Merrivale. 'Why do you put up with it, herald? According to what I hear, you have precious little reason to be grateful to them.'

'Whom do you advise me to hate?' Merrivale asked. 'Edward of Woodstock had not even been born when misfortune struck my family. His father the king was only nine years old. Those who harmed my family are long dead. And I have learned, Sir Roger, that there is very little profit in hating the dead.'

'And the living bear no responsibility? They get off scot-free?'

'I did not say that. But consider this. Perhaps, in his own clumsy, awkward, boyish way, the prince is also seeking... not redemption, that is the wrong word, but restitution. Perhaps by taking you into his service and knighting you, he is trying to make up for the loss you have suffered.'

'You give him too much credit,' Mortimer said. His voice had suddenly gone thick, as if he was having trouble speaking. 'I know you mean well, herald, but please leave me.'

Silently Merrivale turned and walked out into the night. He stood for a while watching the torches flickering along the causeway and on the distant ramparts of Carentan. He remembered again the rain and the mud and the rotting sheep; the linen-swathed bundles that had once been his sisters and mother being lowered into the ground and the earth covering them; the bailiffs arriving to arrest his father for failure to pay his rents and seize his dark, drowning lands.

Nine years old, he thought. I was nine then too, the same age as the king. No child should have to see what I saw. And yet the world shows no sign of changing.

What had John Sully said? Do what your conscience tells you, and damn the rest. That's the only thing a man can do.

Sighing suddenly, the herald turned away towards his own tent.

6

In the end, the siege engines were not needed. At first light, the trumpets sounded and the army came down off the heights and hurried along the repaired causeway towards the town. As the vanguard drew closer, they saw the gates standing wide open, the ramparts empty of defenders. Unlike at Valognes, there was no procession of burgesses waiting to surrender and pledge their allegiance to the king. Carentan had been abandoned.

Yelling with delight, the leading companies began smashing doors and windows and breaking into houses. Smoke and flames were already rising from a dozen points by the time Warwick and the Prince of Wales entered the town. Swearing violently, Warwick directed his under-marshal to arrest as many looters as possible, but it was too late. The sounds of shouting, drunken singing, splintering wood and smashing glass and crockery echoed through every street and alley.

In the main square they found the Red Company, the only company to have maintained its discipline, standing guard over the church of Notre-Dame. Richard Percy walked forward, sheathing his sword, as Warwick and the prince rode up. 'Most of the townspeople have fled,' he said. 'But there are refugees inside the church, about thirty in all. People who were too slow, or too old and infirm, to escape.'

'Protect them as best you can. Any sign of the enemy?'

'The castle is still holding out. The gates are shut and there are men on the ramparts, including at least one crossbowman.'

'Is Bertrand there?'

'There's no sign of his banner.'

A row of arcaded shops along the eastern side of the square was burning, smoke pouring from windows and doors, tiles cracking as flames licked up through the roofs. The prince watched the destruction, his followers nudging each other and laughing. They cheered when a roof caved in and a shower of sparks danced up through the smoke. Their horses stirred, restless.

More men rode into the square, iron-shod hooves hammering on the cobbles, the red and gold banner of Harcourt floating over their heads. Harcourt rode up to Warwick, gesturing towards the fires. 'What is this? The town has surrendered. It should be under the king's protection.'

'If the burgesses had remained, we could have protected them. Once the troops realised the town was empty, there was no stopping them. Why did the townsfolk flee, Godefroi? You sent them letters urging them to surrender, did you not?'

'My messenger was ambushed and killed before he could reach the town. Another is missing too, Jean de Fierville. That son-of-a-whore Bertrand knew my men were coming and set traps for them.'

Warwick looked at the herald, seated on his palfrey amid the Prince of Wales's household. Warin the groom was behind him, mounted on a shaggy pony. 'Your pardon, my lord,' Merrivale said. 'But I saw Jean de Fierville last night in Saint-Côme-du-Mont. He was looking for you.'

Harcourt glanced at him sharply. 'Did he say what his errand was?'

'Only that it was urgent. I told him he could find you at Coigny, and he rode away.'

'He never reached Coigny,' said another of the Normans. It was the man who had threatened Merrivale the night after the landing. 'You are right, my lord. He must have been ambushed too.'

'Bertrand's men are still holding the castle,' Warwick said. 'We need to prise them out. Godefroi, take your men around to the Saint-Lô gate and hold it. If the garrison tries to break out from the castle, stop them. John, Richard, leave a detachment of your men to guard the church, and follow me.'

The streets were full of clouds of choking yellow-white smoke, bearing drifting embers on the currents of air like flotsam on the tide. The horses snorted and sweated with fear, and the men-at-arms had to use spurs to force them on.

Somewhere nearby another roof caved in, flames glaring red through the smoke. The herald's horse reared up, front hooves flailing. For a moment he clung to the saddle, unable to do anything but hold on, and then Warin rode up alongside him and grabbed the reins, pulling the beast down. By the time they had the horse under control again, Warwick and the prince and his household had vanished into the rolling smoke. Merrivale looked around, trying to see which way they had gone. From somewhere close by, invisible in the smoke, a woman screamed.

Merrivale stiffened. 'Where did that come from?'

The voice screamed again, an inarticulate shriek of terror and anger. Warin pointed down an alley leading off the street. 'That way, sir,' he said urgently.

'Come on.' The alley was too narrow for horses; they jumped from the saddle and ran. The houses had not yet begun to burn, but the narrow street was still clogged with acrid smoke. Again the woman screamed. They rounded a bend in the lane, and stopped.

Two men stood facing them, archers clad in russet, one with a leather cuirass over his jerkin. Their bows were slung across their backs and they had knives in their hands. Behind them was a third archer, a big man with a shining bald head bisected by a red scar running across his scalp where someone at some point in the past had tried to carve his head open and failed. In one hand he held a short sword; his other arm was wrapped around a woman, barefoot, with long, dishevelled hair, who struggled violently, trying to get free.

The big man swore at her. 'Hold still, bitch!'

In reply, the woman grabbed his hand, pulled it to her face and bit him hard on the wrist. The big man yelped, raising his arm, and the woman darted away, running towards Merrivale. Fast as a cat, the man was after her, grabbing her by the shoulder and tearing her gown, then throwing her hard down onto the cobbles. He stood over her, sword pointed at her throat.

'Leave her alone,' Merrivale said sharply.

One of the archers shook his head. 'You don't give the orders here, herald.'

'I speak in the king's name. Let the woman go.'

The big man looked up. He was breathing heavily, and blood dripped from his wounded wrist. 'The king isn't here,' he said. 'And the bitch is ours. Get out of here, if you want to live.'

The other two raised their knives and started walking towards Merrivale. Warin stepped forward, drawing his own knife, but Merrivale waved him back. 'I am the herald of the Prince of Wales,' he said calmly. 'And you cannot touch me.'

'Herald to the Prince of Wales, is it? You owe us three shillings, herald. For the information we gave to that black man of yours.'

'I will pay it,' Merrivale said. 'As soon as you let the woman go.'

'No,' said one of the other archers, and he smiled a broken-toothed smile. 'The price has just gone up, mate. Hand over your purse, and that ring on your finger too. Nice and easy, now.'

The ring was his seal ring; it was one of the few things he had been allowed to inherit from his father. 'Don't be damned fools. If you harm me, you will hang. Step back now, and let the woman go.'

'Do as he says,' a soft voice said behind him.

Merrivale turned. Two more archers stood in the narrow street, wearing the dark red iron caps of the Red Company. Both had arrows at the nock, ready to draw and shoot in an instant. He recognised the fine-featured, serious young faces at once; Matt and Pip, the two men Sir John Grey had sent after Edmund Bray.

The Lancashire men hesitated. Their bows were still slung; Matt and Pip could shoot two of them before they moved, and probably the third before he could bring his bow into play. The big man with the scarred head snarled at them. 'I'll kill the woman. Lower those bows and walk away, or I'll cut her throat and let you watch her bleed to death.'

A blur of movement, almost too fast for the eye to see; Matt drawing his longbow, pulling the nock back beside his ear and loosing. Humming, the arrow shot past the big man's head, so close that the barb drew blood from his ear. He shouted, clapping his hand to his head for a moment and then looking at the blood on his fingers. 'You bastard,' he said ominously.

'I missed you deliberately,' Matt said. Already he had another arrow at the nock. 'I won't miss again. It is you, soldier, who will walk away. You and your friends, now.'

A long, tense moment passed, and then the big man raised his sword. Blood ran from his ear down his neck and dripped onto his jerkin. 'Come on,' he said to the others. 'There'll be easier pickings elsewhere, I reckon. Aye, and prettier ones too.' He kicked the woman as she lay on the ground, then turned and strode away through the curtain of smoke. His companions followed him.

Merrivale turned to the two archers. 'Thank you. But why are you here?'

'Sir John realised you were missing, and thought you might have got lost in the smoke,' Matt said. 'He sent us to find you. If I was you, sir, I'd be going soon. Your horses are still out in the street, unattended and pretty much inviting someone to steal them.'

Again there was that confidence, Merrivale thought. These were no ordinary archers. 'Just a moment,' he said. The woman was sitting up, and he hurried to her, taking her hands and lifting her to her feet. '*Madame*, are you hurt? Are you injured?'

She raised her head. Her face was a mask of dirt and grime and her dark red hair fell in tangled clouds around her shoulders and over her face. Her gown had once been fine, but it was soiled and ragged now, and one sleeve had been half torn off, the points ripped and dangling. Her feet were dirty too, and he could see blood on one of them. She was young, he realised, no more than twenty.

'Thanks to you, I am unharmed,' she said. Her voice was shaky but strong. 'May I know the name of my saviour, *monsieur*?'

'I am Simon Merrivale, herald to the Prince of Wales. Who are you, *madame*, and where did you come from?'

'It is *demoiselle*. My name is Tiphaine de Tesson, and I have been imprisoned in the castle of Carentan for the past two years. When your army advanced on the town, I escaped and came here hoping to find your commanders. You must take me to them, *monsieur*. It is urgent.'

He saw the desperation in her brown eyes. Questions could wait, he thought. 'We have horses waiting. Are you well enough to ride? Good, come with me. Warin, give her your pony and follow us on foot. Lead the way, *demoiselle*.'

–

The castle lay in the southern quarter of the town, not far from the Saint-Lô gate. The streets here had not yet begun to burn. They found Warwick and his officers crouched behind the corner of a jettied stone house, looking out at the castle on the far side of the square. The prince and his knights and serjeants of his bodyguard waited further back, out of range of enemy crossbows. No one was visible now on the ramparts of the castle, but the gates were still firmly shut.

'My lord Warwick!' the herald called, sliding out of the saddle and reaching up to help Tiphaine down. 'This lady has recently escaped from the castle. She says she has urgent news.'

Warwick rose and came towards them. The other officers followed, armour and mail clanking. 'Who are you, *demoiselle*?' the marshal asked.

'I am Tiphaine de Tesson. My father was the lord of La Roche Tesson, whom King Philippe executed for rebellion and treason two years ago. I was arrested along with my father, and I have been held in prison in Carentan castle ever since. My cell was in the walls, directly under the ramparts, and I often overheard officers of the garrison talking. This morning when your army began to advance, I heard Messire Robert Bertrand giving orders to the commander of the castle.'

'One moment, *demoiselle*. How strong is the garrison? How many men?'

'Not more than twenty. Messire Bertrand has withdrawn with the rest to Saint-Lô.'

'Only twenty?' said Edward de Tracey. 'We can storm the place easily.'

John Grey nodded. 'No need to wait for the mangonels. A simple ram will break the gates down.'

The woman shook her head violently, her tangled hair swinging around her shoulders. 'No, *messire*! A trap is waiting for you!'

'A trap?' Warwick said sharply. 'What sort of trap?'

'I do not know, *messire*. I only heard Messire Bertrand say to the commander, "Wait until they enter, then spring the trap. Once it is done, escape with your men as best you can." And the commander said, "Do not fear. They will be destroyed."'

'What is the name of the commander?' Merrivale asked.

'He is called Raoul de Barbizan. He is one of King Philippe's officers.'

Merrivale turned to Warwick. 'Let me parley with this man, my lord. Once I am inside the castle, perhaps I can discover what this trap is.'

Warwick frowned. 'Herald, you are an ambassador, not a scout. You would be overstepping the bounds. If Barbizan were to discover what you are up to, he would be perfectly entitled to kill you.'

The flames were drawing nearer; a gust of smoke swirled in the street around them. 'He will not discover it,' Merrivale said.

'Perhaps not,' said Nicholas Courcy, stepping forward. 'But all the same, herald, I think Donnchad and I will come with you. I'm thinking you might need a little assistance.'

Donnchad was a shaggy mountain of a man, bigger even than the Lancashire archer Merrivale had faced down a few minutes earlier. 'I do not need assistance,' the herald said. 'I can gain entrance to the castle without difficulty.'

'I am sure you can. But I fancy you might need a wee bit of help getting out again.'

-

The rest of Carentan was fire and chaos, but the square before the castle was silent as death. The loudest sound was the boots of the three men rasping on the cobbles. The herald walked straight towards the gate, hands at his sides, his tabard shining in the smoke-tainted sunlight. Courcy and Donnchad still wore their swords, but they held their hands out wide, away from their weapons.

A man appeared on the roof of the gatehouse, resting a crossbow on the ramparts and levelling it. His voice echoed hollow off the stone walls around him. 'Who are you? State your business!'

'I am Simon Merrivale, herald to the Prince of Wales. I wish to speak to the Sire de Barbizan.'

'What do you want with him?'

'Carentan has fallen. We know your defences are weak and you cannot withstand an assault for long. I am here to negotiate your surrender.'

The crossbowman said nothing. He remained motionless, his weapon pointed at the three of them. After some little time, a postern gate in the wooden door swung open.

'You may enter,' the crossbowman said.

Merrivale stepped through the postern, Courcy and Donnchad following. Glancing up at the gate arch, he saw that the portcullis had been raised. Courcy noticed it too. 'That's a curious thing.'

'Yes.' If the defenders were preparing to resist an assault, the portcullis should have been lowered.

A single man stood waiting for them in the courtyard of the castle. He wore full armour, but in the heat of the day he had removed his bascinet and pulled the cowl of his mail coat down so he was bareheaded. His sweat-damp hair clung to his forehead in curls. Glancing back at the gatehouse as they passed, Merrivale saw a wooden door standing open. A cart was parked before it, tipped forward and resting on its shaft. The crossbowman stood on the gatehouse roof above them, crossbow pointed at their backs.

'Drop your swords,' said the man in the courtyard.

Courcy and Donnchad drew their swords and laid them on the cobbles. Out of the corner of his eye, the herald saw Courcy glance once at Donnchad, and saw too the almost imperceptible lift of the other man's head.

'Who are these men?' the Frenchman demanded.

'My escort,' Merrivale said. 'Sir Nicholas Courcy of Kingsale and his attendant. Have I the honour of addressing Messire Raoul de Barbizan?'

'I am he. What do you want?'

'Robert Bertrand stripped the garrison when he withdrew this morning,' Merrivale said. 'We know you have only a few men. You cannot hope to resist our army. Surrender now, and save your lives. You and your men will be fairly treated. I give you that assurance in the name of the Prince of Wales, my master.'

Barbizan considered this for a moment. 'You underestimate us,' he said. 'You have seen how strong this castle is. Twenty men could hold it for a week.'

'If you refuse, the offer will not be repeated.'

Barbizan said nothing. Merrivale bowed. 'So be it,' he said. 'Farewell, *messire*. I salute your courage.' He turned away towards the gate.

'Wait,' Barbizan said.

The herald waited. 'I will surrender only to the king,' said Barbizan. 'He must come here in person. I will kneel to him and offer him my sword and the keys to the castle. To him only, herald. No one else.'

Merrivale shook his head. 'The king has not yet entered the town. But the Prince of Wales is near at hand. You may surrender to him if you wish.'

'The prince? I do not kneel before children,' Barbizan snapped.

Merrivale let a few moments pass. 'The prince will receive your surrender outside the castle,' he said firmly.

Barbizan hesitated, glancing towards the gatehouse. 'No. I demand that the surrender takes place here, inside the castle.'

'Why?' demanded Merrivale. 'Why is that so important?'

'I do not answer to you, herald. Only to your master.'

'Then I am afraid we are at an impasse,' said Merrivale, and he turned away again.

Something hit him in the back like a battering ram: Donnchad, slamming into him and shoving him bodily behind the cart just as a crossbow bolt smacked into the cobbles where he had been standing and ricocheted away in a shower of sparks. Courcy pulled a knife from the sleeve of his leather tunic and threw it, and Barbizan collapsed with blood gushing from his throat. The Irish knight picked up the two swords, throwing one to Donnchad and pointing up at the crossbowman on the roof. *'Téigh! Críochnaigh é, go gasta!'*

Donnchad ran through the door into the gatehouse and they heard his boots pounding on the stairs as he raced towards the roof. The crossbowman was already reloading; they had about twenty seconds before he shot again. There was a strange smell in the air, and after a moment Merrivale recognised it as sulphur. Looking inside the cart, he saw traces of fine pale grey dust on the floorboards, glistening a little in the strong sun.

'Sir Nicholas!' he called. 'Come quickly!'

Shouts sounded from the roof of the gatehouse; Donnchad was fighting with the crossbowman. Courcy hurried over to the cart, and Merrivale pointed to the powder. The Irishman shut his eyes for a moment, and the herald saw him go pale under his sunburn. 'Oh Jesus,' he said.

'They used this cart to transport the gunpowder,' Merrivale said. He turned and began to walk towards the gatehouse door. After a moment's hesitation, Courcy ran up alongside him. 'Stand back, herald,' he said grimly. 'This is a job for a fighting man.'

Silently Merrivale followed him into the gatehouse. Just inside the door, the stairs rose in a steep spiral towards the roof, where the clatter of swords could now be heard. Another door led to the guardroom. Courcy tried the latch, but it did not budge.

'Barred on the inside,' Merrivale said.

'Not for long.' Courcy stepped back and kicked the door hard, then again, and again. On the fourth blow they heard wood begin to splinter, and on the fifth the door sprang open, bouncing off the stone wall behind. Sword in hand, Courcy shouldered his way through.

Sword blades clashed, steel rasping on steel, and someone shouted with pain. The herald pushed through the doorway into sudden gloom; the guardroom was lit only by shafts of sun coming through the arrow slits. In the dim light he saw Courcy fighting desperately, holding off two men, one of them bleeding but still coming on. Behind Courcy stood a third man, armoured but with the visor of his bascinet raised so he could see more clearly. His surcoat was white with a red lion rampant, combatant. His sword was raised for a killing stroke.

The sword was already descending when Merrivale grabbed Jean de Fierville's arm with a grip of iron and spun him around so that the blow intended for Courcy's head clattered off the stone floor of the guardroom. Before Fierville could raise his weapon again, Merrivale punched him hard in the face. The Norman staggered, his nose streaming blood, and Merrivale hit him twice more, driving him back against the wall of the guardroom. On the far side of the room was a row of stacked wooden barrels, with something hissing and fizzing on the floor in front of them: a powder train, already burning. The air stank of sulphurous smoke.

One of the men Courcy was fighting was down, clutching at his chest, dying. Merrivale hit the Norman again, a powerful back-handed blow that broke his jaw with a sickening crack, and then tore the sword from his grasp. Ripping Fierville's bascinet off, he clubbed the other man hard over the temple with the pommel of the sword. Fierville's eyes rolled back in his head and he slumped to the floor with a clatter of metal. Behind him, Courcy feinted high and low, then closed in and kicked his opponent hard on the knee. He doubled over in pain and Courcy stabbed him through the chest, stepping back to let the body slide to the floor.

'Holy Mary, Mother of God,' Courcy said breathlessly, and both men ran across the guardroom towards the barrels. A trail of flame snaked across the floor, breathtakingly fast, eating up the powder train. It was less than a foot away from the stacked barrels of serpentine; only a few heartbeats between them and oblivion. Then Courcy's boot came down hard on the flame, stamping and stamping, snuffing it out, while the herald kicked away the rest of the powder to scatter the train. More smoke wafted into the air, but the flame died.

'It has stopped,' Merrivale said.

'Jesus,' Courcy said again. He was white as a sheet now, bent over and rasping for breath. 'Faith, that was as close as I ever want to come. I am not yet ready for paradise, herald. And I am pretty damned sure paradise isn't ready for me.'

Boots thundered on the stairs and Donnchad burst into the room, bloody sword in hand. 'You took your time,' Courcy said. 'Go find out where the rest of the garrison are, you great ox, and this time hurry back.'

Donnchad disappeared. Courcy turned to Merrivale, wiping the sweat from his face. 'You're a fraud,' he said, grinning.

'What do you mean?'

'A true herald shouldn't know how to fight like that. Coats of arms are his profession, not weapon craft.'

'I wasn't always a herald,' Merrivale said.

'Oh? What were you?'

Merrivale said nothing. *What do I say?* he thought. *That once upon a time I was a small boy who fought other boys for scraps of food? That I was a king's messenger and fought for my life more times than I can count?*

'Look out!' Courcy shouted.

Fierville was on his feet, face a mask of blood, a dagger in his hand. He hurled it at Courcy, who ducked just in time; the dagger missed him by a hair's breadth and thudded into one of the casks of serpentine. The Norman ducked through the guardroom door and ran outside. Merrivale followed him, but by the time he reached the courtyard, Fierville was already sprinting across the cobbles towards the donjon on the far side.

Two men ran up beside the herald, archers with arrows nocked. 'Stop him!' Merrivale shouted without thinking.

One of the archers raised his bow, drew and released. The bowstring hummed; the arrow, a blur of motion faster than sight, hit Fierville in the back, slamming through his backplate and driving deep into flesh and bone. He stumbled once, pitched forward and fell onto the cobbles. In that shattering moment, the herald saw how Edmund Bray had died.

–

Fierville was still breathing when Merrivale reached him, but his eyes were closed and his face was pallid. His armoured limbs twitched a couple of times and then relaxed into death.

Merrivale rounded on the archers. It was the Red Company men again, Matt and Pip. 'Why did you kill this man? We needed him alive!'

'You ordered us to stop him, sir,' Pip said. 'You didn't say how.'

The fact that it was his own mistake only made Merrivale more angry. 'What the devil are you doing here?'

'Sir John's orders, sir. When you failed to return, he sent us to investigate.'

'Why did he pick you?' Merrivale demanded.

'We don't know, sir,' said Matt. As usual, his confidence bordered on insolence. 'You would have to ask Sir John.'

Merrivale bit back his anger. 'Tell Sir John the garrison have refused to surrender. Five are dead, but there are still fifteen to be accounted for. I suspect they are trying to escape through a postern gate. Fierville was running to join them.'

Matt nodded. 'We will tell him, sir. Er... the lady was asking after you, sir. The one you rescued. May we tell her that you are safe?'

'Tell her whatever you wish,' the herald snapped, and walked back into the gatehouse.

Courcy was still in the guardroom, staring at the barrels of powder. 'I am not the only fraud in this room, Sir Nicholas,' Merrivale said.

Courcy turned towards him, face full of resignation. 'No,' he said. 'You most certainly are not. How did you work it out?'

'It was not exactly difficult. Those barrels have the arrowhead mark branded on them. They come from the Tower armoury. English gunpowder, Sir Nicholas. Powder that was in your custody.'

'Yes,' said Courcy.

'Fierville and Barbizan set a trap for us. Once the surrender was accepted and the army had advanced through the gates, the powder train was to be set alight. The explosion would blow out the walls of the guardroom and bring the entire gatehouse down on the men beneath it. Scores could have been killed. When they realised we had seen through the plan, they set light to the train anyway in hopes of killing us, at least, and destroying the evidence.'

'Yes,' Courcy said again.

Merrivale faced him. 'You sold the serpentine to Fierville, didn't you?'

'As God is my witness,' Courcy said, 'I had no idea this was his intention. I thought he was on our side. He told me he wanted the powder to arm some ships.'

'Ships?'

'Apparently he is a shipowner, and some of his ships are armed with guns. *Pots-de-feu*, they call them in these parts. He was powerful knowledgeable about powder, quite put me to shame. I thought he was a fellow professional.'

'So you sold him the powder, no doubt for a tidy profit. What next? You're an alchemist, you said. You intended to make more powder yourself, and offer it to the king's officers to replace the missing stocks. Once again, for a profit.'

'I saw no harm in it,' Courcy said. 'Making gunpowder is easy, herald. You only need three ingredients: sulphur, charcoal and saltpetre. Getting hold of the sulphur is easy if you know the right people. Charcoal is cheap and plentiful, and if you want saltpetre, all you have to do is piss in a bucket. The king would have had all the powder he needed in a day or two. I swear on my mother's grave, I intended no evil.'

Merrivale regarded him for a long time. 'I am sorry to hear of the loss of your mother,' he said finally.

'Don't be. She's as hale and well as I am. Her grave is already marked out and paid for in Kingsale church, nice and close to the altar so she'll go to heaven all the faster. Unlike my father, who is headed in the opposite direction.' Courcy sighed. 'What happens now?'

'We are alone,' Merrivale said, watching his eyes. 'You could try to kill me and then make a run for it.'

'I could. But the problem is, you saved my life just now. Killing you would be damned ungrateful, wouldn't it?' Courcy tossed his sword in the air, grabbed it around the blade just below the crossguard and handed it to Merrivale hilt first. 'Receive my surrender,' he said.

The herald took the sword, considered it for a few moments, and handed it back. 'Return the serpentine to the king's stores,' he said. 'How you do it, I do not care. What story you invent to account for its reappearance, I do not care. But make it so.'

The other man hesitated. 'And then what? We carry on as if nothing happened?'

'Not quite. If you transgress again, I will inform the king and the constable and let you take the consequences.'

Courcy thought about this. 'Fair enough,' he said. 'Rather more than I deserve, in fact. People have always told me I am not worthy of my friends. I won't say you can rely on me, because clearly you cannot. But I will do my best to keep my nose clean. You have my oath on that.'

'There is one more thing,' Merrivale said. 'Help me discover who killed Edmund Bray. Do that, and I will use whatever influence I have to help you find you a position, something with a stipend attached that will give you the means to live. What income do you have now?'

'Income? Faith now. I own a tavern in Carbery, back in Ireland, but it costs more to run than it brings in. From which you may gather that I am not a great success as a tavern keeper. I came to the war hoping to recoup my losses. So far, without much luck.'

'And yet despite the wrong you did, you also proved your worth today,' said Merrivale. 'And you saved young Mortimer's life last night. You deserve better, I think.'

'Not everyone would agree with you. But I thank you for the kind sentiment, and if I can help you, I will. You have my oath on that too.' Courcy paused. 'You've probably heard this question before, herald. Why does this matter so much to you?'

'Bray was killed because he witnessed a meeting between Fierville and a French knight,' Merrivale said. 'But I doubt that Fierville killed him. And if he did not, that means Fierville has accomplices in the army, men who are both traitors and murderers. I intend to discover who they are.'

'Traitors and murderers,' Courcy repeated. 'You're playing with fire, herald.'

'I know,' said Merrivale.

7

Carentan, 20th of July, 1346
Evening

Smoke boiled from the ruins of Carentan. A few stone walls still stood, but the stink of burning filled the air for miles.

Godefroi d'Harcourt's tent stood on rising ground east of the city walls, overlooking the flooded marshes. Merrivale stopped outside and spoke to the guard, a Norman serjeant in an iron helmet with an old-fashioned nose guard. 'Ask his lordship if he will receive me.'

The guard stepped into the tent. There was a brief murmur of conversation, and then he reappeared. 'You may enter.'

Harcourt was seated before a wooden table, reading letters. 'What is it?' he asked curtly.

'Jean de Fierville is dead,' Merrivale said, and waited.

'How?' Harcourt asked after a moment.

'He and Barbizan, the captain of the garrison, attempted to destroy the gatehouse of the castle with gunpowder, but they were foiled by Sir Nicholas Courcy. Both were killed.'

Harcourt looked up sharply. 'Fierville was working with the enemy?'

'Probably for some time, since before the army departed from Portchester. He was a conduit between Bertrand and other French agents embedded in our army. He passed on messages to a French knight named Macio Chauffin.'

'Christ Jesus,' said Harcourt, and Merrivale saw the bitterness in his scarred face. 'I also employed him as a messenger to send letters to my allies in the countryside inviting them to join us. And he betrayed them to Bertrand. All of them have been arrested and executed.'

'I suspect that is why he came to report to you in Saint-Côme-du-Mont: to tell you they were dead. I dispatched him to find you at Coigny, but he must have known I was suspicious of him, and he joined the enemy instead.'

A long silence ensued. 'My attempt to rouse the Norman nobles has failed,' Harcourt said. 'My friends, on whom I counted for support, are dead. The rest of the nobility have been persuaded, or threatened, into continuing their allegiance to Philippe. Not a single man will come over to me now.'

He slammed his hand down on the wooden table so hard the parchment sheets jumped and fell to the ground. 'I have failed, utterly. It is over.'

'Surely not yet, my lord. Our army is strong.'

'If you think fifteen thousand men can defeat France, you are a fool.' Abruptly, Harcourt rose and walked out of the tent.

–

'Good evening, Sir Thomas.'

Thomas Holland turned and glared at the herald. A group of young men had gathered around the Prince of Wales, who was rolling dice. They shouted and waved their wine cups when they won, and the prince, as always, laughed uproariously when he lost. He could afford to, Merrivale thought. He didn't have to pay the bills. When he ran out of money, he applied to his treasurer, and his treasurer applied to the Exchequer. Job done.

'You are not joining them?' Merrivale asked, indicating the gamblers.

A jongleur was playing a lute, rather well. No one was paying him the slightest attention. 'I cannot afford it,' Holland said brusquely. 'I am not a rich man, herald. In case you hadn't noticed.'

Merrivale pursed his lips. 'I had. But some of your men seem to be doing rather well. There is one party of looters from Wigan who are making sizeable profits. Perhaps you know them. Their vintenar is a big man, bald, with a scar across his head.'

'I know who you mean. So?'

'They are professional looters. Did you know they were out on the Valognes road the day Bray was killed?'

Holland stiffened. 'What are you insinuating?'

'They might have seen what happened to him. Did they say anything to you?'

'I don't gossip with common soldiers.'

'Will you make enquiries on my behalf?'

'I will not. I owe you no favours, herald, and I don't give a damn about what happened to Bray. I told you, I couldn't stand the little turd.'

'Then let me ask you another question. How well do you know Macio Chauffin?'

Holland stared at him. 'What has that to do with anything?'

'Chauffin was out on the Valognes road too, at the same time as your archers. Did you try to send him a message? Using Jean de Fierville as the messenger, perhaps?'

For a moment he thought Holland was going to reach for his sword, but unusually, the one-eyed knight managed to control his temper. 'If you have an accusation to make, herald, then make it.'

'No,' said Merrivale. 'But if you want to allay my suspicions, you could try answering my question.'

'Not that it is any of your business, but I met Macio in Prussia. He was serving with the Count of Eu.'

'The Constable of France.'

'Yes,' Holland said impatiently. 'There was a truce between England and France at the time, if you recall. So we all went to Prussia to fight the pagans. We were in Königsberg, and then out on the frontier at Allenstein and Rössel. We served together for about a year, all told. I haven't seen Macio since we left Prussia.'

'But you remain on friendly terms.'

'Yes. Is that a crime?'

'No,' said Merrivale. 'So long as friendship is all that passes between you.'

'Go to hell,' said Holland, and he turned on his heel and walked away.

The prince had just lost a sizeable stake to his friend Salisbury. He yelped with laughter and called for more wine. Sir John Grey came and laid a hand on the herald's shoulder. 'You appear to have provoked Sir Thomas,' he said.

'I fear it takes very little to do so,' said Merrivale. 'He is an angry and bitter man.'

'He has no monopoly on either anger or bitterness,' Grey said unexpectedly. 'But some of us manage to control our emotions rather better than he does. You had a couple of close shaves today. I came to see if you were well.'

'I am, thanks to your forethought. Did you find the rest of the garrison?'

'As you suspected, after Barbizan was killed, they fled through a postern behind the donjon. We caught them in the streets before they could get to the Saint-Lô gate. Thank you for sending Matt and Pip with the message.'

'Tell me something, Sir John. When you decided to send your men after me, why did you choose those two?'

'Because they are the best I have,' Grey said.

'Tell me more about them. You said they come from Warwickshire.'

'Yes. Their father was a gamekeeper and forester on the Clinton estate at Kenilworth. Their mother died long ago, and their father reared them and taught them to shoot. When he died last year, the Kenilworth steward turned them out of their home. They were wandering vagabonds when my master bowman found them. He recruited them, and they have served us well ever since.'

In his mind's eye Merrivale saw Fierville stretched dead on the cobbles, shot in the back in exactly the same manner as Edmund Bray. The similarities between the two killings were shocking, and yet they were not identical. He remembered what Pip had said at Quettehou. *We wouldn't have wasted a second arrow. One would have been enough.*

Grey was watching his face. 'If you think they had anything to do with Bray's death, you are barking up the wrong tree. I have no doubts whatever about their fidelity.'

'I am pleased to hear it,' Merrivale said. 'Thank you once again, Sir John.'

'No thanks are necessary. I wish you good night.'

Grey departed. Merrivale watched the gamblers for a moment longer, and then he too walked away towards his tent.

–

Tiphaine de Tesson was waiting for him. Her red hair hung in ragged locks around her neck; rather than attempting to disentangle the matted, filthy tresses, she had cut most of them off. Her ruined gown had been discarded too, and she wore a man's green tunic over a plain shirt, and baggy, wrinkled hose with a pair of soft leather boots. She looked tense and suspicious. 'Your servants brought me here and found me some clothes,' she said. 'I assume they did so at your orders.'

'Yes,' said Merrivale. 'You need shelter until we can take you to a place of safety.'

She shifted from one foot to the other. 'For me, there is no place of safety.'

He regarded her, seeing the suspicion and fear still dark in her eyes. 'Have you no family or friends to whom you could go?'

She shook her head. 'Many are dead. Most of the rest are scattered, in hiding or in exile. Those who remain are known and watched, and have been threatened with dire punishment if they consort with rebels. Even to admit me to their house would be a sentence of death.'

Merrivale frowned. 'If you have been in prison for two years, *demoiselle*, how do you know this?'

'Two friends of my father were captured and brought to Carentan in March. They told me that Robert Bertrand was sending riders all across the country, saying that the English were coming and threatening retribution to any who aided them. My father's friends were arrested and executed as an example to the others. Then, after the landing, Bertrand arrested several more men whose loyalty was suspect and sent them in chains to Caen. They too now have been executed. Barbizan told me this,' she said, anticipating his question. 'He wanted me to know that the Norman revolt had failed.'

The executed men would be the friends that Harcourt had spoken of. His hopes truly had been crushed. 'I am sorry,' Merrivale said.

'Do not be.' Her chin came up a little. 'Barbizan was wrong. There are other Norman lords, powerful and in high places, who have long contemplated revolt. The Count of Eu, the Constable of France, is one of them. The Queen of Navarre is another. One day, Normandy will throw off the French yoke and be a free state once more.'

Merrivale digested this. 'These others, the Count of Eu and the lady of Navarre. Can they not help you?'

'Even if they would help me, which I doubt, how would I get to them? Your soldiers are marauding and plundering everywhere. And you will not be on hand to rescue me again.' She shivered. 'If this is indeed a rescue.'

'I have no designs on your person,' Merrivale said calmly. He turned to Mauro. 'Find the lady a cot and some bedclothes and… whatever else she needs. And rig a curtain across the tent so she has some privacy.'

'Yes, *señor*.'

'You are very kind,' Tiphaine said, and there were sudden tears in her brown eyes. 'I am sorry that I doubted you.'

Merrivale bowed. 'And now you must forgive me,' he said, a little abruptly. 'I fear I have work to do.'

—

Inquisition into the death of Edmund Bray, knight, near the village of Quettehou in Normandy on the XIIth day of July, in the nineteenth year of the reign of King Edward III. This report was composed on the XXth day of the same month.

Two possible reasons for Sir Edmund's death remain. The first is that he was killed by looters, and the second is that he was killed deliberately following his witnessing a meeting between Jean de Fierville and the French miles Macio Chauffin.

Item, as to whether he was killed by troops whom he encountered looting. I can now exonerate Sir Nicholas Courcy of Kingsale and his men. However, a second body of plunderers, soldiers in the retinue of Sir Thomas Holland, were also in the area. They are also archers, and Sir Edmund was killed by two arrows from a longbow. However, there is no firm evidence that they killed him.

Item, it is therefore probable, in my view, that while scouting on the Valognes road, Bray encountered Fierville in the act of passing information to Macio Chauffin. It follows that Bray may have been killed to prevent him from disclosing Fierville's treachery.

Item, it remains unclear who actually killed Bray. A search of Fierville's baggage found no sign of a bow or quiver. I believe that the killer remains at large and that he was, and in all probability still is, among the ranks of our army.

Simon Merrivale, heraldus

-

It was a short walk to the king's big pavilion, glowing red with lamplight. Michael Northburgh's tent was next to it, guarded by a single serjeant. Beyond the camp, the walls of Carentan stood black, silhouetted against the still-glowing embers of the town behind them.

Northburgh read the report, frowning. 'So Fierville was a traitor all along?'

'Yes, but not the only one. The maid who helps look after the king's cattle overheard two men talking at Freshwater, planning to send a message to Robert Bertrand. Both were English, she says. And the *demoiselle* de Tesson has told me that Bertrand began arresting and intimidating suspected rebels as early as March this year.'

'March! For God's sake, the final decision to invade Normandy was only taken in February. The French must have had the news almost as soon as we did!'

'There is something else you need to know,' Merrivale said. 'The *demoiselle* claims that the Count of Eu and the Queen of Navarre may also be considering rebellion.'

Raoul de Brienne, Count of Eu and Constable of France, came from one of the highest families in the land; one of his ancestors had been King of Jerusalem and Emperor of Constantinople. Jeanne of Navarre was King Edward's cousin, and like him had a reasonable claim to the French crown. 'You didn't put that in your report,' Northburgh said.

'My commission is to enquire into the death of Edmund Bray. I am telling you so that you may pass this news to the king. And claim the credit, if you wish,' Merrivale added.

'Very generous of you. What have you done with the *demoiselle*?'

'She remains with me for the moment, until I can find a safe place for her.'

'Ah.' Northburgh winked. 'Is she comely?'

'That question is beneath you, Michael,' the herald said stiffly.

'Come, come, old friend, I am joking. These archers of Holland's. You reckon Bray wasn't killed by looters, but one of these men might have been acting on orders from Fierville, or the other traitors. Shall we arrest them and put them to the question?'

Merrivale shook his head. 'I have no actual evidence against them. Besides, I have always had doubts about torture as a means of persuasion. Men will say whatever they think the torturer wishes to hear. As a result, we get the answers we want, but not the answers we need.'

'I suspect you are probably right.' Northburgh opened his strongbox and placed Merrivale's report inside. 'I would get some sleep if I were you. We march at first light, to Saint-Lô.'

Merrivale raised his eyebrows. 'We are continuing? Even though the Norman revolt has failed?'

'His Grace hopes that if he can win a victory over the French, the Normans will change their minds, and what you have just told me about Eu and Navarre will strengthen his determination. Bertrand is in Saint-Lô. Word is he intends to make a stand there.'

'Saint-Lô is reputed to be the strongest fortress in Normandy,' Merrivale said. 'Taking it will not be easy.'

'Yes, well. The king has determined that this is what shall happen, and so it will happen. Bertrand will be captured and paraded around Normandy to persuade other nobles to forswear their allegiance to the adversary and join us instead. His Grace and the lord of Harcourt have offered a reward to the man who captures Bertrand. Five thousand marks of silver.'

'Five thousand marks? I thought the treasury was empty.'

'It is. God knows where the money will come from. Thankfully, that's not my problem. Get some sleep, my friend. And if you should dream of your Norman *demoiselle*... well, do come and tell me all about it, won't you?'

–

Walking back through the camp, Merrivale spotted a shadow moving ahead of him, a man going carefully and staying out of the firelight. Something about him seemed familiar; after a few moments he realised it was Holland's vintenar, the man with the scarred head. Shrugging off his bright tabard, he rolled it up and tucked it under his arm, and followed the man across the camp and out beyond its eastern limits. Soon they had passed beyond the watchfires and were deep in shadow. Out on the marshes, moonlight glowed bright off stagnant pools. The calls of night birds echoed across the water.

The big man stopped. Another shadow joined him almost at once, another archer with his bow over his shoulder. There was a brief whispered conversation, too far away for Merrivale to hear, and then the two men parted. On impulse, rather than going after the vintenar, he followed the other man back through the firelit camp. He was a lean, long-limbed man, and he walked furtively past the tents and banners, hunched over a little and often looking around him, so that the herald was forced to keep his distance.

Not far from the Saint-Lô gate, the man came to a campfire. Other archers sat around it, playing dice on a blanket laid on the ground. They grinned up at him. 'Roit, me 'ansom,' said one of them in Devon dialect. 'How be 'ackin'?'

'We're to Saint-Lô tomorrow, boy,' said the tall man. 'Bate told me all about it just now. Time to fill our purses when we get there. What you playing, boys?'

'Hazard, me 'ansom,' said the first man. 'Farthing a stake.' He grinned again. 'You want to fill your purse tomorrow, Nicodemus, you'll need to empty it first.'

Standing in the shadows, the herald saw a shield outside a tent further along: two red bends, diagonal bars, on a yellow field, the arms of Edward de Tracey from Dunkeswell. These men were presumably from his retinue. The man called Nicodemus sat down on the ground, folding his long legs and leaning forward.

'Here, boys,' he said, lowering his voice a little. 'You know what else Bate told me? He and the Lanky lads found a nice little pullet in town this morning.'

The other archers chuckled. 'Did they swyve her?' one asked.

'They was all set to, but then that herald came along and took her off 'em. Bate, well, he ain't happy.'

This made them chuckle still more. 'Bate's in a bate?' suggested one, and they all roared with laughter. 'Now you listen, boys,' Nicodemus said urgently. 'This is serious. Bate says he's going to send that herald across the river.'

The laughter stopped. 'Send him across the river?' said the man who had spoken first. 'Has Bate gone mad? You don't go round killin' your own folk, me 'ansom. Especially not a herald. They'll hang him so high he'll be able to see England from the gallows.'

'Not if they don't know who did it,' said Nicodemus. There was a moment of silence. 'Now you keep quiet about this, all of you,' Nicodemus warned. 'You never heard anything. That means you, Jakey boy. Keep your trap shut.'

'So we're just going to sit and do nothing?' the other man said, the unhappiness plain in his voice.

'That's right,' Nicodemus said. 'We keep out of it. The master wouldn't like it. Understood?'

'Understood,' the man said finally, and the others nodded.

8

Long and haunting, the notes of the trumpet echoed over the silent marshes. Listening to the call, the herald thought the silvery notes were like the sound of dawn, perfectly matching the ethereal light that seeped into the eastern sky and swallowed up the stars.

Swiftly the army formed up and prepared to march. By sunrise, the vanguard had crossed the marshes on the far side of Carentan and was already turning south, following the road to Saint-Lô through rolling hills patterned with hedgerows and clumps of trees. Spurred on by the thought of five thousand marks, the companies of Holland, Tracey, Despenser and the Red Company raced each other for the lead, but there was no doubt as to who would win; the Red Company were mounted, while the other three were on foot. By mid morning, Sir John and Sir Richard and their men were nothing more than dust clouds on the southern horizon.

Four miles short of Saint-Lô, the Red Company came to Pont-Hébert, a bridge over the River Vire with a hamlet of wood and stone houses at the far end. The marshes were far behind now, and the Vire ran through a steep valley a hundred feet deep; there was no other way across. And Robert Bertrand had left a detachment of crossbowmen on guard here, with orders to prevent the enemy from crossing.

He had reckoned without the Red Company. Dismounting, they drove the enemy back with showers of arrows and charged over the bridge, shooting or stabbing anyone who tried to resist. Assuming that the crossbowmen had been broken, Grey and Percy remounted their men and rode on towards Saint-Lô. But the remaining defenders were made of tougher metal. Waiting until the Red Company were out of sight, they came out of the houses where they had hidden and attacked the bridge with axes and hammers. By the time the Prince of Wales and the rest of the vanguard arrived at Pont-Hébert, the bridge was nothing more than broken timbers lying scattered on the banks of the river below.

'If the Red Company are already over the river, that means they are cut off,' said the prince. His young face looked worried. 'Should we not try to rescue them, Lord Marshal?'

'The Red Company know how to look after themselves, Highness,' said Warwick. He turned to his esquire. 'Fetch Master Hurley and his carpenters, and ask Sir Nicholas Courcy to join us too. We shall need his engineering expertise once more, I think.'

The esquire turned his horse and galloped away. The prince raised a gauntleted hand, shading his eyes against the sun. 'The enemy are still there, on the far side of the river,' he said. 'Should we not drive them off first before we begin to rebuild the bridge?'

White-coated crossbowmen could still be seen lurking in the houses of Pont-Hébert, weapons levelled and pointed towards the ruined bridge. Warwick just managed to keep the surprise out of his voice. 'Very good, Highness,' he said approvingly, and turned to Holland and Tracey. 'Sir Thomas, Sir Edward, you heard your prince. Drive those varlets off. At once, if you please.'

Spreading out, Holland and Tracey's archers scrambled down the steep slope towards the bridge, lean figures in green and dun brown and russet pulling arrows from their quivers as they ran. In Pont-Hébert, more white-coated figures rose from their places of concealment. Crossbow bolts streaked through the air, dark blurs in the sunlight. Two archers went down, one clutching his leg, the other falling face forward and sliding down the slope for a moment before lying still. The other archers halted and raised their bows.

There was a moment of pause, long enough for an intake of breath, and then the first flight of arrows rose and arched over the river. The second followed almost before the first had reached its target, and then came the familiar pattern of nock-draw-release, nock-draw-release, fifteen times a minute, the thrum of the bows and hiss of feathered shafts vibrating in the air. In Pont Hébert the arrows fell like rain, embedding themselves in thatched roofs and wooden walls, skidding off the cobbled street, pinning the enemy as they tried to load their crossbows and staining their white tunics with blood. In less than a minute, a thousand arrows had been shot into Pont-Hébert, and the only crossbowmen visible now were fleeing up the opposite hill towards Saint-Lô, or lying twitching on the ground.

He had seen it before, but even so the power of the massed long-bows left Merrivale a little shaken. The crossbowmen had stood no chance; what had happened just now was not so much a skirmish as a massacre.

He turned to the sound of hoofbeats, and saw Lord Rowton riding up the road from Carentan, followed by his esquire and a little party of men-at-arms. A moment later Rowton reined in beside them, raising his visor and saluting the marshal and the prince.

'How long will that take to repair?' he asked, looking at the ruined bridge.

'I'm waiting for Courcy to tell us,' Warwick said. 'But I doubt it will be much before midnight.'

The archers were coming back up the slope, carrying two dead men and supporting a third, who hobbled with a black bolt protruding from his leg. He would survive, Merrivale thought, providing the wound did not become infected. In this heat, it very well might.

Rowton looked dubious. 'His Grace insists on reaching Saint-Lô by nightfall.'

'His Grace must needs be disappointed,' Warwick said. He grinned. 'You have his ear, Eustace. You can break the news to him.'

'Thank you very much,' Rowton said wryly. 'Is there anything I can tell him to sweeten the medicine?'

'The Red Company are over the river. If I know John and Richard, they are already raising hell, and Bertrand will have his hands full. Tell the king we will be able to cross at first light, and will be at the gates of Saint-Lô by sunrise. Then all we have to do is find some way of taking the strongest fortress in Normandy... what the devil is that noise?'

Someone was shouting further along the riverbank, and now more voices joined in, raised in anger. The prince turned in his saddle. 'Herald, find out what that commotion is, and put a stop to it. Remind the men that we are fighting the enemy, not each other.'

He had said much the same to his quarrelling knights in Valognes, Merrivale reflected. It sounded like a phrase someone had put in his mouth.

Further along the bank, archers from Holland and Tracey's companies had gathered in an angry circle surrounding two men: Bate, the scar-headed vintenar from Lancashire, and Nicodemus, the archer from Tracey's company. Yesterday evening at Carentan they had met and talked in apparent amity; now they stood crouched, glaring at each other and ready to fight. Bate had drawn a short sword, while Nicodemus held a slender-bladed poignard with a long, wickedly tapering point.

Dismounting and shouldering his way through the press, Merrivale saw another man lying on the ground between them. His head was twisted horribly to one side, and his green tunic was bright with blood. More blood covered his face and matted his hair. His throat had been slashed open from ear to ear, the gory wound revealing his severed jugular vein and windpipe.

Despite this, it was still possible to recognise him. It was Jakey, the Devon man who had been playing hazard outside Carentan last night.

At the sight of the herald's tabard, the shouting was replaced by an uneasy silence. 'By order of his Highness the Prince of Wales, I command you to cease and desist,' Merrivale said. 'Put away your weapons, both of you.'

Neither Bate nor Nicodemus moved. 'The punishment for raising a weapon without permission is amputation,' Merrivale said. 'If you want to keep your sword hands, put up your weapons. *Now!*'

Sullenly Nicodemus slid his dagger back into its sheath. Bate turned towards the herald, his sword flashing in the sunlight. He was sweating heavily and the scar on his head pulsed a deep livid red. Looking into his eyes, Merrivale saw pure hatred.

'You wish to kill me,' he said calmly. He held his hands out from his sides, showing that he was unarmed. 'Very well. You are welcome to try now, if you wish.'

A murmur ran around the circle of men. Merrivale ignored it. He saw the rage in Bate's eyes fade a little, replaced by uncertainty. After a moment, the vintenar raised his sword, then slammed it down point first into the grass at his feet and stood back, breathing heavily.

Merrivale pointed at Jakey's body. 'What happened to this man?'

'He was killed by the enemy,' Bate said, his voice rasping in his throat.

That provoked another outcry from the Devon men. 'Like hell he was!' Nicodemus shouted. 'The enemy were over the river, shooting crossbows! Are you telling me one of them swam across, cut Jakey's throat and swam back again, without nobody seeing him?'

'Happen all you Devon coneys are blind,' said one of the northern men.

The shouting increased in volume. 'Silence!' Merrivale ordered, and slowly the noise died away again. 'Did anyone see what happened?'

A long silence followed. 'He was down at the bridge with the rest of us,' one of the Devon men said. 'I saw him there. But when we got back to the top of the bank, he was gone.'

'Had he quarrelled with anyone?'

'No,' said Nicodemus. He glared at Bate again. 'Jakey was a good lad. Everyone liked him.'

'I had nothing to do with this,' Bate said. 'Nor did any of my men.'

'You're lying, Bate. One of you Lanky bastards killed him. And when I find out who it was, I swear to God I'll cut *his* throat, just like you did to poor Jakey here!'

'God rot you!' Bate roared. 'We didn't do it, I tell you!'

'And another thing, Bate,' said Nicodemus. 'We're not trading with you no more. You want a buyer, you look elsewhere. We don't have dealings with murderers. You got that, boy?'

Red with rage, Bate reached down for his sword, but Merrivale kicked the weapon away, sending it spinning across the grass. Bate glared at him, clenching his fists until the knuckles were white. The scar on his head throbbed again. Calmly the herald waited, watching the emotions flicker through the vintenar's savage, red-rimmed eyes. Time seemed to stop; the men around him held their breath.

Bate threw back his head like a bull and shouted at the sky, an inarticulate bellow of rage and frustration, and turned and walked away. Men scattered out of his path. The herald turned to Nicodemus. 'Take your friend and bury him. The rest of you, return to your posts. Go.'

–

Nicodemus and another man carried the body away. The rest of the men scattered, some still muttering. Merrivale turned to see Lord Rowton sitting on horseback, watching him. 'I thought you might need help,' Rowton said. 'But clearly you had the situation under control.' He paused. 'That big man wanted to kill you. Why didn't he? He had a sword, and you were unarmed.'

'Perhaps that is the reason,' Merrivale said. 'Someone cut the man's throat, my lord. It wasn't a neat job either, but a wild hack with a heavy blade that nearly took his head off. As you saw, and heard, Tracey's men think one of Holland's archers did it. I have my doubts.'

He waited for Rowton to ask him what those doubts were. Instead, the other man shook his head. 'This is not your business, herald.'

'The man was murdered, my lord.'

'He was one of Tracey's men. Let Tracey deal with it. Concentrate on finding out who killed Bray.' Rowton lifted the reins of his horse. 'Come, it is time we returned to his Highness.'

Pont-Hébert, 21st of July, 1346
Evening

At day's end, the English army made camp on the high ground above the Vire, listening to the thump of hammers and the rasp of saws echoing along the riverbank. Most of the kitchen wagons were still on the road from Carentan, so dinner was a simple affair of stockfish and salt salmon, boiled and served with bread and pickles. After the meal was finished, the prince and his knights settled down to their usual evening amusements of wine and dice. Hugh Despenser, who had apologised profusely to the prince after the incident at Valognes – but to no one else – was among them, apparently now in high favour. Merrivale wondered about this.

Tiphaine was waiting outside his tent when he returned. 'When shall we reach Saint-Lô?'

'Not until tomorrow morning, I fear.' He took a closer look at her face, tense and drawn. 'Why is that important?'

'My father was executed there,' she said abruptly, and turned and went into the tent.

Merrivale stood for a moment wondering whether to go after her. A voice hailed him, and he turned to see Sir Edward de Tracey coming towards him. 'I heard what happened this afternoon,' Tracey said. 'I wanted to thank you in person. You prevented what could have been a very nasty incident.'

'Have you discovered what happened?'

Tracey grimaced. 'I'm afraid it turns out one of my own men is responsible. The fools were gambling last night and Jake Madford, the dead man, got into debt and couldn't pay. There was an altercation, and he and some of the others came to blows. Madford finally promised to pay after we took Saint-Lô – presumably he was hoping for a share of the loot – and my vintenar thought the matter was closed. But it looks like someone saw a chance during the fighting today to settle his account for good.'

'Do you know who the killer is?'

'They closed ranks, of course, and refused to say, but it is perfectly obvious who it must be. Another of my archers, Jack Slade, disappeared this afternoon and hasn't been seen since.'

'I am sorry to hear it,' Merrivale said.

'Don't be. Slade was not only a thief and a liar, he was also a terrible shot. My company is better off without him. I daresay he has gone over to the French by now, and if we catch him at Saint-Lô, I will have the pleasure of hanging him myself.'

Merrivale bowed. 'Thank you for letting me know, Sir Edward.'

Tracey departed.

Jakey was a good lad. Everyone liked him. Clearly that was not true. But if Slade had killed him, why did Nicodemus and the others accuse Bate?

-

Later that evening, Lord Rowton sought out the herald. 'I have read the reports you submitted to the king's secretary. May I ask if there has been any further progress?' He paused. 'I am thinking of Edmund's family.'

Merrivale shook his head. 'I think he saw Fierville meeting with Chauffin, and was killed to silence him. But I have no proof.'

'Are there other possibilities?'

The herald paused for a moment. 'Sir Thomas Holland admits that he and Bray quarrelled at Portchester,' he said finally. 'He makes no secret of the fact that he disliked Bray. But enough to kill him? I am not certain.'

Rowton frowned. 'What was the subject of their dispute?'

'Holland says that Bray insulted his wife. Or rather, the woman he claims as his wife.'

'Ah, the fair and divisive Joan... I had not heard of this. It may interest you to know, however, that while at Portchester, Bray also had an altercation with Sir Hugh Despenser.'

Merrivale looked at him. 'You witnessed this, my lord?'

'Yes, I did. Curiously, this quarrel too was about gambling debts.' Rowton shook his head. 'Gambling is an absolute curse in this army. We have more disputes and affrays over games of chance than any other single cause. If I had my way, I would ban gambling throughout the army, and put any man who transgressed into the stocks.'

'I suspect that would not be practical,' Merrivale said.

'Of course not, given that the Prince of Wales is the biggest gambler of the lot.'

Earlier in the year, Merrivale had helped the prince's treasurer settle the young man's debts, which had risen to around sixty-five pounds;

much of it owed to his mother, Queen Philippa. The problem was that the prince loved gambling for its own sake; he simply did not care whether he won or lost, with the result that he lost far more often than he won. 'Had Bray run into debt?' Merrivale asked.

'No, but his friend Mortimer had. Despenser bought the debt from someone else, possibly as a way of putting one over on Mortimer, and demanded repayment. Bray interceded, asking Despenser for more time. When Despenser began to insult Mortimer, Bray stood up for him.'

'As a true friend would.'

'Indeed. However, some quite harsh words were said, and Bray made comments about Despenser's character and parentage that I daresay an older and wiser man would have eschewed. At this point I intervened, ordered them both to apologise, and sent them away. But I fear Despenser is the sort of man who carries a grudge.'

'Yes. Thank you for informing me, my lord.'

'There is no need to thank me. I am sorry I did not tell you earlier.'

Rowton took his leave. Merrivale stood for a moment, thinking. Despenser's company had also been ashore early at Quettehou. And Despenser had many archers in his retinue.

Despenser is the sort of man who carries a grudge. But who in that tortured generation, stained with their fathers' crimes and their fathers' blood, did not? How could anyone have survived that grim decade of famine and anarchy and come through it unmarked? He himself had not.

But… had he been wrong all along? He had become convinced – or, he admitted, he had convinced himself – that Bray had been killed because he had discovered Fierville was working with the enemy. But what if that was not the case? Bray had been a well-liked young man, but he had also made enemies along the way. *Perhaps I am wrong about Holland*, Merrivale thought. *Perhaps he did allow his anger to get the better of him. Or perhaps Despenser, brooding over past histories and past wrongs, had snapped and decided to end the life of the man who had confronted him.*

Sunset was a fading fire. Overhead, stars broke out in the darkening sky. Somewhere in the camp, a man played a lute and sang a *lai* by

Marie de France. The herald recognised the song at once; he had heard it sung before, years ago, in another country.

> *The lives of the others are done.*
> *Their love has cooled.*
> *Yet I remain alive*
> *and my destiny is to be with the woman I love*
> *without ever knowing the bliss I seek.*
> *I cannot possess her. I long for her embrace*
> *and with every breath I draw I suffer.*
> *I envy the others wrapped in death.*

9

Seen from a distance, the walls and towers of Saint-Lô were like a gigantic ship floating above the trees and hedgerows. Surrounded on three sides by steep valleys and on the fourth by massive ramparts and gates protected by towers and bartizans, the city was virtually impregnable. The vanguard moved forward cautiously, hobelars trotting across the fields in little groups to scout, archers spreading out on the flanks, men-at-arms riding in glittering, bright-coloured streams up the centre with the standard of Wales in the lead.

They could see no banners flying from either the ramparts of the town or the castle perched at its far end. The gates were wide open, and the men standing guard outside them wore red iron caps on their heads. The impregnable city had fallen.

'It was another ruse,' said Sir Richard Percy, who came down to meet them at the gate. 'Bertrand left about fifty men to defend the place, and pulled out with the rest. We seized the gates yesterday afternoon, and took the town without a fight. The garrison at the castle held out for most of the night, but this morning we persuaded them to surrender.'

'Persuaded them?' said Warwick. 'How?'

Percy smiled. 'That was John's doing,' he said. 'He claimed we had captured a supply train with all the silver that was meant to pay their wages. They opened the gates and walked out a few minutes later.'

'Where has Bertrand gone?'

'According to the prisoners, he withdrew further up the valley towards Torigni. But we think that too is a deception. We reckon he's retreated to Caen.'

Caen was the second city of Normandy, even bigger than Saint-Lô; it lay about thirty-five miles to the east. 'Why do you think this?' asked the prince.

He was, Merrivale thought, beginning to ask some rather sensible questions. 'The prisoners told us the Count of Eu has just arrived in Caen, Highness,' Percy said. 'He has summoned all the Norman men-at-arms to join him there. Also, there is no other defensible place west of Caen.'

Nicholas Courcy had ridden with the prince's knights. Despite his shabby appearance, he was well regarded at court now, thanks in part to his successful return of the stolen gunpowder. 'So that is where Eu will make his stand,' he said. 'I've been to Caen, and it's a powerful place. I'm thinking the cannon might come in useful.'

The prince looked up at the gatehouse, pointing at three round, pale objects hanging suspended by chains. 'What are those?'

'They are skulls, highness,' said a female voice. They turned to see Tiphaine de Tesson dismounting from a horse. 'Skulls,' she repeated. 'All that remains of the last Normans who tried to start a revolt against our French overlords. Their leader was my father, Jean, Sire de la Roche-Tesson. He and his friends were beheaded here two years ago and their heads hung over the gate as a warning to other traitors.'

No one else spoke. Tiphaine looked at Warwick and the prince. 'I should like to see my father.'

Warwick nodded. 'Bring them down,' he said.

-

Carefully and with great respect, the skulls were brought down from the gatehouse and placed on a blanket on the ground. Time, wind and carrion birds had picked away all vestiges of hair and skin; only the bones remained, eye sockets full of shadow in the sunrise, teeth grinning broken and yellow. Tiphaine knelt before them, studying them intently, oblivious to the men watching her in absolute silence. Roger

Mortimer bit his lip and turned suddenly away. Nicholas Courcy shifted a little, his face full of sympathy. 'The pity of it all,' he said softly.

'What do you mean?' Merrivale asked quietly.

'The fair maiden gazing on the face of death.'

Tiphaine lifted one of the skulls and held it up to the light. 'This one,' she said. 'This is my father.'

Her fingers traced the line of one cheekbone. Closing her eyes, she kissed the skull on the forehead, and then rose to her feet still holding it in her hands. 'The rest of the body was dismembered and scattered,' she said. 'This is all I have of him. I wish to bury him, so that he might at last find rest.'

'Send for Brother Geoffrey,' Warwick said. 'Ask him to conduct the service.'

They gathered in the church of Notre-Dame overlooking the ramparts and the valley of the Vire. The prince and his knights removed their bascinets and stood bare-headed in the apse, watching with a mixture of respect and fascination while Nicholas Courcy and Matthew Gurney prised up one of the flagstones and heaved it to one side. 'Well,' said Gurney, looking down. 'He'll not want for company.'

Beneath the flagstone were other graves of unguessable age, full of brown decaying bones. The men bowed their heads as Tiphaine walked forward cradling the skull of her father in both hands. There came once again to Merrivale's mind the image of Bertrand de Born carrying his severed head before him. Jean de la Roche-Tesson too had sown discord, and paid the price for it.

Tiphaine's face showed no sign of emotion. Silently she knelt and laid the skull among the other bones, then rose and stepped back. At a sign from Warwick, two more men came forward carrying the other skulls and laid them quietly to rest beside the first. Geoffrey of Maldon lifted the crucifix hanging around the neck of his black Augustinian robes and recited the burial prayers. 'I wish to leave money for a mass to be said for his soul,' Tiphaine said at the end.

'I will arrange it,' said Merrivale.

'No,' said another voice. 'Allow me.'

It was Godefroi d'Harcourt who had spoken. Merrivale had not seen him enter the church, but now he limped forward, taking one of Tiphaine's hands in his own and raising it to his lips. 'Your father was my friend,' he said. 'I can do little else for him, or you. But allow me this much at least.'

Tiphaine nodded, unspeaking. Harcourt bowed and walked away, dragging his bad leg. Merrivale watched him for a moment. Tiphaine needed a protector, and he had thought of asking Harcourt; but now, with all the Norman's plans and schemes in ruins and so many of his friends dead, it was Harcourt himself who was likely to need protection.

—

The prince and most of his knights departed. Courcy lingered a little, talking quietly with Tiphaine. Merrivale felt a hand descend on his shoulder and turned to find Sir John Sully standing beside him, regarding him with what the herald could only describe as benevolent mischief. His dog stood behind them, regarding the gravestone with interest.

'Why are you smiling at me?' Merrivale asked.

'Now what reason would I have to smile?' Sully asked. 'She is a comely maid,' he added, nodding towards Tiphaine. 'But why have you dressed her as a boy?'

'This was the best my servant could do.'

Sully's smile grew broader. 'What are you planning to do with her?'

'Find her a place of safety. If necessary, I will send her to England.' Merrivale looked at the older man. 'Unless you would care to take her off my hands?'

'Me? No, boy, I am far too old. I don't hold with these May and December romances. You keep her. Look after her well.'

'Who said anything about romance?'

Sully winked, snapped his fingers to summon the dog and walked away. Courcy raised Tiphaine's hand and kissed it, lips lingering rather longer than was strictly necessary, and followed. Merrivale walked over to where Tiphaine stood staring down at the gravestone. 'Are you all right?' he asked gently.

She raised her eyes to his, liquid and dark brown. 'I have given him peace,' she said. 'Now I must avenge him.'

Merrivale did not answer. She continued to stare at him. 'Have you a father, herald?' she asked.

'Yes.' It was true, although the old man no longer recognised his own son, or knew who he himself was. Time and horror had destroyed his memory.

'If someone killed him, what would you do?'

'I don't know,' Merrivale said. He paused for a moment. 'But I know how terrible it is to lose a parent. You must give yourself time to grieve.'

'Grieve? Why should I grieve for him? I barely knew him. My mother died when I was young, and I was raised by nuns at the Abbaye aux Dames in Caen. I lived with them until I was arrested. I rarely saw my father and I never knew my true home.'

'And yet you wish to avenge him.'

'I am Norman,' Tiphaine said. 'That is what we do.'

Again it was impossible to answer this. 'What did Sir Nicholas want?' the herald asked.

'To offer his condolences, and to exercise his charm on me. Do not worry. I am proof against men like him.' She smiled, the first time he had seen her do so. 'The nuns trained me well.'

A thought struck Merrivale. 'You could go back to them for shelter.'

'The Abbaye aux Dames is one of the richest houses in the land, filled with the daughters of nobles and kings. Do you think they will accept the penniless child of a traitor back into their midst? And in times like these, do you think nunneries will be spared?'

They walked out into the morning sun. 'Are you married, herald?' Tiphaine asked suddenly.

'No.'

'There is no woman in your life?'

'No.'

'No? Has there ever been one?'

With every breath I draw I suffer. Merrivale let the question die in the air between them. 'We must find you some more suitable clothes,' he said after a moment. 'I will see if something can be arranged.'

'I am quite comfortable as I am, thank you.' There was an edge of anger in her voice. 'If I need anything further, I shall ask Mauro. I have found him to be most helpful.'

She walked away down the street. Merrivale wondered briefly if it was safe to let her go alone, but unlike Carentan, the occupation of Saint-Lô had been largely peaceful; the Red Company had seized the town ahead of the rest of the army, and its disciplined soldiers could be seen on every street, maintaining order. The pillaging of the town had begun, but this time it was organised and led by the king's purveyors, working methodically to seize stocks of food and wine and merchandise.

Returning to the town gates, Merrivale found Sir John Grey talking urgently to one of his officers, a craggy-looking man in a mail tunic, carrying a heavy spear. 'There's a thousand tuns of wine in those warehouses on Rue des Fossés,' Grey was saying. 'For God's sake put a strong guard on them, Jacques, until the king's men can come and take over. If the army gets hold of that wine, we'll have fifteen thousand dead-drunk men, and Bertrand will be able to walk back in here and take over whenever he pleases.'

'It shall be done,' the spearman said, touching his red iron cap in salute. He was about twice Grey's age, the herald thought, but he took orders from the young knight without question.

'Thank you.' Grey turned towards Merrivale. 'Sir Herald. May I have a word?'

'Of course.'

The spearman departed. 'I heard about the fracas at Pont-Hébert,' Grey said. 'The rumour says that one of Tracey's archers got his throat cut by someone from our side.'

'Yes. It was a quarrel over gambling debts, it seems.'

'Oh?' Grey's gaze was steady. 'That's not what I heard. According to the gossip one of my men picked up this morning, the archer was talking about a plot by one of the Lancashire men. A plot to kill you, in fact.'

Merrivale said nothing.

'Were you aware of this?' Grey asked.

'Yes.'

'And what are you doing about it?'

Sir Edmund Bray had found Grey irritating. Merrivale was beginning to understand how he felt. Grey had won a great reputation on the Scottish borders over the past couple of years, but his calm arrogance grated on the nerves. 'The man you refer to is a vintenar in Sir Thomas Holland's company,' the herald said. 'His name is Bate. I have confronted him, and he knows I am aware of his intentions. He will be more circumspect now, I think.'

'Perhaps. But Bate also has some very unpleasant friends. They killed Tracey's man to stop him from talking, and they'll kill you if you give them half a chance.' Grey paused. 'We can protect you, if you wish.'

'I am a herald,' said Merrivale. 'I do not need protection.'

'A lot of dead heralds have said the same. Don't be foolish. I will send men to guard you.'

'Thank you, but no,' Merrivale said. 'My own men are sufficient.'

Grey looked at him for a long time. 'Very well,' he said. 'That is your choice.'

–

Mauro said much the same thing. 'This is madness, *señor*,' he said as he and Warin pitched the tent. 'I have seen these men. They are not ordinary soldiers. They are veterans of many wars, who know no restraint and no pity. The fact that you are a herald will not stop them. You should have accepted Sir John's offer, *señor*.'

Dust boiled in the air. The king's division had arrived at Saint-Lô, and now the rest of the baggage train was moving up, a steady stream of wagons and carts turning off the Carentan road and settling in the fields east of the town. A small herd of cows wandered among them, lowing, and he spotted the little cowherd chivvying them along with her stick.

'Sir John would have sent those two archers, Matt and Pip. They are the best he has, he says. But I do not trust them.'

'They saved you and Warin at Carentan, *señor*. And *la señorita*.'

'They also killed Fierville. And they were not far away when Bray died.'

'I've been asking around about them, sir,' said Warin. He hammered in the last tent peg and stood up. 'They are well respected by their comrades.'

The herald shook his head. 'There is something odd about them. Mauro, when you are finished, set up the table and my writing case. I have work to do.'

—

*Inquisition into the death of Edmund Bray, knight, near the village of Quettehou in Normandy on the XII*th *day of July, in the nineteenth year of the reign of King Edward III. This report was composed on the XXII*nd *day of that month, at the town of Saint-Lô.*

Item, it remains my view that Sir Edmund Bray was killed after witnessing a meeting between Jean de Fierville and the French miles Macio Chauffin. However, there is still a lack of direct evidence. Archers of the Red Company and Sir Thomas Holland's company may have been eyewitnesses, but all deny seeing the killing. The only other potential eyewitness, Macio Chauffin, is in the retinue of the Count of Eu, and is presumably in Caen.

Item, it has come to my attention that Bray quarrelled on separate occasions with Sir Thomas Holland and Sir Hugh Despenser. Holland has already denied any involvement in Bray's death, but the presence of his archers in the field when Bray was killed cannot be discounted. I have yet to speak to Despenser. It should be stated that there is absolutely no direct evidence against either man.

Outside, a high-pitched voice was calling his name. Mauro opened the tent flap to admit one of the king's pageboys in red and gold livery. 'Sir Herald? His Grace has sent for you. He wishes to see you at once.'

–

The king had taken up residence in the Abbey of Saint-Croix, outside the town walls to the east. Merrivale followed the pageboy through the cloister and up a stone stair to the abbot's solar. The boy stopped and knocked at a heavy wooden door. 'Enter,' the king's voice commanded.

The solar was a bright, vividly painted room with rush mats on the floor. A Greek ikon, a blue-robed Virgin on a gold background, hung on the wall opposite the brick fireplace. The king had removed most of his armour and was standing by one of the windows, looking out across the valley of the Vire. Lord Rowton and Michael Northburgh were the only other people in the room.

Merrivale bowed. 'This is my latest report on the inquisition into the death of Sir Edmund Bray,' he said.

The king held out his hand. Merrivale gave him the parchment and the king scanned it quickly before passing it to Northburgh. 'Very well,' he said abruptly. 'Bray may have been killed because he discovered Fierville's treasonable plot. Or he may have been killed as a result of rivalries between the knights. Which is it?'

'I do not yet know, sire. I believe the former, but the latter cannot be discounted.'

'Mmm. This incident with the gunpowder at Carentan. Was that an attempt to kill me or my son?'

Thankfully, the king had not asked where the powder had come from. 'I suspect it was,' Merrivale said. 'Barbizan insisted that he would only surrender to yourself or the prince, and that you must come in person to the castle. It all fits.'

'Will there be another attempt?'

'Very likely, sire. Assassination is one of the oldest weapons in war.'

'Mmm.' The king looked out of the window, tapping one long forefinger against his chin. 'I am concerned about this friction between my knights. Holland and Despenser and Gurney are fine fighting men, but they can be troublesome.'

Merrivale cleared his throat. 'I was surprised that the lord marshal posted them all to the vanguard, sire, along with Mortimer and the Earl of Salisbury. Putting them in close proximity would seem to be doing Discord's work for her.'

The king continued to gaze out of the window. 'My son asked for them all to be placed under his command,' he said.

'Do you know why, sire?'

'God alone knows what goes on in that boy's head.' Realising that he had just criticised his son and heir in front of one of the prince's own servants, the king checked. 'But if they endanger the prince, then I will have no mercy on any of them.'

He paused for a moment. 'Could one of them be the traitor? The man who was working with Fierville?'

'I believe there are at least two traitors,' Merrivale said. 'One from the West Country and one from the north.'

'Gurney is from Somerset,' Rowton said thoughtfully, 'and Holland comes from the north. Mortimer is from a Marcher family, and the Despensers have lands there too. It is possible, sire.'

'It is,' the herald agreed, 'but I confess, sire, that I struggle to understand what motive these men might have. All have much to lose. My lord of Salisbury has everything he could want: lands, riches, the friendship of the prince. Why would he turn his back on it all? The others surely hope to restore their reputations and regain their families' lost lands and titles; and Holland, of course, still wishes to recover the woman he claims as his wife.'

'But it is for precisely these reasons that they may have turned traitor,' Rowton said. 'You spoke of Discord, herald. Anger, jealousy and the desire for revenge are all arrows in her quiver.'

'My lord, we have no evidence against these men,' Merrivale pointed out. 'If you are thinking of arresting them for treason, you risk a grave injustice.'

'And it would be bad for the temper of the army,' the king said. 'Holland and Despenser are well liked by their men, and Gurney is popular too. If we punish them, the men of their retinues may become disaffected and start to desert, and that rot could spread quickly.'

'I made no mention of arresting anyone,' Rowton said sharply. 'But we must consider the safety of the prince. And indeed, sire, your safety as well.'

'You may trust me to look after my own safety, Eustace,' the king said. 'Is my son well guarded?'

'Yes, sire,' said Merrivale.

'Good.' The king turned away from the window. 'I summoned you, herald, because I have another task for you.'

'I await your command, sire.'

'Your lady friend, the Demoiselle de Tesson. She said that Eu and the Queen of Navarre are contemplating a rebellion of their own. How reliable is she?'

'She has spoken nothing but truth so far,' Merrivale said.

'Good,' said the king. 'It seems we have been presented with a new opportunity. We have written before to the queen and received no reply, but we wish to try again. And we shall approach Eu as well. We will guarantee Norman independence from France, in exchange for armed support against Philippe de Valois. Harcourt's scheme may have failed, gentlemen, but this is a second chance.'

He looked at the herald again. 'I am sending Geoffrey of Maldon to Caen as my emissary. He will carry a formal letter to the authorities, there demanding the surrender of the city. I want you to go with him.'

Merrivale paused. Macio Chauffin was in Caen, and it was quite possible that he had witnessed the murder of Edmund Bray. There might be a chance to identify Bray's killers. On the other hand, there was bound to be more to this mission than met the eye. There always was, with kings.

'Brother Geoffrey is an experienced and highly skilled ambassador, sire. What role am I meant to play?'

'Once the letter is delivered, your task is to seek out the Count of Eu and negotiate with him. Persuade him to hand the city over to us, and to join our cause.'

'Easier said than done, sire,' Rowton said drily. 'And if Robert Bertrand finds out about these secret negotiations, he may accuse Brother Geoffrey and Master Merrivale of spying. In which case, I do not give much for their chances.'

'Brother Geoffrey is a priest and Merrivale is a herald. Their status protects them. Well, Merrivale? Can you do this?'

Merrivale bowed. 'As you wish, sire.'

'Then make it so. Once we are within striking distance of Caen, Northburgh will send word to you.'

10

Cormolain, 24th of July, 1346
Morning

The roof of the barn was roaring with flame by the time the first rescuers reached it. The door had been blocked by a heavy wagon pushed up against it; Courcy and Matthew Gurney rolled the wagon away and pulled the door open, but the interior of the barn was full of acrid smoke. Covering their faces, they plunged inside and began dragging out the bodies.

'How many?' asked the herald, arriving on the scene.

'Seven,' said Courcy. 'For some, a lucky number. Not for these fellows, though.'

He coughed, his face and hands blackened with soot. Gurney stood bent over with his hands on his knees, gagging as he tried to clear the smoke from his lungs. Donnchad, the big Irish gallowglass, knelt on the ground beside them, vomiting onto the grass.

'Any survivors?' asked Merrivale.

The roof of the barn collapsed with a crash, a shower of sparks, flames and smoke belching skyward and staining the dawn sky. 'No,' said Gurney.

The herald looked at the row of corpses. The clothes of some were still smouldering. 'Did anyone see what happened?'

'Donnchad spotted men dressed like local peasants running away,' Courcy said. 'I saw the barn was on fire and knew some of our lads were inside. We called for help, and Matthew arrived with some of his men. But we were too late.'

'And so the resistance begins,' Merrivale said slowly. 'People will have heard about Montebourg and Carentan and all the other places we destroyed. They are turning against us.'

Courcy looked at him. 'We need to talk,' he said. 'Somewhere private.'

They walked away from the burning barn, leaving Gurney and Donnchad and the others to watch the flames. 'The men who died in that barn were Lankies,' Courcy said when they were out of earshot. 'They were Bate's men. And it wasn't locals who killed them.'

'I am listening,' Merrivale said.

'I did as you asked and started looking around for clues about what happened to Bray. Like you, I thought of Bate and his men. As a fellow plunderer, I was able to get close to them, and I learned something of interest. Bate and his fellows don't carry their booty around with them. They sell it on quickly, and then go out and hunt for more.'

'Who buys it?'

'Nicodemus. Now there's an interesting fellow. A defrocked priest, he is. No one knows why, but it must have been something serious, like pissing on a bishop. Anything less, he'd have bought his way out of it.'

It was true, Merrivale thought. Absolution could always be had, at a price. 'And so he became an archer for hire.'

'Not at first. He worked as clerk to a banker in Southampton, but then when the French attacked in '38, the banker was killed and Nicodemus absconded with the banker's gold and the banker's wife. He popped up in Tracey's retinue in Flanders in '40, and has been in his service ever since.'

The fire in the barn was dying down. 'It's a smart enterprise,' Courcy said. 'I wish I had thought of it myself. He must have learned a lot from that banker, or his wife. Nicodemus buys stolen goods at a discount; the pillagers are happy to sell cheaply to get ready money. That way they don't have to haul the goods around with them. Nicodemus sends the booty back to England and sells it on for a profit. He works with at least a dozen companies, right across the army, and he's acquiring more customers as word gets around. He'll buy and sell anything from anyone.'

He paused. 'Now this is where it gets really interesting. Bate and his lads realised how much money Nicodemus was making, and decided to set up in competition. When Nicodemus found out, he was furious. He thought one of his own men was spying for Bate, and killed him.'

'Madford.'

'Exactly. Then he accused Bate of the murder, hoping to cover his tracks. That's what that little scene at Pont-Hébert was all about. You intervened and spoiled that plan, so he came up with another. He invented the story of the gambling debts, and one of Tracey's archers, Jack Slade, became the scapegoat. The guessing is that he's still out there somewhere, and still working with Nicodemus.'

'Did Slade kill Madford?'

'Could be. Or Nicodemus did it himself.'

Jakey was a good lad. Everyone liked him. The human capacity for deceit really knows no bounds, Merrivale thought. 'Is Tracey aware of Nicodemus's activities?'

'Of course he is. According to Bate's boys, he set up the entire scheme. Nicodemus is like a steward or a factor; he runs the operation. But the profit goes to Tracey.' Courcy's smile had little humour in it. 'It looks like old Jeremiah was right,' he said. 'A leopard can't change its spots.'

'Yes.' Everyone knew the unsavoury history of the Tracey family, but over the past few years, Edward de Tracey had emerged as a competent and reliable captain who had won the respect of his fellow knights and the favour of the king. But had he really left the past behind him?

'And so this morning, Nicodemus's men, disguised as locals, tried to get rid of their rivals?'

'I think you have the right of it. Nicodemus learned that some of Bate's lads were sleeping in the barn, and probably hoped Bate himself was with them, only he wasn't. Someone is stirring the pot, herald.'

'What do you mean?'

'Madford wasn't spying for Bate. All the Lankies swear to that. And they don't know how Nicodemus discovered their enterprise. I reckon someone is trying to set these boys against each other. And that is dangerous.'

Merrivale nodded. 'An army that is divided against itself will not fight well.'

'I meant dangerous for you. Bate still hates you. Watch your back, and remember, if they kill you, they'll take that pretty young lady away as well. They reckon she's unfinished business.'

In the distance, a trumpet sounded, rousing the men to march. 'Thank you,' Merrivale said. 'You have well repaid my trust in you.'

'It's not over yet. You still haven't discovered who killed Edmund Bray.'

'Not yet. But I will.'

Saint-Germain-d'Ectot, 24th of July, 1346
Late evening

The last of the sunset glow had faded, bringing a night full of fire. Caen was less than twenty miles away and the vanguard's camp was bright with watchfires, flotsam on a sea of flame. The countryside around them was flooded with pulsing orange light as villages and farms blazed. Out on the coast the northern horizon flickered and glowed like some unholy aurora as the English fleet burned its way east, targeting every ship and coastal port in its path.

In the camp at Saint-Germain-d'Ectot, the prince and his companions ate and drank and shouted and rattled the dice. As usual, the prince lost; as usual, the more he lost, the louder he laughed. Merrivale waited until they were all roaring drunk and then slipped quietly away. He found Tiphaine standing outside his tent looking at the fires. 'The world is burning,' she said quietly.

'Yes. It is the king's order. He has reversed his earlier edict and ordered the destruction of every town and village. He knows the smoke and flames will be seen in Caen.'

'Your commanders hope this will persuade the citizens to surrender, lest their own city suffer the same fate.'

Sparks danced like fireflies in the night. 'Do you think that is likely?' Merrivale asked. 'Will the citizens be dismayed by what they see?'

'The citizens may, but the Count of Eu will not. Why should he care? It is not his lands that are burning.'

The herald said nothing. Tiphaine turned and looked at him, her eyes clear in the firelight. 'I wish to apologise for my behaviour at Saint-Lô,' she said. 'I was rude to you, and that is unpardonable. I owe you everything, including my life.'

'I am troubled for your safety,' Merrivale said, 'and this army is no place for you. If I can find you passage to England, will you go?'

'England? What would I do there? I have no money, no friends, nowhere to live.'

'We could find you a place, I am sure.'

'Where?'

'A convent, perhaps.'

'Another prison? No thank you. I am staying here.'

Merrivale shook his head. 'Be reasonable, *demoiselle*. We must find a place of safety for you.'

She turned on him, almost fiercely. 'I do not care about safety. I told you at Saint-Lô. I intend to avenge my father.'

'How?'

'I do not yet know. But like the spider, I am patient.'

–

The shouting began a moment later, coming from the direction of the prince's pavilion. Gripped by sudden apprehension, Merrivale turned and ran towards the scene. The knights and esquires and serjeants of the prince's household had gathered, all staring in astonishment. He pushed through the crowd, not caring who he shouldered out of the way. It was only when he saw the prince standing swaying a little with wine cup in hand, but definitely unharmed, that he let out his breath.

Hugh Despenser was in the middle of the group, holding up a longbow arrow fletched with goose feathers and tipped with a gleaming broadhead; a hunter's arrow, designed to embed itself in flesh and bone and not be withdrawn. 'This was shot at me when I left the prince's pavilion a few moments ago. It missed me by no more than an inch.' His voice rose. 'Some coward has tried to shoot me in the back!'

The prince stared, glassy-eyed. His tutor, Bartholomew Burghersh, stepped forward. 'What are you saying, Sir Hugh?' he asked sharply. 'Are you accusing someone?'

'Yes!' Despenser spun around, pointing at Roger Mortimer. 'I am accusing you, you treacherous bastard! My father, my grandfather, my great-grandfather have all been butchered by Mortimers! Are you trying to add a fourth generation to the tally?'

Mortimer had gone pale in the firelight. 'Don't be ridiculous, Despenser. I can't shoot. I don't even own a bow.'

'No, but your friends do. Gurney! You have a longbow, don't you? I've seen you at the butts with your men, shooting like some damned peasant.' Despenser threw the arrow down at Gurney's feet. 'Is that yours?'

'No,' said Gurney, and his voice was cold. 'Be very careful what you say, Sir Hugh.'

'Or what? Or I too will end up with a poker up my arse? Or with an arrow in my back, like Bray?'

'Sir Roger is right. You *are* ridiculous,' Gurney said. 'Bray was my kinsman and I would never have harmed him. Seek your enemies elsewhere, Sir Hugh. You have plenty to choose from, after all.'

'Enough,' said Merrivale.

Silence fell. The herald walked forward until he stood between Gurney and Despenser, his ornate tabard glittering in the firelight. 'Must we repeat that dismal scene at Valognes, when you embarrassed your lord the prince and humiliated yourselves?'

No one answered. 'Sir Hugh, if you have evidence that either Sir Roger or Sir Matthew was behind an attempt to assassinate you, then lay it before his lordship the constable, whose duty it is to oversee discipline. Have you such evidence?'

Despenser said nothing.

'Then I think you should all retire and get some sleep,' Merrivale said. 'At dawn we advance on Caen.'

Burghersh cleared his throat. 'You heard what the herald said, gentlemen.'

Despenser spun on his heel and walked away. Swaying a little, the prince returned to the pavilion. The others dispersed, talking in low voices. Merrivale waited until they had gone, and turned to Burghersh.

'I know what you are thinking,' the prince's tutor said before Merrivale could speak. 'Why do I let them get out of hand? Why don't I exercise more control over the prince?'

'I have a feeling you are going to tell me.'

'The king's orders. This campaign will turn his son from a boy into a man, he says. But the prince has to be given his head and allowed to make his own decisions.'

'Including bringing those who are mortal enemies into his household and expecting them to work together in amity?'

Burghersh nodded. 'He must make his own mistakes, and learn from them. In his Grace's words, "let the boy win his spurs".'

'A harsh approach to fatherhood,' Merrivale observed.

'But not necessarily the wrong one. The king is wiser than he sometimes appears. And he has been a better father to his son than his own father ever was to him.'

'Of that there can be little doubt,' the herald agreed. 'Good night, Sir Bartholomew.'

–

Just as the fires began to die down, a night wind came, fanning them back into life once more. Merrivale found Gurney standing outside his tent staring into a night ripped apart by flames. 'What do you see?' the herald asked quietly.

'The pits of hell.'

That might be a metaphor, Merrivale thought, or it might not. 'May I ask you a couple of questions, Sir Matthew?'

'If you wish.'

'You said Bray was your kinsman. How were you related?'

'We were cousins,' Gurney said. 'His mother was my aunt.'

'Your family are from Somerset?'

'Yes. My father held the manor of Gurney Slade, not far from Wells.'

'Slade,' the herald said. He paused for a moment, thinking. 'An archer named Jack Slade deserted at Pont-Hébert.'

'Yes, I know him. His father was the miller in Gurney Slade. I tried to recruit him for my retinue, but he went to Edward de Tracey instead. Tracey has deeper pockets than me, and offered a larger bounty.'

'You sought him out deliberately. Was he a good man?'

'Yes, I thought so. Careful, reliable, and a good shot, too. I was very surprised to hear he had deserted.'

He was also a terrible shot, Tracey had said. For a moment, the herald wondered if they were talking about the same person. 'Have you seen him since?'

Gurney gave him a hard stare. 'Of course not. If I had, I would have arrested him and handed him over to the constable.'

'Of course,' Merrivale said. 'Was there any bad blood between you and Bray? Any ill feeling?'

'You mean beyond the normal revulsion most people feel for the son of a regicide? No, none. In fact, Bray was more polite to me than most.' Gurney's eyes met the herald's. 'I did not kill him, and I did not shoot at Despenser. And I don't believe Roger Mortimer had anything to do with it either.'

Someone is stirring the pot, Courcy had said this morning. He was right, and it wasn't just the archers; someone was setting the knights against each other, provoking quarrels, casting suspicions; and more than that. Someone had tried to drown Mortimer on the causeway at Saint-Côme-du-Mont; now, someone had narrowly missed shooting Despenser.

The Despensers and the Mortimers had been at feud for eighty years. Who had suggested to the prince that he bring them together under his command, along with other equally divisive figures like Holland, Gurney and Salisbury? Surely the prince would never have thought of this himself; but who had put the idea into his head?

'No,' Merrivale said. 'I do not believe it either. Good night, Sir Matthew.'

Outside the door of his tent he paused, suddenly tense. Something had moved in the night, a rustle right on the edge of hearing. He stood silent, straining his ears and listening, but no sound came.

For the second time that night, an archer cloaked in shadow raised his bow and lined it up on the back of his target. Silently he drew an arrow from his quiver and nocked it, drawing back the bowstring until the nock and flights were resting just in front of his ear.

In the split second before he released, someone grabbed the herald's arm and pulled him hard to the ground. The arrow whirred over his head and punched through the canvas wall of the tent. 'Stay down, *señor*!' Mauro hissed, and rolled over with his knife in his hand, holding it by the blade ready to throw as he searched for the hidden archer.

'There he is,' a voice said. 'In the shadows. Take him.'

'A pox on it, he's seen us. He's running.'

'After him, then.' Two men raced past, longbows in hand, running hard in pursuit of a third man fleeing through the firelight and shadows. The herald sat up and watched them for a moment, and then slammed his hand on the ground in anger. 'Damn the man,' he said quietly. 'Why can't he mind his own business?'

The light was poor, but he had no difficulty in recognising the two archers from the Red Company, Matt and Pip.

Saint-Germain-d'Ectot, 24ᵗʰ of July, 1346
Night

'Splendid,' said the man from the north. 'The knights are quarrelling among themselves. This is going very well, my friend.'

'I still don't see how it profits us,' said the man from the West Country.

'Isn't it obvious? The more they fight each other, the less will and energy they will have for fighting the French. And their mood will spread to their retinues and supporters. Soon the army will begin to fall apart.'

'If you say so, but it's taking too damned long. I wish that scheme at Carentan had worked. If the king was dead, all this would be over and we could move on with the rest of the plan.'

'Well it didn't work, and neither did the attempt at Quettehou. Never mind. Be patient, my friend. We have plenty more schemes in hand. We can afford to fail, many times, because we only need to succeed once.'

'Very well. What next?'

'The king still cherishes hopes of starting a Norman revolt, and he has learned about the Count of Eu and the Queen of Navarre and what they are plotting. Geoffrey of Maldon and Merrivale are going to Caen to persuade Eu to surrender the city and join the English cause.'

'Then we must stop them. There *will* be a Norman revolt, yes, but guided by us, not the king. We have already poured enough money into supporting Eu and the queen, and buying their loyalty. If the king steps in and takes over now, all our effort will be wasted.'

'Never fear. Eu has personally assured me of his loyalty. And Brother Geoffrey and Merrivale's mission will fail. They will be executed as soon as they reach Caen.'

'Good. That damned herald is starting to annoy me.'

'After that, Eu will hold the castle at Caen, which is impregnable. He has four thousand men, he says, and the storerooms are full; he can withstand a siege indefinitely. King Edward will suffer a humiliating defeat and be forced to withdraw.'

'Giving us a chance to lay another snare for him,' said the West Country man.

'Exactly. And then, my friend, our time will come.'

Saint-Germain-d'Ectot, 25th of July 1346
Morning

'Where are you going?' Tiphaine asked.

'Caen,' Merrivale said. He pulled his embroidered tabard over his head and shook out the folds. 'King's orders.'

Northburgh's letter was on the table beside him. Crumbs of red wax from the broken seal lay dark on the wood, like little drops of blood in the dawn light.

She watched him steadily. 'You are walking into a trap.'

'I know. I have done this before. If you need help, seek out Sir John Sully.'

Tiphaine continued to watch him. 'Are you not afraid?'

He considered the matter for a moment. 'No,' he said finally. 'Not yet. But I am sure there will be plenty of time for that later.'

—

Outside the Prince of Wales's pavilion, a lone figure stood waiting for him. 'Stay a moment, herald,' the prince said. 'I wish to speak with you.'

Merrivale reined in, bowing from the saddle. 'How may I serve you, Highness?'

'Lord Rowton told me about your mission to Caen. It is dangerous, is it not?'

'Do not fear, Highness.' Merrivale touched his tabard. 'As your father said, I am protected by my station. The French are honourable men. They will do no violence against a herald.'

'All the same, I wish my father would send someone else. Why can't Clarenceux go instead of you?'

'Andrew Clarenceux is a fine man, Highness, and a master of all things to do with armorial bearings and coats. But I have experience and skills he does not possess.'

'But what if you don't come back? Herald, I depend on you.'

'You have many fine servants, Highness.'

'But they cannot do what you do. I watched you last night, bringing my knights to heel, and... I envied you. I wish I could do that.'

'You will learn in time, Highness.'

'Will I? I know they think I am still a child. I know what they say about me behind my back. I took them into my service, even knighted some of them. I let them win my money at hazard. What else must I do to win their respect? I look at my father, and how easy he makes it look, how he barely has to lift a finger to command the loyalty of men like Warwick and Northampton and Rowton. What must I do to do that?'

'Be yourself, Highness,' Merrivale said. 'Do not put on a pretence for them, and do not try to be your father. Be your own man, and in time they will respect your fine qualities and look up to you. It will come.'

'I hope you are right.' The prince raised his hand. 'God go with you,' he said. 'Return safely.' Then he turned abruptly and walked away.

Geoffrey of Maldon waited for him at the edge of camp, his angular frame wrapped in a long black cassock. Behind them, the vanguard was forming up. The village of Saint-Germain had been saved from burning last night because some of the men were sheltering there, but now it too was on fire, smoke boiling up to join the dark skeins already staining the sky. The sunrise glowed livid orange.

Brother Geoffrey raised a hand in greeting as the herald rode up. 'Well, old friend? Shall we stick our heads in the lion's mouth once more?'

Despite the plain cassock, Brother Geoffrey was much more than just a canon and a priest. Over the past decade, he had visited half the courts of Europe, acting as ambassador, building coalitions of support for King Edward, paying out pensions and bribes and gathering information. Merrivale had been the hard-riding king's messenger who supported him, carrying coded letters to and from the offices of state in London.

'You make it sound like it might be the last time,' the herald said.

Brother Geoffrey laughed. 'Every time might be the last time.' He picked up the reins of his horse, nudging it with the heels of his sandalled feet. 'Very well. Let us go.'

Behind them, towers of smoke climbed hundreds of feet into the sky. Ahead lay the walls of Caen, church spires rising behind them. The massive bulk of the castle brooded against the skyline. To its left stood the great abbey church of Saint-Étienne, the burial place of William the Conqueror, surrounded by cloisters, outbuildings and a cluster of houses. Further east, beyond the castle, they could see another big abbey on a low hill; La Trinité, the Abbaye aux Dames, resting place of the Conqueror's wife Queen Matilda. The place Tiphaine had once called home, and to which she refused to return.

Brother Geoffrey shaded his eyes with his hand. 'The district next to the castle is the old town, the Bourg-le-Roi. To the south is the Saint-Jean quarter. That, we are told, is the richest district of the city. As you can see, it is surrounded by water, and there are marshes further south. A strong position, would you say?'

Merrivale studied the defences. 'I am not sure. Bourg-le-Roi is walled, but apart from the water, Saint-Jean is protected only by a wooden palisade. That will keep wild beasts out, but not our army.'

'What about the castle?'

'That is another matter.' The castle stood on rising ground at the northern edge of the Bourg-le-Roi. The stone walls were high and looked thick, sprouting towers and turrets and bartizans. The big gatehouse probably had at least two portcullises, with murder holes to deal with any attacker who managed to get through them. It too was surrounded by a wet moat. No, taking the castle would not be easy.

Brother Geoffrey pointed. 'We have been spotted.'

A column of men-at-arms rode out of the gates of the Bourg-le-Roi. Their leader bore an unusual device, a white mastiff on a field of red. Twenty more men rode behind him, all heavily armed and armoured.

The man with the mastiff device made a circular motion with his hand. At once the men-at-arms fanned out, sweeping around to encircle the two Englishmen and then closing in, lowering their lances as they did so. Brother Geoffrey and Merrivale halted their horses and dropped their reins, raising their hands to show they were unarmed. 'We come in peace,' the canon said. 'We are emissaries from King Edward, with a message for your commanders.'

The leader inclined his head. 'Very well. Come with us.'

The Englishmen picked up their reins once more and, still surrounded by the men-at-arms, rode forward towards the open gates of the city. Crossbowmen covered them from the ramparts, and more men-at-arms watched them from the shadows behind the gates. The city streets were deserted. The hooves of their horses echoed in an empty silence.

They came to the castle, crossing a drawbridge over a broad moat full of brackish water. More armed men crowded the wall-walk overhead, staring down at them. In the courtyard, they dismounted, and the man with the mastiff device gestured towards a big stone hall. 'This way,' he said.

They climbed the wooden stair to the door of the hall, and the leader ushered them inside. They found themselves in a long room with a beamed ceiling, timbers stained with smoke from two centuries of hearth fires. Banners, some old and faded, hung from the walls. A group of men sat around a long oak table, some in clerical black, one wearing a bishop's mitre. Some of the others were well dressed; one wore several rings on his fingers, gold set with amethysts and lapis lazuli.

A white-haired man in a surcoat with a green lion rampant on gold, his face scarred and his arm in a dirty sling, sat opposite the bishop. This was Robert Bertrand, the man they had been fighting for the past twelve days. Bertrand gazed at the two Englishmen with eyes that radiated hate. The hairs on Merrivale's neck rose in sudden alarm. Tiphaine had been right, this was a trap, but it was too late. They were surrounded by armed men. There was nowhere to run.

The bishop rose to his feet. 'Who are you?' he demanded. 'State your names and purpose.'

'We are emissaries from King Edward,' the canon said. 'I am Brother Geoffrey of Maldon, canon of the Augustinian order. My companion is Simon Merrivale, herald to the Prince of Wales. We carry a letter from the king, addressed to the commanders of the garrison of Caen.'

He laid the king's letter on the table. The bishop broke the seal and held it up to the light. His face flushed dull red with anger. 'It is, as we suspected, a demand for surrender,' he said. The man with the rings laughed. Bertrand spat with contempt.

'What answer do you give, my lords?' Brother Geoffrey asked patiently.

The bishop tore the parchment in half, ripped each piece in half again and threw the fragments on the floor, grinding them under the heel of his boot. 'That is our answer!' he snarled. 'We know who you are, Brother Geoffrey, and why you have really come here. You are spies, both of you, and you will meet a spy's death. Take them outside and hang them.'

11

Caen, 25th of July, 1346
Midday

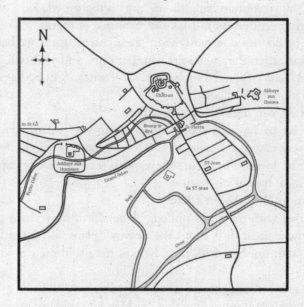

Hard hands gripped their arms and pinned them behind their backs. 'No,' said the man with the rings, and he rose to his feet. 'These men are protected.'

The bishop slammed his fist down on the table. 'You fool! They are *spies*, I tell you! Hang them!'

Bertrand stood up too, cradling his wounded arm. 'My brother is right, Constable. You heard the messenger yesterday. Maldon and Merrivale have been sent to spy and report back to King Edward.'

'Then we shall prevent them from doing so,' the man with the rings said calmly. 'Brother Geoffrey, Master Merrivale, your lives will be spared, but I fear we must detain you. Once your army retreats from Caen, you will be released.'

'This is monstrous,' Merrivale said sharply. 'We are ambassadors. You cannot interfere with us.'

'Oh, don't go quoting the laws of war at me, herald,' the man with the rings said wearily. 'Ambassadors are also spies; always have been and always will be. It is part of their job. I didn't need the messenger to tell me that.' He paused for a moment, stroking his chin.

'I still say we should hang them,' the bishop growled.

'I agree,' said Bertrand. 'Make an example of them.'

'Your bellicosity does you credit, gentlemen. But if we hang their ambassadors, then they will start hanging ours, and so it will go on… I'm afraid we do still need such men, sometimes. And perhaps we can turn this to our advantage.'

'What do you mean?' asked Bertrand.

'First, let us separate them. Keep Brother Geoffrey here in the castle. I will take the herald to one of the towers on the bridge of Saint-Pierre. He will be secure there, with no chance of escape, and I shall question him at my leisure.'

'Question him? About what?'

The man with the rings smiled. 'A herald to the Prince of Wales must know a great deal about the enemy's plans and intentions. By the time I am finished with him, he will have told me everything he knows.'

'You said you would spare our lives,' Merrivale said.

'And I shall. But more than that, Sir Herald, I will not promise you.' He waved his hand, purple and blue light flashing from his rings. Two men-at-arms took hold of Brother Geoffrey. 'Good luck, old friend,' Geoffrey murmured. 'May God watch over you.'

'And you also,' Merrivale said quietly.

The men-at-arms marched the black-robed canon away. Merrivale wondered if he would ever see him again. Two more men took his own arms, and the man with the mastiff device tapped him on the shoulder. 'Come with me,' he said.

The guards took Merrivale to a room high up in one of the squat towers that guarded the southern end of the bridge of Saint-Pierre. Below he could see the bridge itself lined with half-timbered houses, some hanging out over the surging brown river. This was the Odon, which divided the two halves of the city. The river channel was broad; the tide, he guessed, was nearly full. The coast was only about ten miles away.

The single door into the chamber was locked from the outside. Even if he could get through it, the only way out was down the narrow spiral stair to another door at the foot of the tower. That door, as he had seen when they brought him in, was heavily guarded.

The windows were narrow, little more than arrow slits. Different angles showed him small parts of the city. Beyond the bridge to the north stood a big church, Saint-Pierre, its windows and buttresses rising above the riverbank; beyond it were the crowded buildings of Bourg-le-Roi. The towers of the abbey of Saint-Étienne could be seen in the distance. To the south was the district of Saint-Jean, streets lined with fine houses backing onto gardens. A pleasant, prosperous city, the herald thought, and big, too; not so big as London, but still powerful.

Everywhere he looked, he saw preparations for war. At the foot of the bridge a strong barricade had been thrown up, and he could see a host of defenders behind it, armour flashing and sparkling in the strong sunlight. Dozens of shallops and coracles were coming up the river on the incoming tide, all crowded with crossbowmen wearing white tunics.

White was the colour worn by Genoese mercenaries. Until now, apart from the detachment that had been overwhelmed at Pont-Hébert, they had seen nothing of these feared crossbowmen and their powerful weapons. Now, hundreds of them floated on the river, weapons at the ready. Merrivale wondered why they had been so late in arriving. Had Bertrand commanded this many crossbowmen earlier in the campaign, the outcome at Carentan and Saint-Lô might have been different; indeed, the English army might never have got ashore at Saint-Vaast.

Off to the west, smoke clouds billowed like the wall of a storm, lit from within by the red lightning of burning villages, coming steadily closer.

The room itself was not uncomfortable. There was a bed with a straw mattress and wool blankets, a painted wooden chest and a *jeu de table*, a small table inlaid with triangular patterns of dark wood and bone. Opening a drawer at one end, the herald found a stack of gaming pieces and a pair of dice. Thoughtfully he pulled up a wooden stool and arranged the pieces, then began rolling dice against himself, moving the pieces around the board.

He was halfway through a game when a key rattled in the lock and the door opened. The man with the rings walked into the room, closing the door behind him. He was about Merrivale's own age, thin-faced and long-nosed, with an air of careless arrogance that came from generations of breeding and power. He wore an embroidered doublet and hose partly covered by a flowing silk surcoat bearing his arms: a gold lion on a blue field, quartered with an ornate gold cross on white. Of course, the herald thought with professional detachment; one of his ancestors had been King of Jerusalem.

'I assume you know who I am,' the man said.

Merrivale bowed. 'Raoul de Brienne, Count of Eu and Guînes and Constable of France,' he said. 'I am at your service, my lord.'

'A curious turn of phrase,' Eu said. He surveyed his prisoner for a moment. Merrivale studied him in turn, waiting.

Eu pulled up another stool and sat down, studying the gaming table. 'Are you fond of games of chance, herald?'

'I dislike gambling, my lord. I prefer calculation.'

'You dislike gambling? That must make you unique at King Edward's court.' The count gestured for Merrivale to sit. 'Life itself is a gamble, herald. You wagered *your* life, when you came here to spy for your king.'

He rolled the dice and moved one of the white counters, and sat back looking at Merrivale again, his gaze steady.

'Someone told you we were coming,' Merrivale said. 'Who was it?'

'Do you really believe I will answer that question? Tell me instead why you came here.'

'I have a message for you, my lord. And whoever told you we were spies was trying to stop that message from getting through. He hoped you would hang us out of hand, as the bishop and the Sire de Bertrand urged you to do.'

Eu stroked his chin, still watching him. 'This message. What is it?'

'Once I have told you, what then?'

'That depends on the message,' the count said, 'and who it is from.' He gestured towards the gaming table. 'Your move.'

Merrivale rolled the dice, moved a black piece and pushed the dice back across the table. 'My message is from the king,' he said.

The count studied the game. 'Ah,' he said after a moment, 'I see.'

'But you had already guessed this,' Merrivale said. 'That is the real reason why you intervened to stop the bishop from killing us. You wanted to hear what I had to say.'

'Let us just say your arrival was not unexpected.' The count picked up the dice and rolled them. 'And what does Edward Plantagenet want with me?'

Merrivale did not answer directly. 'You will know by now, my lord, that Godefroi d'Harcourt's revolt against King Philip has failed.'

'Yes. It appears that Harcourt has fewer friends than he thought. Even his own brother has turned against him, and gone to join the royal army mustering at Rouen.'

'As a loyal Frenchman, this must be pleasing to you,' the herald said. 'The threat of rebellion is averted and Normandy's loyalty to the French crown has been secured.' He paused. 'Of course, my lord, it depends on who you really are. A Frenchman, or a Norman.'

Eu rolled the dice, studied the table for a long moment and finally moved a piece. 'And what does your king want from me?' he asked.

'His Grace knows that you and the Queen of Navarre are planning a rebellion of your own. This revolt would be much more dangerous than Harcourt's failed uprising. The queen is King Philip's cousin. Your ancestors fought for the Holy Sepulchre, and the blood of kings and emperors runs in your veins. Where you lead, thousands will flock to follow you.'

The count said nothing. He picked up one of the gaming pieces, examined it for a moment, then put it back on the board.

'If you rebel, His Grace will support you,' Merrivale said. 'He has fifteen thousand men, and more will come from England. You will need English support if you are to defeat King Philip and his royal army.'

'What does Edward suggest I do?'

'Join forces with him,' Merrivale said. 'When his army approaches Caen, open the gates of the city and bring your men over to join us.'

Eu made an impatient gesture. 'If I do, King Philippe will declare me a rebel. All my lands and estates will be forfeit, and I will be no better off than Harcourt. What happens if I refuse Edward's gentle offer?'

'Then his Grace will storm the city,' Merrivale said.

The count gestured towards the windows. 'Look again, herald. Do you think that will be easy?'

'The walls of Bourg-le-Roi are old and weak, and will be easy to undermine. Saint-Jean's only protection, apart from these towers on the bridge, is the river and a wooden palisade. But the river can be swum or forded, and a child could climb over the palisade. Caen will fall, my lord, no matter how stoutly you defend it.'

'Ah, but you have forgotten the castle. It is impregnable, and its storerooms are full. And I have four thousand men at my command, including a thousand crossbowmen. Even if the city falls, I can hold the castle for weeks.'

Merrivale nodded. 'Ah, yes. You will hold out until the royal army arrives from Rouen to relieve you. King Edward will be forced to retreat, and the power and prestige of King Philip will grow stronger. The dream of rebellion and a free Normandy will recede into the distance. It would appear you have made your choice, my lord. You *are* French, after all.'

The count rose to his feet and stood looking down at him. 'I told you earlier that you were gambling with your life,' he said. 'By speaking to me as you have done, you have forfeited your immunity as a herald. I could hang you right now.'

'You could,' Merrivale agreed. 'But as I said, my lord, I prefer calculation to gambling.'

'Well, let us see if you have calculated correctly. Is there anything you desire?'

'Yes, my lord. You have in your service a man-at-arms named Macio Chauffin. I should like to speak with him.'

'Chauffin? Why?'

'An English knight was murdered shortly after we landed at Saint-Vaast, by one of our own men. I think Chauffin may have witnessed the murder. I would like to ask him what he knows.'

The count raised his eyebrows a little. 'Why should I care if one of your men was killed? One less of the enemy to worry about.'

'If indeed we are the enemy,' said Merrivale. 'But, my lord, this is a matter of murder, not warfare. And the principles of justice apply equally in France as they do in England, I think.'

Eu considered this. 'You are bold with your demands,' he said. 'Perhaps I should take the bishop's advice and hang you.'

A cold finger of doubt crept down Merrivale's spine, and he wondered if he had overplayed his hand. 'That is your lordship's decision,' he said.

'It is,' Eu agreed. 'I wish you a good evening, Sir Herald.'

Caen, 25th of July, 1346
Evening

Time passed, and the wall of smoke grew closer. The sun, dipping into the west, was obscured by its clouds. Today, dusk fell early in Caen.

Macio Chauffin was the man who had arrested them outside the city walls. He had stripped off his surcoat and most of his armour, but still wore a mail tunic over a padded doublet. His balding head was fringed with dark hair like a monk's tonsure. Merrivale guessed he was in his early forties.

'Thank you for coming to see me,' the herald said. 'I am sorry I have no refreshment to offer you.'

'I am here at my lord's command,' Chauffin replied. His face and voice were both wary, like a man expecting to be attacked.

'If you will permit me, I have a few questions for you. I believe you met with Jean de Fierville on the road from Quettehou to Valognes the day we landed, the twelfth of July. During this meeting, did you see anyone else?'

Chauffin looked surprised, as if this was not the question he had been expecting. 'Yes, I did. Just as we were finishing our... conversation, another English man-at-arms came riding up from Quettehou. I wasn't expecting him, and I could see Fierville wasn't either.'

'What did you do?'

'I thought it might be a trap, and I turned my horse and rode away. But I had only gone about a hundred yards when I heard Fierville calling me back. I turned again and saw the other man lying on the ground. He was dead by the time I rejoined Fierville.'

'Did you see the men who killed him?' Merrivale asked.

'Yes,' Chauffin said. 'I did not see the actual shooting, but there were two archers standing only a few yards away, with strung bows and arrows at the nock. It was obvious that they were the killers.'

A gust of wind wafted through the windows, smelling of smoke. 'Could you identify them?' the herald asked.

Chauffin shook his head. 'They wore no badges or blazons.'

'Did either of them wear a red iron cap?'

'No, they wore no headgear. I am positive of it.'

The caps could have been removed, of course. 'Was one of them bald? With a scar across his scalp?'

Chauffin shook his head again.

'What happened next?' Merrivale asked.

'Nothing. Fierville told the two archers to go, and they ran off. We debated about what to do with the body; he wanted to hide it, but there wasn't time. Bertrand's men were already coming down the road and hell was about to break loose. So we rode away and left him. Poor fellow,' Chauffin said. 'So young, too. His family will miss him.'

Merrivale looked at him sharply. 'Did you recognise him?'

'No.' It was said so quickly and abruptly that the herald was quite certain he was lying.

'You met Fierville by arrangement, I assume. Who told you where and when to meet him?'

Chauffin scratched his ear. 'Does this have anything to do with the murder?'

'It might.'

'The letter arrived a week earlier,' Chauffin said. 'It came from someone in your camp, but I don't know who.'

'Might it have been Sir Thomas Holland?' the herald asked.

Chauffin's head jerked back in shock. 'I don't know who you are talking about.'

'You and Sir Thomas and the Count of Eu served together in Prussia,' Merrivale said. 'You were together for about a year, first in Königsberg and then out on the frontier. At Allenstein and Rössel, I believe.'

Chauffin stared at him, lips clamped tightly together.

'I am a herald,' Merrivale said. 'I know Fierville gave you information, and I know Sir Thomas Holland is betraying his country, but these matters do not fall within my jurisdiction. All I want to know is who killed that young knight.'

'Holland is not a traitor.'

'Fierville and yourself were go-betweens,' the herald said, continuing as if Chauffin had not spoken. 'Fierville carried messages from Holland to you, and you passed them on to the count; who, let us not forget, is also Constable of France. If this correspondence had come to light, Holland would have been attainted and executed. He would do anything to stop that from happening. His archers were keeping watch when you met Fierville that day, and when Sir Edmund Bray discovered the two of you together, they killed him.'

Chauffin's eyelids flickered.

'Yes, that was his name,' Merrivale said. 'You recognise it, don't you?'

'Yes,' Chauffin said quietly.

'How? Where had you heard it before?'

'Fierville told me. When I rode back to join him.'

Another lie, Merrivale thought. 'You are quite positive that you did not recognise these archers? They were not from Holland's retinue?'

Chauffin stood up and walked to the door. 'I know most of Holland's trusted men,' he said. 'They were with us in Prussia too. The men I saw that day I had never seen before in my life. And you are wrong, Sir Herald. What Sir Thomas did was not treason.'

Merrivale raised his eyebrows. 'No? But then treason is so often a matter of perspective, don't you think? Did you know that, as well as delivering messages to you, Fierville was also reporting directly to Robert Bertrand?'

The look of astonishment on Chauffin's face gave him the answer. 'Fierville betrayed Godefroi d'Harcourt's plans to the enemy,' Merrivale said. 'You must pray, *messire*, that he did not also know about the plot your master is hatching with the Queen of Navarre. Because if he did, that plan is also known to Bertrand, and probably by now to King Philip in Rouen. Tell your master this, and ask him where he wishes to place his bet.'

Caen, 26th of July, 1346
Morning

Now the smoke was very close, hanging over the faubourgs of the city and drifting in clouds above the castle and the Bourg-le-Roi. Looking through the narrow windows, Merrivale could see the sharp glitter of flames on the high ground west of the city. The storm was about to break.

Down on the bridge, the men around the barricade were alert, swords drawn, spears braced, crossbows ready. He could hear more men moving around on the roof of the tower overhead. Another column of men-at-arms and crossbowmen came down past the church of Saint-Pierre to the far end of the bridge and took up position in the half-timbered houses that lined the span, crouching in doorways or climbing up to lean out of windows The tide was nearly out, the river crowded with boats shrunk to a narrow channel with gleaming expanses of mud on either side.

Once again a key rasped in the lock and the door swung open. The Count of Eu walked into the room, clad in brilliantly polished metal armour with his bascinet tucked under one arm. The lion and cross on his surcoat were stitched with gold thread. Other men-at-arms followed him. One of them was Chauffin. Unlike the others, his face was pale and sweating and he looked sick with fear.

'My apologies for disturbing you,' the count said. 'This room gives an excellent vantage point from which to survey the defences. My men and I will take post here.'

Merrivale bowed. 'Do you wish me to withdraw, my lord?'

'Stay. I may have need of your services before this is over.'

And what did that mean? the herald wondered. Eu had apparently made his choice; he seemed determined to fight.

'I am at your service, my lord,' he said. 'If I may be so bold as to ask, is there any news of my friend Brother Geoffrey?'

'He is in the dungeon at the castle. The Sire de Bertrand and the bishop have decided to remain there with their men. They will not join the defence of the city.'

'We should all be in the castle,' one of the other men-at-arms said. 'We could hold it for weeks, long enough for King Philippe to arrive.'

'And hand over the city and all its people to the enemy? We must make some attempt to defend them, Tancarville.'

'But then why have you abandoned Bourg-le-Roi? At least it has walls.'

'The walls are old and weak and easily undermined,' Eu said, without looking at the herald. 'Saint-Jean is an island, and easy to defend. Most of the population of Bourg-le-Roi have already fled here. We shall protect them.'

'An island?' Tancarville persisted. 'See how low the water is! The enemy can cross the Odon with ease.'

Eu pointed to the boats full of crossbowmen drifting on the tide. 'The river and the bridge are both strongly defended. Be at ease, Tancarville. The enemy shall not pass. We can hold Saint-Jean, and we will.'

Outside, the hot sun glared off the rooftops and the brown waters of the Odon. Up in the tower, the French men-at-arms waited, sweating in their armour as they watched the far end of the bridge and the lanes around the church of Saint-Pierre. Merrivale glanced again at Chauffin and saw terror plain in the other man's face. He knows Eu is wrong, the herald thought. He knows the city will fall.

What has made the count change his mind? Why has he chosen to make his stand here, in practically defenceless Saint-Jean? Does he not know what will happen?

'Here they come,' someone murmured.

Three, four, five the archers came, distant figures in russet and green slipping around the apse of Saint-Pierre and staring out towards the river. In the tower they heard the distant clack of crossbows as the men in the boats began to shoot. One of the archers fell, rolling down the riverbank onto the gleaming foreshore. He tried to get up, but two more crossbow bolts slammed him back into the mud. The others vanished.

Voices murmured in the tower, almost whispering. 'Have we seen them off?'

'No. That was just a reconnaissance party. Those were only archers. The men-at-arms will come next.'

'Our crossbowmen will see them off.'

'No. Wait.'

More movement at the far end of the bridge, archers running out of cover and shooting at the men posted in the houses, dodging back again as the crossbow bolts lashed at them. Two fell kicking and twitching in the street, but suddenly there were more archers, and more, and the shower of arrows became a steady hail, thumping into the wooden walls and sticking out like porcupine quills. Beyond the bridge the watchers in the tower could see gleaming armour and bright shields, the English men-at-arms running forward to reinforce the archers, and Merrivale saw a flash of red and gold. Warwick the marshal was there, leading his troops from the front.

Streaks of flame arched through the air, fire arrows falling in swarms, plunging into walls and roofs tinder dry in the summer heat.

Smoke rose almost at once, spreading across the bridge. Half a dozen French men-at-arms bolted from one burning house, running towards the shelter of the barricade at the southern end. The archers rose from cover and shot them as they ran, and their bodies tumbled down with arrows protruding from the joints of their armour. None reached safety.

Out on the river, the crossbowmen shot steadily, black bolts streaking through the air. Archers fell, their bodies littering the foreshore, but more and more were piling into the fight, shooting fast and accurately, and hundreds of grey-feathered arrows hissed like dragon's teeth, shredding the air above the waters of the Odon and thudding into wood and flesh and bone. The showers of arrows scythed the Genoese down, some collapsing back into their boats and lying still, others falling overboard and drifting slowly downstream on the receding tide.

Some of these arrows were fire-tipped too. Already several boats were burning, and crossbowmen dived into the river to escape the flames; the archers shot them as they struggled in the water. The survivors crouched behind the gunwales of their boats and shot back desperately. Some archers were running out into the mud now, seeking to close the range, and now they were so close the crossbowmen could not miss. More archers fell and died, but the deadly rain of arrows continued.

In the tower room the voices whispered again. 'No matter how many of them we kill, they keep coming. They do not stop.'

Welsh spearmen, men from Merioneth and Caernarvon, ran down the bank and plunged into the river, half wading and half swimming towards the boats. The fire arrows streaked out again and another boat began to burn; its crew dived into the stream, and then the Welsh were on them, spears rising and falling until the brown waters of the Odon were streaked with blood. In the boat nearest the bridge a handful of crossbowmen were still shooting steadily, and a Welshman reared back clutching at a bolt protruding from his chest, and slid under the water. His comrades reached the boat, stabbing wildly inside with their spears, the Genoese clubbing at them with the butts of their crossbows;

the boat capsized and pitched them all into the water, men stabbing and grappling with each other in a shouting, screaming frenzy until the bodies of friend and foe alike went still and began floating away towards the sea.

The houses on the bridge were burning fiercely now, flames roaring and sparks shooting into the air. One collapsed, spilling flaming timbers into the river. A few more French defenders broke cover and ran, preferring a quick death in the street to burning slowly in their houses, but most stood fast. The clatter of metal sounded through the smoke as the English worked their way from house to burning house, clearing the defenders, still covered by those deadly clouds of arrows. More English men-at-arms ran forward across the bridge.

'I see Northampton's colours,' said one of the French knights, looking out of the lancet window. 'The English constable is here. And Warwick, and Thomas Holland as well.'

'Holland,' said the Count of Eu. His lips twisted into a smile. 'My old friend from Prussia. How ironic.'

Tancarville turned on him. 'Your old friend who is going to kill us all! The defences are collapsing, Constable! They are eating us up! We might as well defend a sand dune against the tide!'

'The barricade will hold firm,' the Count of Eu said. Chauffin had closed his eyes, his lips moving in silent prayer.

An arrow rattled against the stone wall of the tower and bounced away. 'I recommend you stand away from the windows,' Merrivale said quietly.

'Don't be ridiculous,' the man watching the bridge said. He wore an open-faced helmet rather than a visor. 'The window is narrow and high. Their archers cannot possibly hit it.'

A rushing hiss and a noise like a storm of sleet, arrows hammering at the wall outside, and the man who had spoken fell back into the room with four arrows protruding from the bloody wreckage of his face, their points driven deep into his brain. More arrows flew through the window, streaks of death seeking their target, and another man gagged, clutching at his throat. He collapsed across the gaming table, which broke and smashed beneath his weight, and lay sprawled on the splintered wood with blood spurting around the feathered shaft. Everyone else ducked, while the storm went on and arrows continued to fly in showers into the room. Screams and shouts overhead told them the defenders on the tower roof were being picked off.

In the street below, all was chaos, men shouting and screaming, the hammer of weapons reverberating off the walls, smoke and flames blowing everywhere, and then the cry went up: 'England! Saint George, Saint George!', a shout of victory ripped from a thousand throats. 'The barricade has fallen,' Tancarville said, and he drew his sword. 'We are next.'

He had barely finished speaking when something smashed hard against the door of the tower. Merrivale looked at the Count of Eu. 'The city is lost, my lord,' he said. 'There is no point in further resistance. Let me parley on your behalf. I will speak to the earls of Warwick and Northampton and ask them to accept your surrender.'

Eu smiled wryly. 'Find me Thomas Holland instead. I wish to surrender to him.'

The door reverberated like the stroke of doom. The English were using rams; it would not be long before they broke the door down and swarmed inside.

'Why?' the herald asked.

'He saved my life once in Prussia,' the count said. 'This is the least I can do for him.'

Chauffin leaned against the wall, eyes closed. Spent arrows crunched under Merrivale's feet like kindling as he walked across the room. Descending the spiral stair, he heard the ram smashing into the lower door again and again; by the time he reached the bottom of the tower, the wood was already splintering around the hinges. He raised his voice.

'I am Merrivale, herald to his Highness the Prince of Wales! I am sent by the Count of Eu to parley!'

The hammering on the door ceased, and he heard a confused muttering outside. Drawing a deep breath, he lifted the bar of the door, swung it open and stepped outside. Swords and spear points raised to confront him lowered slowly – and, he thought, not without a little disappointment – when the men saw his herald's tabard. The bridge around the barricade and the street behind it were covered with bodies, some still, some moving feebly. A wounded Frenchman waved a hand, struggling to sit up, and one of the English archers ran over to him, pulled his head back to expose his throat and plunged a knife into his neck. The air stank of smoke and fresh blood. Gurney and young Mortimer were there, breathing hard, their armour dented, bright surcoats splattered with blood. 'Where is Sir Thomas Holland?' Merrivale asked.

'Here.' Holland pushed through the crowd of men around the door. 'What do you want with me?'

'The Count of Eu is within,' Merrivale said. 'He asks that you receive his surrender. Will you accept it?'

Holland pushed his visor up. 'Eu wishes to surrender? To me?'

'Yes,' Merrivale said.

Holland closed his eye, and for a moment Merrivale wondered if he intended to refuse. Then he opened his eye and smiled broadly. 'Of course,' he said, and he turned to his esquire. 'Go and find my lord of Warwick. Tell him the battle is over. The city is ours.'

One by one the defeated men came down the stairs, handing over their swords. Eu was the last but one, and when he saw Holland, he unbuckled his sword belt and knelt and laid it at the English knight's feet. With surprising kindness, Holland took the other man's hand and raised him up, handing back his sword. 'Fortune did not smile on you today, Raoul,' he said.

'Whereas it glows on you like the sun, my friend. I think you will achieve all that you desire now. I give you my parole that I will not attempt to escape.'

'Of course. Is there anyone else inside?'

'There is still one,' the herald said.

Slowly, dragging his feet as if he was suddenly very weary, Macio Chauffin stepped out of the tower into the light, holding his sword belt in one hand. He had closed his visor to hide his face, but the mastiff on his surcoat was plain for everyone to see. Holland drew his breath with a sudden sharp hiss. But before he could move, Matthew Gurney stepped forward and took Chauffin's sword.

'Well met, Macio,' he said softly. 'Welcome home.'

12

Caen, 26th of July, 1346
Early afternoon

For Caen, the agony had only just begun.

The prisoners were led away, Holland walking beside the Count of Eu and both talking cheerfully. They might have been discussing the weather, the herald thought. Chauffin followed them, silent, head down. The houses on the bridge still burned, and down in the Odon bodies drifted on the tide. Up by the barricade, men were already stripping the corpses of the dead.

Chauffin had lied, repeatedly. He had lied about not knowing who Bray was, he had lied about not recognising Holland's archers, and he had lied when he said Holland was not a traitor. What game Holland and Eu were playing, and why the count had insisted on surrendering to him, Merrivale did not know. But he was certain now that Bate and his men had killed Edmund Bray, and he was certain too that Thomas Holland was responsible.

Roger Mortimer had taken no prisoners. He stood, still holding his sword in his hand, staring at the bodies around the barricade. The marks and bloodstains on his armour showed he had been in the thick of the fighting, but now the fierce rush of battle was wearing off and reaction was setting in. Merrivale tapped him on the shoulder. 'I need your help.'

Mortimer looked at him wearily. 'What is it?'

'I know who killed your friend. Come with me.'

He did not know where Bate was, but he knew how to find him; anywhere plunder could be found, Bate would be there. Followed by Mortimer, he walked away from the bridge and the dead men, down through the pall of smoke hanging over the streets of Saint-Jean. Flames roared, and he heard the sound of screaming men and women.

A man-at-arms came out of the smoke, sword in hand, and Mortimer moved up quickly on Merrivale's shoulder, but then they saw the colours, red eagles on white, and relaxed a little. Nicholas Courcy walked forward, followed by Donnchad and the rest of the gallowglasses, their leather armour battered and some of them bleeding. They too had been in the thick of the fighting.

'Herald. What are you doing here?'

'I am looking for Bate,' Merrivale said. 'Have you seen him?'

'I know where he is, yes.' Courcy hesitated. 'It will not be pleasant.'

'That is to be expected. Take me to him.'

Caen had resisted, and so, according to the laws of war, Caen was being ravaged. Over and over again the question ran through the herald's mind. Why had Eu come out of the castle to defend the city? What he had said yesterday was correct; with four thousand men, he could have held the castle until the royal army arrived. Instead, he had chosen to make his stand in the most indefensible quarter of the city, Saint-Jean.

I may have need of your services before this is over. Had Eu intended all along that Caen should fall? Had he sacrificed the city and allowed himself to be captured?

They found the first bodies of the townspeople soon after, men and some women too, lying in the street or the gutter where they had been shot or cut down. Some had been stripped; the clothing of the others was too mangled and bloodstained to be worth salvaging. Mortimer stopped for a moment, staring in horror at the dead women, and the herald touched his arm. 'Come. There is nothing we can do for them.'

'Why kill the women?' Mortimer asked.

'Some of our boys broke into Saint-Jean through a postern gate,' Courcy said. 'It was undefended. When the people realised our troops were inside, they came out of their houses and started fighting. Some of the women took up arms alongside the men.'

'Arms. Wooden mallets and besoms against spears and longbows,' Mortimer said. 'They didn't have a chance.'

Donnchad growled deep in his throat. 'Ní dhéanfadh ach na Sasanaigh mná a mharú.'

Courcy shook his head. 'No, my friend. It is not only the English who slaughter women. They have been men's victims since the beginning of time.' He looked at Mortimer. 'This is your first war, isn't it?'

'Yes.' More corpses lay in the street ahead, a man lying across the threshold of a door, another woman hanging over a windowsill above him, body pierced by arrows. Mortimer swallowed. 'I suppose I will get used to it.'

'Pray to God you do not,' Courcy said.

—

The square church tower of Saint-Jean loomed out of the smoke. 'Bate's men were working their way down this street when I saw them,' Courcy said. 'I expect by now they are inside the church.'

The west door of the big church was open. High pillars marched in shadow towards the altar, where painted angels danced on the ceiling. An archer knelt on the altar table, hacking gemstones out of the crucifix behind it with a long knife. Another man smashed open the wooden doors of an ambry and pulled out a small iron-bound casket, while two more came out of the vestry carrying armfuls of embroidered robes. Piled on the floor before the altar was a heap of gold and silver vessels, chalices and ciboria, patens and pyxes, a gold monstrance, a couple of reliquaries studded with garnets, the jewelled wooden covers of a bible. The parchment pages of the bible lay strewn across the floor.

'Stop!' the herald said sharply. His voice rang in the dark vaults overhead, but the looters around the altar ignored him. The man by the ambry raised the casket over his head and hurled it down on the floor. The casket broke, the iron bands splitting apart, and silver coins danced and spun across the flagstones, shining in the dim light. The man whooped, kneeling down to scoop up the money. 'Hoy! Look what I found!'

The man attacking the crucifix turned. It was Nicodemus, Edmund de Tracey's bank clerk-turned-archer. 'What you got there, Hobby?'

'French deniers, boy!' Hobby shouted, stuffing coins into his tunic. 'Must be five hundred at least!'

Merrivale opened his mouth to repeat his order, but before he could speak, a bowstring twanged behind him and an arrow hissed up the nave, hitting Hobby and driving him back against the painted wall of the church. He sat for a moment, clutching at the shaft protruding from his chest, and then slumped over onto his side. Bate stalked up the aisle, holding his bow with another arrow already at the nock. His hands were red with fresh blood, and more was caked on his tunic. His archers followed him, shadows in russet and grey moving through the church.

'Drop that knife, Nicodemus,' Bate said. 'All the rest, put down your weapons.'

The knife clattered to the floor. The men carrying the vestments dropped them and spread their hands wide, showing they were unarmed; their bows stood propped against the wall behind them.

Bate turned to Courcy. 'That means you, *Sir* Nicholas!' he snarled. 'And your Irish hogs!'

'This is a damned shame, Bate,' Courcy said, laying his sword on the flagstones. 'And here was me thinking we were friends.'

Bate spat, and gestured towards Mortimer. 'You too, boy.'

The herald felt Mortimer stiffen, sword hand clenching. 'No,' he whispered urgently. 'This is not worth dying for.' After a moment, Mortimer nodded, unbuckled his sword belt and dropped it on the floor. Bate pointed towards the pile of gold and silver.

'We'll have all this. And that money, too.'

Nicodemus jumped down from the altar. 'God damn you, Bate, this is ours! There's plenty other churches in the city. Go and find one of them!'

Bate smiled. The scar on his head was like a dark line of blood across his scalp. 'Nah,' he said. 'I'd rather steal from you, you ugly bastard. Go on, boys, gather it up. Any of them tries anything, give him a shaft through the guts.'

Something whispered in the air behind Merrivale, a hint of movement in the nave, unseen. He raised his voice. 'This is a holy place, Bate. Touch those vessels or that money, and you will bring God's anger down on your head. You and all your men.'

Silence fell in the church. Slowly Bate turned to face the herald. 'Not worth dying for?' Courcy murmured out of the corner of his mouth.

Merrivale ignored him. 'Go,' he said to Bate. 'Walk out of here now, and nothing will happen to you.'

Bate's voice was dark in his throat. 'You know something, herald,' he said, raising his bow. 'I've had just about enough of you.'

The arrow, a sharp bodkin point, was levelled straight at Merrivale's chest. He watched Bate's face, and saw none of the uncertainty of Pont-Hébert; now, there was only the sick madness that came with bloodshed. This man had killed recently, and was ready to kill again.

'There are witnesses,' the herald said. 'Shoot me, and you will have to shoot them all.'

'I don't mind,' said Bate, and he drew back the bowstring just as an archer in a red iron cap stepped out from behind the nearest pillar and shot him through the body.

Bate screamed, dropping his bow and sinking to his knees. Another Lancashire man lifted his bow, and a second red-capped archer shot him too, the arrow driving deep into his shoulder and spinning him around with the force of the blow. More men came running through the church, archers and spearmen together, and Merrivale saw the gold lion on blue of Northumberland, Sir Richard Percy striding up the nave after his men with a drawn sword in his hand. 'Drop your bows,' he shouted at the Lancashire men, his voice ringing in the vaults. '*Now!*'

They obeyed at once. Merrivale walked over to Bate. The scar-headed man had fallen onto his back; he lay loose-limbed, gazing up at the cold-eyed angels overhead. Fresh blood welled around the arrow embedded in his body, and when he coughed, more blood trickled from the corner of his mouth. 'I warned you,' the herald said.

Bate coughed again. 'Go to hell.'

Merrivale knelt on the floor beside him. 'You are dying, Bate. This is the end.'

The bloody mouth twisted. 'Tell me something I don't know.'

'I cannot give you absolution. But if you tell me what I want to know, it may count in your favour when the moment of judgement comes.'

Bate's back arched in a sudden spasm, and the blood flowed.

'Did you kill Sir Edmund Bray?' the herald asked.

'No.' Already the voice was sinking to a whisper.

'Do you know who did? Was it one of your men?'

'No. I swear on the body of Christ, it wasn't us.'

'But you were out in the field that day. You saw Fierville meet Chauffin. Why were you there?'

'We were doing Sir Thomas's work. But we didn't know anything about... the meeting... we had... no reason... to kill Bray.'

'Sir Thomas's work? What do you mean?'

'Stealing. Looting. Raising money. Sir Thomas... needed money. Lots of money.'

'Why?'

Bate's lips moved, but no sound came. His eyes froze, staring lifelessly up at the angels guarding the gates to eternity.

Silently, Merrivale closed the man's eyes with his fingertips and rose to his feet. The Red Company men were already herding Nicodemus and his two comrades out of the church, followed by the remaining Lancashire men. Richard Percy walked over to the herald.

'What did he have to say?'

Merrivale shook his head. 'It was a dying man's confession.'

'Please yourself. I'll have to ask you to leave now. You and your men too, Sir Nicholas. We're about to barricade this church and put a guard on it.'

Merrivale looked at him. 'Why?'

'Because we're restoring order, or trying to. His Grace has issued another proclamation. No more looting, women and children not to be harmed, places of worship to be unmolested, the usual clart. We've been sent to enforce it.'

'No more looting? The troops won't like it.'

'His Grace reckons they've had their fill. He wants the rest of the spoil for himself.' Percy glanced at the pile of altar vessels. 'This campaign has to be paid for somehow.'

They walked towards the door, Courcy and his men following. 'Who were the archers who shot Bate?' Merrivale asked.

'Need you ask? Matt and Pip. Sir John heard you had been freed, and sent them to find you.' Percy chuckled, glancing up at the ceiling. 'You're a lucky man, herald. You have your own private guardian angels.'

I wanted to talk to Bate, Merrivale thought, and they shot him before I could do so. Just like Fierville. I was lucky to get the few words I did.

'Indeed,' he said aloud. 'Kindly convey my thanks to Sir John.'

Caen, 26th of July, 1346
Evening

The nuns of the Abbaye aux Dames had fled as soon as they heard of the English advance. The Prince of Wales's household had taken over the abbey, the prince himself settling in the abbess's lodgings and the senior knights and nobles occupying the dortoir, while the rest camped in the abbey grounds. The herald's tent had been pitched near the crest of the hill, looking out towards the castle and the silent, empty Bourg-le-Roi. The wreckage of Saint-Jean still smouldered beyond the bridge and its towers. In the distance, the masts and sails of ships could be seen; Huntingdon's fleet had sailed upriver as soon as the tide turned to cut off any French retreat. Very few of the Count of Eu's four thousand men had survived.

French banners still flew over the castle. Bertrand and his brother the bishop had refused to join Eu in his doomed defence of the city, and were still holed up there with several hundred men-at-arms and crossbowmen, defying the enemy. There too, presumably, was Brother Geoffrey of Maldon.

Merrivale walked up the hill towards the tent. Mauro and Warin were waiting for him, and so was Tiphaine, relief plain in all three faces. Tiphaine took a couple of steps towards him and stopped. 'Welcome back,' she said.

'Thank you. I have some news you will want to hear. Bate is dead. He will trouble us no more.'

'I am glad,' she said, and he remembered what she had said about Normans and vengeance. 'Was Bate the man you were looking for?'

The herald shook his head. 'Warin, I have a task for you. The two archers from the Red Company, the brothers Matt and Pip. I want you to watch them whenever their company is in camp. If they say or do anything unusual, report to me.'

Warin touched his forehead. 'And me, *señor*?' Mauro asked.

'I need more information about one of Sir Edward de Tracey's men, an archer named Nicodemus.' He could have asked Courcy to do this, but Bate had grown suspicious of the Irishman, and others might have done so as well. 'Ask around the camp and find out who he deals with, and from which companies they come. Be discreet, and be careful. These are dangerous men.'

'Yes, *señor*.'

'And both of you, keep your ears open for word of an archer named Jack Slade. He deserted from Tracey's company at Pont-Hébert, but I am guessing he is still in contact with Nicodemus. Try to discover if anyone has seen him.'

'What about me?' Tiphaine asked. 'Have you no task for me?'

The herald smiled briefly. 'Your task is to stay safe,' he said.

She planted her hands on her hips. 'You think I am incapable of helping you?'

Merrivale stared at her in surprise. 'I did not know you wanted to help,' he said finally.

'No,' Tiphaine said. 'I don't suppose you did.' She turned on her heel and walked into the tent. Mauro shook his head gravely.

'Forgive me, *señor*,' he said. 'But I think you chose your words unwisely.'

'Yes,' Merrivale said. 'So do I.'

Sir Matthew Gurney's tent was pitched on the outskirts of the camp, looking out towards the other abbey, Saint-Étienne. In the distance, the royal standard could be seen floating above the Logis du Roi, the King's House, just outside the abbey gates.

'Is your prisoner here?' Merrivale asked.

Gurney nodded.

'I would like to speak to him,' the herald said. 'Alone, if possible. I give you my word he will not escape.'

'He has already given his parole,' Gurney said. 'But I think I should stay. I can guess what questions you wish to ask him, and they concern me as well.'

Macio Chauffin sat on a wooden bench inside the tent, leaning forward with his head in his hands. He did not look up as Merrivale and Gurney entered. Merrivale pulled up another bench and sat down. 'You know why I am here.'

'Yes. I lied to you about Bray.'

'And Holland.'

'No.' Chauffin raised his head. 'I told you the truth about him.'

'The truth,' said the herald. 'Then tell me the truth this time. All of it.'

'Ah, what a strange and nebulous commodity truth is… all of it, you say. Very well, let us start with myself. I am, or was, an Englishman. My family name is Chaffin, and I was born and bred in Dorset. My father was a gentleman, though not a knight; my mother was the daughter of a Portuguese ship's captain. At a young age I entered the service of one of our neighbours, Sir John Maltravers.'

The herald sat still, watching the other man.

'I see I have your full attention now,' Chauffin said wryly. 'Maltravers was a loyal servitor of Roger Mortimer, the Earl of March. When the old king was imprisoned at Berkeley Castle in 1327, Maltravers was appointed his keeper.'

'And you were still in his service?' asked Merrivale.

'I was, along with Matthew's father, Sir Thomas Gurney, and Edmund Bray's father, Sir John Bray of Huxley in Cheshire. He too was a strong supporter of Mortimer.'

'You were there at Berkeley when the old king died,' Merrivale said.

Chauffin looked down at his hands. Merrivale glanced at Gurney, who nodded. 'Nothing you will say will go beyond this tent,' the herald said. 'You have our word of honour on that. But, *messire*, I must know what happened to Bray.'

'I will tell you what I know. Whether that will help you in your quest, I cannot say.'

'Go on,' Merrivale said.

'I was on duty at Berkeley Castle on the night of the twenty-first of September. Sir Thomas Gurney was in command of the night watch, and I was his deputy. It was late, nearly midnight. I remember how cold it was...' Chauffin shivered a little with memories. 'I heard the couriers come in. I looked out into the courtyard and saw them in the torchlight, three of them. A few minutes later, two came upstairs with Maltravers. I didn't recognise one of the men, but I knew the other. It was Sir Robert Holland of Upholland, Thomas Holland's father.'

He swallowed suddenly. 'Holland and Maltravers were arguing. Christ, Maltravers said, we can't do this! Holland just shook his head. Those are the Earl of March's orders, he said, and the queen has given her assent. Maltravers was still objecting, and the other man grabbed him by the shoulders and shook him. Damn you, he said, do you not understand? Mortimer has ordered this! Obey orders, or you will be executed... God, I'm parched. Is there any wine?'

Gurney poured wine into a wooden cup and added water. Chauffin wiped the sweat from his forehead and took a quick sip. 'They sent the other guards away, and then Maltravers turned to Thomas Gurney and me. Do it, he said. Make it quick. So we went into the cell. The king was sleeping, lying on his back, snoring a little. Sir Thomas picked up a cushion. Hold his feet, he said to me. So I held his ankles while Sir Thomas put the cushion over his face and pressed down. The king started to kick and struggle, and it was all I could do to hold him.

I remember the noise he made in his throat, struggling for breath… then he went still.'

Matthew Gurney turned his back and walked to the door of the tent, staring out over the city.

'Why did you obey the order?' the herald asked.

'What the other man had said was no idle threat. Old Mortimer was a bitter and vengeful enemy, and he did not take kindly to being crossed. From the moment that order was given, it was the king's life or ours.' Chauffin paused, staring into space. 'Except, of course, that our lives were forfeit anyway.'

'What happened next?'

'Just as we were coming out of the room, John Bray came upstairs. He had heard of Holland's arrival and was looking for him. He looked into the cell and saw what had happened. He raged at us, calling us murderers and regicides, which of course we were. Holland explained Mortimer's orders, and instructed him to keep silent on pain of death. Sir John was still furious. I will keep silent, he said finally, but I will consort with you no longer. Late though the hour was, he packed his bags and rode away with his esquire and groom.'

'What did the rest of you do?'

'It was obvious we had been lined up as scapegoats. As soon as the king's body was found next day, we would be accused of murdering him. Mortimer would kill us, to deflect attention from himself and eliminate witnesses. And it would be no easy death, either. Remember the Despensers? They took the old man down from the gallows and then cut his body into pieces and fed it to the dogs, and they dragged his son naked through the streets and castrated him before they drew and quartered him. We didn't fancy the same fate.'

Sometimes, the herald reflected, one forgot why Sir Hugh Despenser was so angry with the world. 'So you fled.'

Chauffin nodded. 'Robert Holland decided to stay in the country, trusting to his influence at court to keep him safe, but he was murdered the following year. John Maltravers, Thomas Gurney and I were all attainted and fled the country, each of us going our separate way. I ended up in Normandy.'

'Where you made a new life for yourself,' Merrivale said.

'Yes, Our Lady smiled upon me. Only she knows why, given the crime I helped to commit. I married well, and my wife inherited some land. I became a *gentilhomme*. The Count of Eu took me into his service and I prospered. Until now.'

'You could have gone back,' Merrivale said. 'Maltravers made his peace with the king and returned home, his lands and positions restored.'

'Maltravers is rich and powerful. Gurney and I were small fry, no use to anyone. If I returned, I would have got a knife in my ribs, like Holland. Or Thomas Gurney. That's what happened, isn't it, Matthew? They say he died of illness in Spain. But that's not true, is it?'

'No,' Gurney said. 'My father was killed to silence him. If he had been brought back to England for trial, he would have told the truth about who was behind the king's assassination. But the men of power could not let that happen. You were right to hide, Macio.'

'The man who came in with Holland. Are you sure you didn't recognise him?'

'No. His surcoat bore three black chevrons on yellow, but I had never seen the device before. From his accent I would say he was Flemish, or from Hainault, perhaps. That is all I know. I never saw him again.'

'And the third man?'

'He never came upstairs. I only saw him once in the courtyard, and the torchlight was dim. He wore no device.'

The herald nodded. 'And John Bray? What happened to him?'

'He stayed behind like Holland. How he survived, I don't know. But I never saw or heard from him again.'

'Yet you knew his son.'

Chauffin shook his head. 'No. But when I saw the body, I recognised the device. I asked Fierville who he was, and he told me. It felt like the past was coming back to stick its claws into me.'

Silence fell again. 'Only you, Matthew and Holland know who I am,' Chauffin said. 'If you tell anyone else, I am a dead man. Mortimer is long in his grave, but there are still others with secrets to protect.'

'Do you know who they are?'

Chauffin shook his head. 'I was a lowly esquire. Maltravers did not confide in me. Matthew's father knew, I think.'

'He did, but he did not tell me,' Gurney said. 'I suspect he felt that confiding in me might have put me at risk also. Then when the tensions with France began, the king and his advisers decided to sweep the whole affair away, pretend it never happened, so everyone could forget about the past. Old sins were forgiven. Edward II had died of heart failure, it was suggested, or there was even a rumour that he was still alive, living in exile.'

He turned back from the door. 'So it never happened. All the king's knights now live in amity and brotherhood, united by their desire to slaughter Frenchmen. You see, Macio, you could have come home after all.'

Chauffin shook his head again. 'The herald is right, I had made a new life. The past was over for me. Until now.'

'There is one more thing,' Merrivale said. 'You are positive Sir Thomas Holland is not a traitor. What makes you so certain?'

'Because I know the content of the messages he sent the Count of Eu. He betrayed no secrets and he sent no word of your plans.'

'Then what message did he send?'

'He wanted to borrow money,' Chauffin said.

–

In the silence that followed, Gurney poured wine into another cup and drank it down in a single draught, slamming the cup back onto the table.

'What happens to me now?' Chauffin asked.

'That depends on Sir Matthew,' the herald said. 'You are his prisoner. Presumably he will ask for a ransom, and if you agree terms and continue to honour your parole, you can go free.'

'I don't want your money,' Gurney said abruptly. He motioned towards the door. 'Get out of here. Go.'

Chauffin stared at him. 'What do you mean?'

'I don't want your money,' Gurney repeated. 'I wish to God you had died, along with my father and Robert Holland. I wish we had all died, so none of us would have to live with this stain. Go on, Macio. Go back to your Norman wife and your other life.' He picked up Chauffin's sword and scabbard, standing in a corner, corner and tossed them to him. 'Live out the rest of your life, and stay away from me.'

Chauffin rose to his feet, holding the scabbard in one hand. 'I have not told you anything about Edmund Bray,' he said to the herald.

Merrivale shook his head. 'You have told me something important, I think. But I am not yet certain what it means. Journey safely, *messire*.'

After Chauffin had gone, Gurney poured another full cup of wine and drained it. He offered the flask to Merrivale, who shook his head. 'During the time we were camped at Portchester, did you see much of Bray?' he asked.

'No. We were cousins, but not especially close. In part because of the history you have just heard.'

'What about Jean de Fierville? Were you friendly with him?'

'No. He joined the prince's games of hazard sometimes, that was all. He usually won.'

'And Bray? Were he and Fierville friendly?'

'They talked together, but I don't know how close they were. Why do you ask?'

'I have a hypothesis,' Merrivale said. 'But I shall need to test it.' He rose, laying a hand on Gurney's shoulder. 'The sins of the father are not always visited on the son, you know.'

'Try telling that to Hugh Despenser,' Gurney said wryly. 'The guilt remains, herald. I feel sometimes like the blood is on *my* hands, as well as my father's.'

'We all carry the burdens of the past,' Merrivale said. 'The fact that I could not save my mother or my sisters from the famine burns like hot iron in my soul. Nothing will ever erase those memories.'

Gurney turned to face him. 'Why, herald? Why does God allow us to be so tormented? Is this the act of a kind God, a loving God?'

Merrivale smiled a little. 'I do not know,' he said. 'I am a herald, not a theologian. Good night, Sir Matthew.'

13

Caen, 26th of July, 1346
Evening

Merrivale found Holland in front of the west door of the Abbaye aux Dames. 'I wish to speak to you in private, Sir Thomas,' he said without preamble. 'Shall we go into the cloister?'

The colonnades of the cloister were silent and shadowy, lit only by a few lamps in the falling dusk. 'You are attempting to raise a large sum of money,' Merrivale said. 'And you are using some rather unusual means to do so.'

'What of it?' Holland asked sharply.

'I wasn't sure of your purpose at first, but then I realised the answer is obvious. You intend to ask the pope to adjudicate on your marriage to Countess Joan. But bringing cases to the papal court is expensive. His Holiness and his lawyers are... acquisitive.'

'Rapacious would be a better word,' said Holland. 'You know the old saying. "Verily, verily, you shall not enter into the kingdom of heaven until you have paid unto the last farthing."'

'And so you embarked on various ventures,' Merrivale said. 'One of these was looting. Your vintenar Bate was highly skilled at finding plunder, and you took your share of the spoils. When he told you about Nicodemus and Tracey and their scheme, you decided to do the same.'

'And why not? Tracey has already made enough to cover his campaign expenses, and more besides.'

'But you reckoned you would need even more. Prosecuting a case before the curia in Avignon will require thousands of pounds. So before the campaign began, you resolved on another, rather more risky stratagem. You decided to approach your old friend the Count of Eu, whom you knew to be one of the wealthiest men in France, and ask if he would lend you the money.'

Holland was quiet for a moment. 'You have worked it out,' he said finally. 'How very clever of you.'

'As a matter of interest, why go to the count? Why not approach one of the English bankers, like Tracey's brother Sir Gilbert, or Sir John Pulteney? Surely that would have been much easier, and safer.'

'Need you ask? These men lend money to the Crown. If the king found out they had given me a loan so I could claim his cousin as my wife, they would suffer for it. But if I borrowed the money from Raoul, no one would know. Or so I thought.'

'I see. As an Englishman, you had no qualms about taking money from the Constable of France? When England and France are at war?'

'So what? This was a private transaction. It had nothing to do with the war, or the king's claims to the French throne, or anything else that is anyone's business.'

There was sweat on Holland's forehead now; he knew he was walking a tightrope. He must be truly desperate, the herald thought. How much does Joan of Kent really mean to him?

'You knew direct contact with the count could be dangerous, so you decided to use Jean de Fierville as an intermediary. Why did you choose him?'

'I knew he was one of the couriers Godefroi d'Harcourt used to contact his friends in Normandy. He agreed to carry a personal message for me and deliver it to Macio Chauffin, who would pass it on to Raoul. I tell you, herald, I did nothing wrong! Even in wartime, one can still send a message to a friend.'

'Did it never occur to you that Fierville was also spying for the French? Did you know that he betrayed Harcourt's entire scheme to Robert Bertrand?'

'No. And you have no proof that I did.'

'You quarrelled with Edmund Bray at Portchester. You said he made a slighting reference to your wife. But there was more to the quarrel than that, wasn't there?'

Holland said nothing.

'Bray knew Fierville,' the herald continued. 'Back in Portchester, they were seen talking together several times. Somehow Bray found out about your arrangement. He accused you of treasonable correspondence with the enemy. I shall take your silence as assent.'

Holland stared at him. A gust of wind fluttered the lamps, shadows dancing off the columns and the painted acanthus leaves on their capitals.

'Fearful that Bray might denounce you as a traitor, you explained your real purpose,' Merrivale said. 'He expressed his disgust, and that was when he made his comments about Countess Joan.' He paused. 'But, of course, that was not the beginning. Bray already disliked you. He knew what had happened on the twenty-first of September 1327.'

Holland looked around quickly to see if anyone was nearby. 'My father killed no one,' he said, low-voiced. 'Bray knows that.'

'No. But he was one of those who carried the message to Berkeley Castle, and he persuaded Maltravers to order the old king's death. He shared the guilt. Did Bray imply that you do also?'

'Yes. That was when I hit him. For God's sake, herald, I was just a boy when the king was killed!'

'In some people's minds, that doesn't matter,' the herald said, thinking of Matthew Gurney. 'Bray accused your father of being a regicide, and you of being a traitor. You had plenty of reasons to kill him, or have him killed.'

'But I didn't,' Holland said. 'I told you at Valognes. I disliked Bray, but I would never have soiled my hands by killing him. Or asked my men to do so either.'

'Perhaps. When we landed at Saint-Vaast, Fierville went to meet Macio Chauffin. Did you send some of your archers to follow him? Bate, perhaps?'

'No. He and his men went out plundering, just before Bertrand attacked us at Quettehou. When they came back, they told me they had seen Chauffin meeting another man-at-arms, but they didn't know who it was. I knew it was Fierville, of course, and told them to forget what they had seen and keep quiet. That was all.'

'Bray accused you of being a traitor. Are you?'

'No.'

The answer was blunt, unequivocal, almost challenging. Merrivale watched the other man for a while, studying his face. 'And so all your problems are now solved,' he said. 'You can ransom the Count of Eu for a fortune, enough to pay for your case at the papal court. Eu knew that, of course. That was why, when all was lost and surrender or death were the only choices, he decided to hand himself over to you. He told me it was the least he could do for you.'

'Raoul is loyal to his friends,' Holland said quietly.

'And he was right. Fortune smiled on you today, but you could just as easily have ended up with your head on a spike.'

'I told you. I have done nothing wrong.'

'No? I have not asked what you promised the Count of Eu as collateral for his loan. You claim you are not a traitor. Would you swear an oath that this is true? Would you stake your immortal soul on it?'

The silence that followed seemed to last for a very long time. Finally Holland looked away. 'I swear on the blood of Christ that I have never betrayed my country. But... the offer was there.'

'Who made this offer?'

'Fierville. He said something was in the wind, something much bigger than the Norman revolt or our war with France. He said there were powerful forces at work, not just in England and France, but all over Europe. He didn't say what these forces were or who was behind them. But he told me there was a place for me if I wished to join them.'

'What did you reply?'

'I said I needed time to think it over.'

'And have you thought it over?'

'All I want is my wife. Once I have her, I will be the king's loyal servant unto death. I will swear to that, too.'

The herald nodded. 'Then I wish you good fortune with your court case,' he said. 'Good night, Sir Thomas.'

Inquisition into the death of Edmund Bray, knight, near the village of Quettehou in Normandy on the XIIth day of July, in the nineteenth year of the reign of King Edward III. This report was composed on the XXVIth day of that month, at the city of Caen.

Item, I have now interviewed the French miles Macio Chauffin, who confirms that Sir Edmund Bray was shot by two English or Welsh archers. Chauffin was unable to identify the archers, who bore no distinguishing badges.

Item, evidence has emerged that suggests Bray may have grown suspicious of Fierville, and his appearance at this meeting was no accident. He had volunteered for the reconnaissance at Quettehou in hopes of finding Fierville.

Item, it also remains to be seen who gave the archers their orders. It is possible that they were employed directly by Fierville and accompanied him as guards, but I feel this is unlikely. Someone else therefore must have had an interest in this meeting between Fierville and Chauffin.

Item, Sir Thomas Holland has given me a full account of his relations with Bray. I also spoke to Holland's vintenar, shortly before the latter's death in Caen. I am satisfied that this man had no part in Bray's death, and that Sir Thomas himself can be exonerated from any involvement.

Item, several of the people involved in this case have connections to the foul and unnatural death of his Grace the king's late father. This includes Bray, whose father Sir John Bray of Huxley was present at Berkeley Castle at the time. I do not know whether this has any connection with Bray's murder, but I feel the matter warrants further investigation.

Simon Merrivale, heraldus

At the Logis du Roi, Merrivale waited while Michael Northburgh read the report. 'Sir Thomas is cleared,' the clerk commented. 'The king will be pleased.'

The herald raised his eyebrows. 'Have you heard?' asked Northburgh. 'He has bought the Count of Eu from Holland for eighty thousand florins.'

'Thirteen thousand pounds. More than enough to allow Sir Thomas to fight his court case,' Merrivale said. 'But what does the king get for his money?'

'Two things. Control of the Count of Eu with a chance to renew the Norman rebellion, and Holland's loyalty. A bargain, I would say.'

'I see. The king has changed his mind about Sir Thomas?'

Northburgh smiled. 'Don't underestimate his Grace. He is cleverer than he sometimes seems. He understands the minds of men quite well.'

'And the Earl of Salisbury? What will he think of this news?'

'It doesn't matter. The deal is done. Salisbury will be compensated in other ways. For example, he might find a new wife, one who actually likes him.' Northburgh laid the report on his desk. 'Speaking of which, how is your little *demoiselle*?'

Caen, 26th of July, 1346
Night

'Well that didn't exactly go to plan,' the man from the north said drily.

'Eu played us false,' said the West Country man. 'He was supposed to hold Caen until Philip's army arrived. And now we have lost Holland as well.'

'We don't need him. Let him go.'

'This is the herald's doing. We must get rid of him.'

'You've already tried, and failed. Let me deal with him. I know how it can be done without attracting notice.'

The West Country man grunted. 'Eu let himself get taken deliberately. Why?'

'Oh, it was cleverly done,' said the man from the north. 'He can hold up his hands and protest his innocence; he tried loyally to defend the city, and surrendered only when all was lost. In reality, of course, he has changed sides and gone over to King Edward.'

'He will regret it. All we have to do is inform Philip's court, and Eu will be attainted as a traitor.'

The man from the north shook his head. 'Not yet. Let's keep our options open. Once Edward is finished, the Count of Eu will need a new sponsor. Meanwhile, you must send word to the Queen of Navarre, and the cardinals. Tell them we need to meet, urgently.'

'Clearly you have some new scheme in mind,' the man from the West Country said.

'It's the same scheme as the old one, with some new twists.' The northern man paused. 'I have a copy of Philip's plans for an invasion of England back in '38. It makes interesting reading.'

'What do you mean?'

'The raid on Southampton in October that year was meant to be just the beginning. The plan was for a thousand ships and forty thousand men to descend on England, landing all along the south coast. Edward would be deposed and Philip's son would sit on the throne of England. The English barons would be dispossessed and their lands distributed among the French nobles.'

'Christ,' said the man from the West Country. 'How did you come to learn of these plans? I've never heard of them before.'

'That's because the document is a forgery. I wrote it myself, and sealed it with a copy of the French royal seal.'

'God's teeth! Where did you get that?'

'Never you mind. The document is hidden in the Logis du Roi, and I will ensure Edward's clerks discover it tomorrow morning. By midday, the whole army will know about it. Edward will go up in flames, and even if he doesn't, the barons and knights will. And then they will march straight out to confront Philip.'

'Fifteen thousand men against the entire French royal army? They won't have a prayer.'

'That's not how they see it. After the fall of Caen, the hot-brains think they are invincible. And, of course, we shall continue to stir up trouble between the knights.'

'And King Philip? What do we do about him?'

'Nothing, for the moment. But once he has won his victory, we will undermine him in turn. That is where the Queen of Navarre and the cardinals come in. Especially Aubert. He is the key man.'

'What about the others?'

'Not yet. We will bring them in when the time is right. For the moment, we still have work to do.'

Caen, 27th of July, 1346
Midday

'The king is busy,' Lord Rowton said, a little abruptly. 'What did you want?'

'It was his Grace who summoned me, my lord.' The message had come that morning, a single line in Northburgh's writing and sealed with the privy seal.

Rowton made an impatient gesture. 'Yes, I had forgotten. He wanted to discuss your latest report, the one you sent to Northburgh last night. But I'm afraid he won't be able to see you now.'

They were in the courtyard of the Logis du Roi. Voices could be heard inside, shouting and arguing.

'Has something happened, my lord?'

Rowton paused for a moment, then shrugged. 'Everyone will know soon enough. One of the royal clerks found a document in the palace this morning. It purports to be some sort of French plan for the conquest of England, complete with provisions for forcing the king to abdicate and seizing the lands of the English nobility.'

'I see. And the nobility are angry about this.'

'The nobility have taken leave of their senses,' Rowton said angrily. 'They want to ride to Rouen and challenge the French royal army to do battle. Warwick and Northampton and I, and young John Grey, are trying to talk them around.' A fresh outburst of shouting erupted inside the building. 'But I fear they are not listening.'

Merrivale frowned. 'Is this document genuine, my lord?'

'Who knows? It's either a forgery or some half-baked idea that the adversary never seriously considered putting into practice. Either way, we are letting ourselves be gulled.'

'What does his Grace say?'

'He is angry too, understandably so. But he also knows that you can only lead men where they already want to go. If we merely stand fast now and defend the gains we have won – which, from the point of view of military logic, is exactly what we should do – his prestige will suffer. The men are spoiling for a fight. They are thinking with their hearts, not their heads.'

Rowton shook his head. 'However. To come back to your report. You mentioned some connection with the death of the king's father. I should drop that if I were you.'

'May I ask why, my lord?'

'Because the king doesn't want to hear it. The past is the past, dead and buried. His Grace even thinks it is possible that his father didn't die at all, but was helped to escape after he signed the letter of abdication.'

I remember the noise he made in his throat, struggling for breath. 'That seems unlikely,' Merrivale said.

'I would have said impossible. Nevertheless, I think you should let it lie.'

'I will, my lord. But may I ask one question? Did you know Sir John Bray was present at Berkeley Castle the day the old king died?'

Rowton paused for a long time. 'I did,' he said finally. 'But he had no part in the king's death. After that night, Bray stayed out of sight. He remained on his own lands and took no part in life at court. That was my advice to him: keep your head down, and let everyone forget you. It worked, too.'

'Until Edmund Bray joined the Prince of Wales's household,' Merrivale said. 'At which point, all those rivalries and animosities broke surface again. He had quarrelled with Holland and Despenser even before we sailed from Portchester. Mortimer and Gurney have been dragged in too.'

'What are you saying, herald?'

'Someone is trying to drive wedges into this army, my lord, in order to split it apart. I think the same person, or people, is behind the murder of Edmund Bray.'

They looked at each other in silence for a moment. 'Is there any word of the fate of Brother Geoffrey?' the herald asked.

'Not yet. Andrew Clarenceux is at the castle, trying to parley with Bertrand and his brother the bishop, but they refuse to answer. As soon as we do get a response, I will see that you are informed.'

14

'Nicodemus is now buying plundered goods from nearly every company in the army,' Mauro said. 'He also buys from archers and men-at-arms in the prince's own retinue. Only two companies refuse to do business with him.'

Tiphaine sat quietly in a corner of the tent, listening. 'One will be the Red Company,' Merrivale said.

Mauro nodded. 'The other is Lord Rowton's retinue. His lordship has forbidden his men to plunder and threatened dire punishments for any who sell stolen goods to Nicodemus. The word is that he wants them to be more professional, after the example of the Red Company.'

'I wish some of the other captains would do the same,' Merrivale said. 'Anything else?'

'Yes, *señor*. Nicodemus also visits the royal kitchens. He has been there twice in the last three days.'

It had been four days since the battle of Caen, during which time the rich and powerful city had been stripped to the walls. The great market halls had been emptied and private houses ransacked of everything they contained: gold and silver plate, jewellery, furniture, clothing, even tools and kitchen utensils. Every day, wagonloads of spoil rolled away towards the river and the nearby port of Ouistreham, where the goods were loaded aboard ships and sent to England.

'Is there any sign of Slade?' Merrivale asked.

'No, *señor*. Perhaps he has returned to England.'

'Very well. Warin, have you anything to report?'

'I've been watching Matt and Pip as you asked, sir. It hasn't been difficult, as they spend most of their time loitering around here. They're definitely keeping watch, but whether they're watching us, or keeping an eye out for someone else, it's difficult to tell.'

'Do they meet or speak to anyone?'

'No one but members of their own company, sir. There's a couple of others sometimes come and keep watch when they're absent. Another archer, and a big fellow with a spear.'

That sounded like the man Sir John Grey had been talking to in Saint-Lô. 'Very well, continue to keep an eye on them. Well done, both of you.'

—

Mauro and Warin bowed and departed. Merrivale sat for some time after they had gone, staring into space. Eventually Tiphaine walked across the tent and pulled up a wooden stool, sitting down opposite him.

'You are pensive,' she said. 'What are you worrying about?'

'I am no further ahead than I was the day Bray was murdered. I still do not know who killed him, or why.'

She shook her head. 'You must know something, or at least have suspicions.'

'I *think* Bray volunteered for the reconnaissance party at Quettehou because he believed Fierville was riding out to meet the enemy and wanted to catch him in the act. In his youth and pride, he decided to do this alone, not telling anyone else or asking for help. His pride cost him his life.'

'That is a harsh judgement. Have you never done anything rash and stupid? Like ride unarmed into an enemy citadel with only an old monk for company?'

'Brother Geoffrey is a canon, not a monk.'

Tiphaine rolled her eyes. 'So. Those who employed Fierville realised Bray was suspicious. When he followed Fierville that day at Quettehou, they sent archers to shoot him. Yes?'

'That is what I believe,' Merrivale said.

'You have tried to identify the archers who carried out the killing. But you have failed, I think.'

Merrivale studied his hands for a moment. 'I was convinced Bate was the killer, but he denied it and I believe him. Men find it hard to lie when death is in their eyes.'

'And the other two? The ones from the Red Company?'

'By their own admission, they were near the scene when Bray was killed. On the other hand, they also chased away the man who tried to shoot me at Saint-Germain-d'Ectot and saved my life at Saint-Jean. I genuinely do not know whose side they are on.'

Tiphaine glanced at the patch on the canvas wall of the tent where the arrow had pierced the fabric. 'They could be on both sides, of course. Taking money from more than one master.'

'They could,' the herald agreed. 'Sir John Grey has assured me they can be trusted. But there is something about them that continues to rouse my suspicions.'

'And the other man Mauro mentioned, Nicodemus. What about him?'

'He seems interested in nothing but making money.'

'Then perhaps someone paid him to kill Bray.'

'Perhaps. But he is one of Tracey's men, and Tracey's company had only just come up from the beach and were still in Quettehou when Bray was killed. Nicodemus would have had no opportunity.'

'Then why ask Mauro to follow him?'

'Because I do think that Nicodemus was responsible for the death of Jake Madford, the archer who was killed at Pont-Hébert.'

Tiphaine's eyebrows rose. 'All this fuss for an archer?'

'He was a man, with the same right to justice as any other,' the herald said. 'And these events did not happen at random.'

'You think there may be a conspiracy,' Tiphaine said.

Merrivale studied her face for a moment, searching her eyes. 'Why do you say that?'

'As I told you, when I was in prison in Carentan, I heard people talking. Perhaps they did not know I could overhear them. Or perhaps they thought that, being a woman, I was too stupid to understand.'

'What did you hear?' Merrivale asked quietly.

'Fierville and Barbizan were involved in more than one plot. There is the one you know about, the betrayal of Harcourt's revolt and the attempt to kill your king or your prince at Carentan. But there is another, against King Philippe of France. And both are guided by the same hand.'

Merrivale paused for a moment, thinking. 'You mean the second Norman revolt,' he said. 'The one to be led by the Count of Eu and the Queen of Navarre.'

'No,' said Tiphaine. 'The Normans are pawns, Barbizan said so himself. The real conspiracy is close to the French king, right at the heart of power.'

The herald thought for a moment. *There are powerful forces at work*, Thomas Holland had said, and he had spoken of a conspiracy engulfing both France and England. 'Why did you not tell me this before?'

'Because you did not ask. You confide in Mauro and Warin, even in Sir Nicholas Courcy, but not in me. I am no more than a piece of furniture,' Tiphaine said bitterly.

Merrivale said nothing. Tiphaine rose to her feet. 'I can help you, if you wish,' she said.

Merrivale glanced at the patched hole in the canvas, and shook his head. 'It is too dangerous.'

He saw the anger and disappointment in her face. 'Why do you think danger matters to me?' she demanded. 'Why shut me out? What offence have I ever given you?'

'None,' the herald said quietly. 'You have committed no offence. It is I who am at fault.'

Without another word, Tiphaine turned and walked out of the tent. Merrivale sat for a moment listening to her rapid footsteps fade away. Then he rose and picked up his herald's tabard, his armour against all weapons and woes, pulled it over his head and walked out into the hot afternoon sun.

—

Stopping at the kitchen in the Abbaye aux Dames, Merrivale procured a thick wedge of cheese and then walked down past the crumbling walls of Bourg-le-Roi towards Saint-Étienne. In the distance he could see men prowling the ramparts of the castle. Bertrand's green and gold colours still flew defiantly above the donjon.

In the meadow behind Saint-Étienne the royal livestock grazed, the king's war horses mingling with cattle and sheep. Chickens clucked in their crates and pigs grunted in wooden sties. Some of these were the original beasts that had crossed the water from England; others had been purchased or plundered along the way. He found the little cowherd sitting on the grass, shoes off in the sun and stick resting across her knees, watching her cows.

She jumped to her feet when she saw him and curtseyed. 'Good day to you, sir. Can I be of assistance?'

'You can, Mistress Driver.' He offered her the cheese, and she stared at it with wide eyes. She still had the rind of the cheese he had given her in Saint-Côme-du-Mont; it resided in her pocket, stiff with lint, and every so often she took it out and sniffed it, inhaling the memory of its flavour. She had never expected to receive such bounty again. She took the cheese now and gazed at it, the expression on her face suggesting she was holding the keys to paradise.

'Do you know an archer called Nicodemus?' he asked. 'From Sir Edward de Tracey's company?'

'Him that buys all the things the archers steal?'

'Yes. I am told he sometimes comes around to the royal kitchens. Have you seen him there?'

'Yes, sir,' she said, staring at the cheese and wondering if it would be rude to start eating it now. 'Some of the kitchen staff sell him things they have despoiled, just like the soldiers do. The sauce-maker, Master Clerebaud, he's a great one for pillaging. There's another one too, one of the scullions. He was only hired on a few days ago, but he knows where to find all sorts of things, gold and silver and everything.'

Merrivale smiled. 'Not tempted to join them?'

She looked indignant. 'Sir! I'm not a thief!'

'Congratulations. You are one of the very few people in this army who is not. Have you heard Nicodemus speak? He is from Devon. I wondered if he could be the man with the West Country accent you heard that night at Freshwater.'

Nell gave this serious thought. 'No,' she said finally. 'I don't think so. The voice didn't sound the same.'

'The Norman knight you pointed out to me at Saint-Côme-du-Mont, Jean de Fierville. Did you ever see him with Nicodemus?'

'No, sir. I can't say I did.'

The herald nodded. 'When Nicodemus came to the kitchen, did he speak to Master Clerebaud both times?'

'Yes, sir. And to the scullion.'

'This scullion. You say he is new. Where did he come from?'

'He was a sailor, sir, with the fleet. He got left behind when his ship sailed back to England, so he came to the army looking for work. Master Coloyne the yeoman hired him to guard the cooking pots.'

'Do they need guarding?'

'Oh yes, sir. Those archers are terrible thieves. They come right into the kitchen, trying to take food out of the pots when no one is looking.'

The herald rubbed his chin. 'Do you know the scullion's name?'

'Curry, sir. Riccon Curry.'

Merrivale nodded. 'Thank you, Mistress Driver. As always, you have been most helpful.'

—

He found Michael Northburgh hard at work at his desk in the Logis du Roi, sheets of parchment before him. 'Letters home,' the secretary said. 'His Grace is writing to Queen Philippa and all the bishops, telling them about the capture of Caen. The letters will be read out before the populace, who will rejoice at the great victories won by their king and rush out to pay their taxes. How may I serve you, Simon?'

'I need an audience with the king. A brief one, I assure you.'

Northburgh shook his head. 'He is closeted with his council. Have you heard the news? We are marching tomorrow, on Rouen.'

There was a moment of silence. Merrivale shook his head. 'This is a blunder,' he said. 'We have won half of Normandy; now we need to hold it.'

'I know it. You know it. Warwick and Northampton and Rowton know it, and frankly, I think the king knows it too. But the rest are clamouring for battle. If we don't march, the men will start to desert. Why do you want to see his Grace?'

'It concerns Brother Geoffrey,' Merrivale said. 'I assume the French are still holding him.'

'Yes.' Northburgh rubbed his chin. 'What do you expect his Grace to do about it?'

'Negotiate with Bertrand. Offer to pay a ransom. Anything that will set him free.' When Northburgh did not answer, Merrivale said, 'You know Geoffrey well, Michael. Should he really be abandoned?'

Northburgh rose. 'I will see if his Grace can spare you a few minutes.'

A page ushered Merrivale into a solar. He waited, bathed in diamond patterns of sunlight coming in through the window. A door opened and the king walked in, robed in red. He looked hot and angry. 'What is it?' he demanded.

'Three days ago, Lord Rowton told me measures were being taken to procure Brother Geoffrey's release,' Merrivale said. 'May I ask, sire, has there been any progress?'

'None. Bertrand won't negotiate.'

'Forgive me, sire, but how hard have we tried?'

A painted wooden chest stood on the rushes below the window. The king sat down on it, arranging his robe around him. 'Still haven't lost your taste for insolence, I see,' he said. 'The last time Clarenceux went to negotiate, they shot at him. They missed, but one of the clerks went out yesterday morning to try again and got a crossbow bolt in the leg. He may not live.'

'I am sorry to hear it,' the herald said.

'It takes two to negotiate, Merrivale. If Bertrand refuses to talk, there is nothing we can do.'

Merrivale looked down at his hands. 'When I was in your service, your Grace, we had one simple rule. We never left one of our own behind.'

'Then it was a damned stupid rule,' the king said. 'Men are left behind on the battlefield all the time. Men are expendable, Merrivale. You know that.'

'There will be no further steps to save him?'

'For Christ's sake, herald! We have lost one man already because of Brother Geoffrey, and I don't intend to lose any more. We move on. Understood?'

The herald bowed. 'Yes, your Grace.'

'Good. Dismissed.'

Caen, 30ᵗʰ of July, 1346
Late afternoon

Word of the orders to march had already spread by the time Merrivale returned to the Abbaye aux Dames. In the camp, the archers waxed their bowstrings and checked the fletchings of their arrows, while esquires and servants polished armour plate and strained at the cranks of sandboxes, turning the heavy mail coats to remove stains and rust. The tap of a farrier's hammer sounded among the tents.

For once, the Prince of Wales was neither playing dice nor drinking. When Merrivale was shown into the abbess's solar, the young man was poring over a parchment map spread out on a table. Salisbury and Bartholomew Burghersh the tutor were with him. 'Have you heard the news, herald?' the prince asked excitedly. 'We are to march against the adversary! Three days' march to Lisieux, and three more from there to Rouen. When we arrive, the adversary is certain to give battle. It will be a gallant contest of arms, will it not?'

'Perhaps, Highness,' the herald said. 'Let us not forget that Rouen is on the far side of the broad River Seine. To bring the adversary to battle, it will be necessary to force a crossing.'

'Oh, that will be done,' said the prince, glowing with the confidence of youth and inexperience. 'You wished to see me, herald?'

'Yes, Highness. Brother Geoffrey of Maldon is in the dungeons at the castle. It seems we are to march away and leave him behind.'

The prince's brow furrowed. 'But that would be dishonourable! Brother Geoffrey is a good servant and a brave man. Go and see my father, herald, and ask him to arrange for Geoffrey's release.'

'I have already done so, Highness. His Grace says there is nothing more to be done.'

'He says that? I cannot believe it of him.' Suddenly angry, the prince thumped his fist on the table. '*I* shall speak to my father. Do not fear, herald, he will listen to *me*.' The prince hurried out of the chamber and ran downstairs, followed by Salisbury. Burghersh looked at the herald. 'I hope you know what you are doing.'

'Geoffrey was your friend too, I recall,' Merrivale said.

15

Troarn, 31ˢᵗ of July, 1346
Evening

The black-robed body of a monk lay outside the door of the big abbey church, two arrows still protruding from his corpse. He was one of a handful of Benedictine brothers and townspeople of Troarn, eight miles east of Caen, who had tried to resist the English army; the leading companies of the vanguard had swatted them away like flies. Now the abbey buildings and the little town were swarming with English troops. Smoke rose once more, grey and sour, into the evening air.

Beyond the town and abbey lay the tidal estuary of the River Dives, gleaming with water. Warwick rode up the hill from the river followed by a handful of knights including Salisbury and Mortimer. Northampton, the constable, stood waiting for them. 'There is a ford,' Warwick said as he dismounted, 'and the vanguard can cross in the morning. The wagon train will have to wait until midday, once the tide is out, and we'll have to use faggots to build a causeway over the deeper streams. But once we cross, we can move straight up the road to Lisieux.'

He and the constable moved away, talking quickly. Everyone ignored the dead monk. Merrivale caught Salisbury's eye, and the young earl walked over to join him, armour clanking softly. 'Has he spoken to you yet?' Salisbury asked.

The herald shook his head. The prince had returned yesterday from his interview with his father looking sullen. All through the march from Caen, eight miles of heat and dust, he had not spoken a word to Merrivale, nor glanced in his direction.

'He is embarrassed,' Salisbury said. 'He feels that he has let you down.'

'It is Brother Geoffrey who has been let down, not I. What happened?'

Salisbury grinned. Most people still saw him as the prince's lapdog, but as the campaign progressed, he was beginning to emerge as a confident young man, showing some of the qualities that had marked out his late father. 'He and the king stood toe to toe and shouted at each other until they ran out of breath. Then his Grace told him that unless he obeyed orders, he would be relieved of his command and sent back to England.'

'I see. I hope I have not been the cause of any rupture between them.'

'I couldn't speak for his highness. But when I looked back, the king was smiling.' Salisbury grinned again. 'Give the prince a couple of days, herald. He will come around. I'm sorry about Brother Geoffrey, though. He was a good man.'

'Yes,' said the herald. He glanced back at the body of the dead monk. 'He was.'

—

The other archer and the big man with the spear had come to relieve Matt and Pip. They exchanged a few words, and then the two young archers walked away. Warin followed them through the camp and down the hill to the bank of the Dives. All was calm and peaceful here; the stream rippled softly in the evening light, and a few ducks quacked in the reeds that grew along the water's edge. Further upstream, not far from the line of the ford, there was a stand of big willows, the wind rustling their long, trailing branches. Matt pointed to these and the two men walked into the shelter of the trees. Silently Warin followed them.

The archers knelt on the riverbank and cupped their hands in the water, lifting them to drink. After a moment, Pip said something to Matt, who nodded. Reaching under his tunic, Pip pulled out a small strip of red cloth and dropped it into the water, washing it slowly and carefully until the colour began to fade. Matt watched him for a few moments, and then stood up and pulled his tunic off over his head. His torso gleamed pale in the sunset light.

Warin did not wait to see more. Backing away, he turned and hurried back to the camp, where he found the herald and related what he had seen. Merrivale stared.

'Are you quite certain?'

'Yes, sir. There is no doubt about it.'

'Well,' Merrivale said, half to himself. 'That explains some things, at least. Wait here. I am going to see Sir John Grey.'

—

'Their names are Matilda and Philippa Forrester,' Grey said. He seemed amused. 'Otherwise, it is exactly as I told you. Their mother died when they were small, and their father raised them as boys and taught them to shoot and live out of doors. After their father died, they were homeless, until we recruited them.'

'How long have you known?'

'Since very shortly after they joined the company.'

'And you made no objection?'

'Why would I? I told you, they are the best we have. Our master bowman once shot a man through the heart at three hundred and twenty-five yards. I thought he was the best I had ever seen, or ever would see. Then I met these two.'

'Do the rest of your company know?'

'I would imagine they do.'

'You imagine?'

Grey raised one eyebrow. 'We have never discussed it,' he said. 'Why would we?'

Merrivale nodded. 'I owe you an apology,' he said. 'And them also. I felt all along that there was something not right about them, something not… authentic. I see now what it was.'

'You're wrong. They *are* authentic. Matt and Pip are archers of the Red Company, accepted by their brothers in arms, and that is all that matters. Do you have any objection to their keeping watch over you?'

'On the contrary,' said the herald, 'I am profoundly grateful. Thank you, Sir John.'

Night was falling as Merrivale walked back through the camp towards his own tent. He saw two figures in front of him and realised suddenly who they were. One, still in his battered leather jerkin with the three red eagles on his faded surcoat, was Sir Nicholas Courcy; the other was Tiphaine. They were talking together, both smiling, and after a moment Tiphaine threw back her head and laughed.

Merrivale had never heard her laugh before, and he could not tell why the sound should irritate him so much. He started to move towards them, and then realised that someone else was watching them too, a man-at-arms in armour that looked like it had been made for some long-ago war: a mail tunic, battered vambraces and dented greaves, a heavy iron breastplate and an ancient pot helm with a narrow slit for a visor. He wore a sword but no surcoat or device of any kind. When Courcy and Tiphaine walked away, the other man followed them.

Alert, the herald shrugged off his all-too-conspicuous tabard and went after them, keeping his eye on the man-at-arms. It was impossible to tell who he was watching, Courcy or Tiphaine. They passed a group of West Country archers roasting rabbits on spits over a fire, felt a warm glow of charcoal heating a portable forge, saw men unloading wagons by torchlight and carrying bundles of faggots down to the river to build Warwick's causeway. Further on was Sir John Sully's tent, the dog curled up outside the door. It raised its head when it saw Merrivale and wagged its tail, then went back to sleep.

It might have been the dog that betrayed his presence, he could not be certain. But suddenly the man-at-arms wheeled around and looked straight at him. The visor of his helm was a black line, but Merrivale could feel the invisible eyes behind it, boring into him. For a moment the other man's hand went to the hilt of his sword. Then he turned and walked away, quickly swallowed up in the gathering shadow.

In the morning, the vanguard splashed across the shallow waters of the Dives and climbed the gentle slope on the far side, pushing on through fields and hedgerows past the village of Rumesnil. The king's division followed more slowly, and both halted to wait while the wagon train made its tortuous way across the muddy estuary. By the time the wagons arrived it was nearly evening, and the army made camp once more. In the open-air kitchens the cooks began preparing for the Lammas feast. Lammas, the Loaf Mass, was the traditional first day of harvest and a time for celebration, even for an army in the field, marching through enemy country and burning and despoiling crops as it went.

Nell milked her cows in a nearby field, watching the beasts with a critical eye. They had lost weight during the march from Saint-Vaast to Caen; they had put some of it back on again during the halt at Caen, but Marigold in particular was looking thinner already, and there was an unhappy look in her soft brown eyes. The other milk cows were restive too, and Garnet lowed unhappily. Of course, their mood was not helped by the fact that those idiots the butchers were cutting up beef carcasses only a few yards away, and her cows could smell the blood. She would have to speak to Master Coloyne, she thought, about procuring better fodder and asking the slaughterers to move somewhere else. Otherwise the cows might stop giving milk at all, and no milk meant no butter for the king's table.

She loaded the foaming buckets of milk onto a handcart and pushed it across the field towards the kitchen. The bakers had already lit fires under their ovens, and further on Master Clerebaud the sauce-maker was hard at work cutting up onions and fresh herbs. He winked at her as she passed, as he usually did. He was a nice man, Master Clerebaud, always friendly but not *too* friendly, and sometimes he gave her sauce bowls to lick clean. The new man, Curry, prowled around the cooking pots on guard, a knife at his belt and a cudgel in his hand. Nell had her doubts about him. He seemed diligent and good at his job, but she had grown up within sight of the sea, and she thought he didn't look like much of a mariner.

She delivered her milk to the scullions and heard the heavy thump of the butter churn begin almost at once. The woman in charge of the dairy gave her a piece of bread and honey and Nell sat down to eat it, wiping the honey from her chin with one finger and licking it. Out of the corner of her eye she saw Curry talking with the archer Nicodemus, the one the herald had been interested in. They spoke for a few moments, then Nicodemus handed something to Curry, who tucked it swiftly inside his tunic. Nicodemus said something else, and Curry nodded. The archer departed.

Curry looked around to see if anyone was observing him, and Nell quickly bowed her head, concentrating on her bread and honey. She watched from under her eyebrows as Curry walked over to the sauce-maker's table. He said a few words to Master Clerebaud and laid something down on the table; Nell could not be sure, but she thought she caught a gleam of gold. Then he turned away and went back to watching his pots. Master Clerebaud looked down at the table for a moment, then picked up his knife and began peeling cloves of garlic. When Nell walked past him to return to her cows, he did not look up.

Léaupartie, 1ˢᵗ of August, 1346
Evening

Further east, at the Prince of Wales's camp, the knights of the vanguard gathered for the Lammas feast. There was a little hamlet nearby, which someone said was called Léaupartie; on its edge was an old stone chapel where the feast would be held.

Merrivale and Sir John Sully walked through the camp, where the archers were already making merry with wine they had looted from Rumesnil as they passed. 'There will be sore heads in the morning,' Sully commented.

'There always are after Lammas,' Merrivale said. He never enjoyed Lammas; the feasting and celebration always reminded him of those terrible years when the harvest had failed. He saw once again the bodies wrapped in white being lowered into the ground, the thin, wasted faces of the survivors watching and wondering when their turn would come.

Sully nudged him. 'Isn't that your *demoiselle*?'

Tiphaine had returned to the tent late last night, and departed this morning before the army marched, without saying a word. Now she was with Courcy again, her hand resting on his arm, smiling at him.

'She is making free with Sir Nicholas,' the older man commented. He turned to look at Merrivale. 'Should you allow that to be happening?'

'She is not my property,' the herald said irritably.

'You rescued her, boy.'

'She is not obligated to me, or I to her.'

'Some might see it differently.'

'She needs a protector,' Merrivale said. 'Perhaps she has found one.'

'Sir Nicholas Courcy? The greatest rascal in the army?'

'No. Believe me, there are many worse.'

Something moved in the corner of his eye; the man-at-arms he had seen last night at Troarn was stalking slowly forward, his hand on the hilt of his sword. Merrivale started forward, but he was too late. Courcy bowed to Tiphaine, then raised her hand to his lips and kissed it. The man-at-arms leaped forward, raised one fist and punched him on the jaw. Startled, Courcy fell to the ground, and the man-at-arms stepped forward and kicked him hard in the ribs.

Tiphaine started towards him, but the man-at-arms turned on her. 'Get away from him, harlot! And stay away, or I'll cut out your liver and lights and feed them to the crows!'

Tiphaine stopped.

'Who are you, sir?' Merrivale demanded. 'And how dare you threaten this lady?'

'I think I can explain,' said a voice from the ground.

Everyone looked at Courcy, who sat up rubbing his jaw. 'Faith,' he said. 'That's one hell of a punch you have there, my darling.'

'Darling?' said Sully blankly.

Courcy nodded. 'Take off that ridiculous helm and show yourself,' he said to the man-at-arms.

Slowly the helm was removed. The face beneath it was haughty, with high cheekbones, a long nose and a grimly set mouth, all framed by a tied-back mass of curling hair the colour of a raven's wing. Blue-grey eyes, like the sea in storm, glared at Courcy.

'Allow me to make the introductions,' Courcy said, rising to his feet. 'Demoiselle de Tesson, gentlemen; may I present to you the lady Gráinne MacCarthaigh Riabhach, daughter of the Prince of Carbery – and my wife.'

–

'What in the devil's name are you doing here?' Courcy demanded.

'Looking for you, you lazy, useless, pox-brained piece of goat shit,' said Lady Gráinne. 'You went off and left me without so much as a word, so I followed you. I assumed I'd probably catch you fornicating with some whore, and so I have.'

'I have not fornicated with anyone!' Courcy protested. 'Least of all with that lady!'

Tiphaine slapped Courcy hard across the other cheek and marched away. Merrivale thought about going after her, but did not.

'Lady, is she?' demanded Gráinne. 'So why have you dressed her up as a boy? Is that where your tastes lie? Well, you'll fancy me now, won't you?'

Men were gathering around them, watching open-mouthed. Merrivale turned to them. 'Sir Nicholas and his wife have been reunited after a long parting,' he said. 'Grant them some privacy.'

Reluctantly the bystanders moved on. Courcy rubbed his jaw again. 'Where did you get the armour?' he asked.

'My brother. I traded him the tavern for it.'

Courcy's eyes opened wide. 'The tavern? You got rid of that godforsaken tavern? Ah, Gráinne, you are a miracle worker!'

'Don't try to soften me up!' she snarled. 'He took the tavern because he felt sorry for me. The armour is worth twice as much.'

'Sweetheart,' he pleaded. 'You know I only went to war because we needed the money. I hoped I could make our fortune and we would be free to leave that wretched hovel and roam the world together, as we once dreamed of doing.'

'Then why didn't you tell me you were going?'

'Because I thought you would try to talk me out of it.'

Gráinne hit him again. 'Of course I would have tried to talk you out of it, you witless fool! You might have got yourself killed, and then where would I be? I cut myself off from my father, I abandoned a life of wealth and privilege, all for the love of you. And you repay me by deserting me and going off to fuck some French bitch behind my back!'

'You can stand there and hit me all night,' Courcy said with injured dignity. 'But I have never been unfaithful to you.' He looked her up and down, and a slow smile spread across his face. 'And you're right,' he said. 'That gear does suit you. Do you know what, sweetheart? I've never loved a lady in armour before.'

'Oh, God's curse on you!' Gráinne snapped. 'I swear by the bones of Christ I have never hated anyone so much as I hate you!' And stepping forward, she took Courcy's bruised face between her gloved hands and kissed him, grinding her mouth hard and powerfully into his.

—

The floor of the chapel had been laid with rush mats, and long trestle tables had been set up in the nave; the prince's servants had even climbed up and hung branches of greenery and sheaves of wheat stalks from the capitals of the pillars. Candles flickered in silver and gold candlesticks and torches burned in sconces along the walls. Model ships, artfully made from bread with straw rigging, sat in the middle of each table with ornamented silver salt cellars resting on their crusted decks.

'First the two Red Company archers, and now this,' Merrivale said. 'How many more women in armour have we among us, I wonder?'

'I wouldn't care to speculate,' said Sully. He sat opposite the herald, his dog curled up beside his feet. 'It happens in every army, boy. When the men go off to war, the women don't always remain behind.'

'Has that been your experience, Sir John?' asked Edward de Tracey, smiling.

'Aye. I counted twenty-six maids amongst the Welsh archers at Halidon Hill, and one of Ralph Ufford's grooms was a damsel of good birth from Rutland who had run away from her family. And you remember Algeciras, Simon? That young Moorish crossbowman, Jalid?'

'Yes,' Merrivale said warily.

'I never told you, but *he* turned out to be a *she*. Her real name was Durr. It meant pearl, she told me. Aye, well,' Sully said nostalgically. 'Enough said about her.'

'You were at Algeciras?' asked Mortimer. The question, to the herald's mind, rather missed the point of the anecdote, but he was glad of the change of subject. He wondered where Tiphaine was.

'I was, lad. So was the herald here, though he held no such lofty post back then. It was a grim siege and a bloody one, with all the forces of Morocco and Granada arrayed against us. I'll never forget the bodies floating in the water after the battle on the Rio Palmones.'

'I imagine Durr helped you forget the hardships,' said Hugh Despenser, seated beside Merrivale and pointedly ignoring Mortimer. 'How did you come to meet a Moorish woman? Wasn't she one of the enemy?'

Sully shook his white head. 'Spain is a land of complicated loyalties, Sir Hugh. There were many Moors serving in King Alfonso's army, just as there were plenty of Spaniards serving with Sultan Yusuf. Durr's father had been executed by the sultan, so she changed sides.' He grinned at Merrivale, lined face lively with mischief. 'Just like your *demoiselle*.'

'She is not my *demoiselle*,' the herald said.

Servants were carrying food into the chapel, and the smell of roasted meats and hot bread floated among the candles. Despenser pulled a plate of roast goose towards him and began cutting slices of breast meat and laying them on his trencher. 'That's not what the gossip says.'

'I am not interested in gossip, Sir Hugh. And neither should the rest of you be. You are men-at-arms, not fishwives.'

It had come out more sharply than he intended, and even Mortimer smiled. Despenser put a spoonful of salt on the edge of his plate next to the trencher and picked up the sauce pot, pouring brilliant green sauce over his meat. The smells of wine and garlic and fresh parsley rose to their nostrils. 'I think we have touched a nerve, gentlemen,' he said. 'You should have brought her with you, herald. I'd like to hear her side of the story.'

He stabbed a piece of meat with his knife and raised it to his lips, then stopped, wincing in pain as Merrivale's hand took his wrist in a crushing grip. 'No,' the herald said.

'What in hell's name are you doing?' Despenser demanded.

'If you eat that, you will die.'

Letting go of the other man's arm, Merrivale picked up his napkin and used it to remove something from the sauce. He held it up to the light, and saw a chunk of bulbous root, about an inch long, dripping thick blobs of green sauce back onto the table. Around them, everyone had stopped eating.

'Do not eat the juvert sauce!' Merrivale said sharply. 'If it is already on your trencher, push your plate away and do not touch your meat!'

'What is it?' Tracey asked.

The herald dropped the root on the table. 'Wolf's-bane,' he said.

A gasp went up around the room. 'Aconitum,' said John Sully thoughtfully. 'Poison, said to come from the mouth of Cerberus, the dog that guards the entrance to the underworld. Just what is it doing in the juvert?'

'And what is it doing on my plate?' demanded Despenser.

Merrivale upended the sauce pot on the table, spilling green sauce across the cloth. There, plain to see, were several more pieces of wolf's-bane. 'Check the others,' he said.

There were three other pots of juvert on the tables, but none of them contained any trace of the root.

Despenser was staring hard at Mortimer. 'A craven attempt to poison me. Who could be behind such a thing, I wonder?'

'Who can tell?' snapped Mortimer. 'Christ knows you have enough enemies, Sir Hugh.'

'But not all of them are cowards,' said Despenser.

Mortimer kicked the table over and reached for his sword just as Despenser slapped his hand on his own hilt. Before Merrivale could move, another man stepped between them, standing over the wreck of the table and holding up one hand. A hush fell in the chapel.

'Hands off those hilts,' said the Prince of Wales. His voice was high-pitched with nerves, but his young face was set hard. He drew his dagger from his belt, blade twinkling in the light. 'Hands off, gentlemen! Or before God, I will cut them off.'

Slowly, sullenly, Despenser and Mortimer removed their hands from their swords. 'Every man in this room is aware of the enmity your ancestors bore each other,' the prince said. 'But we are not our fathers, nor our grandfathers. We are the men we are here and now.'

Absolute silence had fallen. The candles flickered in a sudden waft of wind. 'The past is gone, gentlemen, and you will leave it behind you. Do you hear me?'

'With great respect, Highness,' Despenser said through clenched teeth, 'someone has just tried to poison me.'

'An inquisition will be established,' the prince said. 'Whoever is responsible will be found and punished.'

Sir Thomas Holland bowed. 'May I make a suggestion, Highness? Your herald, Master Merrivale, is a skilled inquisitor. Perhaps he should undertake this task.'

Merrivale looked at him sharply. Holland met his gaze, an ironic gleam in his eye. Was this a form of polite revenge, wondered the herald, or did the man have some other purpose? He bowed. 'If it pleases your Highness, I shall of course undertake an inquisition.'

'Good,' said the prince. 'It is settled. Sir Roger, Sir Hugh, you will apologise for the harsh words you have spoken. Now.'

Grimly, Mortimer and Despenser uttered words of apology.

'Have the servants clear away and reset the table,' the prince said. 'The rest of you, return to your seats. The feast will continue.' He slapped his dagger back into its sheath and threw up his hands. 'Music, that's what we need! Where are those musician fellows? I want to hear them play.'

Quietly, a little subdued, the prince's knights returned to their seats. The prince paused for a moment and looked at Merrivale. 'How did I do?' he asked softly.

'For a moment, Highness, you reminded me of your father.'

'I did, didn't I? Do you know, herald, I think I am beginning to understand.'

Head high, he walked back to his place. The musicians took up their instruments and began to play a roundelay. Sully came up beside Merrivale and rested a hand on his shoulder. 'What do you think happened just now?'

'At the moment, your guess is as good as mine,' the herald said. 'You called Spain a land of complicated loyalties, Sir John. You should take a closer look at England.'

16

'The sauce came from the king's kitchen,' Mauro reported. 'I spoke to the prince's servants and they all said the same thing. It was sent over as a Lammas gift, along with the model ships and the salts. The prince's head cook said it was an excellent juvert, the best he had ever tasted. Master Clerebaud is a wizard with sauces, he said.'

'He tasted it? With no ill effects?'

'None, *señor*. The sauce was put into four sauce pots and distributed around the dinner tables.'

'And only one contained traces of wolf's-bane.'

'It might not have been intended for Sir Hugh,' Warin said. 'With respect, sir, they might have been trying to kill you.'

'The thought had occurred to me,' the herald agreed.

They were standing on the bridge outside the west gate of Lisieux, bathed in hot sunlight. The river beneath their feet stank of dung and urine, effluent from the tanneries that lined its banks. Behind them the tile roofs of the town climbed up the hill towards the towers and flying buttresses of the cathedral. From nearer at hand came the sounds of splintering wood and smashing crockery and glass as the troops ransacked the city.

There was still no sign of Tiphaine.

'Which of the servants handled the sauce?'

'The head cook decanted it into the sauce pots, *señor*,' Mauro said. 'The scullion who drove the cart from the king's kitchen helped him.

The servants then took the pots directly into the chapel and set them on the tables.'

'Could one of the servants have slipped the wolf's-bane into the sauce?'

'It would have been difficult, *señor*, as they were in plain view the entire time.'

'What about this man who drove the cart?'

'His name was Riccon. The cook did not know him, nor did any of the others.'

'Riccon Curry. I know who he is. And the cook himself? Could he have done it?'

Mauro looked doubtful. 'He has been in the prince's service for eight years, *señor*, and he values his position very much. It seems unlikely.'

'Watch him all the same, both of you, and as many of the other servants as you can. Note anything unusual, where they go and who they speak to.'

—

Nell scrambled up from her milking stool as the herald approached. 'Please,' Merrivale said, 'continue your work. I will not detain you for long.'

Obediently Nell sat down again and leaned forward, taking a firm hold on the cow's teats and pulling. Milk streamed into the wooden pail. Around them the royal household was making camp in the fields, a safe distance from the city. Most of the population of Lisieux had fled at the English approach, but the bishop and his armed retainers still held the cathedral and its precinct, shooting bolts at any English soldier who came too close.

'Did Nicodemus call at the kitchens yesterday? At any time before the evening banquet?'

'Yes, sir. I saw him when I brought in the evening milk. He spoke with Curry, just like before, and then he gave him something. I couldn't see what it was.'

'Did he talk to Master Clerebaud as well?'

'No, sir, but after he left, Curry went to speak to Master Clerebaud. He gave him some money, three nobles. I saw them on the table as I walked past, sir.'

Three gold nobles was twenty shillings; a useful sum of money, but hardly a fortune. Part payment, perhaps? For services rendered, or about to be rendered? Merrivale nodded. 'Thank you, Mistress Driver. Once again you have been most helpful.' He smiled. 'I owe you another piece of cheese.'

He found Coloyne, the yeoman of the kitchen, and asked to speak to Clerebaud. The sauce-maker came, his eyes full of fright, twisting his hands with nerves. Everyone else in the kitchen pavilion paused to watch him. 'You know what happened last night,' the herald said. 'How do you explain it?'

'I swear before God, sir, I do not know.'

'Did you prepare the sauce yourself? Did anyone help you?'

'No, sir. I prepared all the ingredients and made the sauce myself, just as I always do.'

'Do you know where the wolf's-bane might have come from? Do you keep stocks of it?'

'No, sir! This is a kitchen! We would never keep anything so deadly here.' His voice trailed off and he looked down at his hands.

'Curry gave you money yesterday evening, three nobles,' Merrivale said. 'What was it for?'

The hands twisted again. 'It was money Nicodemus owed me, sir. Curry collected it from him.' Clerebaud swallowed. 'It was a gambling debt, sir.'

'You won three gold nobles at dice? You must have been playing for high stakes.'

'I had a run of luck, sir. You know how it is sometimes.'

'Look at me,' the herald said.

Unwillingly Clerebaud raised his eyes and met the herald's gaze.

'Are you speaking the truth?' Merrivale asked. 'The money was to settle a gambling debt, nothing else? For example, did Nicodemus want you to perform a service for him?'

The hand-wringing increased. 'I swear to God, sir! I am innocent of any crime!'

Merrivale watched him for a long time. 'Then you have nothing to fear,' he said finally. 'You may go.'

–

Riccon Curry was a big, truculent man with shaggy dark hair, missing the last two joints of his left index finger. 'Did you help Master Clerebaud prepare the juvert sauce last night?' Merrivale asked him.

'No.'

'Did you drive the cart from the royal kitchen over to the prince's camp?'

'Yes.'

'You helped the prince's cook decant the sauce. What did you do?'

'Held the pots while he poured the sauce in. Then I left.'

'How well do you know Nicodemus?' the herald asked.

One shoulder lifted. 'A little.'

'Only a little? You have spoken to him three times in the past week.'

The shoulder lifted again. 'Commerce,' said Riccon Curry. 'We're in the same trade.'

'Looting, you mean. Nicodemus gave you something yesterday evening. What was it?'

'Money,' said Curry. 'He owed me for a purchase he made a couple of days ago. And he asked me to pass on some money to that sauce-maker. For settling a debt, he said.'

Well, thought Merrivale as he rode back to the Prince of Wales's camp, all that proved was that they had arranged their stories before-hand. On the other hand, it seemed impossible that either of them could have introduced the poison into the sauce, given that the prince's cook had tasted it before it was decanted and the wolf's-bane was found in only one pot.

Logically, the poison must have been introduced at the prince's kitchen, and that left two choices: the kitchen servants, or someone who sitting at the table. But Mauro was positive that it was not one of the servants, and he trusted Mauro's judgement; and the others sitting around them – Mortimer, Despenser, Sully, Edward de Tracey – had been in plain view the whole time. Despite Despenser's accusation,

Merrivale doubted Mortimer hated him enough to want to poison him, and neither Sully nor Tracey had any motive.

Wolf's-bane was a powerful poison, but it was also rare and expensive. Whoever had procured it had the wealth and the means to do so, and also knew that sauce from the king's kitchen was due to be served at the prince's table. Merrivale made his way to Sir Nicholas Courcy's tent.

–

The gallowglasses were sprawled on the grass outside the tent, some of them asleep in the sun. The giant Donnchad sat cross-legged, honing the edge of his sword on a whetstone. 'Is Sir Nicholas here?' Merrivale asked.

Donnchad motioned silently towards the tent. Merrivale opened the flap and stepped inside. 'Sir Nicholas? Pardon the intrusion, but I have a question for you—'

A turmoil of heaving, glistening skin on the palliasse in the corner of the tent, two bodies thrashing against each other like flails on the winnowing floor; then a woman's voice said, '*Máthair Dé!*' and hands scrambled to snatch blankets from the floor beside the bed. From outside came a sound like two slabs of granite scraping together, which Merrivale realised was Donnchad laughing.

After a moment, Courcy sat up, holding one of the blankets around his waist. 'Herald,' he said. 'What can I do for you?'

'Tell him to frig off!' snapped Lady Gráinne, still covering herself.

Merrivale held up a hand. 'My profuse apologies. I shall wait outside.' He walked back out into the sunlight, where Donnchad lay flat on his back, still laughing. 'You did that on purpose,' the herald said.

'He understands English, but he doesn't speak it,' said Courcy, stepping out of the tent. He had pulled a tunic over his head, and he mopped the sweat from his forehead with the back of his hand. 'And yes, he did it on purpose, the evil old bastard. How may I help you?'

'You told me once you were an alchemist.'

'I wouldn't go so far. But I have studied the subject.'

'If you wanted to procure wolf's-bane, enough to poison someone, how would you go about doing it?'

'Most apothecaries carry a stock. It is used in preparing certain medicines.' Courcy considered for a moment. 'There were apothecary's shops in Caen, and Saint-Lô.'

'Someone might have stolen the wolf's-bane from one of those shops.'

'They might, but you would really have to know what you were doing. Even touching the stuff can be dangerous. And only an educated man would recognise aconitum for what it is. Like an alchemist,' he added.

'Or a priest?'

'Only if he had studied medicine as well as theology. But that is not unknown at the universities.' Courcy paused. 'An educated man who is skilled at looting. Are you thinking of Nicodemus?'

'Possibly.'

'I heard what happened last night. Are you investigating this as well as young Bray's death?'

'Yes.' The herald nodded towards the tent. 'I am pleased to see that you and your wife are reconciled.'

Courcy grinned. 'Oh, we're all of that. Ever since we arrived at Lisieux we've been reconciling the arse off each other. Now, if you'll forgive me, I said I wouldn't be long.'

-

The red and yellow colours of Tracey were clearly visible in the distance. Beyond them was the camp of the Red Company, neat and orderly amid the haphazard jumble of tents. Tracey's esquire greeted the herald with an air of polite curiosity. 'I wish to speak with your master,' Merrivale said.

Tracey came out of the pavilion at once. 'Leave us,' he said curtly to the esquire. The young man walked away and Tracey faced the herald. 'What?'

'Tell me more about your archer Nicodemus,' Merrivale said.

'Is this about last night?'

'Of course.'

'Why do you suspect Nicodemus was involved?'

'I did not say I did. I asked you to tell me about him.'

'He came into my service back in '40,' Tracey said. 'I don't know a great deal about him.'

'Did you know he was a defrocked priest?'

'I heard something about that, yes.'

'And he then worked as clerk to a banker?'

'Yes. I believe his master was killed when the French attacked Southampton.'

Merrivale nodded. 'So he is not just an archer. He is also your factor. He buys spoil from the soldiers at cheap prices for ready money, and you transport the goods back to England and sell them at a profit.'

Tracey gazed at him. 'I take it you disapprove.'

'It is not my place to approve or disapprove,' Merrivale said. 'Nicodemus deals in stolen goods of all kind, and it is conceivable that those goods included aconitum. He has connections with two people in the royal kitchen, including the man who made the sauce, and he visited the kitchen yesterday evening while the feast was being prepared.'

'And you think one of those men poisoned the sauce? Then have them arrested!'

Merrivale shook his head. 'The poison was added in the prince's kitchen or at the banqueting hall, and only to the pot intended for our table.'

'Then Nicodemus didn't do it. He returned to my camp before the feast and spent the evening here working on accounts. My esquire was with him the entire time.'

'I did not accuse him of administering the poison. But he may have procured it.'

'You are barking up the wrong tree, Merrivale. For God's sake, I was at that table too! It could have been me they were trying to poison, not Despenser.'

'All the more reason, surely, to find out if Nicodemus was involved. Perhaps he was intending to betray you.'

'Nonsense. He has served me faithfully for years.'

'Money does strange things to a man, Sir Edward, and I imagine this venture of yours involves a great deal of money. Perhaps he got greedy and wanted it all for himself.'

Tracey shook his head in exasperation. 'My venture has brought in a few hundred pounds, herald, no more. Not a fortune, and certainly not enough to kill a man for.'

That was not the picture Mauro had painted. 'Really? I have known men to plot murder for far less. If you are shielding him, Sir Edward, I would advise you to be very careful...'

—

Inquisition into the attempted poisoning of Hugh Despenser, knight, near the village of Léaupartie in Normandy on the Ist day of August in the nineteenth year of the reign of King Edward III. This report was composed on the IInd day of that month, at the city of Lisieux.

Item, the poison, a form of aconitum known as wolf's-bane, was introduced into a single pot of sauce. This almost certainly happened at the prince's kitchen or in the banqueting hall, not the royal kitchen. However, it remains to be seen how this was done.

Item, at no time was his Highness the Prince of Wales in danger.

Item, the source of the wolf's-bane has not been identified, but I have lines of enquiry to pursue.

Simon Merrivale, heraldus

Lamps glowed all around the royal pavilion. In the field outside, trestle tables were being unloaded from carts and set up, with benches arranged around them. Candles flickered like fireflies in the falling dusk.

The king read the brief report, the rings on his fingers glittering in the candlelight before handing the parchment to Northburgh. Lord Rowton watched him in silence. 'This was not an attempt on my son's life', the king said.

'I do not believe so, sire,' Merrivale said.

Lord Rowton shook his head. 'Perhaps Despenser put the poison there himself so he could accuse Mortimer and continue their feud.'

'That is possible, my lord,' the herald acknowledged.

The king growled under his breath. 'When will these damned fools stop raking up the past? For Christ's sake, we have a war to fight.'

'A point made by your son with admirable clarity, sire,' Merrivale said. 'He commanded Mortimer and Despenser to apologise to each other.'

'Good. Keep an eye on this Nicodemus.'

'You wish me to continue my inquisition, sire, alongside the investigation into Bray's death?'

'No, you can drop that. Time to make an end, I think.'

'Sire?' said Merrivale. He looked at Northburgh, who avoided his gaze. 'May I ask why?'

'You said at Saint-Vaast that you would find the killer quickly,' the king said. 'That was more than two weeks ago. What progress have you made?' Merrivale said nothing. 'Make an end,' the king repeated. 'We have matters of greater moment. Did you hear that we have received an embassy?'

'No, sire. From the adversary?'

'From the pope, but that amounts to the same thing. Étienne Aubert is their leader. We are preparing a banquet to welcome him.'

The herald stared at him. 'The Cardinal of Ostia? He is here?'

'Along with another cardinal, Ceccano from Naples,' Rowton said. 'They come bearing an offer of peace, or so they say. They arrived an hour ago.'

'Aubert knows you,' the king said to Merrivale. 'Clarenceux will handle the formalities, but I want you at the banquet too. Talk to his staff and tell me what you learn. They claim to want peace, but why are they really here?'

'They are here at the behest of the adversary,' the herald said. 'While you halt and engage in peace talks, he wins more time to prepare and assemble his army at Rouen.'

'Obviously,' the king said impatiently. 'But they may have another purpose as well. Aubert is close to the Queen of Navarre, remember. And I want to meet with her. I have been sending messages to her home in Évreux since before we sailed from Portchester, but there has been no reply.'

'You are still determined to start a new Norman revolt, sire? With her Grace and the Count of Eu as leaders?'

'Of course. If we can set Normandy alight, we can squeeze that bastard Philip between the jaws of a vice. But we need Jeanne of Navarre. Try to find out where she is and what she is doing. There is something going on deep below the surface here, and I want to know what it is.'

–

There are powerful forces at work, Thomas Holland had said, and now the king had said something similar. Merrivale wondered how much His Grace already knew. Impatient, arrogant and bellicose though he often was, Edward III was no one's fool; unlike his son, he was an accomplished gambler and adept at the long game, and he had many sources of intelligence.

Merrivale stood behind the Prince of Wales as the latter was presented to the distinguished guests. Étienne Aubert's cold eye fell on him. A tall man with black hair streaked with grey, wearing red robes that blazed with embroidery, the Cardinal-Bishop of Ostia spoke with a nasal accent and clipped vowels suggesting his mother tongue had been Occitan rather than French. 'Simon Merrivale, in a herald's tabard. How times have changed.'

'They have indeed, your Eminence,' said the herald, bowing. The other cardinal, Ceccano, looked at him suspiciously as if he suspected him of insolence. Aubert waved an airy hand, his seal ring flashing red fire, dismissing the herald as being of no account. But he had taken note of Merrivale's presence all the same, and it was no coincidence that Merrivale found himself placed at dinner next to Aubert's secretary, Raimon Vidal, a rotund tonsured man in the brown habit of a Franciscan friar.

'Well met, my friend,' Vidal said cheerfully. 'I see fortune's wheel has turned in your favour.'

At the high table, the king and the cardinals were seated, and the rest of the company pulled out their benches and sat also. Stars gleamed high overhead; in the distance they could see lamps burning in the towers of the cathedral, where the bishop and his men kept watch.

'And you also,' Merrivale said. 'You have landed a good post. His Eminence will be the next pope, they say, when Clement receives his reward in heaven.'

'Heaven? If you say so. Most of us in Avignon assume the Holy Father will travel in the opposite direction. How fare you, my friend? I have not seen you since Savoy. Geoffrey of Maldon was there too, of course. How is the good brother? Is he here tonight?'

'No.' Briefly Merrivale told Vidal what had happened in Caen. 'I don't suppose you could persuade his Eminence to secure his release.'

Vidal looked amused. 'Secure the release of Geoffrey of Maldon? You do remember what happened in Savoy, don't you?'

'Regardless of the past, Brother Geoffrey is a cleric who went to Caen as an ambassador. It was dishonourable of Bishop Bertrand to arrest him.'

'So it was. I shall speak to his Eminence and see if something can be arranged.'

Dishes were set before them: cod with peas, stockfish with sauces made from verjuice, minced chicken decorated with thick sauces brilliant with colour and tasting of almonds; it was Wednesday, a fast day, so no meat was served. Wine splashed into their cups. Merrivale and Vidal added water to theirs. 'You would never know there was a war being fought,' the Franciscan said.

Merrivale looked at the watchful lights on the distant cathedral. 'Some people would,' he said. 'Did you have a good journey?'

'Atrocious,' said Vidal, carving a duck leg with his knife. 'As if the discomforts of the road were not bad enough, on approaching the town we were set upon by some of your barbarian archers and robbed of our horses and baggage. I trust his Grace will see them returned.'

'I am certain he will. But why come all this way and endure such hardship?'

'Do you not know?' Vidal looked at him guilelessly. 'The Holy Father desires most earnestly that the kings of England and France be reconciled with each other. He has instructed the Cardinal-Bishop of Ostia and the Cardinal-Archbishop of Naples to do their utmost to make peace. So we have come to open talks.'

'Have you a peace proposal?'

'Yes, but it is not one your king will want to hear. Restoration of the position *ante bellum*. Everyone gets their lands back and we pretend the last nine years never happened.'

'Reset the pieces,' the herald said. 'And start the game again.'

'Precisely. Edward will never agree, and everyone knows it. But,' the Franciscan shrugged, 'those are the Holy Father's wishes.'

'You mean they are King Philip's wishes,' Merrivale said.

'Why do you say that?'

'Oh, come, Raimon. It is a distinction without a difference. The Holy Father lives in luxurious imprisonment in Avignon, surrounded by French cardinals like your master who spy on his every move. When King Philip orders him to jump, he does not question the order but merely asks how high the bar is set. We have both been in this game long enough, my friend, to know what this visit is really about.'

Vidal smiled, lifting his wine glass. 'Perspicacious as ever. The spy still lurks beneath the herald's tabard.'

'I was a messenger, not a spy.'

Vidal's smile grew broader. 'It is a distinction without a difference.'

'Every hour we are delayed, more French troops arrive in Rouen and Philip grows stronger,' Merrivale said. 'But surely he has strength enough already. His army is far more powerful than ours. Why does he delay?'

'Who knows what goes on in the minds of kings?'

'Oh, come now.' Merrivale helped himself to a piece of fish, considered adding sauce and changed his mind. 'I think we can do better than that, Raimon. Philip is afraid of conspiracies, he always has been. He sees them at every turn. Only this time, he is right. This time, someone really is conspiring against him.'

It was a shot in the dark, but he saw Vidal's eyes flicker. 'Why do you say that?'

The real conspiracy is close to the French king, Tiphaine had said, right at the heart of power. 'I have my own sources.'

'I am certain you do. And who are the leaders of this conspiracy, I wonder?'

'I think you know perfectly well who they are,' Merrivale said.

'Do you? You credit me with far too much wit.'

Up at the head table, Aubert was talking gravely with the king, both resplendent in red. Beside them Ceccano sat stuffing himself with chicken, almond sauce dripping from his ringed hands. The prince looked openly bored. He will need to work on that, Merrivale thought. He watched Vidal for a moment, and said, 'I wonder where the Queen of Navarre is right now.'

'Safely at home in Évreux, I should imagine. Hoping the barbarian English do not despoil her lands.'

Merrivale shook his head. 'She is King Edward's cousin. Her lands will be safe.'

Vidal lowered his voice a little, resting his knife on his plate. 'Especially if King Edward still desires to win the allegiance of the Normans.'

'Precisely,' said Merrivale.

'Hmm. Alone, the Normans are no threat to King Philippe. He has already shown he can deal with them. Your conspiracy will need to be stronger than that.'

'I agree,' Merrivale said. 'But you asked who the leaders are. There are plenty of other candidates, are there not? Philip's own nobles, who grow impatient with his failure to crush England. His brother, Charles of Alençon, arrogant and ambitious. The papacy, chafing in its Babylonian captivity and, like the Normans, desiring freedom. Jeanne of Navarre could ally with any or all of them.'

Vidal smiled. 'You have an active imagination, my friend. But then you always did. It was what made you such a dangerous enemy,' he added softly.

Merrivale nodded towards the high table. 'What is Ceccano's role? To secure the allegiance of the Italian commanders, Doria and Grimaldi?'

Vidal snapped his fingers. 'Of course, you know them both, don't you? You are right. The cardinal is here to hold them to their promises and ensure they remain loyal to France.'

'That is not what I meant,' Merrivale said.

'I know precisely what you meant.' Vidal picked up his knife again. 'Will you try the duck? It is quite delicious, beautifully cooked. I had not realised English cooks were so skilful.'

'You do not deny there is a conspiracy,' Merrivale said.

'My friend, there are always conspiracies. Even the cats and dogs are plotting, each seeking to overthrow the other. But I am only a humble Franciscan friar, and the secular world does not concern me. Now, I really do urge you to try the duck.'

Lisieux, 2nd of August, 1346
Midnight

'Welcome,' said the man from the north. 'I must apologise for the humble surroundings. This is about the only building the peasants have not yet burned.'

While the king and cardinals feasted, the archers had scoured the countryside around Lisieux. A stiff east wind had blown most of the smoke away, and the embers of burnt-out buildings flickered like corpse candles in the moonlight. The farmhouse in which they stood was built of timber and cob, with a low-beamed roof, furnished only with a wooden table and benches beside the hearth. There were five of them in the room, four men in black cloaks and a woman with a hood concealing her face.

'It does not matter,' said Étienne Aubert. 'Why have you summoned us here?'

'To advise you that there has been a change in plan,' said the West Country man. 'We intended to confine Edward to western Normandy until the French royal army could arrive, but as you know, he defeated the French at Caen.'

'Thanks to the Count of Eu's treachery,' said the woman with the hood.

'That may yet work in our favour,' said the man from the north. 'Now Edward has broken out and is advancing towards Rouen, with the intention of challenging Philip to battle.'

'Then he is a fool,' said Cardinal Ceccano, picking his teeth. 'Philip is mustering forty thousand men, with allies coming from all over Europe. Edward will be crushed.'

The man from the north nodded. 'Precisely, monsignor. That is the new plan. Edward will be defeated, but not just yet. His army will reach Rouen in a few days' time. When it does, Philip must refuse to give battle.' He looked at Aubert. 'We rely on you, your Eminence, to ensure that he does so.'

'That will not be difficult. What is he to do instead?'

'Block the crossings of the River Seine, all of them. Break down every bridge between Rouen and Paris, or else man the fortifications so that they are impregnable. Edward must not be allowed to cross the river.'

'Ah,' said the woman in the hood, thoughtfully. 'I begin to see.'

'I do not,' said Ceccano. 'Explain.'

'If Edward cannot cross at Rouen, he will advance upriver looking for a bridge. Within a few days he will arrive at Paris. Philip can cross the river himself, trap Edward against the walls of Paris and destroy his army. The king and the prince will be killed or captured, and England's power will be broken.'

'And Philippe?' asked the woman.

'He will not enjoy his triumph for long. The damage the English will do as they advance on Paris will be laid at his door. Also, letters will be published in the city bearing the king's personal seal. They will make it clear that Philip's failure to give battle was due to the treachery of his councillors and his own vacillation and cowardice. His reputation will suffer and the people will begin to murmur against him. That is where you come in, your Eminences, and your Grace.'

Queen Jeanne of Navarre threw back her hood. Candlelight gleamed off fair hair and a long Norman nose. 'These letters will be forgeries, of course.'

'Of course.'

'And the royal seal? How did you get it?'

The man from the north hesitated.

'Do you desire that we trust you?' the queen asked. 'Then you will need to demonstrate that you trust us also. The seal, I assume, is a copy. Who procured it for you?'

'John of Hainault, Lord of Beaumont, was my father's faithful friend for many years,' said the man from the north. 'Now he is mine.'

The other three looked at each other, and Ceccano snorted with sudden laughter. 'The treachery of his own councillors,' he said. 'Well. It appears at least one of Philippe's councillors really *is* a traitor. I am impressed.'

'You see now how far our power extends,' said the man from the West Country.

'Indeed,' said the Queen of Navarre. 'And so, what do you offer me?'

'Normandy, as a free and independent principality,' said the West Country man. 'Normandy allied with Navarre will be a force to be reckoned with, especially with England and France laid low. The balance of power will shift towards you.'

Jeanne said nothing.

'And what do I stand to gain?' asked Aubert.

'A great deal of money,' said the West Country man. 'Which you will need, I am sure, to launch your campaign for the papacy when Pope Clement finally departs this life. How are the Holy Father's kidney stones?'

'Somewhat improved, I am sorry to say.'

'It need not be kidney stones that kill him,' the man from the north said. 'And of course, when you do sit on the throne of Saint Peter, our friend Cardinal Ceccano will be at your right hand.'

'Of course,' said Ceccano. He rubbed his hands. 'What do you want us to do?'

'Her Grace should gather her forces quietly, in Navarre and here in Normandy. Monsignor Aubert, your task is to make sure Philippe adheres to our plan. Monsignor Ceccano, you control the Genoese mercenary captains in French service, Grimaldi and Doria.'

Ceccano shook his head. 'Grimaldi, yes. Doria, I am not so sure. He takes his loyalties seriously.'

'Then offer him more money,' said the man from the West Country. 'As much as he wants. But make sure he does our bidding. When the time comes, we want the Genoese on our side.'

Ceccano shrugged.

'What about you?' Queen Jeanne asked the two Englishmen. 'What do you stand to gain from this?'

'What everyone wants,' said the man from the north. 'Power, influence and wealth. We shall show the rest of Europe that we can bend events to our will. A new game is beginning, and we are its masters. Kings and emperors will see our power and respect it. And we shall grow very, very rich.'

There was a pause. 'I spoke earlier of trust,' the queen said. '*Can* we trust you?'

'You have no choice,' said the man from the north. 'We can make you powerful, your Grace. But if you turn against us, we will break you.'

Bernay, 3rd of August, 1346
Early morning

Riding east, the Queen of Navarre and her escort reached the Benedictine abbey at Bernay just before dawn. 'We will rest here for a few hours,' she told her captain. 'Then we will return to Évreux.'

Jeanne had inherited the mountain kingdom of Navarre from her father, but she rarely visited it. Her power and wealth came from her wide lands in eastern Normandy, including Bernay. She climbed the steps to the guest lodgings wearily, thinking about the conversation the previous evening and pondering its implications. The Englishmen had been right: the power of Normandy and Navarre combined would be formidable. And she knew Étienne Aubert well. She could work with him.

The sleepy monk who guided her stopped before the door of the chamber, fumbling with his keys. It is, after all, a family quarrel, Jeanne thought. Edward of England, Philippe of France and myself; cousins, grandchildren of Philippe le Bel. Perhaps instead of fighting each other, we should band together, unite in the face of the enemies that conspire against us. But that will never happen. We are united only by our hatred of each other.

Well; that is not quite true. Edward and I agree that Philippe is a usurper. Both of us have better claims to the throne, Edward through his mother, I through my father. But the law in France says that a woman cannot inherit the throne. The law is nonsense, of course, but men use it to protect their power.

The door opened and the monk stepped back, bowing. Jeanne walked into the room, followed by her tirewoman. A single candle burned in a bronze candlestick on the table. Beyond it stood a figure in ragged tunic and hose, with rough-shorn red hair. Just for a moment Jeanne knew fear, but then she saw the figure was alone and carried no weapon. Despite its garb, it was also unmistakably a woman. She set her lips in a thin line and snapped, 'Who the devil are you?'

'I am Tiphaine, the Demoiselle de Tesson, your Grace. The daughter of the Sire de la Roche Tesson. I would speak with you alone, if I may.'

Jeanne turned to her tirewoman. 'Go. Tell the monk to give you the keys and send him away. Stand watch over the door.'

The door closed behind the servant. 'You escaped from prison in Carentan and joined the English,' Jeanne said. 'Did you know there is a price on your head?'

'It does not matter. Your Grace, I am here to warn you.'

'Against what?'

'King Edward has sent messengers to find you. He wants you to join him and lead a new Norman revolt against King Philippe. Your Grace, you must not do so. Not yet.'

Jeanne took her time about answering. 'I am a loyal subject of France. I have no intention of rebelling against my king.'

'Of course not, your Grace,' Tiphaine said. 'But King Edward will continue to press you. The time may come when you must choose between England and France.'

'Indeed. It would seem you have already made your choice. Like Godefroi d'Harcourt and Raoul of Eu, you have opted for England.'

'No,' Tiphaine said. 'I have not. My heart and my soul belong to Normandy, and always will. I will do whatever it takes to free my country from the French yoke.'

Silence fell for a moment. Jeanne took off her riding gloves and dropped them on the table, flexing her long fingers. 'You say this, but then you advise me against rebellion. Why?'

'Because the time is not right, and because Edward of England is an unreliable ally. He is domesticating the Norman lords. Harcourt is his already. He will turn Eu into his servant as well, and desires to do the same to you. His intention is that the three of you will rule Normandy as English puppets, exchanging one master for another. But without you, his plan will fall apart.'

'And we will go merrily on as before,' Jeanne said. 'Normandy is ruled by Philippe and his idiot son and their corrupt councillors and *huissiers* and *greffiers*, who rob and plunder us at will. What I said earlier was wrong. I think I might prefer Edward as my master.'

'But if you fight France now, you will be betrayed,' Tiphaine said emphatically. 'Just like Harcourt. The French received word of his intentions months ago. Did Jean de Fierville work for you?'

'...Yes.'

'Fierville was also reporting to Robert Bertrand. Now Harcourt's friends are dead and his power is broken. He can remain as Edward's lapdog, or he can return and make his peace with Philippe; those are his only choices. Eu tried to make a secret deal with England, abandoning Caen and allowing himself to be captured. But the enemy know about this too, or they will very soon. Someone is working to undermine us, and has been for years. If you rebel now, death or exile will be your fate.'

Jeanne stared at the ragged figure before her. 'You know a great deal, for one so young.'

'I learned much while I was in prison, and more since I have been with the English army. There are many plots and conspiracies, your Grace. Against us, against King Philippe and against King Edward. They are all connected and guided by a single hand. Is Rollond de Brus still in your service?'

In the back of Jeanne's mind an alarm bell began to ring. 'What do you know about Brus?'

'I used to know him well,' Tiphaine said. 'He was your servitor then, or pretended to be. Where is he now?'

'He is in Rouen,' Jeanne said. 'He has taken service with the king's brother, the Count of Alençon.'

Tiphaine's eyes opened wide. 'Of course. Alençon is conspiring to overthrow the king, and Brus is your link to him.' Jeanne said nothing. 'If you join them, they will betray you,' Tiphaine went on. 'Alençon has no more intention of allowing a free Normandy than the king has. This is the season of danger, your Grace. Your best hope is to lie low and let it pass.'

The Queen of Navarre stood for a long time staring at the candle flame, lost in thought. 'Your father was a wise man,' she said eventually. 'I see he bred some of his wisdom into his daughter.'

Tiphaine's mouth twisted. 'His wisdom did not prevent him from being killed. Or mine from following in his footsteps.'

'What do you intend to do?'

'Philippe must not succeed,' said Tiphaine. 'But neither must the conspirators. I intend to stop them both. Then it will be your time. Then is the moment to come out of hiding and strike.'

17

Duranville, 4ᵗʰ of August, 1346
Evening

The army had remained for a day at Lisieux, camped in the smoky fields outside the town while the king and the cardinals discussed the peace proposals. It was a farce, of course, and everyone knew it. 'Do I really have to go through with this nonsense?' the king had asked before the talks started.

'Your Grace must decide that for himself,' Merrivale said. 'But I believe Étienne Aubert is playing some game of his own. It might be useful to listen to him and try to discern what it is.'

'I agree,' said the Bishop of Durham. 'His Eminence is an influential man. It would not be wise to offend him.'

That was not what Merrivale meant and the king knew it. He looked at Rowton. 'What do you think, Eustace?'

'Talk to them, sire,' Rowton said. 'A day will make very little difference.'

So they engaged in talks. Politely and with great courtesy, Cardinal Aubert laid out the papal peace terms, and with equal politeness and courtesy the king tore them to shreds. Vidal, sitting behind his master, looked at Merrivale and rolled his eyes. Another banquet followed, during which the cardinals and their entourage were reunited with their stolen baggage and horses, and in the morning they departed, jogging away towards Rouen to report the failure of their mission to King Philippe.

Even before they were out of sight, the English troops were moving. Progress from Caen to Lisieux had been leisurely, but now Edward gathered his army and, with furious energy, flung it forward fifteen miles across the rolling plain, leaving Lisieux burning behind them. Evening brought them to a dry camp outside the village of Duranville, the sky behind them orange with dust and smoke. Baggage wagons were still rolling in, the tired troops of the rearguard marching up after them, when the king sent for Merrivale.

'I know what you did at Caen, by the way. Using my son against me to try to force me to free Brother Geoffrey.' He held up a hand. 'No, don't bother. The boy showed he had backbone. He stood up for what he thought was right. Good for him.'

'That was not my intention, sire.'

'I know it wasn't. But your action had some positive benefits all the same. You said you thought Étienne Aubert is playing some game of his own. What is it?'

'I don't know, sire. But I am told there is a conspiracy against the adversary, and I believe that he and the Queen of Navarre are both involved. That could explain why the queen has not responded to your messages.'

'Perhaps she is playing more than one game at a time,' the king said.

'Perhaps, sire. I would venture a small wager that the Count of Alençon is involved. And I would guess that the Count of Eu was as well, before he came over to us.'

'Yes.' The king stroked his chin, and Merrivale could almost see the wheels of calculation turning in his mind. 'This wants some careful thought,' he said. 'Do you know, Merrivale, I doubted the wisdom of advancing east from Caen. We are taking a risk, there is no doubt about it. But if Philip's enemies really do attempt to remove him from power, there will be bloody chaos. And if we're camped on his doorstep when it happens, I reckon we are well placed to profit from that chaos.'

The king paused, deep in thought. He was so preoccupied that he did not even notice he had called his adversary by name, something his own court was forbidden to do. 'We'll bring the Count of Eu back into play,' he said. 'By God, that's it. Start a civil war in Normandy and it will spread through all of France. Then we'll seize our chance.'

'Yes, sire. Ideally, though, we need to know more about the conspiracy. At the moment, I only have word from two sources, neither of whom are wholly reliable.'

Thomas Holland had told the truth, but had he told all of it? And Tiphaine's disappearance meant that doubt was growing in the herald's mind. 'Jean de Fierville was involved in both Norman conspiracies,' Merrivale continued. 'And I believe that Edmund Bray knew something about this. If I can discover who killed Bray, then the trail will lead us to the conspirators.'

'For Christ's sake. You're not still harping on about Bray, are you?'

'Yes, sire, I am. Bray's killers, Fierville's partners in treason, the men who planted the gunpowder in the gatehouse at Carentan and tried to poison some of your son's knights; they are one and the same. There is a third conspiracy, sire, directed by the same people, and this one is aimed at England.'

After a moment the king said, 'Who are these people? And for Christ's sake don't say "I don't know".'

'Allow me to continue my inquisition into Bray's death,' the herald said, 'and I will find them.'

'By God, Merrivale, you are stubborn as a cross-grained mule.'

'Yes, sire. Permit me to say that I have also observed the same trait in your Grace.'

'Damn your impertinence. Do whatever it takes, herald, but find these traitors.'

Neubourg, 5th of August, 1346
Evening

There was a new urgency in the air now, a sense of bristling alertness as the troops swung off the road and made camp in the fields around the little town of Neubourg. Today's march had been a punishing one, twenty miles in blistering heat, and now they were nearing Rouen, capital of Normandy and the place where the adversary was gathering his army.

'Behold the hand of brotherly love,' said Sir John Sully wryly, staring at the western sky. Columns of smoke rose towards the sun, burning towns and villages set alight by the army as it passed. They had marched that day through the lands of the Count of Harcourt, Godefroi's elder brother and the leader of the Norman party loyal to King Philip, and the lord Godefroi had taken special pleasure in destroying his brother's lands.

Despite the failure of his plans, Harcourt remained with the army and in high favour. Whatever else one might say of him, King Edward was loyal to his friends.

'And the king has made no objection,' Merrivale said. 'They burned the abbey of Le Bec, too. So much for protection for houses of religion.'

'All wars begin with the best of intentions,' Sully said. 'A clean fight between adversaries, with the innocents protected. It never lasts for long. In the end, it is the innocents who suffer most.'

'And brotherhood amounts to nothing,' Merrivale said. 'What we see here is simply an act of revenge. Burning his towns will not compel the Count of Harcourt to change sides, and Godefroi knows it. This is pure spite.'

They stood in silence for a while, watching the smoke and ignoring the bustle of the camp around them. 'May I speak to you privately, Sir John?' Merrivale asked.

'Of course.' They walked away from the camp, Sully's dog at his heels and Matt and Pip trailing them at a discreet distance. Matt and Pip; even now, Merrivale found he could not think of them as Matilda and Philippa. He wondered how Nicholas Courcy was faring. He had seen Courcy and his wife together on the march, laughing with the gallowglasses, apparently inseparable. Human nature is a strange and peculiar thing, he thought.

For the hundredth time, he wondered where Tiphaine was, and whether she was safe.

'What troubles you, boy?' Sully asked.

'History,' Merrivale said.

'You might have to narrow it down a little.'

'The year 1327,' Merrivale said. 'Bray's father was at Berkeley Castle, along with Robert Holland and Macio Chauffin. Mortimer's grandfather had already killed the Despensers, and he sent Holland to give the order to kill the king. With him was another man, with a device of three black chevrons on yellow.' He looked steadily at Sully. 'Do you remember him?'

'Aye,' said Sully quietly. 'I do. John of Hainault, Lord of Beaumont and uncle of our Queen Philippa.'

'I didn't remember him at first, when Chauffin mentioned him, but I had just started as a messenger and was often away from court. I only saw him once or twice. But you knew him, I think.'

'He was a comrade in arms, of sorts. We served together at Berwick, and Halidon Hill. Then he went back home to Hainault.'

'Tell me about him, Sir John.'

'When the Earl of March and the King's mother, Queen Isabella, returned to England, Hainault commanded the army that escorted them. He was Mortimer's loyal lieutenant, helping him hunt down supporters of the king and the Despensers. For a time, anyway.'

'What do you mean?'

'There were many rumours flying about. Some said Hainault's real master wasn't Mortimer, but the King of France, who was controlling events from the shadows. Isabella, after all, was the French king's daughter.' Sully paused. 'And now you say he was there at Berkeley that night.'

'So I have been told. These rumours you speak of. Did they link him to the king's death?'

'There were whispers,' Sully said. 'And perhaps that he had a hand in the execution of the old king's brother, Edmund of Kent. After that, it was pretty obvious what the plan was. Once his father and uncle were dead, the young king would die too, and Isabella and Mortimer would rule, with Hainault as the French pro-consul, guiding their hands. Fortunately the king had a wise head on young shoulders, and pre-empted them.'

'After the queen and Mortimer were arrested, what did Hainault do?'

'Changed sides at once, of course, and pledged his loyalty to the king. He was instrumental in helping the king become reconciled to some of his late father's enemies. For example, it was he who procured a pardon for Sir John de Tracey of Dunkeswell and his sons.'

'Did Hainault remain long in the country?'

'A few years. Then he went back home, in hopes of wresting control of Hainault and Holland from his brother. When that failed, he went to France and joined the court of the adversary. He is now one of King Philip's most trusted councillors.'

The man who had brought the orders to kill the King of England standing now at the right hand of the King of France. The herald gave an involuntary shiver. Sully glanced at him. 'What's wrong, boy? Someone walk over your grave?'

'Perhaps,' the herald said. 'Or perhaps it wasn't my grave.'

Neubourg, 6th of August, 1346
Late afternoon

'It was a trap, of course,' Sir John Grey said. 'They abandoned the southern faubourgs and let us burn those, while they were concealed in the towers at the south end of the bridge. Then they waited until we were within crossbow range and shot us to pieces.'

All around them men were riding back into the camp outside Neubourg, the remnants of the reconnaissance party Godefroi d'Harcourt had led out towards Rouen that morning. Some were pale with pain, black crossbow bolts still embedded in their armour. An esquire led a horse with the body of an armoured man draped across the saddle, arms dangling loose. The horse had been wounded too, and its blood and that of its dead master leaked together onto the ground. 'John Daunay,' said Grey. 'A good man, or at least he was.'

'How many did you lose?' asked Merrivale.

'Of our company? None. But there's at least two men-at-arms dead, and a score of hobelars and archers.'

'And the bridge?' asked Nicholas Courcy. 'Can we force it?'

Grey shook his head. 'The centre of the span has been broken down, and there is a barricade and more towers at the north end. Even if we managed to repair the bridge under fire, our losses would be disastrous, and we would then have to fight our way through the streets of Rouen against the French army.'

'Are there other bridges?' asked Gráinne.

The appearance of the Lady Gráinne MacCarthaigh Riabhach had caused a stir in the army, but the sensation had been brief. The troops were already used to the sight of Courcy's wife in her antiquated armour and now paid her little attention. Gráinne herself seemed determined to stay with her husband, though whether this was due to infatuation or mistrust, the herald was not quite certain. Probably a mixture of both, he thought.

'Downstream, no,' Grey said. 'The river broadens out into a tidal estuary, and is unbridgeable and unfordable. Upstream, there are six bridges: Elbeuf, Pont de l'Arche, Vernon, Mantes, Meulan and Poissy.'

'Then we'll have to seize and cross one of them,' Courcy said.

'Yes,' Grey said. 'I will wager any amount of money you care to name that every one of those bridges has been broken down or is heavily defended, or both. I said this was a trap. And we have advanced towards it willingly and stuck our neck into its jaws.'

'We could retreat,' said Roger Mortimer, who had just joined them. He had a dent the size of a goose egg in his breastplate where a crossbow bolt had hit him but failed to penetrate his armour.

Grey shook his head. 'If the king gives the order to retreat now, the army will melt away. By the time we reach the coast, there won't be one man in five still with the banners. You have studied history, Sir Nicholas; you know what happens when an army retreats.'

'I have,' Courcy agreed. 'Our only choice is to advance, and hope to Christ we can find a way across the river.'

'And then bring the French to battle,' Mortimer said. 'Surely we will defeat them easily.'

Courcy's voice was weary. 'My boy, you have no idea. We took losses at Caen, and we left garrisons there and in Carentan, and that's not counting the ones who deserted after Caen to go home and count their loot. We've barely thirteen thousand men left now, out of the fifteen thousand we started with. And we're ranged against the French royal army, plus God knows how many Genoese crossbowmen and all of France's allies from around Europe: the Empire, Bohemia, Savoy, Majorca. We stand about as much chance as a snowflake in hell.'

'Then what are we going to do?'

'Find a way across the Seine,' Courcy repeated. 'Then evade the French army and escape north to Flanders.'

Grey agreed. 'If we can join the Flemish rebels and the English forces in the north, we might just have enough men to stand up to the French. The question is, how are we going to get across this goddamned river?'

No one had an answer. Mortimer departed, holding his side. He would have a serious bruise where the crossbow bolt had hit him, Merrivale thought, and quite possibly a cracked rib or two. Courcy and Gráinne followed him. Grey looked at the herald. 'Are my watch-dogs giving good service?'

'There have been no further attempts to kill me,' Merrivale said. 'You called our situation a trap.'

'Of course it is,' Grey said. 'We have been manoeuvred into it ever since we left Caen. Keep us penned up south of the river, let us batter ourselves to pieces against the bridges, and when we grow weak, cross the river and smash us. We have been gulled, herald. Haven't we?'

Merrivale said nothing. Grey looked him directly in the eye. 'Is someone betraying us to the French?'

'Yes,' Merrivale said.

'And are the traitors the same men who persuaded the army to advance from Caen?'

'Yes.'

'I am relieved to hear it,' Grey said sarcastically. 'The other option is that the king and his captains are bungling idiots who know nothing whatever about war, a prospect I find profoundly depressing. Thank you, herald. You have restored my faith in human nature.'

The English raid on the southern faubourgs two days previously had caused panic in Rouen. Most of the population had fled, taking with them anything they could carry. The only things that moved in the streets were the herds of semi-wild pigs that lived by scavenging in the gutters, and royal men-at-arms on patrol. Slipping through the back streets wrapped in a dun cloak with her hood pulled over her face, Tiphaine de Tesson was not sure which were the more dangerous.

Most of the army was quartered in the vast French camp on the high ground north of the city. Earlier, Tiphaine had walked through it, seeing the ranks of pavilions and the glittering coats of arms of the high nobility of France; Blois, Aumale, Lorraine, Hainault, Charles d'Alençon, the king's brother. Down in the river, the galleys lay moored rank upon rank, sails furled and oars at rest, flying their own banners, the red cross of Genoa and the red and white lozenges of Grimaldi, the lord of Monaco. Only at the end of the day did she finally spy the banner she was looking for: the red saltire on gold of the Seigneur de Brus. The sight of it sent a shiver down her spine.

She lingered, steeling herself, and then approached the pavilion and asked the servant outside where his master was. The servant stared at the woman in boy's clothes. 'Why do you want to know?'

'Mind your own business,' Tiphaine said.

The man looked her up and down. 'I don't suppose you'd like to—'

'No. And if you suggest it again, I will kick you where it really hurts.'

The man lost interest. 'He's at the castle. Attending on the Count of Harcourt. But you won't get in there. They close the gates at sundown.'

He was right. As at Caen, the castle at Rouen was located just outside the city walls to the north. Tiphaine arrived outside the Port-Levis, the main gate, just as the chains began to rattle and the massive drawbridge was winched up, the gates slamming shut behind it, leaving her stranded outside. There were bakeries in the northern faubourg;

she stole a loaf of bread from a passing cart and then slipped into the deserted city, where she made herself comfortable for the night in an empty stable. In the morning, dusting off her clothes and picking the hay out of her hair, she made her way back through the city and loitered outside the Port-Levis, a non-descript figure in ragged tunic and hose, waiting for her chance.

A wagon loaded with firewood rumbled past, heading towards the gate, slowing as the driver made the sharp turn onto the drawbridge over the fosse. She ran after it, scrambling onto the back and burrowing in among the wood while the wagon rolled through the gatehouse and came to a halt outside the kitchens. Dropping onto the cobbles, she looked around at the tall towers and the massive cylinder of the donjon, where the hated fleur-de-lys standard streamed in the morning breeze. She drew a deep breath and stopped the first passer-by.

'I have an urgent message for the Seigneur de Brus. Where can I find him?'

The man, a Dominican friar with cold grey eyes, looked at her impassively. 'You will find him in the Tour de Gascon,' he said, pointing.

Guards with spears in mail coats barred the door to the tower. 'What is your business here?' one demanded.

'I wish to speak to the Seigneur de Brus. Tell him Tiphaine is here.'

After five minutes of waiting, with the clatter and bustle of an army preparing for war all around her, the door opened and Rollond de Brus stepped out into the courtyard. Tiphaine studied him critically, hoping to see signs of imperfection or ageing: a receding hairline, perhaps, or wrinkles around his eyes. But no, he was the same as ever: tall, smooth-skinned with an overlay of sunburn, his fair hair fashionably curled, his doublet and hose uncreased and unstained. He looks more like a wall painting than a real man, she thought, but then he always did. He had about as much personality, too.

His blue eyes widened. 'Tiphaine! How intriguing to find you here.'

'I need to talk with you,' she said. 'Privately.'

'Come with me.' He led the way inside, up to a bare little chamber on the first floor of the tower; it had a single narrow window. 'Sit down,' he said, pulling up a bench. 'Tell me what I can do for you.'

She sat, gazing up at him as he stood by the door. 'Truly? You are willing to help me?'

Brus smiled. The first time she had seen that smile, it had melted her heart. By the end of their romance, it had been like a file rasping on her nerves. There had only ever been one thing between them, and so far as she was concerned, that fire had soon died.

'You must have known I would be willing,' he said. 'Otherwise, you would not have come here. What do you need? Say the word.'

Tiphaine fought to control the trembling in her legs. 'I need to know about Jean de Fierville.'

'Ah.' Brus stroked his chin for a moment. 'My late and unlamented cousin. What do you wish to know?'

'Who was paying him when he died?'

'My dear, everyone was paying him. He was in Godefroi d'Harcourt's retinue, but he was also receiving a retainer from the Queen of Navarre and, of course, from Robert Bertrand. Jean was like that. Loyalties did not bind him, faith did not hold him. All that interested him was gold.'

Brus paused, looking at her. 'Why does it matter, now that he is dead?'

'He betrayed Harcourt this year, and some of my father's friends along with him. I wonder if he betrayed my father as well.'

'I would not answer that even if I could. Your father and I were on opposite sides. Remember?'

'But you and I were not,' Tiphaine said. 'There was a time when we were inseparable. Remember?'

'And then you left. You ran away.' Brus paused, 'I missed you, you know.'

'I am sorry,' Tiphaine said. 'I never intended to cause you hurt.'

'But you did, all the same. You should have stayed with me, Tiphaine. As my wife, you would have been untouchable.'

'Do you think that is all I care about? My own safety?'

Brus said nothing. 'When did Fierville first have dealings with the English?' Tiphaine asked.

'Why should I answer that question? Are you here to make amends? Do you wish to come back to me?'

Tiphaine steeled herself. 'If you answer my questions, I will return to you,' she said. 'I will be your lover again, if you wish it. Even your wife.'

Brus stared at her for a long time, and then a slow smile spread across his face. She could see the joy dancing in his eyes.

'Jean led a contingent of Norman ships that joined the French fleet in the summer of 1338,' he said. 'They burned their way along the south coast of England, sacked Portsmouth and then took Southampton. Jean had some sort of spy in the city, a man who helped him rob one of the biggest moneylenders of all his gold and silver. He sold slaves too, girls mostly, but some boys as well, and got a very good price for them. There are parts of the world where English slaves are very much sought after.'

Tiphaine shivered. 'What happened to them? The slaves?'

'As I recall, he sold them in England. He had a dealer there, already lined up.'

'He sold English slaves to another Englishman?'

'I know. I have always said the English have no morals. Perhaps slavery is all they are really good for.'

'Who was this agent?'

'Tiphaine, I fail to see why this is so important. Jean is dead. He is no longer a danger to anyone.'

'No, but his masters are. You were wrong, Rollond, he was loyal. He served his true masters faithfully to the end.'

Brus's eyes narrowed a little. 'His true masters?'

'The ones who betrayed Harcourt and my father. The ones who will betray Jeanne of Navarre. And the ones who will betray King Philippe and bring him to his death.'

'Ah.' Brus's eyes narrowed a little. 'And these masters. Do you know who they are?'

'Not yet. But tell me who Fierville's contact in England was and I may be able to find them. When I do, I will tell you, and you can get the credit for saving the king.' Tiphaine watched his face. 'Unless, of course, you too are one of the plotters.'

A long silence followed. Dust motes glinted silver in the sunlight falling through the window.

'Jean sold his slaves to Sir John de Tracey,' Brus said finally. 'Ah. I see the name means something to you.'

'Perhaps,' Tiphaine said. 'I don't know.'

'Don't you? Well, never mind. As I said, it hardly matters now.' Brus walked towards the door and opened it. 'So. Will you keep your word? Will you come back to me?'

Tiphaine swallowed. 'Yes. If that is your wish.'

'If that is my wish,' Brus repeated, and the same slow smile crossed his face. She saw the look in his eyes, and realised with horror what she had done.

'Do you know what hurt most when you left me, little Tiphaine?' he asked. 'The mockery of my friends. They made me into a jest, the man who could not keep a woman, not even a plain little scrap of a thing like you. You never had the power to wound me, but my friends, oh yes. It took a long time for their mockery to fade.'

'You never cared for me,' Tiphaine said. 'You had no intention of marrying me.'

'You were good for one thing only. One thing, and you weren't even very good at that. As for marriage, I would sooner have married a pox-ridden whore lying in a ditch than the daughter of a traitor.' He opened the door and called down the stairs. 'Seize her! Take her to the count!'

The great hall of Rouen Castle was full of activity, clerks carrying stacks of parchment, messengers and pages bringing in muster rolls and returns of supply. At the high table, a tall man stood staring down at a map unrolled before him, chess pieces weighing the corners to keep them from curling up. Despite the heat of the day, he wore a heavy blue robe powdered with gold fleurs-de-lys and an ermine collar. 'The English failed at Elbeuf,' he was saying to the man beside him. 'Now they are attacking Pont de l'Arche, but du Bosq and Mesnil will hold them. That means they will move on to Vernon. Are the defences in place, Montmorency?'

'Yes, your Imperial Majesty. We have put two thousand men-at-arms and a thousand crossbows into the town. And the walls of Vernon were repaired only last year.'

'Good, good. Keep pushing the English east towards Paris. That's where we'll pin them down. We will finish this at Poissy, just as we planned. By God, Cousin Edward is playing into our hands. I thought he was a better commander than this.' The tall man looked up sharply. 'Yes, Brus? What is it?'

Brus bowed. 'May I have a moment of your time, your Imperial Majesty?'

'Of course.' Charles, Count of Alençon and Perche, also claimed the title of Emperor of Constantinople, and liked people to use it. It also annoyed his brother the king, who was simply styled 'your Grace' and resented Alençon's attempt to outrank him. 'What is it?'

Two soldiers dragged Tiphaine forward and threw her onto the flagstones in front of the table. 'We caught this woman creeping into the castle, disguised as a man,' Brus said. 'Fortunately, I recognised her. She is Tiphaine de Tesson, daughter of the executed traitor Jean de la Roche Tesson. I have reason to believe she is also an English spy.'

'Oh? Why?'

'I interrogated her before I brought her here, your Majesty. She was asking questions about Jean de Fierville.'

'Fierville! How does she know about him?'

'Doubtless the English told her, your Majesty, which is clear proof of her guilt. I ask that she be placed on trial as a spy.'

Alençon raised his eyebrows. 'There is no need. Have you forgotten? Since her escape from Carentan, she is attainted. She can be executed without trial.'

'Then shall we carry out the sentence?'

'Not yet. We're too busy dealing with the English, and I want to be there when she dies. The king will wish to be there as well. Take her to La Roche-Guyon, and see she is held securely. And make certain there is plenty of firewood in store at the castle. We shall need it.'

Tiphaine raised her head then, staring up at Alençon in horror. 'Yes,' the count said, and he smiled. 'You know the penalty for treason, *demoiselle*. For a man, it is drawing and quartering. For a woman, it is burning alive.'

18

'Christ!' said Sir Thomas Holland through clenched teeth. 'Pull it out!'

The one-eyed knight lay sprawled on the grass, a black crossbow bolt protruding from his shoulder, punched deep through armour and doublet and embedded in the flesh beneath.

'I can't, sir,' said his esquire. 'It is wedged in too tightly.'

'Take off his armour,' the herald instructed. 'The spaulder and the rerebrace both. Quickly now, lad. Cut the straps if you must. The longer that bolt is embedded in the flesh, the more likely it is the wound will become contaminated.'

Pale, his hands already stained with blood, the esquire obeyed, casting aside the shoulder and arm guards and taking a fresh grip on the bolt. Holland gasped and slammed his fist on the ground with pain, but this time the bolt gave up its grip and pulled free. Blood flowed, ruby red in the sunlight. 'Staunch the wound,' the herald instructed. 'Then wash it out with a mixture of vinegar and clean water. It will be painful, but it will keep the infection at bay.'

The esquire looked helpless. 'Where do I find vinegar, sir?'

Merrivale looked around. A column of wagons was passing down the road towards Vernon, followed by a herd of cattle chivvied along by a girl with a stick. 'That is the royal kitchen,' he said. 'Find Master Clerebaud, the sauce-maker. He will give you vinegar.'

The esquire scrambled onto his horse and rode away after the wagons. Merrivale studied the flow of blood from the wounded shoulder and watched it began to slow. 'Shouldn't you put a compress on that?' Holland asked.

'Later, after the wound has been washed. Rest easy, Sir Thomas.'

The stink of burning filled their nostrils, just as it had done for weeks. Behind the English army lay a trail of ruins twenty miles wide, hamlets and farms, rich towns and monasteries, all reduced to rubble and glowing embers. Close at hand the town and castle of Gaillon were burning fiercely while the English archers and Welsh spearmen hunted the last French defenders to annihilation among the ruins. But they had held up the vanguard for several hours and Thomas Holland was only one of many casualties. Up ahead, more smoke rose as the king's division, bypassing the fighting at Gaillon, began smashing its way through the suburbs of Vernon, hoping to break through to the bridge.

As the English army had moved east, the French had left Rouen and tracked them along the north bank, ready to throw them back should they manage to gain a foothold across the river. Any hope of aid from Jeanne of Navarre had been dashed too. As the herald knew, message after message had been sent to Évreux. No reply had come.

Holland stirred a little, and when he spoke, his voice was slurred with pain. 'Did I hear you send my esquire to ask the king's sauce-maker for vinegar?'

'Yes.'

A note of humour etched its way through the pain. 'Better hope he doesn't put wolf's-bane in it. Are you any closer to finding out who did that? Or do you believe this story that Despenser put it there himself to get even with Mortimer?'

Merrivale wondered how widely this tale was circulating in the army, and whether Despenser had heard it yet. 'No,' he said. 'I do not believe it. As a matter of interest, Sir Thomas, why did you recommend that I be put in charge of this inquisition?'

'You won't believe it, but if there is an assassin among us, I think you are the best person to track him down. I know from experience how goddamned tenacious you are. And I also know you are honest.'

The herald smiled a little. 'Thank you for the compliments.'

'Take them. They're the last you're likely to get from me... God, my arm feels like it's on fire.'

'Perhaps a little light conversation would distract you.'

'Oh? What subject did you have in mind?'

'The twenty-first of September 1327,' the herald said.

'Oh Christ, not that again. You really are like a dog with a bone, aren't you?'

'Three men rode to Berkeley Castle, carrying Mortimer's orders to kill the king. One was your father. The second was John of Hainault, Lord of Beaumont and the enforcer of Mortimer's will. Who was the third?'

'I don't know. I wasn't there.'

'Of course. How well did your father know John of Hainault?'

Holland considered the matter for a moment. 'Fairly well, I suppose. It was Hainault who interceded to get his lands restored. Not that it did much good. Six months later, he was dead.'

'Who else was close to Hainault? Who did he consort with?'

'At the time of the old king's death? I don't know. Later, after Mortimer was gone, he helped a number of men to be reconciled with the king. Lord Rowton was one of them.'

Merrivale stared at him. 'Eustace Rowton?'

'No, his father. Gerard Rowton had been one of Mortimer's supporters after he returned, although I believe they quarrelled not long before Mortimer's fall from grace. Holland grimaced. 'Jesus, this hurts. Where is my damned esquire?'

'He is coming,' Merrivale said.

The esquire pulled his horse to a halt and jumped down holding a flask and a pannier. Merrivale took them from him, poured vinegar from the flask into the pannier and added water from a waterskin, then gently drizzled the liquid across the wound. Holland stiffened, biting his lip in agony. 'Now dry the wound and bind it closely,' Merrivale said to the esquire. 'Change the dressing regularly, and if you smell putrefaction in the wound, repeat the treatment with vinegar and water.'

'Yes, sir.' The esquire began drying the wound with a square of linen.

'How are your men faring?' Merrivale asked Holland. 'They must be missing their vintenar.'

'We all miss him. Bate was a good soldier. We would have taken Gaillon quicker if he had been there.'

'And the others? Are they still selling their plunder to Nicodemus?'

'I don't know,' said Holland. 'And what is more' he added, with the insouciance of a man with eighty thousand florins in the bank, 'I no longer care.'

Vernon, 9th of August, 1346
Evening

Blackened with smoke, the walls of Vernon stood intact, French banners waving from their towers. Beyond the walls, the bridge could be seen, lined with houses and watermills, stretching away to the north bank. And up on the escarpment overlooking the far end of the bridge, the French royal army waited, rank upon rank of mounted men-at-arms in bright surcoats and glittering armour, thousands of white-coated Genoese crossbowmen all looking across the river and watching; powerful, ominous, waiting.

Overhead, the clouds drifted, thunder rumbling distant in the heavy air. Clouds of flies buzzed around, feasting on sweat and blood.

At the water's edge, the grange of the abbey of La Croix was a sheet of flame. Fire was beginning to take hold in the cloister too, roof tiles cracking and sliding to the ground. 'We won't be crossing at Vernon,' said Sir Edward de Tracey, his face and hands black with smoke. 'We set fire to every building in the faubourgs, right up to the walls, in hopes of tempting them out to fight, but they won't budge.'

'And even if they did, it would not matter,' said Hugh Despenser, wiping blood from his face. 'We would still have to fight our way through the town and across the bridge, with no room to deploy our own archers and those goddamned Genoese sweeping the span with crossbows. It is hopeless.'

'It is worse than hopeless,' said John Grey, his voice cold with anger. 'It is folly. We failed at Rouen, we failed at Elbeuf, we failed at Pont de l'Arche, and now we have failed at Vernon. There are three more bridges, gentlemen. Then what?'

No one had an answer. Grey departed to join his company, and Despenser followed him. The two red-capped archers remained behind, lurking watchfully in the middle distance.

'May I have a moment, Sir Edward?' Merrivale asked.

Tracey turned to face him, eyes wary. They had not spoken since their meeting outside Lisieux a week ago. 'What is it? Which of my archers do you want to question me about now?'

'I want to ask about your late father,' Merrivale said.

'My father? He was a callous, murdering old bastard who would have cut your throat for the price of a firkin of ale. I tried to have as little to do with him as possible.'

'He was attainted for a time, was he not? When did he receive his pardon?'

'I think it was 1332,' Tracey said reluctantly. 'The king needed his money, of course, to pay for the Scottish wars. I saw him seldom after that, until the day his horse threw him and he broke his neck. I like to think the beast did it on purpose.'

'When was that?'

'1339, the feast day of Saint Hilarius. Apt, I have always thought.'

'How did he procure his pardon?'

'I have no idea.'

'What about your brother? Might he know?'

Tracey shook his head. 'Gilbert loved our father even less than I did, if such a thing is possible. He was already settled in London by the time the old man went down to hell.'

The roof of the cloister caved in, flames rushing up from the wreckage and sparks dancing in the air. 'Are you certain there is nothing more you can tell me?' Merrivale persisted.

'Mary, Mother of God!' Tracey exploded. He pointed to the burning abbey. 'Here we are, death and destruction all around us, the army fighting for its life, and all you can think about is things that happened twenty years ago.'

'Yes,' said the herald quietly. 'We are fighting for our lives. And yet you and Nicodemus still trade in plundered goods, and you're making more than just a few hundred pounds. I have some idea of how wide your trading network is, and I reckon you have both made a fortune. Or should I say another one, as well as the land you own? Do you need the money so badly, Sir Edward?'

'Rents from land don't pay for a man's upkeep, herald. You of all people should remember that. I have investments in commercial ventures from one end of England to the other, iron mines in the Weald, sea coal in Yorkshire, salt from Nantwich. This is just another venture. Now kindly leave me alone.'

Longueville, 9th of August, 1346
Night

In just a few days, the mood of the army had changed. The attack on Caen and the plundering of the city had sent spirits soaring; the march east to Rouen had been triumphant, confident of victory. But now, everyone in the army knew the obstacle that faced them. They stood along the riverbank, archers and men-at-arms, grooms and farriers, Welsh spearmen and Irish gallowglasses, looking at the watchfires of the French army camped on the heights. The fires, hazy in the smoky air, extended to the horizon in both directions. 'Blessed Jesus,' an archer whispered, 'there's thousands of them. Tens of thousands.'

'*Támid marbh,*' said Donnchad, and he spat on the ground and turned away.

Lightning flickered on the southern horizon, and thunder boomed again just as the herald reached the king's pavilion. 'If you want an audience, I should wait,' Michael Northburgh said as he entered. 'He's angry as a bear. Rowton and the Bishop of Durham went in to see him just now, urging a retreat to Caen. He tore them both to shreds.' The secretary gestured towards the inner chamber. 'They're still in there, trying to calm him down.'

A few raindrops pattered on the canvas overhead. 'It was actually you I came to see, Michael. Sir John Tracey of Dunkeswell was killed while out riding in January 1339. Do you happen to recall the details of his *inquisition post mortem*? I know the records are back in London at the Tower, but I hoped that fine memory of yours might recall their contents.'

Northburgh frowned. 'I remember his death, of course. A controversial man, to say the least. He was killed while riding, you say?'

'Yes. I wondered if there were any further details.'

The secretary shook his head. 'I really don't remember, I fear. But Sir John Sully was escheator for the county of Devon that year. Try him.'

'I had forgotten that. Thank you, Michael, I shall seek him out.' The door of the inner chamber opened and Lord Rowton strode out, still in full armour, his face red with anger. Behind him the king and the bishop could be heard, still arguing. 'My lord,' Merrivale said quickly. 'Might I have a word in private?'

For a moment he thought Rowton was going to ignore him, but his lordship motioned with his hand. 'Come with me,' he said curtly.

Outside, they walked away until they were out of earshot of the guards. The army's campfires flickered around them, a tiny cluster compared to the endless blaze of lights along the north shore. Rowton stopped and took a deep breath. 'What is it?'

'This may seem an odd question to ask at this time and place, my lord. But how well did your late father know John of Hainault?'

Rowton stared at him. 'You are right. That is a damned odd question. Why do you want to know?'

'I have a theory that Bray's death is connected to the events of 1327,' the herald said.

More lightning flashes, and the air growled with thunder. 'Then you already know the answer to your question,' Rowton said.

'I have heard that Hainault helped reconcile your father and the king after Mortimer's death.'

'He did,' Rowton said. 'I was already in the king's household, along with Montacute and Bohun – or Salisbury and Northampton, as they later became – and I asked for clemency for my father. When the king hesitated, I appealed to Hainault. He stepped in and persuaded his Grace.'

'You supported the king, and your father had supported Mortimer. Was that a source of friction between you?'

'Yes,' Rowton said. 'It was. But my father behaved honourably in the end, and was the king's loyal servant until his death.'

Sudden and sharp in the distance came the noise of fighting: men shouting, swords clashing on armour. A trumpet called urgently, blowing the alarm. Before Merrivale or Rowton could respond, a crossbow bolt came winging out of the darkness, hitting Rowton's vambrace and whirring away into the shadows. He shouted with pain, stumbling to his knees and clutching at his arm. Hooded men in dark clothing were swarming up from the river, dim silhouettes against the watchfires, and more shouts and screams broke out. Merrivale turned to call for Matt and Pip, but there was no need; they were already at his shoulders, shooting fast and accurately into the press of men. Three went down, two more clutched at arrows embedded in their bodies. Another crossbow bolt hissed past Merrivale's ear, and then the dark figures were surging around them.

'*Fág a' Bealach! Fág a' Bealach!*' Out of the darkness came the gallowglasses, slamming into the enemy and pushing them back. Merrivale caught a glimpse of Courcy, swinging his sword, and beside him Gráinne raising her blade and driving it through the chest of a crossbowman just as he lifted his weapon to take aim. More men came flooding in; these wore the caps of the Red Company, a solid hedge of spearmen with archers behind. As suddenly as they had come, the enemy melted away, leaving a scattering of bodies on the ground.

Merrivale bent over Lord Rowton. 'My lord. Are you badly hurt?'

Rowton wrenched off his dented vambrace and tried to flex his fingers, grimacing in pain. 'God, it's broken, Those bastards broke my fucking arm. Who the hell were they? Where did they come from?'

'The river,' said Sir Richard Percy, coming through the press with a bloody sword in his hand. 'They came across by boat. We spotted them landing just below the camp of the prince's division, and drove them back into the river. But while we were busy, this lot slipped past us and attacked the king's camp as well. Thank God you and his lordship spotted them before they could reach his Grace.'

'They didn't attack the king's pavilion,' Merrivale said. 'They attacked us. Without your two watchdogs and the arrival of Sir Nicholas and his men, we would be dead.'

The Red Company were dragging the dead men together. Matt and Pip pulled arrows out of the bodies and began carefully cleaning the arrowheads. Merrivale followed them, looking down at the dead men. 'Who were they?' he asked.

'An excellent question,' said Percy. 'They're not French or Genoese, not with those weapons. Those big crossbows look like Flemish arbalests. And those short, broad-bladed swords could be Spanish, but many Spanish blade-makers have settled in Flanders.'

Something glinted in the firelight, a clasp brooch on one of the dead men's cloaks. Reaching down, Merrivale unfastened it and held it up to the light. Crudely painted on metal was a badge, black chevrons on a yellow field.

'Flanders?' he asked. 'Or Hainault, perhaps?' He turned to Rowton, who was on his feet again, cradling his broken arm, his face set with pain. 'My lord, I think you should see this.'

Rowton glanced at the badge. 'John of Hainault,' he said slowly.

'Yes. We appear to have summoned the devil. One moment we are talking about Hainault, and the next his men are coming out of the night to kill us. What might we have done to attract his attention, do you suppose?'

–

The Prince of Wales's camp, when Merrivale returned, was in uproar. More fires had been lit and men were milling about in confusion, some dragging bodies away through the drizzling rain. Among the dead were several English archers and spearmen. Sir Thomas Ughtred, the under-marshal, confirmed what had happened. 'While the Red Company were driving the main body back, small parties slipped into the camp. There was some bloody fighting before we drove them off.'

Lightning flashed, far away; the storm was moving on. 'What do you think their purpose was?' the herald asked. 'To sow confusion?'

'Oh, that all right, but some captains were deliberately attacked. Warwick, myself, Sully, Holland, Despenser and Tracey all appear to have been targets. Tracey in particular was hard pressed. He lost two men before young Mortimer and some of the prince's knights came to his aid.'

Tracey was cleaning blood off his hands when Merrivale found him. 'It was an assassination,' the Devon knight said. 'They cut my men down and were inside my tent almost before I could draw sword. I was fighting for my life when Mortimer arrived.' He bowed to the younger man. 'I owe you a debt, sir.'

'Think nothing of it,' said Mortimer, still breathing deeply.

Another man was suddenly alongside them, drawn sword in hand, and they realised it was the Prince of Wales. 'What has happened here?' Tracey told him.

'Two good men,' the prince said. 'Very well, I want the night guards doubled from now on. We must have no more such incidents. Sir Edward, I am very glad to see you are safe.' He laid a hand on Mortimer's shoulder. 'As for you, Roger, very well done.'

The prince walked away through the camp, calling out to his men. Bartholomew Burghersh, following him, glanced at the herald and their eyes met briefly before Burghersh moved on. Merrivale looked at Mortimer and saw conflicting emotions in his face: the old bitterness, mixed with something raw and confused.

One of Tracey's archers ran up, touching his forehead in salute. 'The rest of them got away, sir. We took no prisoners.'

'Where is Nicodemus?' Tracey asked.

The archer looked worried. 'I'm afraid he's gone, sir.'

'Gone? What do you mean, gone?'

'He's vanished, sir. There ain't a trace of him, nowhere.'

Freneuse, 10th of August, 1346
Afternoon

The previous night's storm had done nothing to lessen the heat and humidity. The army sweated and toiled in the heat as it pressed on upriver towards the next bridge at Mantes. Across the river, the vast French army matched it step-for-step, banners waving and spear points shining like a bright forest, flowing along the north bank past the massive walls and keep of the castle of La Roche-Guyon.

'After Mantes, there are only two more bridges,' the Earl of Salisbury said. 'And Paris is only forty miles away.'

'Never mind,' said the prince. 'We will gain the victory in the end. My father will find a way.'

'I am sure he will, Highness,' said Salisbury, but his was not the only face that looked dubious. Mortimer remained silent, watching the French across the river.

The wind died away, and the heat increased still further. The herald turned his horse and, followed by Warin, rode back along the column until he came to Sir John Sully's company, the ermine and red chevrons hanging limp in the lifeless air. The old knight greeted him with his usual good cheer.

'I'm glad to see you well, boy. I hear you had a close call last night.'

'It felt like it at the time. Now I am not so sure. Are you?'

Sully studied him for a moment as they rode side by side. The dog trotted between them, glancing up at his master from time to time. 'So. Those men last night were play-actors? Putting on a piece of mummery for our benefit?'

'They didn't press home their attacks. They could have killed Lord Rowton and myself with ease, but they hung back.'

Sully nodded. 'My men put them to flight easily enough.'

'And yet the attack was meticulously planned. But for the alertness of the Red Company, we would never have seen them coming. Whoever organised them was careful to give them Flemish weapons, knowing that Hainault and Flanders are adjacent. And in case we missed that point, one of the dead men wore a brooch with John of Hainault's colours.'

'That's hardly surprising, though, is it? Hainault is the enemy.'

'Yes. Sir John, I have another question for you. When you were escheator of Devon, did you conduct the *inquisition post mortem* into Sir John de Tracey of Dunkeswell?'

'I did.'

'Do you recall the cause of death?'

'He was out riding, as I recall. A hunting party, I think. His horse threw him, and he broke his neck when he fell.'

'Was there anything suspicious about his death? Tracey had plenty of enemies. Even his own sons disliked him.'

'You're right, and hunts are notoriously good places for disposing of men and making it look like an accident. There were no witnesses who saw him fall. His other son, Gilbert, discovered the body and worked out what had happened. No tears were shed at his funeral.'

One of the royal serjeants rode up alongside them, raising his visor and saluting. 'Sir Herald? His Grace summons you.'

Nodding farewell to Sully, Merrivale turned his horse and followed the serjeant back towards the village of Freneuse on the riverbank. Grey and white columns of smoke rose all around them, but Freneuse itself had not yet been burned. He saw the royal standard there, and alongside it the banners of the two cardinals, Étienne Aubert and Annibale Ceccano. The two men stood conversing calmly with the king, their red robes like splashes of flame against the green river beyond.

As Merrivale dismounted, handing over the reins to Warin. Raimon Vidal laid a hand on his shoulder. 'In the name of God, it is hot,' the Franciscan said, wiping the sweat from his face with his brown sleeve. 'How are you, my friend? I think things do not go so well for your army, no?'

'We have not given up,' Merrivale said. 'Do the cardinals bring new peace proposals?'

'No, it is the same old dish, reheated and served on a new plate. I doubt if your king will be so polite as he was the last time, and I suspect we will soon be on our way once more. While we wait for our exodus, I have some news for you. Some good, some perhaps not so good.'

'One cannot have everything,' Merrivale said.

'Indeed, it is so. The good news first. Your friend Brother Geoffrey of Maldon has been released from prison in Caen.'

Merrivale did not attempt to disguise his relief. 'I know I have you to thank for this.'

'I merely spoke to the cardinal. He did the rest. Brother Geoffrey is on his way back to England. He is a little worse for wear, but I am assured that Bishop Bertrand's gaolers did him no permanent damage.'

'I am very glad to hear it.'

'I was certain you would be. You may not be so sanguine, however, when I tell you my next piece of news. King Philippe's men arrested an English spy in Rouen a couple of days ago.' Vidal watched the herald's face. 'A woman,' he said.

'What was her name?' Merrivale asked quietly.

'She is called the Demoiselle Tiphaine de Tesson. I fear things will not go well for her. Since she escaped from Carentan and joined your army, she is under sentence of death as a traitor. That sentence will shortly be carried out.'

'I see,' Merrivale said. 'Where is she now?'

Vidal pointed to the grey stone fortifications of La Roche-Guyon, towering grim on the north bank. 'She is there. Locked up in a cell from which there is no escape, inside a powerful castle. Ironic, is it not? You are so close, but you cannot see her, or she you. But if you rise early in the morning, you might able to see the smoke from her pyre rising over the castle walls.'

Vidal paused for a moment. His voice, when he resumed, was entirely neutral, but there was a trace of sympathy in his dark eyes. 'If you watch closely, you might even catch a glimpse of her soul as it goes, rising towards heaven.'

19

The pyre was already prepared in the upper courtyard, a wooden platform with a tall stake in its midst, and faggots of dry wood stacked all around. The smell of pine resin was thick in the air. She shivered a little, and one of her guards noticed and laughed.

'The wood smells sweet, doesn't it? Not half so sweet as you'll smell burning, you traitorous bitch.'

Rollond de Brus strode down the steps from the entrance to the donjon. He had ridden on ahead to prepare her reception, and had taken advantage of the moment to change out of riding clothes into courtly doublet and hose. Of course, he had, Tiphaine thought. Vanity is what this man lives for. That is why I am to be burned; to heal his injured pride.

'Bring her inside,' Brus said curtly. 'Our hostesses want a look at her before she goes down to her cell.'

The guards dragged her down from the saddle and stood her upright, still in her filthy tunic and hose with her hands bound tightly in front of her. Her hands tingled and her wrists were rubbed raw by her bonds. One of the guards shoved her in the back and she followed Brus up the stairs and into the donjon, through an antechamber and into a dark circular chamber. Despite the evening's heat, the stone tower was cold, and a fire burned in the grate at the back of the room. Lamps flickered in sconces around the whitewashed stone walls.

The hall was crowded with people. She saw a couple of priests in black robes, but the rest were women: noblewomen in gowns and cauled headdresses with jewels sparkling darkly in the light, nuns in black habits and wimples, all staring at her in a mixture of fear and anger. Brus bowed to them with a flourish, bending one knee.

'*Mesdames*,' he said. 'Allow me to introduce our guest, the Demoiselle de Tesson. I regret the inconvenience of housing her here, but do not fear; she will not outstay her welcome.' He smiled. 'She will, ah... how shall I put it? She will *depart* in the morning.'

Some of the women laughed openly. One of the nuns, her face hard as a slab, walked up to Tiphaine and slapped her across the face, twice. Tiphaine's head rocked back and she felt the blood rush to her bruised cheeks.

'You accursed harlot!' the nun snapped. 'You whore of Babylon! You have brought the English upon us! My convent has been despoiled and burned, my nuns dispossessed, our lands ruined and our tenants robbed of all they possess.'

'I did not bring—'

The nun slapped her again, then spat in her face. Held rigid between her guards, Tiphaine could not move or respond. She felt the spittle running down her forehead. 'Silence!' the nun screamed. 'Do not speak, harlot! Go to your cell and wait until the hour of your execution! Do not expect us to pray for your soul, for that would be blasphemy. You sold your soul to the English and the devil!'

'Take her down,' Brus said to the guards.

'Farewell, *demoiselle*!' shouted one of the noblewomen. 'Tomorrow I shall enjoy watching you burn!' Others joined in the clamour. Brus motioned with his hand and the guards seized Tiphaine's arms and dragged her down the spiral stair into the darkness below, her heels bumping on the stone steps.

At the bottom of the stair was a heavy door. Brus unlocked it and pushed it open, and the guards shoved Tiphaine inside, so hard that she stumbled and fell sprawling on the damp cobbled floor. The door slammed shut and the key turned in the lock.

She lay for a moment, gasping in the pitch blackness, and then sat up. Her hand touched something metallic and flaking with rust, and after a moment she realised it was a length of chain. She pulled it towards her, gathering the links in her hand. Suddenly the chain pulled taut. Feeling her way along its length, she bumped into the stone wall of her cell. Her hands groped around the end of the chain and found it affixed to the wall through a metal eye.

The stone around the eye was damp too, and crumbling. Sudden hope seized her. Grabbing the chain in both hands, she heaved with all her strength, hoping to pull it out of the wall. Nothing happened. She tried again, this time bracing her feet against the wall and throwing all of her weight against the chain. Again and again she pulled, straining, arms aching, gasping with effort.

Nothing happened. The chain did not budge.

She stopped, leaning her forehead against the wall and sobbing for breath. It was hopeless; she simply wasn't strong enough. But in the back of her mind, a flame began to burn. No, she thought, I did not survive two years in prison in Carentan in order to end like this. Drawing a long, deep breath, sucking the damp, fetid air into her lungs, she set herself against the wall once more and began to pull.

Freneuse, 10th of August, 1346
Evening

'I need your help,' the herald said.

'For what purpose?' asked John Grey.

'The Demoiselle de Tesson was captured in Rouen, and is now imprisoned in La Roche-Guyon. The French intend to execute her at dawn. We need to bring her out.'

Richard Percy smiled. 'A damsel in distress?'

'I believe she was spying for us when she was taken.'

'You believe?' said Grey.

'She did not confide her plans to me. But if she has information about the French and their movements, we need to hear it.'

'If?' said Percy. 'What if she was caught before she learned anything at all?'

'Then the expedition to free her will be pointless and futile,' the herald said.

John Grey smiled. 'What do you think, Richard?'

'Sounds like the perfect task for the Red Company,' Percy said. He looked at La Roche-Guyon. 'How do we get across the river?'

'Boats. We need to talk to Llewellyn.'

'Which one?'

'Ap Gruffud, the one from Conwy. His men stole some boats at Elbeuf, remember, when the rest of us were trying to force a passage across that godforsaken bridge. Ask if we can borrow them, and some men to row them.'

'All right. I'll bring the boats up and meet you north of Freneuse.'

Percy departed. 'Jacques, François, Rob!' Grey called. 'Get the men together, as quickly as you can. We have work to do.'

Suddenly the camp was full of quiet, purposeful movement, archers and crossbowmen and spearmen collecting their weapons and gathering around their vintenars. 'Are you going to ask Warwick or Northampton for permission?' Merrivale asked.

'No,' said Grey. 'They wouldn't give it, so why bother? Do I take it you are intending to come with us? I can lend you a sword.'

Merrivale shook his head. 'Thank you, but no.'

'Please yourself.' Grey turned to a tall young man in armour with a sword at his belt and a longbow and quiver strapped across his back. 'This is my esquire, Harry Graham. He, Matt and Pip will look after you. Jacques, are we ready? Good, let's get moving. I want to be over the river before Warwick realises we have gone.'

Freneuse, 10th of August, 1346
Night

The sky overhead was inky black, but the lights of campfires and the watchful torches on the walls of La Roche-Guyon reflected off the dark river. The boats lay huddled along the bank, invisible in shadow. Behind them the ground rose sharply into low chalky cliffs, pierced here and there by the doors and windows of troglodyte houses, all deserted.

'Llewellyn agreed to lend us his boats,' Percy said, 'but on one condition.'

'That we come with you,' said Llewellyn. He was a broad-shouldered man in mail corselet with a breastplate over top, armed with a sword and a heavy stabbing spear. 'We haven't had a proper fight since Caen. We're getting bored, man.'

The Welshmen behind him nodded. 'And you'll need more muscle if you're going to crack that castle,' a voice said. Nicholas Courcy stepped forward, the eagles on his faded surcoat almost black in the dim light. Gráinne was beside him, along with Donnchad and the other gallowglasses. He grinned at Merrivale. 'For a herald, you have a knack for getting into trouble.'

'He does,' Grey agreed. He turned to his master bowman. 'Rob, you've scouted the place. What did you see?'

'There's a cluster of wooden houses at the water's edge,' said the archer. 'I saw sentries there, and I wouldn't be surprised if there are men posted in the houses. Immediately behind the houses is the lower bailey, with a strong gatehouse. The gates are open at the moment, but the portcullis is down. The upper bailey is about a hundred feet above the lower, at the top of a vertical cliff face. There are two ways up, an open stair and a covered passage carved through the rock. At the top is another gatehouse, and a high curtain wall around the donjon. All the walls and towers are manned.'

'I doubt they would keep Mistress de Tesson in the lower bailey,' Percy said. 'I reckon she'll be in the donjon.'

'Trust the French to make things difficult for us,' said Courcy, peering up at the dark tower.

'Indeed,' said Merrivale. 'How do you propose to break into the castle, Sir John?'

Grey looked at Percy. 'What do you think, Richard?'

'There is a time for subtle and clever stratagems,' Percy said. 'This isn't one of them. Clear the houses, sweep the wall, cut through the portcullis and then hard and fast up the stair and tunnel. Hold the donjon long enough to get the *demoiselle* out, and then back to the boats.'

'That sounds simple enough,' said Llewellyn. 'So, what are we waiting for?'

La Roche-Guyon, 10th of August, 1346
Night

'There they are, my lord. You can see them now.'

Rollond de Brus squinted into the darkness, staring at the faint shimmer of the river. He had not believed the sentry at first when he claimed to have seen boats moving on the water, but the man had persisted. And there they were, a column of shallops moving under oars along the river, shadows against the greater shadow of the south bank.

'Are they ours, or theirs?' he wondered aloud.

'Can't tell from this distance, my lord.'

Silence fell. The night air had cooled a little but was still clammy with humidity. Brus mopped the sweat from his forehead, straining his eyes into the night as he watched the boats continue upriver. No, wait... was the lead boat turning? Yes, it was... by God, they were all turning, rowing hard now for the north shore and aiming to land just below the lower bailey.

From down the hill he heard a trumpet blowing the alarm. Further uphill the call was repeated, and he heard men running across the cobbles and up the stone steps to their posts on the walls. La Roche-Guyon was powerful and well defended, he thought; why would the English attack it now? The answer came on the heels of the thought; they were here to rescue their spy.

He looked down at the pyre waiting in the courtyard. By God, we'll see about that, he thought. She'll not cheat the executioner, not this time. Alençon would have to be disappointed. Turning, he ran down the spiral stair, shouldering men out of the way as they climbed up to man the defences, and on down to Tiphaine's cell. He knew he needed to go and put on his armour and take command of the defence, but that could wait. This was more important.

Unlocking the door, he drew his sword and stepped inside, peering around in the darkness. Tiphaine, who had been standing behind the door, smashed him across the back of the head with a length of heavy iron chain, and he staggered forward. A second blow, delivered with furious force, knocked him unconscious, and he fell heavily onto the cobbles.

—

'Now,' Richard Percy said quietly. 'Boatmen, turn towards the castle and pull like hell. Crossbowmen, make ready.'

The boats turned and began driving across the water towards the flickering torches of La Roche-Guyon. The men around him crouched in the boats, waiting. Harry Graham sat beside the herald, bow resting on the thwarts beside him. Young though he was, he exuded a calm confidence that Merrivale found reassuring, and Matt and Pip, seated behind them, were ruthless killers. Grey was right, he thought. I have stopped thinking of them as women. They are archers of the Red Company, and I am glad I have them at my back.

Something whipped through the air and struck the water beside the boat with a hard splash. More followed, crossbow bolts hitting the river or thudding into the boats, and one of the Welshmen shouted with pain and dropped his oar, clutching at his bloody arm. The longbowmen of the Red Company were hampered by the crowded boats, but the crossbowmen, crouching in the bows, shot back, picking off the enemy on the waterfront. Steadily the boats pushed on across the dark waters of the Seine.

Keels grated on shingle. The men were over the side in seconds, splashing in the shallows and running up into the town. Harry Graham turned and courteously offered Merrivale a hand. My God, the herald thought, how old does he think I am? They ran up the bank, Matt and Pip flanking them and nocking arrows as they went.

A street lined with half-timbered houses led to the gatehouse. The gates were still open, but they would not be for long. Crossbow bolts continued to fly, shot from the windows and doorways of the houses.

'Clear them out,' said Percy. 'Llewellyn, take the left side, Courcy the right, Red Company straight up the middle. Stop for nothing.'

They ran, a solid corps of spearmen leading the way, the rest following. Genoese crossbowmen leaned out of the windows to shoot at them, and the Red Company's archers fanned out across the street, picking off most of them before they could pull their triggers. A couple of spearmen fell wounded, tumbling down onto the cobbles, but the rest ran on, the air full of flying arrows and bolts, men shouting and yelling, the sounds of screaming behind them as the gallowglasses and the Welsh ran from house to house, smashing down doors, stabbing and killing.

Ahead loomed the gatehouse, gates already swinging shut. John Grey and the leading spearmen charged into the rapidly closing gap. There was a brief flurry of violence and the gates slammed open again. Men were still shooting from the ramparts, but clouds of arrows rose and a Genoese fell from the wall into the street, half a dozen arrows protruding from his body. More bodies lay in the arch under the gatehouse where Red Company men were attacking the portcullis with axes.

'Ware the murder holes!' someone shouted, and they all dodged to one side just as long lances stabbed down through holes in the ceiling, grating on the cobbles. A door in the stone wall slammed open and French men-at-arms charged out into the archway. For a moment Merrivale found himself hemmed against the wall by the mass of struggling, shouting men around him. Then Richard Percy crashed into the press, a dozen spearmen at his back, and the Red Company began howling their war cries – '*Rouge! Roooouge!*' – and they drove French through the archway and out into the open courtyard beyond. The enemy turned to run, and the archers, stepping over the bodies of men bleeding on the ground, shot them one by one, steel points smashing through armour and flesh and bone and stretching the men-at-arms dead or dying on the cobbles.

They were in the lower bailey now, the cliff climbing above them towards the torchlit donjon dark against the clouds. At the top of the hill a trumpet was blowing the alarm, over and over. Close at hand a bowstring twanged, and Merrivale turned to see another crossbowman fall from the ramparts, transfixed by an arrow. Calmly, Pip nocked a fresh shaft and shot another man racing up the stairs towards the upper bailey. Courcy, Gráinne and the gallowglasses ran into the courtyard, followed by Llewellyn and his spearmen. 'Everyone ready?' asked John Grey. 'Now comes the hard part.'

'We'll take the stair,' Percy said. 'The rest of you, up the tunnel. You too, herald. Rob, archers out in front this time.'

Heavy stones came crashing down the stair, hurled from the ramparts above, and the Red Company archers raised their bows and shot at the men silhouetted against the orange clouds, arrows black streaks in the unearthly light. Smoke began to boil up from burning houses below, sparks whirling around them like fireflies. Under cover of the smoke, the archers inched up the stairs, crouching, nocking arrows, rising, shooting and then ducking down again. The stones still fell, but less thickly than before.

Courcy nodded to his men and led the rush into the tunnel, the gallowglasses following with Merrivale and the Welshmen crowding behind. The tunnel was high and steep, the cobbles smooth and worn by the passage of wagon wheels and iron-shod horses, and the men around gasped and swore as they struggled to maintain their footing.

Torchlight flared ahead, the French shouting their own war cry, 'Montjoie! Montjoie Saint-Denis!', and heavily armoured men-at-arms ran down the slope, hurling themselves bodily into the gallowglasses. Courcy was knocked off his feet; Gráinne stood over him, her helm off, bleeding from a cut above one eye, slashing around her. A French knight raised a heavy mace, aiming a blow at her head, and paused in surprise when he realised she was a woman; and in that second of hesitation, Gráinne drove her sword point through his neck. Courcy was up again, the gallowglasses stabbing and slashing, the Welsh pressing forward, men screaming, the stench of hot blood strong in the air, and then they were moving again, driving the French back up the steep slope towards the top of the tunnel.

Gasping and bleeding, they broke out into the open space before the gatehouse. The Red Company were running up the stair, the ramparts were silent above them. A few bodies lay on the ground, pierced by feathered shafts. The gates were shut; the last of the French men-at-arms, with nowhere to run, turned and fought and died. Even as they fell, Red Company men were throwing grapnels over the ramparts of the gatehouse and beginning to climb. A crossbowman leaned over the wall to shoot at them; a dozen bowstrings twanged and the Genoese dropped his bow, which clattered to the ground in front of the gate. His body slumped against the rampart.

The first men reached the rampart and climbed over. There was a brief clatter of fighting beyond the wall, followed by a tense silence; then the gates swung open and the Red Company swarmed inside, followed by the rest. They ducked under the partly lifted portcullis and ran into the upper bailey, the archers picking off the last defenders as they tried to flee. A woman screamed, and Merrivale turned in sudden horror.

Tiphaine stood on the platform above the pyre. She held a sword in her hand. Facing her was a half-circle of nuns in black habits, their faces hard and implacable under their wimples, barring her escape. Below, more nuns with torches were lighting the faggots. In several places the fire had already taken hold.

Merrivale ran towards the pyre. One of the nuns turned towards him, swinging her torch viciously at his head, but he ducked under it and rammed her with his shoulder, knocking her off her feet. Running up the steps to the platform, he found the other nuns barring his way. He tried to dodge past them to reach Tiphaine, but they seized his arms, screaming curses at him and trying to push him over the edge of the platform. Bracing himself, he tore free and shoved the nearest woman hard, throwing her onto her back. Another nun ran at him, spitting in his face and clawing at his eyes; he stepped sideways to avoid her and she tripped on the hem of her long habit and fell, toppling over the edge of the platform into the fire below.

Then Graham was alongside him, and Matt and Pip with arrows at the nock. At the sight of their grim faces, the other nuns hesitated. 'Get back!' the herald commanded.

'English devil-spawn!' one of the women screamed. 'Burn, all of you, burn! Roast in hell for eternity!'

Merrivale grabbed Tiphaine's arm and pulled her down the steps. She was shaking and trembling as though she had a fever. Graham and the two archers followed, the nuns still screaming abuse at them.

John Grey was in the courtyard, receiving reports from the vintenars. 'That's the garrison taken care of, sir,' said one of them. 'There's no one left but the sisters, and the ladies and their servants in the hall.'

'Leave them be,' Grey said. 'What about the enemy?'

An archer ran up, touching his cap in salute. 'The French camp is arming, sir. And there is already a strong company of men-at-arms and crossbowmen coming this way. They'll be here in a few minutes.'

Grey nodded. 'Is this the lady we came for, herald?'

'Yes,' said Merrivale.

'Signal the men to fall back to the boats. Right, everyone. Time to go.'

20

Mantes, 11th of August, 1346
Midday

Another day, another bridge, the herald thought; and this one more impossible than the others. Mantes lay on the south bank of the river, and its defences were even stronger than those of Vernon. After last night's raid at La Roche-Guyon, the garrison was clearly on alert. From the low hill where he stood, Merrivale could see the ramparts bright with gleaming armour and white Genoese surcoats. Beyond the town, the bridge over the Seine was strongly fortified too, and over on the north shore the French army was drawn up, company after company of men-at-arms with brilliant banners streaming in the wind.

The English had not even tried to take Mantes. The men of the vanguard had circled around the town well out of crossbow range and were moving on east, archers trudging through dust and smoke with their bows over their shoulders. Around them, every hamlet and village for miles was burning, a trail of destruction carved through the heart of France. Ostensibly, this was to lure the French over the river and force them to give battle, but everyone knew that strategy was not working and would never work. No, thought the herald, this is sheer anger and frustration, the lashing out of a king who had been lured into a trap and can see no way out of it.

Tiphaine had been shaking with exhaustion and shock when they returned to camp last night, and she had collapsed into sleep almost at once. Today she was silent, pale under her sunburn, sitting on the grass with her hands clasped on her lap and staring at the army as it marched by. Warin stood quietly behind them, holding the reins of their horses.

Sir Nicholas Courcy and Lady Gráinne rode up the hill, followed by Mauro driving the cart. They dismounted, Gráinne shaking out her black hair. 'Sir Nicholas, my lady, thank you for your help last night,' Merrivale said. 'Sir John Grey bids me tell you he is grateful for your assistance.'

'John Grey acknowledging that he needed help?' said Courcy. 'Now that's not a thing you hear every day. And how are you faring this morning, *demoiselle*?'

'I feel lucky to be alive,' Tiphaine said. She shivered a little. 'I thought last night that my luck had finished. I shall never forget the hatred in their eyes.'

'What happened?' Merrivale asked gently.

'When the attack began, my gaoler came to find me. I managed to knock him out with a length of chain and stole his sword, thinking I could escape. But one of the nuns saw me and raised the alarm, and then all the sisters came running. They forced me out onto the platform and barred my way, while others lit the pyre. They told me they were the instruments of God's punishment, and that they would sooner burn with me than let me escape.'

'You had a sword,' Gráinne pointed out. The cut over her eye had been stitched up, quite expertly; there was, it seemed, no end to Sir Nicholas's talents.

'Could you kill a nun, my lady? A woman of God?'

'Women of God bleed just like the rest of us.'

Tiphaine shook her head. 'I lived in a convent as a child and was reared by nuns. It would have been like killing my own mother. I found I could not do it.'

Silence fell for a few moments. Armour and bright banners gleamed in the sunlight as the army marched on. Just two more bridges remained, Meulan and Poissy.

'Poissy,' Tiphaine said, echoing the herald's unspoken thought. 'They will finish this at Poissy. That is what the Count of Alençon said.'

'Where did you hear him say this?' Merrivale asked quietly.

'In Rouen.'

'And why did you go to Rouen?'

She raised her eyes and looked at him. 'I wanted to know more about Jean de Fierville. I know someone who I thought could give me answers to my questions.'

'And did he?'

'Some of them.' She paused, marshalling her thoughts. 'Fierville was part of three plots; or four, if you count the fact that he was also in the pay of the French. One was Harcourt's rebellion, now ruined. The second was the greater rebellion of the Count of Eu and the Queen of Navarre. That too will not take place.'

'Why not?' asked Courcy. Mauro and Warin stood silent, listening.

'Because I advised the queen against it,' Tiphaine said.

Merrivale considered this. 'You have seen her? Where?'

Tiphaine nodded. 'I went to her after I left Lisieux. I told her what I knew, that she too would be betrayed if she rebelled. The other conspirators wish to push Philippe off his throne, but they have no desire to see Normandy go free.'

'I take it these "other conspirators" are the third plot you mentioned. Who leads it?'

'Charles d'Alençon, the king's brother,' she said. 'Montmorency the marshal, I think. I don't know who else.'

'I can add a few more names,' Merrivale said. 'Cardinal Aubert, of course, and the two Italian mercenary commanders, Doria and Grimaldi.'

Tiphaine nodded. 'I saw Genoese crossbowmen in the camp at Rouen. One of Alençon's chief lieutenants is a Norman baron, Rollond de Brus, the man I went to see. Jean de Fierville was his cousin.'

She told them what she had learned in Rouen. 'This man, Sir John de Tracey, bought English slaves from Fierville. But there was another, who worked for a moneylender. I do not know his name.'

'I do,' Merrivale said. 'He is called Nicodemus.'

Mauro looked dubious. 'Begging your pardon, *señorita*, but Sir John de Tracey died seven years ago.'

'What about his son?' asked Gráinne.

'Sir Edward has always been at pains to distance himself from his father,' Merrivale said. 'He became angry to the point of hostility when I last questioned him. Given what you have told us, *demoiselle*, I understand why.'

He pondered for a moment. 'Very well. Nicodemus is said to have deserted, but I am convinced he is not far away. Perhaps he and Slade, the other deserter, are working together. We need to find them, and soon.'

Aubergenville, 11ᵗʰ of August, 1346
Evening

As the army made camp that evening on high ground overlooking the Seine, Merrivale called on his ever-reliable informant the cowherd. 'You do not look happy, Mistress Driver.'

'No, sir. My poor cows are getting so gaunt and weary with all this marching, and the milk they are giving is so thin, there's hardly any cream at all. Marigold is in real distress, sir. Are we going to be able to escape across the river?'

'I hope so,' Merrivale said. 'I came to ask if you had seen anything of Nicodemus. Has he approached the kitchen in the last few days?'

'No, sir. Folk are saying he deserted. He won't be the last one, either, the way things are going.'

'No.' After the failure at Mantes, the mood of the army was more depressed than ever. The heady aftermath of victory at Caen seemed a long time ago. 'The man who watches the cooking pots, Curry. Has he had any callers, or does he go anywhere?'

'No callers that I have seen, sir, and he never leaves camp, just sleeps on the ground next to the cooking fires. He's fallen out with Master Clerebaud too, I think.'

'Oh?'

'He keeps staring at the poor man. Poor Master Clerebaud has gone all quiet and never talks to anyone now, not even me.'

Something tingled along the herald's spine. 'Does he ever leave the kitchen?'

'Yes, sir, most evenings once dinner is finished. He's either looking for plunder or playing dice with some of the archers. I reckon he goes to get away from Curry.'

Clerebaud had once won money from Nicodemus. Was the defrocked priest still attending these games of dice? the herald wondered. Perhaps in disguise?

'Thank you, Mistress Driver,' he said, handing over a piece of cheese. 'Once again, you have been a wellspring of information.'

—

> Inquisition into the death of Edmund Bray, knight, near the village of Quettehou in Normandy on the XIIth day of July, in the nineteenth year of the reign of King Edward III. This report was composed on the XIth day of August, at the village of Aubergenville.
>
> Item, it seems likely that an archer calling himself Nicodemus, formerly of Sir Edward de Tracey's retinue, was also a conspirator along with Jean de Fierville. Nicodemus deserted the army two days ago, but I believe he is still in the vicinity, possibly along with another deserter, Jack Slade. I have ordered a search for both men.
>
> Item, I have received information that the French intend to strike a blow at our army when and if it reaches Poissy. The nature of the coup they are planning is not known, but I believe this information to be true and correct.
>
> Simon Merrivale, heraldus

Michael Northburgh read the brief report and laid it to one side. 'Tracey? Could he himself be involved?'

'Anything is possible, of course. But he says he had nothing to do with his father's activities, and I have no reason to disbelieve him. And there is another thing.'

'What is it?'

Merrivale outlined the wide-ranging conspiracy aimed at both King Edward and Philippe de Valois. 'Could Edward de Tracey, greedy and rich though he is, organise a coup like this alone? Frankly, I doubt it.'

'Then who could?'

'Of the others I have suspected? None. Mortimer is too young and inexperienced. Holland has the right connections, but the king has already bought his loyalty. Despenser has motive, perhaps, but he lacks the resources, especially money. The same is true of Gurney.'

Northburgh nodded. 'So, to sum up, you have strong evidence of a conspiracy within our army, but have no idea who is behind it.'

'Yes. Which means I am no further ahead than I was before,' the herald said bitterly. 'I know why Bray was killed, but I cannot prove who did it. That is why I must find these two renegade archers. At the moment, they are my only hope.'

Northburgh frowned. 'I will pass on your report to his Grace, of course, but he may not have time to read it. He is too busy worrying about bridges.'

'Is there any hope at Meulan?'

'Warwick and Northampton have gone forward with an advance party to see if a surprise attack can be mounted. If that fails, then it will be one last throw of the dice at Poissy.' Northburgh glanced at the report again. 'Where you say the enemy have something planned for us.'

'I fear that is the case, yes.'

'Well, we shall have to fight our way through somehow and force a river crossing. We cannot stay south of the river forever.' Northburgh smiled. 'On the other hand, you must be glad to have your *demoiselle* back.'

'For the last time, Michael, she is not my *demoiselle*.'

'Of course she isn't,' Northburgh said soothingly. 'Not yet. Be patient, my friend. Ripe fruit will fall from the tree eventually. You must be waiting, ready to seize and pluck it.'

'You are a disgrace to the priesthood,' Merrivale told him. 'Good night, Michael.'

'You too, old friend. Sweet dreams.'

Poissy, 12ᵗʰ of August, 1346
Afternoon

The thump of hammers and rasp of saws echoed over the rippling water of the river. The beams of the central span were being cut down; most had drifted away on the current, but one was still bumping against the stone piers below them.

'Warwick failed at Meulan this morning,' said the man from the West Country.

'Good,' said the man from the north. 'It is exactly as we planned it. Both Edward and Philip have played into our hands.'

The other man looked across the river. 'Why aren't the French guarding the north bank?'

'They will. Philip is anxious to get his army into Paris before the Parisians all die of fright. They're angry enough with him already for failing to stop the English. A force coming down from Amiens has been commanded to guard the bridge. They should arrive tomorrow morning.'

'How strong is this force?'

'Four hundred men-at-arms, as well as crossbowmen and ballistae.'

'Only four hundred? Will that be enough?'

'Of course. The bridge is broken, and anyone trying to swim the river or cross in boats will be shot to pieces.' The man from the north smiled. 'Come. Let us go and meet our friends.'

They turned their horses and rode through the deserted streets of Poissy. All those residents who had not already fled had been taken away to the safety of the walls of Paris that morning. The fine stone and timber houses they passed were silent and empty.

'The herald has been asking too damned many questions,' the man from the West Country said. 'I thought you were going to take care of him.'

'I thought I had,' said the man from the north. 'The king ordered him to abandon the inquisition. Now he seems to have told him to take it up again. I don't know why.'

The man from the West Country looked at him. 'Isn't it your job to know why?'

'I shall assume that is an ill-advised attempt at humour,' said the other man. 'I do not recommend you try it again.' They rode on in silence.

One of King Philip's many hunting lodges in the forests and fields west of Paris lay on the southern edge of Poissy, next to a deserted Dominican priory. Grooms stood in the courtyard, holding the reins of a dozen horses. The door to the hall opened and a young man with a surcoat bearing a red saltire on yellow came down the steps, bowing as the two men dismounted. 'Gentlemen, I am honoured to meet you. I am Rollond, lord of Brus. His Imperial Majesty and the others are waiting for you inside.'

The lodge's servants had fled in haste, without bothering to pack away their valuables. In the hall, tapestries still hung on the walls, red and blue figures of horses and huntsmen in pursuit of a white unicorn with gold horn and collar, all brilliant with sunlight. A fine film of dust lay on the polished wood of the high table. Beneath the tapestries, ten men stood waiting, watching them with calculating eyes. One wore a red cloak bearing the white eight-pointed cross of the Knights of Saint John. The man from the north nodded with satisfaction. They were all here.

He bowed. 'Your Imperial Majesty, my lords. It is a pleasure to welcome you.'

Charles d'Alençon held up a hand. 'Let us wait and see what you have to offer. Only then will we know whether it has truly been a pleasure.'

'I think we can promise you complete satisfaction, your Imperial Majesty,' said the man from the north. 'You see, we have fulfilled our part of the bargain. Edward of England is trapped. Even as we speak, the last bridge over the Seine is being broken. Edward cannot cross the river to the north. Nor can he retreat west through lands he has already devastated, because he is running out of food and needs somewhere to forage. And if he tries to advance east, he will batter himself to death against the walls of Paris.'

'He could march south,' said Cardinal Aubert. 'There is another English army in Gascony. They might try to join forces.'

The man from the north shook his head. 'Edward and his captains will come to Poissy tomorrow,' he said. 'And there they will die. The English army will be left leaderless. The men-at-arms are already quarrelling and demoralised. Without their captains, both they and the archers will soon begin to desert. One or two disciplined units may hold together, but you have more than enough men to overwhelm them. The rest you may round up at your leisure.'

'How do you intend to accomplish this?' demanded another man. He was tall and thickly bearded, and he spoke French with the strong accent of central Europe.

The man from the north shook his head. 'Leave that to us,' he said. 'And make ready. As soon as the English army has been destroyed, you must strike.'

A burly man standing by the wall cleared his throat. 'And where is the Queen of Navarre? We understood from Cardinal Ceccano that she would be joining us.'

'She has changed her mind,' said the man from the West Country. 'She has decided to remain neutral, and no, Signor Doria, I do not know why. However, I strongly suspect that once our coup is complete, she will return to join us.'

A grey-haired older man nodded. 'I think she is wise. I must say I am tempted to remain neutral myself. Yours is a complex plan, my lords, and in my experience, complex plans have a habit of going wrong. You have set a trap for Edward here at Poissy. But what if he should escape from it?'

'He will not,' said the man from the north.

The burly man cleared his throat again but said nothing. The man beside him, weather-beaten and scarred like the cliffs of his homeland in Monaco, growled under his breath. 'What about the money? You offered twenty thousand écus. I want more.'

'And you shall have it, Signor Grimaldi,' said the man from the West Country. 'For you, and also for you, Signor Doria, and for all of you. Count Rožmberk, the high chamberlain of Bohemia. Count Louis of Vaud, the regent of Savoy. Marshal de Montmorency. My lord John of Hainault. Cardinal Aubert and you also, Cardinal Ceccano. – When the deed is done and the Count of Alençon is crowned King Charles V of France, there will be a reward of forty thousand écus in gold.'

'You are doubling the money?' asked Louis of Vaud, the grey-haired man. His face was incredulous.

'We are. Are you tempted now to join us?'

Vaud said nothing. 'And you, Grand Prior?' the man from the north asked. 'I know the Knights of Saint John have forsaken all worldly goods. But monastic poverty can still be endured in comfort, I think. And forty thousand écus would buy you a great deal of comfort.'

'The money would be useful to my order,' the Grand Prior said smoothly. 'More to the point, I believe King Charles V will make a better king than his brother; and, of course, he will look kindly on the Knights of Saint John and will favour them in future. I am with you.'

'And me?' demanded Charles d'Alençon. 'What is my reward?'

'The throne of France, of course. And one hundred thousand écus, to pay off your debts and suppress your enemies. And distribute to your loyal friends, of course,' added the man from the north, glancing at Rollond de Brus.

Montmorency raised his eyebrows. 'You will pay out almost half a million écus, at a time when your king is nearly bankrupt? I did not realise there was so much money in all of England.'

'There are reasons why King Edward has no money,' the man from the West Country said, and he smiled.

'And once this plan is complete, what then?' demanded the bearded Count Rožmberk. 'What is in this for you?'

'We shall make profit out of chaos,' said the man from the north. 'And invite you to join us. In this room are representatives of some of the greatest powers of Europe: the papacy, France, England, the

Knights of Saint John. And others that were once great, and could be again: Genoa, Savoy.' He looked again at Louis of Vaud. 'Savoy is a mere county now. With our support, you could make it a kingdom once more.'

'We have tried that before,' Vaud said. 'We failed.'

'Forty thousand écus, remember? With that amount of money, you could buy the fealty of your fellow rulers. Your kingdom could stretch from Provence to the Rhine.'

The man from the north turned back to Count Rožmberk, the bearded man. 'We are waiting for King Jean of Bohemia. Has his army arrived yet?'

'Indeed. They have joined the royal army at Saint-Denis.'

'King Jean is ambitious and desires further conquests to enlarge his kingdom, but he needs money. We can provide it.'

'And I say again. What do you intend to do?'

'Say rather what do *you* want to do? Unite the embattled kingdoms of Spain and lead them to conquer the Moors? Crush Venice and take over the spice trade? Launch a new crusade to reconquer Jerusalem? Overthrow the Greek empire and restore the empire of Constantinople? Where do your ambitions lead you, my lords? Whatever they are, we can help you achieve them. We are the brokers of power, who will make a new Europe. We call on you to be part of it.'

There was a moment of silence. The man from the north looked around the room for a moment, then drew his sword and held it up by the blade, so the hilt formed the sign of a cross. Beside him, the West Country man touched the hilt and then raised his hand in the air. 'This is our pledge,' he said. 'Join us.'

Jean de Nanteuil, the Grand Prior of the Knights of Saint John, stepped up and touched the hilt, kissing his fingers as he withdrew. Grimaldi of Monaco followed him, and so after a little hesitation did Ottone Doria from Genoa. The two cardinals followed. Alençon looked at Rožmberk and Vaud. 'Well, my lords? It is time to choose sides.'

Silently Rožmberk stepped forward and touched the hilt. Vaud smiled a little. 'Forty thousand écus,' he said. 'It appears, gentlemen, that you have found my price,' and he too touched the sword. Montmorency and Hainault followed, and last of all came Alençon. He rested his fingertips on the hilt, and then suddenly wrapped his hand hard around it, as if he intended to rip it from the other man's hands.

'Do not fail me,' he said.

'We will not,' said the man from the West Country.

A moment passed, and then Alençon relaxed his grip. Without another word he turned and walked out of the room, followed by the others. John of Hainault lingered for a moment, looking into the eyes of the man from the north and smiling a little. 'My congratulations,' he said. 'You have a played a long game with patience and skill.'

'Twenty years,' said the man from the north. 'We have had our setbacks, but we have won through.'

'You have. I hope you get the reward you deserve.'

'I will,' said the man from the north. 'We all will. Are you certain about Alençon?'

'He is a bombastic, arrogant fool,' said Hainault. 'But he is also the king's brother. We must either use him, or kill him. The former is easier and less risky.' He smiled a little. 'Worry not. I shall keep him under control.'

Poissy, 13th of August, 1346
Afternoon

'So much for the last bridge,' Thomas Holland said, staring glumly at the sixty-foot gap that had been ripped out of the middle of the bridge at Poissy. The rest of the span still stood, wooden planks and beams resting on broad stone pillars, but for the heavily armed and encumbered army, the gap in the middle might as well have been sixty miles.

Thanks to the wound he had taken at Gaillon, Holland was still unable to wear his shoulder guard; his arming doublet bulged over a thick wad of bandages. 'What in hell's name do we do now?' he asked.

'We were rather hoping that a veteran soldier like yourself might tell us,' Hugh Despenser said cuttingly. 'And where the fuck is the enemy?'

They stood for a few moments looking out at the empty fields on the north bank of the Seine. Unlike the bright sunlight of the last few days, the sky was dull and grey, the air heavy with humidity and smoke. Behind them, the inevitable fires burned; Bures and Ecquevilly, where they had camped the night before, were blazing on the western horizon.

'There's no sign of them,' said Richard Percy. 'Which is damned odd, given that they have been glaring across the river at us every day since we left Rouen.'

The Prince of Wales pointed to the escarpment, far to the north now and a dim line on the horizon. 'They could be beyond those hills,' he said. 'But why abandon the river?'

'I have no idea, your Highness. But their absence is our opportunity. If we move quickly, we might just have time to rebuild the bridge.'

'Rebuild it?' the prince asked quickly. 'Is that possible?'

Percy pointed to the river. A long wooden beam floated in the water next to the stone piers, pressed against them by the current. 'If we can salvage that, your Highness, we could make a start.'

More horsemen came down the road from the town, Warwick and Ughtred, and with them Northampton the constable. The prince turned eagerly to meet them. 'My lords! Sir Richard believes we can rebuild the bridge. But we must start at once, before the enemy arrive.'

Northampton looked puzzled. 'Where are the French?'

'An excellent question,' Percy said. 'However, his Highness is right. We should get to work straight away, before they reappear.'

Warwick laughed, flipping up the visor of his bascinet. 'Do you know you are beginning to sound damned near as imperious as your brother-in-law?'

'John Grey is a contagion,' Percy said. 'Spend enough time around him and he rubs off on you. What are your orders, Lord Marshal?'

Warwick glanced at Northampton, who nodded. 'Find Llewellyn and tell him to get his boats up here, and then ferry the Red

Company over the river to guard the bridgehead. Tom,' Warwick said to Ughtred, 'find Hurley and his carpenters. Get them up here, now.'

'I would like to volunteer my company to guard the bridgehead, my lord,' Despenser said.

'Certainly. You may cross later, after the Red Company and the carpenters. Very well, gentlemen, make it so.'

Warwick rode away, followed by the prince and his esquires and bodyguard. Northampton lingered, sitting in the saddle, leaning forward a little and watching the flat horizon smudged with haze. Behind him the knights stood muttering. 'Why does the goddamned Red Company always go first?' Despenser muttered.

'Perhaps because, unlike some, their captains actually know what they are doing,' said Mortimer.

Despenser took a step towards him. 'Oh, for the love of Christ!' snapped Matthew Gurney. 'I am sick to death of this. Grow up, both of you!'

Despenser stalked away. Mortimer slammed the visor of his bascinet down and sulked behind it. Merrivale stood watching the boats take the Red Company across to the north bank. The carpenters arrived, driving their wagons full of tools and equipment, and the boats returned and ferried some of them over the river, where they began assembling windlasses with ropes and blocks on the broken ends of the bridge. Slings were lowered and men swam out into the river to loop these around the ends of the beam.

'Right,' said the master carpenter, waving the rest of his men towards the windlasses. 'Put your backs into it.'

The men threw themselves onto the cranks, straining. Gradually the big beam lifted out of the water and inched its way up towards the bridge platform. Time passed with grinding slowness in the murky air. The herald waited, full of foreboding. He could tell by the slope of his back as he hunched in the saddle that Northampton felt the same anxiety.

Someone shouted from the far bank. 'Enemy in sight!'

Out of the haze they came, sparkling specks of colour, a wedge of men-at-arms followed by the unmistakable white coats of crossbowmen, and then a column of carts each with a black tripod shape mounted in the back. 'What are those?' asked Mortimer.

'Ballistae,' said Merrivale. 'They fire stone shot the size of a fist, and will punch through armour at twice the range of an ordinary crossbow.'

Northampton jumped down from the saddle, handing his reins to his esquire, and walked out onto the bridge. 'Master Hurley! How long until that beam is in place?'

The beam was ten feet below the level of the bridge. 'Long enough to say a rosary,' said the master carpenter. 'More or less.'

'Make it less,' said the constable. 'A damned sight less.'

The enemy were coming on quickly now, and the carts with the ballistae were spreading out, men jumping down to load and aim the big weapons. They looked a little like giant crossbows mounted on heavy wooden frames. Despenser ran up to Northampton. 'I need the boats, my lord. I must get my men across the river.'

'There isn't time for the boats,' said Northampton. He gestured at the beam. 'We'll cross as soon as that is in place. Where is Tracey?'

'I don't know, my lord,' said Gurney. 'I haven't seen him since we arrived in Poissy.'

'Never mind. Holland, Gurney, Mortimer, collect every man you can find. Then get ready to follow me.'

Mortimer gazed down at the swirling river, doubtless remembering his near drowning at Carentan, and then back at the beam, a foot wide and dripping with water. 'We're going to cross on that?'

'The rest of us are,' Despenser snapped. 'Come with us, or stay here and soil yourself. Your choice.'

Mortimer stared at him and then turned on his heel. Gurney is right, the herald thought. They are like quarrelling children. Despenser turned away too, shouting to his vintenar, and Holland was calling for his men. More men-at-arms came running up to join them, Courcy and Gráinne among them, the bulky figure of Donnchad following. Harry Percy, Sir Richard's brother, arrived at the run, followed by his own archers.

On the far shore, the ballistae began to shoot, each one making an audible crack as it launched its stone shot. The shot were the size of apples, black streaks rushing through the air. Two punched into the walls of the houses near the bridge, knocking holes in the timber. A third struck a man-at-arms in the head, shattering his bascinet like an eggshell.

'Hurley!' Northampton snapped. 'Get that goddamned beam in place!'

'Nearly there, my lord. A couple more Aves should do it.' One of the carpenters spun around with a crossbow bolt in his side, toppled and fell into the river. Another ran forward to take his place on the windlass. The beam continued to rise with painful slowness. On the far side of the river, a trumpet sounded, and the French men-at-arms lowered their lances and launched forward, charging across the flat fields towards the Red Company through showers of arrows. On the south bank, the English waited. Merrivale found he was holding his breath.

The air vibrated as the French men-at-arms crashed into the Red Company. Standing at the south end of the bridge, the herald heard the shouts and screams of anger and pain, the hammer of metal on metal, the constant twang of bowstrings, and suddenly the hair stood up on the back of every neck as the Red Company began their war cry, '*Rouge! Rooouge! Rooooouge!*' Just for a moment, he was back in Savoy, listening to the howling of wolves in the mountains; but these were men, not wolves, fighting with skill as well as fury, and one by one the French men-at-arms began to go down.

But there were too many of them, and sheer weight of numbers began forcing the Red Company back towards the river. The beam reached the level of the bridge. Harry Percy, whose brother was fighting at the far end, ran forward to help lift it into place. It spanned the gap, a foot wide and shining treacherously wet, twenty feet above the rushing waters of the river. Someone whispered a prayer. Drawing his sword, Northampton jumped onto the beam and began to run.

Encased in armour and mail, knowing that death awaited him in the river below, the constable ran lightly and easily, his arms outstretched for balance. Others followed him: Despenser, Mortimer, Gurney, Harry Percy, then Courcy and Gráinne and Donnchad and the other men-at-arms, running along the beam in single file while the stone shot continued to whip through the air around them. One man slipped and fell, hitting the water with a hard splash. Weighed down by eighty pounds of armour, he sank straight to the bottom. A trail of air bubbles marked the spot where he fell for minute or so, and then stopped.

Northampton reached the far end of the beam and charged forward into the heart of the fighting. The others followed. At first they seemed to make no impact, but as more and more English men-at-arms piled in, the impetus swung and the French began falling back. As suddenly as they had charged, they broke, the Red Company running after them and shooting them down as they fled. The crews of the ballistae tried to reload, but were cut down by arrows and crossbow bolts. Within a few minutes, the surviving French had fled, disappearing into the haze. Someone had already set their carts on fire, and flames rose pale in the dim light.

Northampton walked back across the beam, handing his bloody sword to his esquire for cleaning. 'You may continue your work now, Master Hurley,' he said calmly. 'I want this bridge serviceable and ready for passage as soon as possible.'

'Aye, my lord. We'll do our best.' The master carpenter said something under his breath and then turned to his men.

Hugh Despenser looked grudgingly at Mortimer. 'I was wrong,' he said. 'You didn't soil yourself.'

'Go to hell,' said Mortimer tiredly, and he pulled his bascinet off and stood for a moment, sweat pouring down his face and hair clinging limply to his neck, watching the smoke of the burning carts rolling across the fields.

21

Poissy, 14th of August, 1346
Morning

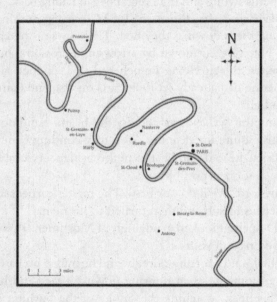

'Well, that wasn't supposed to happen,' said the man from the West Country.

'No,' agreed the man from the north. 'The French were damnably careless. They should have made certain that the bridge was completely destroyed, and ensured there was a decent guard on the north bank.'

'That force from Amiens sent to protect it. Why were they so late?'

'Their orders were delayed in arriving. That is all I have been told.'

They stood on the riverbank downstream from the bridge, watching the carpenters at work. 'However, it hardly matters now,' the man from the north said. 'What's done is done.'

'I wish I had your philosophy.'

The man from the north smiled. 'These things are sent to try us, my friend. Tribulations purify the soul, as Abelard said. Now we must decide what to do next.'

'If all of Edward's army escapes across the river, our entire plan is in ruins,' said the man from the West Country. 'They will march north to Flanders and safety, and Alençon and Hainault cannot attack Philip until Edward has been disposed of.'

The man from the north frowned. 'As always, you exaggerate the danger. First, Edward is not marching anywhere, not yet. It will be some time before that bridge is fully repaired. Second, Philip's army is still at Saint-Denis, north of the river. If Edward does cross, the French can easily cut him off.'

'Will Philip remain at Saint-Denis?'

'No, and there I concede you have a point. There is some risk.' The man from the north pointed towards the columns of smoke rising in the east and spreading out on the soft wind. 'Warwick and Harcourt are burning the suburbs of Paris now, trying to tempt Philip to cross the river and fight. This time, I think they will succeed; Philip has to protect Paris.'

'The Parisians won't forgive him if he doesn't.'

'Indeed. They are already accusing him and his councillors of betrayal. They have managed to get hold of a letter with the king's seal insisting that the army does not have enough men to defend Paris and that the city should be abandoned. They are threatening revolt, and Philip will have to placate them.'

'Where did this letter come from?'

'I wrote it, of course. I have a copy of the seal, remember? The point is that once Philip is over the river, he can move west and trap the English here. We can trust Alençon and Hainault to remind him of this, even if he does not think of it for himself.'

'But this is exactly what I mean. Once Philip is south of the river, that leaves the way open for Edward. All he needs to do is repair the bridge and he can cross and march away.'

The man from the north shook his head. 'By the time the bridge is repaired, it will be too late. All the French will need to do is mop up. We will have already administered the *coup de grâce*, remember? Time to put our plan into effect.'

'Is everything ready?'

'It will happen exactly as we planned it.' The man from the north smiled. 'Just remember not to touch the eggs.'

Poissy, 14th of August, 1346
Late afternoon

'We've done everything we could,' Warwick said. 'We burned every village and manor house and monastery to the ground, Saint-Germain-en-Laye, Montjoie, Nanterre, Saint-Cloud, the lot. Some of our hobelars were within shouting distance of the southern gates.'

'We destroyed three more of the adversary's palaces,' said the Prince of Wales. 'If that doesn't make him come out and fight, nothing will.'

'We don't want him to fight, your Highness,' said Northampton. 'We only want to draw him south of the river and leave us with a free run to the north.'

The prince looked disappointed. 'When shall we fight?'

'When we are strong enough, Highness,' said Lord Rowton. He had come up from the king's headquarters to view the work on the bridge, meeting Warwick and the prince just as they returned from their raid towards Paris. His broken arm was strapped into a sling, and he seemed still to be in considerable pain. 'When we reach Flanders and join forces with the rebels, then we shall be strong enough. Not before then.'

'I think you underestimate the fighting spirit of our army, Lord Rowton,' the prince snapped. 'You should have more faith in our men.'

Rowton turned to him. 'I bow to your superior experience, Highness. But the troops are tired from marching, food is running low, the captains are bickering amongst themselves, and the enemy have four times our numbers. Given all of this, do you think the army is ready to fight a battle, here and now?'

The prince stared at him. 'I would not presume to make such a decision,' he said. 'I would defer to my father, the king. You see, Lord Rowton, I know my place. I am not sure you do.'

Rowton's face went red. Merrivale looked up to see Warwick raise a hand to his face, hiding a smile. Northampton turned to the master carpenter. 'How much longer, Hurley? And tell me in real time, not rosaries or Aves or chanting psalms.'

'The bridge won't be ready today, my lord. I can tell you that much for a fact.'

'Tomorrow?'

'Tomorrow evening, perhaps. No sooner.'

'For God's sake, Hurley!' Northampton said. 'The king wants this bridge repaired *now*. Work through the night if you have to.'

'Now see here, Lord Constable!' The master carpenter glared at him. 'We bloody well did work through last night, and we'll be working through the night to come. But this isn't the Carentan causeway or Pont-Hébert. That gap is sixty feet long, and we'll need two more support beams at least. Which means we have to find an oak tree that's tall enough, fell it, cut two beams and size them, drag them up here and fix them to the supports, and then we still have to cut and plane down the planks to build the roadway and fix them in place. We've run out of nails too, and the blacksmith is sweating his guts out to forge some more, but it all takes *time*. So you tell the king, if he wants the bridge repaired any faster, he can come down here and pick up a fucking hammer!'

Northampton held up a hand. 'Just do your best.'

'I am certain you are working as hard as you can, Master Hurley,' the prince said. Northampton and Warwick looked at each other, eyebrows raised. 'And we are all grateful for your efforts. I shall tell my father as much when I see him.'

He turned and walked away. Merrivale prepared to follow, but Northampton raised his hand again. 'Stay a moment, herald. We need a word.'

Merrivale inclined his head. 'I am at your service, my lord.'

'I am pleased to see that you survived your escapade at La Roche-Guyon unharmed,' the constable said. 'I assume your purpose was to rescue the Demoiselle de Tesson. Was she spying for you?'

'I did not request her to do so,' said Merrivale. 'But yes, in effect that is what she was doing. I should add that I take full responsibility for the raid. I hope you have not rebuked Sir John Grey and Sir Richard Percy.'

'Do you think rebuking them would have made the slightest difference to their behaviour?' asked Warwick. 'The king has shown us your report from the following day.'

Merrivale raised his eyebrows. 'I was not certain that he had read it.'

'He has read it, and he takes it very seriously. Something will happen at Poissy, you said. What?'

'I don't know, my lord. The *demoiselle* overheard the Count of Alençon say this to one of his officers, the Seigneur de Brus. That is all she knows.'

Rowton looked at the bridge. 'Surely it is obvious,' he said. 'The French knew that if they blocked or broke down each bridge in turn, we would eventually arrive at Poissy. Assuming we cannot cross the river, and with the king still unwilling to sanction a retreat to Caen, we would have no choice but to stand and fight. This is where they intend to give battle.'

He looked at Northampton and Warwick. 'Was his Highness by any chance right? Could we offer battle with any real hope of success?'

Northampton shook his head. 'Reluctantly, Eustace, I must agree with you. The men are tired, and apart from a few companies like Grey and Percy's, they are in no condition to give battle. And the terrain is flat, with no defensive features. The enemy would roll over us.'

'Which undoubtedly has been their plan all along,' Rowton said. 'I said as much to the king, but he wouldn't listen. Now all we can do is pray that Master Hurley can finish the bridge before the French army arrives on our doorstep.'

'Oh, we're all doing that,' Warwick said. 'The Bishop of Durham and his priests are in the priory right now, rubbing their knees raw while they pray to the Virgin and every saint in the calendar. But even if we do finish the bridge on time, it is still a hell of a long way to Flanders and safety. And don't forget, gentlemen, before we reach Flanders, there is still another great river to cross. The Somme.'

Poissy, 15th of August, 1346
Late morning

'Is there any word on Nicodemus?' the herald asked. 'Has he been seen?'

Mauro and Warin both shook their heads. 'We have spoken to men from nearly every retinue in the army, *señor*,' Mauro said. 'We did not speak to Sir Edward de Tracey's men, for I do not think they would tell me the truth. But all the others, even some of Holland's men.'

'I also called at the royal kitchen this morning,' Warin said. 'I wasn't very welcome, because they're all running about like chickens without heads, preparing for the feast this afternoon. But I wanted to know if Nicodemus had approached Curry or Master Clerebaud.'

'And had he?'

Warin shook his head again. 'No one has seen Nicodemus, or is prepared to admit it. I did learn one thing, though, from one of the scullions. Master Clerebaud has recently lost a lot of money at dice. He is deeply in debt.'

The herald considered this, wondering what it meant, if anything. 'With whom does he gamble?'

'No one knows, sir. He slips out pretty much every night, once they've cleaned up the kitchen. Only he didn't go last night because they were already hard at work preparing for the feast.'

'The enemy is at hand, food is running out, and your king has ordered a feast?' Tiphaine asked.

Today was the feast day of the Assumption of the Blessed Virgin; along with Lammas, it was the most important celebration of the summer. 'It is a symbol,' Merrivale said. 'To sit down and feast with the enemy gathering in Paris a few miles away shows the army that he is in control. Rather than rush to cross the river by any means possible, abandoning our baggage, we will wait until the bridge is repaired and then cross in an orderly fashion.'

'And you agree with this?'

'As it happens, I do. In times of crisis, the leader must present a calm face to his men. If he is frightened or worried, he must never show it.'

Tiphaine looked dubious. 'I think I would prefer to rush, and get away. But then I am not a king. Or a herald.'

'You may go if you wish,' he said gently.

'Are you going?'

'My duty is here. I am bidden to attend the feast along with the prince.'

Her chin came up. 'If you stay, then I stay.'

'There is one other thing that may be of interest, *señor*,' said Mauro. 'Nicodemus has vanished, but some of Tracey's men are continuing to buy plunder. There has been plenty of spoil in the rich towns and abbeys we have passed. They are still making a great deal of money.'

Silence fell. The herald stared out across the fields towards Paris, where the smoke of yesterday's fires still drifted in the air. The other three glanced at each other. 'What are you thinking?' Tiphaine asked.

'I was right. Nicodemus is here. Warin, find Sir John Grey and Sir Richard Percy. Give them my compliments and ask them to turn out their men. Describe Nicodemus to them and ask them to search the camp from top to bottom. Check the baggage train in particular, any place where he might hide. *Demoiselle*, will you please find Sir Nicholas Courcy and ask him to meet me at the palace? Are Matt and Pip here?'

Warin motioned towards the two archers leaning on their bows thirty yards away. Merrivale turned to them. 'Come with me,' he said. 'You too, Mauro. I may have need of you.'

Coloyne, the yeoman of the kitchen, met them looking worried. 'What is this about, herald? The feast begins in an hour's time and we have much work to do.'

The royal cooks had established themselves in the palace kitchen. Fires roared on the hearths and pots bubbled and boiled, while outside men in bloody aprons butchered beef and mutton carcasses and prepared them for cooking. From the chapel of the priory next door came the sound of chanting; the king and his court were attending mass.

'I must speak to Master Clerebaud,' the herald said.

'Very well, but please do not detain him for long.'

Glancing around the crowded kitchen, Merrivale could see no sign of Curry. Clerebaud was at work at the sauce table, chopping herbs with manic energy and stirring them into a pot over a low fire. He wiped the sweat from his forehead and straightened as Merrivale approached. His eyes were guarded. 'How may I help you, herald?'

'How much do you owe them?' Merrivale asked.

'How much do I... what are you talking about?'

'Nicodemus and his friends. You play dice with them almost every night.'

Clerebaud looked around for a moment, then back at the herald. 'I gamble with a few friends. I don't know what you mean about Nicodemus.'

'How much do you owe?' the herald repeated.

'...Thirty marks, or thereabouts. A trifling sum. I can easily win it back.'

Thirty marks, or twenty pounds, was more than even a skilled professional cook like Clerebaud earned in a year. 'What sauces are you making for the banquet?'

Clerebaud looked startled by the question. 'Cameline for roasting the beef. Sorrel verjuice for the carp. Saffron sauce, ginger sauce, garlic sauce, and a honey mustard glaze for the swan.'

'Show me what you are putting in them.'

The sauce-maker indicated the table where his ingredients were laid out. Merrivale sifted through them, picking up bunches of herbs and examining them, sniffing a bowl of chopped garlic, dipping his finger in a crock of honey. He could see or smell nothing out of the ordinary. 'Mauro? What do you think?'

'Everything seems in order, *señor*.'

The herald turned back to Clerebaud. 'The scullion who watches the pots, Curry. Where is he?'

Sudden terror crept into Clerebaud's eyes. 'I don't know. He was here last night, but I haven't seen him this morning.'

The herald remembered what Nell had said. 'Has Curry threatened you?'

The terror increased. After a moment, Clerebaud nodded. 'He said if they don't get their money, they'll skin me alive.'

Merrivale watched the other man's eyes. 'Curry also made you an offer, didn't he? He asked you to do something in order to pay off the debt. What was it?'

The air in the kitchen was hot and full of steam and smoke, and sweat streamed down Clerebaud's face. 'I don't know what you're talking about.'

'Tell me where Nicodemus is.'

'I don't know. I swear by the blood of Jesus, I haven't seen him.'

'You remember what happened at Lammas,' Merrivale said. 'The poisoned juvert.'

'That was nothing to do with me!'

'No. But if something happens today, it won't be Curry and his men coming to flay you. It will be the king's executioners.'

–

Back in the courtyard, they could hear singing again, the words of the Gloria echoing off stone walls.

Domine Fili unigenite, Iesu Christe,

Domine Deus, Agnus Dei, Filius Patris,
qui tollis peccata mundi, miserere nobis;
qui tollis peccata mundi, suscipe deprecationem nostram.
Qui sedes ad dexteram Patris, miserere nobis.

'He is lying, *señor*,' Mauro said.

'Of course he is. Stay here, and do not let him out of your sight.'

'Yes, *señor*.'

Courcy had arrived, Gráinne inevitably at his elbow. Tiphaine was with them, standing what she judged was a safe distance from Gráinne; Matt and Pip lingered silently a few yards away. 'Sir Nicholas,' the herald said, 'I need your knowledge of alchemy. How many kinds of poison are there?'

'Christ knows,' said Courcy. 'Wolf's-bane, belladonna, arsenic, strychnine, hemlock, opium, to name just a few. Do you want me to recite the entire pharmacopoeia?'

'At Lisieux, you said the poison might have been acquired from an apothecary's shop. Is there such a shop in Poissy?'

'Yes, in the square by the church of Notre-Dame.'

'Take me there, if you please.'

–

The looters had been thorough; every door in the square had been forced open and every building plundered, including the church. The windows of the apothecary's shop had been smashed, fragments of glass and lead crunching under their boots as they entered. Cabinets and chests stood open, but by and large their contents had been left untouched; the looters had been looking for gold and silver or goods they could sell, and powders and tinctures were not considered valuable enough to take away.

Leaving Matt and Pip on guard outside, they searched the shop. 'What are we looking for?' Tiphaine asked.

'Every box or bottle will have a label,' Courcy said. 'That's so the 'pothecary doesn't get the ingredients mixed up and accidentally sell a love potion when he was meant to provide a hair restorer.' He paused for a moment, looking at her. 'Sorry, I should have asked. You do know how to read?'

'I was educated at the finest convent school in Normandy,' Tiphaine snapped. 'I know how to read.'

'Sweet Jesus, you're an idiot,' Gráinne told her husband, cuffing him with one gauntleted hand.

'Not every country believes in educating women, *mo grá*. I wasn't sure how they did things in Normandy.'

They searched the shop, looking into cabinets and lifting the tops of majolica jars to smell the contents, Courcy checking the labels and muttering under his breath in Latin. Finding nothing, they moved through to the storeroom at the rear of the building. Almost at once they discovered what they were looking for, a wooden cabinet full of jars of dark treacly syrup and cloth packets containing roots and seeds. '*Lachryma papaveris*,' Courcy said, pointing to the syrup. 'And here we have *Aconitum napellus*, *Atropa belladonna*, *Nux vomica* and *Arsenicum trisulphide*. These are the poisons.'

'Is anything missing?' asked Merrivale.

'It is hard to tell without an inventory. But the cabinet is well stocked. If someone did steal anything, they can't have taken much.'

'Where else might someone find poisons?'

'Well, we've looted half a dozen towns since Lisieux. Or the poisoner might still have the stock he picked up in Caen.'

Merrivale shook his head. 'They wouldn't carry the poison this far in their baggage. The risk of discovery is too great. They will look for stocks near to hand.'

'Where else in Poissy could they find *aconitum*?' asked Gráinne.

Tiphaine snapped her fingers. 'The priory here is a rich house. King Philippe's sister is the prioress there. They would have their own physician.'

'And the physician will have stocks of drugs,' said Courcy. 'But the king and prince are hearing mass at the priory now. Can we get in?'

The herald touched his tabard. 'This is our passport,' he said.

The kitchen, Mauro reflected, looked a little like one of those scenes from hell's inferno that he remembered seeing painted on church walls back in Spain. Flames crackled, smoke and steam billowed towards the high ceiling. Men crouched over the fires, turning haunches of meat on spits. Pans clattered and pots bubbled. He mopped his forehead, watching Clerebaud adding breadcrumbs to the ginger sauce and stirring to thicken it, his face full of concentration.

Suddenly the sauce-maker frowned, rubbing a hand over his stomach and wincing in pain. He lifted the sauce pot from the fire, and hurried towards the door. 'Where are you going?' Mauro asked.

'Garderobe. Christ, my guts are on fire.'

Mauro grinned. 'Have you been eating your own cooking, *señor*?'

'Very funny. Where are *you* going?'

'I'm coming with you. My orders are not to let you out of my sight.'

The garderobe was in the stair turret next to the stables, a narrow dog-leg passage leading off the stair. 'For God's sake give me some privacy,' Clerebaud pleaded. 'I feel like hell. The last thing I need is you standing there watching me.'

'I've seen worse,' Mauro said, but the garderobe was tiny, with room only for one. He was forced to stand in the passage, waiting and listening to the sounds of distress. His mind was still dwelling on the subject of poison. 'Seriously, *señor*. Was it something you ate?'

'We had tripe sausages for dinner last night. I thought they smelled off.'

'Is anyone else feeling ill?'

'I don't know. Perhaps I just had a bad piece. Oh God, I could shit through the eye of a needle.'

More groans followed, and eventually Clerebaud re-emerged, wiping his hands and looking a little pale. 'Are you all right, *señor*?' Mauro asked.

'I have to be,' Clerebaud said, mopping the sweat from his face again. 'I have work to do.'

At the priory, the communion rite had begun.

Agnus Dei, qui tollis peccata mundi, miserere nobis.
Agnus Dei, qui tollis peccata mundi, dona nobis pacem.

The royal serjeants guarding the priory gates looked dubious when Merrivale demanded entrance. 'The king gave strict orders not to be disturbed during mass, sir.'

'This is the king's business,' Merrivale said. 'I take full responsibility.'

The gates swung open. The chapel lay directly ahead, the cloister to the right, the prioress's lodging to the left. 'The infirmary will be beyond the cloister,' Tiphaine said, pointing. They ran through the colonnade, pushing open doors into chapter house and scriptorium, and found a corridor leading to the kitchen and domestic buildings. 'Here!' Tiphaine called, and they followed her into a whitewashed room with an arched stone ceiling and beds arranged at neat intervals. A wooden table stood at one end of the room, a heavy iron-bound chest and an ambry behind it. The door of the ambry was open.

Courcy rummaged through it quickly. 'Poppy syrup, belladonna, arsenic, all here.' He turned, his eyes narrowed a little. 'No *aconitum*,' he said. 'No wolf's-bane.'

'Would they necessarily keep stocks of it?'

'It is a common treatment for fever and rheum. No well-stocked pharmacy is without it.'

'So Nicodemus has the wolf's-bane,' Merrivale said. 'And the feast begins at nones, as soon as mass is over.' He looked up at the sun. 'We have very little time.'

'That saffron sauce smells good,' Mauro said. 'Saffron always reminds me of home.'

'Spanish saffron is the best,' Clerebaud agreed. 'Far better than what they grow in France. This is to go with the poached eggs. Saffron sauce with eggs is one of the king's favourite dishes.'

Mauro smiled. 'Better that than tripe sausages.'

'Don't remind me.' As if on cue, Clerebaud gave a sudden moan, doubling up and clutching at his stomach. 'Christ, here we go again,' he said, and he lifted the pot from the fire once more and ran out of the kitchen, heading for the garderobe. Mauro followed him. By the time he reached the top of the stair, Clerebaud was already inside the little chamber, groaning with pain.

'*Señor*,' Mauro called. 'Are you all right?'

There was no answer, but the groaning ceased. The silence lasted for half a minute, and Mauro began to grow uneasy. '*Señor!*' he called.

Still no answer. With a shock, Mauro realised what had happened. '*Bastardo*,' he said under his breath, and hurried into the garderobe. The wooden seat had been lifted, and the shaft leading down to the ditch below was empty. There was no sign of Clerebaud.

–

Merrivale hurried into the palace courtyard followed by Tiphaine, Courcy and Gráinne, just as Mauro came running downstairs. 'He is gone. He climbed down the garderobe shaft just a few moments ago. *Señor*, I am sorry.'

'Don't be. Quickly, to the kitchens.'

John Sully was in the courtyard, dog trotting at his heels, and Merrivale stopped for a moment in surprise. 'Sir John! I thought you would be at mass.'

'At my age, mass is irrelevant,' the older man said. 'The fact that I am still alive is proof enough of God's favour.' He looked at Merrivale. 'What is wrong?'

'Someone is trying to poison the king,' Merrivale said, and he ran into the kitchen. The others followed. The pots of sauce stood lined up on the table, ready to be decanted for service. Merrivale bent over them, inhaling their rich aromas. Above the saffron sauce he stopped abruptly and stepped back. 'What do you think?' he asked Courcy.

The Irish knight leaned over the pot, sniffed and nodded. 'I think we've found the wolf's-bane,' he said.

Coloyne was beside them, his face sharp with anxiety. 'What is it?'

'This pot has been poisoned with aconitum,' Merrivale said. 'For whom was this intended? The king's table?'

'For everyone in the hall. We are feeding three hundred people, all the nobles and senior knights. A dish of poached eggs and saffron sauce was to be placed on every table.'

Courcy's jaw dropped. 'Jesus Christ. They intended to kill every single captain. They would decapitate the entire army, and leave it leaderless in the face of the enemy.'

'Yes,' said Merrivale, staring at the pot. 'That was their intention.'

'But what about the feast?' asked Coloyne, his face white with shock. 'The king is due to take his seat in the hall in a few minutes.'

'The other sauces may not have been poisoned,' Merrivale said. 'But we need to find a volunteer to taste the food, and quickly.'

'There is no need to risk a man's life,' said Sully. He turned to his dog, snapping his fingers. 'Sit, boy. Sit.'

'No, Sir John,' Merrivale said quietly. 'I know how much he means to you.'

'Aye, he's a good and loyal companion. But he is still a dog, and his life is not worth that of a man.' Sully picked up pieces of bread from the table and dipped them one by one in the other sauces. The animal looked up at him, brown eyes trusting, and opened its mouth to receive the first piece of bread, swallowing it quickly. The rest followed. Silence fell in the kitchen, everyone turning to watch.

'The poison acts quickly,' Courcy said. 'We will soon know.'

Time passed slowly, the curl of smoke from the fires the only movement in the kitchen around them. The dog looked up at Sully, gave the gentlest of belches and sat back. Raising one leg and lowering its head, it began to lick its own bollocks. Gráinne watched with disapproval. 'I reckon you'd do that, if you could,' she said to her husband.

Sully closed his eyes with relief. Merrivale gripped his shoulder tightly and nodded to the yeoman of the kitchen. 'Master Coloyne, you may serve your feast. The rest of you, come with me. We must find Clerebaud.'

–

The ditch below the garderobe shaft was muddy where someone had landed, and footprints had flattened the grass. Beyond the palace enclosure was another courtyard, surrounded by stone barns, leading to open fields where a few cows grazed in the middle distance, tended by a girl with a stick. To the right lay the picketed horses and rows of parked wagons of the baggage train.

Master Clerebaud the sauce-maker stood in the courtyard, leaning against a wooden water butt. His arms dangled loosely at his sides and his head lolled forward on his chest. Two arrows pinned him to the butt, holding him upright. Blood had welled up around the shafts, staining the front of his smock and dripping bright ruby droplets from its hem onto the ground.

He had been dead for no more than a few minutes. Merrivale ran past the barns and looked out across the fields. A man was running towards the pasture where the cows grazed. He carried a longbow in one hand and had a quiver slung across his back. Beyond the pasture lay a dense belt of woodland, part of the royal hunting preserve at Saint-Germain-en-Laye. If the archer gained the shelter of those trees, it would be impossible to find him.

Movement caught his eye, and he turned to see spearmen from the Red Company emerging from among the parked wagons. He cupped his hands to his mouth and shouted at them. 'Quickly! Stop that man!'

–

Nell Driver heard the herald's shout, and looked up to see Riccon Curry rushing towards her. She had never much liked him, especially after he started to bully her friend Master Clerebaud, and when she heard the herald shout the order to stop him, she did not even think. She drew the knife she carried at her belt and ran towards him.

She was small, but the knife was long and sharp and she knew how to use it; back in Hampshire, she had once had to drive off a wolf that was trying to attack her cattle. Curry saw her coming and reached for an arrow, but before he could draw it from the quiver, Nell was at close quarters, slashing with the knife. Curry dodged the first two blows and then stepped forward and kicked her, knocking her onto her back. He swore at her and raised his heavy bow to club her over the head, but Nell rolled away and the bow thudded into the ground. Curry overbalanced, and Nell rolled over again and stabbed him in the thigh.

The archer shouted, dropping the bow and clutching at his leg. Nell raised the knife again. Curry turned to see the Red Company spearmen charging towards him and realised he was cut off; he could no longer reach the shelter of the forest. He turned and ran back towards the town, sprinting with desperate speed despite his damaged leg, pursued by the spearmen. Drawing breath, Nell hitched up her kirtle and raced after them.

–

Matt raised his bow to shoot, but the herald knocked it aside. 'No!' he commanded. 'This time, I want him alive.'

'Then we had better get after him,' said Courcy.

They ran, but fast as they went, Curry was faster still. The scullion was wounded and leaking blood, but he was also running for his life. Passing the palace, they raced down the high street towards the bridge. Merrivale watched the fleeing man closely; if Curry dodged into one of the narrow lanes that ran off the street, he could hole up in an abandoned house and be hard to discover. But Curry did not turn. Injured, panicked and desperate, he ran without thought, hoping against hope for rescue.

By the time they reached the bridge, injury and loss of blood had begun to take their toll. Hobbling rather than running now, he struggled on towards the gap in the centre of the span. 'Stop him!'

Merrivale shouted to the carpenters. 'Do not let him cross!' The carpenters looked startled, but they picked up their hammers and mallets and turned to face the running man, barring his way.

Curry halted. The herald and his companions halted too, facing him, and Nell came panting up and joined them, still holding her bloody knife. The spearmen fanned out, prowling forward, intent on their quarry.

'Riccon Curry,' Merrivale said. 'By the powers invested in me by the king, I am placing you under arrest for the killing of John Clerebaud.'

'Go to hell,' said Curry. Dragging his wounded leg, he staggered towards the parapet of the bridge.

'You can still save yourself,' Merrivale said. 'Tell us where to find Nicodemus. If you do, I give you my word you will live.'

'I will tell you nothing,' said Curry. He hauled himself up onto the wooden parapet and stood for a moment, swaying.

'Christ!' Merrivale said sharply, and ran towards him, but he was too late. Gathering his strength, Curry turned to face the river, and jumped.

–

The current was strong; by the time Merrivale reached the parapet, Curry was already thirty yards downstream, splashing and floundering in the water. Pulling off his tabard and boots, the herald dived after him. He hit the river with a hard shock, water filling his mouth and nostrils, and kicked out, driving himself back towards the surface. Dimly he could hear people shouting from the bank. He spotted the scullion kicking feebly some distance downstream, and struck out after him.

Merrivale was a strong swimmer, having learned to swim in the cold pools of Dartmoor as a boy, but even so the currents buffeted him and sometimes tried to pull him under. He gained only slowly on the drifting man, and by the time he reached him, Curry had stopped moving. Hauling the inert body after him, the herald edged towards the southern shore. With the last of his strength he pulled the scullion into the shallows, where strong arms reached out and dragged them both ashore.

Mauro bent over him, eyes wide with anxiety. Tiphaine, white-faced, stood behind the manservant. Others gathered around too, a small crowd attracted by the chase and the shouting; he saw Mortimer and Gurney among them. The big leader of the Red Company's spearmen was there too. '*Señor!*' said Mauro. 'Are you all right?'

Merrivale sat up and spat out river water. 'Where is Curry?'

The scullion lay on his belly, eyes closed. Courcy knelt over him, pressing hard on his back and pumping the water out of his lungs in thin streams, but Curry did not move. After a while, Courcy lifted one of his arms and let it fall back limp. 'Gone to feed the fires of hell,' he said, and he turned the dead man over and closed his eyes with gentle fingers. *O God, Son of the Father, who taketh away the sins of the world, have mercy upon us*, the herald thought tiredly.

'Wait a moment,' Gurney said sharply. 'Why did you call him Curry?'

'That's his name, sir,' said Nell, looking down at the dead man with wide curious eyes. 'Riccon Curry. He's a sailor, or so he said.'

'He damned well is not. He's an archer, and his name is Jack Slade. He's the man who joined Tracey's company instead of mine.'

'And deserted at Pont-Hébert after killing his comrade Jake Madford,' the herald said. 'He was working with Nicodemus all along.' He looked at the Red Company man. 'Have you found Nicodemus?'

'Not yet, sir. But we found a wagon in the baggage train where we reckon a man has been sleeping at night. There were clothes and a bedroll, and several pairs of dice. One of them was weighted,' he added.

So that was how they had trapped Clerebaud. They had let him win money at first, and then used the weighted dice to clean him out. Trapped in debt, he'd had no choice but to do whatever Nicodemus and Slade demanded of him.

'It was Slade who poisoned the sauce at Lammas,' the herald said. 'He added the wolf's-bane when he brought the sauce to the prince's kitchen; he must have slipped it into one of the pots after the head cook had tasted it. I reckon that was a test, to see if it could be done. But Slade was not in the kitchens this morning.'

'No, *señor*,' said Mauro. 'I think the poison was hidden in the garderobe. Clerebaud collected it when he went there, and hid it in his clothes when I could not see him. I am sorry, *señor*. I should have made sure.'

Yes, you should, the herald thought, but there was no point in dwelling on it now. 'So, having added the poison to the sauce, Clerebaud then tried to escape, and Nicodemus ordered Slade to silence him.' He looked down at the dead man. 'Was he still hoping to make his own escape when he dived into the river? Or did he prefer death to capture?'

No one answered. Still dripping, Merrivale rose to his feet. Someone else came pushing through the crowd; another of the royal pages, a boy glittering in red and gold livery. 'Sir Herald? The Prince of Wales bids you attend on him. Come quickly, sir. You must make ready for the feast.'

'I will come,' the herald said heavily. 'But I doubt if I will have much appetite.'

22

Beauvais, thirty-seven miles south of the Somme, 18ᵗʰ of August, 1346
Morning

Dawn was a blaze of glory in the east, the sky painted with vibrant colours, and in the brilliant light the flames leaping from the roof of the abbey of Saint-Lucien seemed pale, almost transparent. Two more monasteries burned in the middle distance, smoke rising to cloud the fading stars. Watchfires glimmered on the walls of Beauvais, the city's defenders standing to and waiting for the English assault.

The Prince of Wales and his father were shouting at each other. 'What are they arguing about?' asked Lord Rowton.

'His Highness wishes to attack,' Merrivale said. 'His men are spoiling for a fight, he says, and the city is rich and offers many opportunities for plunder. His Grace says it would take too long and cost too many casualties.'

Rowton snorted. His arm was still strapped in its sling, now dirty with travel and fighting. 'His Grace is right, of course. Spoiling for a fight? Christ, have you seen the men? We've marched thirty miles in two days since Poissy, and they're exhausted. Their boots are wearing out, and we're running low on flour and pottage. I tell you, this army is in no condition to give battle.'

'I am inclined to agree, my lord. What is the latest news of the French?'

'While we were at Poissy, the main body of their army moved to defend Paris as we assumed they would. But King Jean and his Bohemian troops remained at Saint-Denis, and they are already in pursuit. Philip and the main army are a day behind us now, but the

Bohemians are closer, and they have fast light cavalry called *panzerati* that can make up the ground quickly. If the prince wants fighting, he is going to see plenty of it in the days to come.'

The shouting match ended as everyone knew it would; the prince throwing his arms in the air and stalking away in a fury, the king watching him with a small smile of satisfaction on his face. Around them the army streamed past in long columns, skirting the city and pressing on north.

'May I have a moment of your time, my lord?' Merrivale asked. 'There is a rather delicate matter I wish to discuss with you.'

'Is this to do with that unfortunate incident at Poissy?'

'Yes, my lord. Something is rotten in Sir Edward de Tracey's retinue. The deserter, Slade, killed the king's sauce-maker and twice attempted to poison the food. I am certain that Clerebaud was corrupted by Nicodemus, and that Slade was also working to Nicodemus's orders.'

'Have you found Nicodemus yet?'

'No, my lord, but the search by Grey and Percy's company confirmed he is still with the army, probably in some sort of disguise. Unfortunately, I am no longer able to avail myself of their services.' The Red Company were out on the army's eastern flank, ready to ward off the expected attacks of the Bohemians; only Matt and Pip remained behind, continuing their vigil as the herald's bodyguards.

'What do you need from me?' Rowton asked.

'How much influence does Sir Edward de Tracey have with the king?'

By the look on his face, it was clear that Rowton had not been expecting the question. 'How much do you think he has? His brother is the king's banker, after all.'

'I ask, my lord, because someone persuaded the king to stop me from investigating Sir Edmund Bray's death.'

'And you think that might have been Tracey. Why?'

'To protect Nicodemus, who formerly worked for Sir Edward's father, Sir John de Tracey. Among other things, Sir John and Nicodemus bought and sold slaves after the sack of Southampton. Several hundred English children were sold to buyers overseas.'

'Jesus Christ!' Rowton stared at him. 'Can you prove this?'

'At the moment, it is hearsay only. If I could lay hands on Nicodemus, I daresay I could.'

'Have you spoken to Tracey about this?'

'No, my lord. For whatever reason, I believe he is still protecting Nicodemus.'

The golden rim of the sun broke over the eastern horizon, inaugurating another day of fire. 'Leave this with me,' Rowton said. 'I will speak with the king, and with Tracey. If he really is protecting this man, then God help him.'

Grandvilliers, twenty-five miles south of the Somme, 19ᵗʰ of August, 1346
Evening

'The prince's division only made twelve miles today,' said Richard Percy. 'Any idea why?'

Percy had been in the field all day; he had ridden in to report to the king's headquarters at Sommereux, a couple of miles away to the north-west, and had stopped en route to see if there was any news.

'The men disobeyed orders,' Merrivale said. 'They stopped to plunder and burn a couple of towns as we passed.'

'Jesus Christ. Did the prince do nothing to stop them?'

'No.' As at Carentan, the young men had sat on the backs of their horses and laughed at the flames, cheering when roofs collapsed and ignoring the marshal when he tried to hurry them on. 'They are boys,' the herald said, 'and they have a boy's love of fire.'

'Well, they had better start growing up. The Bohemians are *there*.' Percy pointed to the east, where the sky was darkening to periwinkle blue and the first stars were pricking out. 'They drew level with us today, and they are marching faster and harder than we are. If King Jean reaches the Somme and its bridges before we do, then we can bend over and kiss our arses farewell.'

Still angry, Percy rode away towards headquarters. The herald stood for a moment, watching the stars, and then turned and walked into the

Prince of Wales's pavilion. Dinner had finished, though plates littered with fish bones were still stacked on the tables. There were no sauces.

'Highness,' said the herald. 'May I have a brief word?'

The prince paused, dice in hand, and waved to his companions. 'Leave us for a moment. What is it, herald?'

'Your defiance of your father does you credit,' Merrivale said. 'It is good to see you asserting your authority. Independence of spirit is one of the assay marks of a good leader.'

The young face glowed with pride. 'I am pleased to hear you say so, herald. I value your opinion, as you know.'

'Thank you, Highness. However, there must be no repeat of the scenes today.'

The prince's face lost some of its brightness. 'Why not?' he demanded.

'Because while we lingered and watched French towns burn, their army marched. We have now lost all the advantage we gained when we departed from Poissy.'

'The adversary is close at hand?'

'The royal army is still a day behind us, Highness. But King Jean of Bohemia and his troops are far too close for comfort.'

The prince's face lit up again. 'Blind King Jean? The crusader, the greatest general and warrior of our time? Oh, herald! It would be such an honour to match a lance with him!'

'King Jean will not fight us, Highness, not yet. I know his mind and how he thinks. He aims to reach the Somme before us and seize the bridges. If he succeeds, we will be in even greater peril than we were at Poissy.'

'Ah.' There was a pause while the implications sank in. 'Then we shall keep the men moving tomorrow,' the prince said abruptly. 'I will see to it, herald, and I will order the lord marshal to make it so.' He hesitated. 'You say you know King Jean's mind. Have you met him?'

'Once,' the herald said. 'It did not go well.'

'What happened?'

'He ordered me to be tied inside a sack and thrown into a river to drown. It is his favourite way of getting rid of those who displease him.'

The prince's jaw dropped. 'Why did he do that?'

'I brought him a message he did not like. He is a choleric man, and it takes little to anger him.'

'But... a sack in the river, to drown like a rat.' The prince paused, clearly re-evaluating his hero. 'How did you survive?'

Memories were crowding around the herald, and he was growing tired of them. 'I didn't,' he said. He bowed, turned and left the pavilion. Behind him he heard the prince explode into sudden laughter.

Molliens-Vidame, ten miles south of the Somme, 20th of August, 1346
Night

They had eaten Marigold two days ago, the night after the passage around Beauvais. She was the last of the milk cows to go; Garnet had been taken the day after they marched from Poissy. Milk cows were not meant for marching long distances over hard ground, and the poor beasts were so tired and worn that Nell thought it was almost a kindness to slaughter them. A farmer's daughter, she was unsentimental about her cows, or pretended to be, but now that they were gone, she had nothing to care for and no real occupation. She helped out in the royal kitchen where she could, eating leftovers in the evening and sleeping in the open fields with the other servants. She found she was beginning to miss her home.

She knew the danger, of course. They had marched hard today, but the rumours, running fast through the army, said they would never reach the Somme. Already there had been skirmishes out on the right flank. Everyone knew about Blind Jean, the famous King of Bohemia, and the kitchen staff discussed the battles he had fought and victories he had won in hushed, apprehensive voices. Now King Jean and his veteran troops were just over the eastern horizon, poised to reach the Somme before them and cut off their advance. If that happened, her chances of seeing her home again were small.

Kicking off her worn shoes and carrying them in her hand, she walked away from the camp. After the heat of the day, the grass felt cool under her feet. The moon was a thin scimitar already low in the west, and darkness lay heavy over the fields. She stopped after a while, looking up at the stars and seeing the familiar patterns, Arthur's Wain, the Harp, the Archer with his belt. In a moment of whimsy, she wondered where a mere archer had managed to find a belt with so many glowing jewels. Probably looted it from somewhere, she thought.

She realised she could hear voices, very dim and faint, just on the edge of hearing. For a moment she was reminded of being back in Freshwater, waking in the barn with Marigold and listening to the men outside, but these were different voices, speaking with Devon accents; and moreover, she thought she recognised one of them. She strained for a moment, listening to the faint whispers, and realised with a shock that one of them was Nicodemus.

'That's the orders, boy. Do it right away, you hear? There's no time to waste.'

'What about the money, Nic?' whispered another voice. 'When do we see it?'

'Tomorrow, when you've done your work. Ten florins it'll be, for each of you. But no mistakes now. If you fail, there's no money for any of us.'

'Aye, Nic. We'll attend to it.'

The voices ceased. Nell listened, holding her breath. Two shadows detached themselves from the blackness. Neither was Nicodemus; they were too tall and too broad in the shoulder. Taking a deep breath, she followed the two men back towards the camp.

–

Tiphaine was sitting on a bench outside the tent when the herald returned from dinner. 'Have you eaten?' he asked.

'Salt fish. I did not enjoy it.'

'The food at the prince's table was little better. Salt fish and dried mutton are about all we have left. Who is on watch tonight?'

'The younger one. Pip.'

Merrivale turned to see the archer standing in the shadows not far away, motionless and watchful. Since the Red Company's deployment into the field, the two sisters had been keeping watch in turns. Merrivale had offered to send them back to their company, but John Grey had refused. 'Keep them with you,' he had said tersely. 'You are still in danger, perhaps now more than ever.'

'You should be sleeping,' the herald said to Tiphaine.

'Inside the tent it is hot and airless. Out here it is cool. Sit down, if you wish.'

Merrivale pulled off his heavy tabard and sat down on the bench beside her. The night air smelled of smoke and sweat, bruised grass and the scent of horses in the lines nearby. Silence fell. Tiphaine sat gazing towards the east, where the glow of the Bohemian campfires was a thin orange line on the horizon.

'They will be over the river tomorrow,' she said. 'Won't they?'

'Yes,' said Merrivale. 'And we have no way of stopping them. Jean of Bohemia will win the race.'

'And then what?'

'I don't know. It is up to our commanders to devise some way out of this latest trap we have fallen into.'

Another long silence ensued. Merrivale watched Tiphaine's face, faint in profile in the dim light. He saw the long Norman nose, the straight, serious eyebrows and the thin, firm-set mouth. A strong face, he thought, and yet her chin was surprisingly soft, her eyelashes as delicate as silk threads. A perplexing face, a mixture of hard and gentle, like the soul that lay beneath it.

'Why did you go to Rouen?' he asked quietly.

'The queen told me I would find Rollond de Brus there. I thought I could talk to him and he would not betray me. I was wrong,' she added.

'You knew him from before?'

'Of course. His, like mine, is a prominent family. He is a cousin of the kings of Scotland, the Bruces. There was talk of a match between us. I knew Rollond wanted me for his wife. I was less certain.'

'Why?'

Tiphaine looked down at her hands. 'He is a very comely man; many would say he is beautiful. When he suggested we become lovers, I was more than willing.' She glanced up at Merrivale with a wry smile. 'And why not? You would not buy a horse without riding it first, would you?'

'Was this what he said?'

'That is what *I* said. And I will tell you the truth. I found the ride very agreeable at first.'

She waited to see if he was shocked. 'What happened?' Merrivale asked.

'After a time, once the delights of fornication had worn off, I began to realise his true nature. He is beautiful, but no one admires his beauty more than he himself. Narcissus could not rival him for vanity. And he knows the power that his charm gives him over women; oh, and men too, and that is what he lives for. There is not a single particle in his body that has ever given a thought for the happiness and well-being of anyone other than himself. I realised that I was just another mirror, into which he looked in order to admire himself more fully.'

She paused. 'I left him. But when I did so, I did not realise how much I had wounded his pride, or how badly he desired to revenge himself on me. When I walked into the castle at Rouen, he was overjoyed. I was foolish enough to believe that he was delighted to see me once more. Too late, I learned how wrong I was.'

'Yes,' Merrivale said. 'We all learn too late.'

Silence fell. The words lay between them, almost visible in the air, settling like dew on the grass.

'I asked you once if there had ever been a woman in your life,' Tiphaine said. 'You did not answer. I assume that means there was.'

'Yes,' Merrivale said finally. 'There was.'

'Is she still alive?'

'Yes. But she is unobtainable, at least to me.'

'Did you love her?' Tiphaine asked quietly.

He considered the question for a long time. 'Love,' he said finally. 'Such a small and insignificant word. It hardly begins to describe the turmoil of the soul, the terror and ecstasy and lunacy that burn like fever-candles... yes, I did love her. But those words don't do her justice, nor me.'

'Tell me about her.'

'What can I say? She was everything. She was Iseult and Morgana and Blanchefleur all rolled into one. She was the fire and the flame; she was the lily, and the rose.'

Tiphaine's voice was low. 'But it ended.'

'Yes. It turns out that the storybooks are all wrong. Our wishes were not granted. The kindly fates did not bring us together. No Olympian gods turned us into stars and planted us in the night sky to shine for evermore. No smiling Virgin looked down from her ikon and granted us eternal bliss. What we had turned to ashes and left us with nothing. And I still don't understand, Tiphaine. Why give us happiness in the first place, if only to take it away?'

'What happened?' she asked, echoing his own words.

'She was unobtainable. There is really no more to say.'

Tiphaine did not speak again. After a while, she turned and kissed his cheek, her lips soft as a bee's wing as they brushed his skin, and then she rose and went inside the tent.

–

Memories, the herald thought. As if we do not have enough cares in the present world, the past sends its phantoms to plague us as well. He shivered as he shrugged on his tabard once more, and he knew that it was not the cold that made him shiver.

He walked away from the tent, looking out towards the orange glow in the east. Ten miles to the Somme, he thought. Irrational hope suggested that there might still be a way across; after all, they had triumphed at Poissy when all seemed lost. Reason told him this was a lie. Lightning did not strike twice.

Something rustled in the darkness behind him. Nell Driver's voice screamed, 'Sir Herald! Look out!'

That half-second of warning saved his life. Merrivale turned, and the cudgel that had been aimed for the crown of his head hit his left shoulder instead. The padding of his tabard absorbed most of the blow, but it was still hard enough to numb his arm and make him wince with pain. He stumbled, a second blow thudding into his back, and then the man behind him was grappling with him, trying to slip something around his throat. A few yards away Pip was fighting with another man in the shadows. With his good hand, Merrivale caught hold of the bowstring his assailant was trying to use to choke him and pulled it forward, shuffling his boots to locate the other man's foot and then stamping down hard. The man grunted, his grip on the bowstring slackening, and Merrivale ripped it out of his hands and spun around, hitting him with a back-handed blow across his jaw that knocked him onto his back.

Pip was down on her knees, and her attacker had looped his own bowstring around her neck and was pulling hard. Choking silently, she scrabbled at the string, trying to pull it free. Merrivale ran straight into the man, knocking him sideways. The man stumbled but stayed on his feet and swung his fist, hitting Merrivale a powerful blow in the midriff and knocking the wind from his lungs. Gasping, the herald sank to his knees, seeing a dim flash of light as the man pulled something from his belt. Out of the shadows Nell came running, knife in hand, but the man turned to face her, towering over her with his own knife raised for the kill.

A bowstring twanged and an arrow drove into the man's ribs, burying itself halfway to the fletchings. Shot through the heart, he collapsed and fell without a sound, blood pouring black from his mouth as he lay on the grass. Pip walked forward, carrying her bow in one hand and rubbing her neck with the other. 'Thank you, sir.'

'Likewise,' Merrivale said, getting to his feet. His arm was still tingling, but he could feel his fingers again, and when he flexed his shoulder, nothing seemed to be broken.

Tiphaine appeared, followed by Mauro and Warin. The shot man lay lifeless on the ground. 'I'm sorry, sir,' Pip said. 'Looks like we've done it again. You probably wanted him alive to question him.'

'Under the circumstances, you were fully justified. What about the other one?' But there was no sign of the man Merrivale had knocked down. Clearly I didn't hit him hard enough, he thought. He looked at Nell.

'What are you doing here, Mistress Driver?'

'I overheard them two talking with Nicodemus, sir. They were Devon men, I reckon. They called him Nic, like they were friends.'

'From Tracey's retinue,' the herald said grimly. 'Did you see where Nicodemus went?'

'No, sir, but I followed the other two. Nicodemus promised them money to do something, but I didn't realise what it was till now.'

Rowton had said he would speak to Tracey about Nicodemus. This was the archer's response. 'How much did he offer them?' the herald asked.

'Ten florins each, sir.'

'So little? I would set a higher value on my life than that.'

He looked around the little group. 'I think that is quite enough excitement for one night,' he said. 'I suggest we all get some sleep. Tomorrow promises to be a long day.'

Airaines, four miles south of the Somme, 21ˢᵗ of August, 1346
Evening

'That was a damned stupid thing to do,' said the man from the north.

'Someone had to do something,' snapped the man from the West Country. 'You promised you would take care of the herald, but you didn't. He sank us at Poissy, and now we have to go and grovel in front of our partners and explain what went wrong.'

'I said I would take care of him, and I will.'

'Would you care to tell me how?'

'Not yet.'

'What do you mean, not yet? You haven't thought of anything, have you?'

'No, but I will,' said the man from the north. 'Now concentrate on the matter at hand. This is going to be difficult.'

The horizon was full of fire. To the west, watchfires glowed on the walls of the towns of Oisemont and Abbeville; to the east and south lay a long convex arc of orange light marking the positions of the main French army. And ominously, to the north, clusters of twinkling lights showed where Bohemian troops now guarded the bridges over the Somme. The race was over, and the blind king had won.

Closer at hand, the flames of burning farms and villages flickered like candles as the English continued their work of devastation. The lurid light showed five men waiting by a grove of trees, standing by their saddled horses. The man from the north frowned. 'There should be more of them,' he murmured. 'Something is wrong.'

John of Hainault stepped forward and bowed, stiffly and with a muffled clank of armour under his cloak. Nanteuil, the Grand Prior of the Knights of Saint John, was with him. 'Welcome,' Hainault said quietly.

'Where is the Count of Alençon?' asked the man from the north.

'His duties do not permit him to leave the army,' a younger man said smoothly. 'He sent me in his place to represent him. We met at Poissy, my lord. My name is Rollond de Brus.' He gestured to the other two men. 'This is Monsignor Raimon Vidal, secretary to Cardinal Aubert. He represents the cardinals, and by extension Signors Doria and Grimaldi. And this is Vilém Zajíc, herald to King Jean of Bohemia. He represents the interests of Count Rožmberk.'

They don't want to meet us, the man from the north thought in sudden anger. They are fobbing us off with their underlings. The Savoyard, Louis of Vaud had not even bothered to send a representative.

'Tell us what you want,' said Brus. 'Quickly, so that we may be gone.'

'We have a new plan,' said the man from the West Country.

The Grand Prior raised his eyebrows. 'What happened to the last one? You promised us you would cripple the English at Poissy. The king and his captains would die, and – what was your phrase? We could round up the rest at our leisure.'

'That plan failed. We have another one. Must we go over old ground?'

Vidal the secretary cleared his throat. 'Yes,' he said. 'I think we must. My master the cardinal insists on knowing what went wrong.'

'We attempted to poison the food at the feast of the Assumption,' the man from the West Country said. 'We thought the plan was foolproof, but someone found out about it.'

'Someone?' demanded Zajíc the herald. 'Who?'

'Simon Merrivale,' said the man from the West Country. 'The Prince of Wales's herald.'

Zajíc and Vidal looked at each other in the dim light. 'That man is dangerous,' said Vidal. 'You must remove him.'

'For Christ's sake,' said the man from the West Country. 'We have tried to kill him several times.'

'I did not say, kill him,' said Vidal. 'I said, remove him from the game. Or even better, turn him. Bring him over to our side.'

There was a long pause. 'Can that be done?' asked the man from the north.

'I know Merrivale well, as does my friend from Bohemia. We have sparred with him in the past. He is impressive. We could use his services.'

The West Country man was reluctant. 'Killing him would be safer.'

Vidal shook his head. 'But you have failed already, remember? Merrivale is a survivor. And as long as he lives, he will make trouble for you. My advice is to buy him.'

'What do you have in mind?' asked the man from the north.

'Tomorrow your army will attack the bridges on the Somme and try to force a passage,' said Zajíc. 'They will fail, of course. No one has ever defeated the blind king.'

Vidal nodded. 'When the fighting is over, we will send a flag of truce and offer to exchange prisoners. Make certain Merrivale is one of those who comes to meet us. Vilém and I will speak to him then. Be prepared to pay whatever price he asks.'

'Why are you so certain he will betray his masters?' asked the man from the West Country.

'Everyone has his price,' the Grand Prior said. 'You have proven that already, my lords.'

The man from the north nodded. 'We will do as you ask,' he said.

'And then what?' asked the Grand Prior. 'You spoke of another plan.'

'Edward's army is exhausted and running low on food. You must use the Bohemians to hold the bridges, as Master Zajíc suggests, while the rest of the army drives Edward west. Beyond Abbeville, the Somme broadens out into a wide estuary, and there are no more bridges.'

'But there is a ford,' John of Hainault said. 'The White Road across the Somme, which can be crossed at low tide. Remember?'

'We remember. And we will ensure that Edward remembers too. He is running out of ground for manoeuvre. Faced with a choice between starvation and being pushed into the sea, he will attempt the ford. Once his army is in the river, all you need do is stop up both ends of the ford, pin him there and wait for the tide to come in.'

'The entire English army will drown,' said the man from the West Country. 'And that, gentlemen, will be your moment to strike.'

'I think you may rely on us to know when it is time to strike,' said the Grand Prior. He moved towards his horse and stepped up into the saddle. 'Come, it is dangerous to linger here. Have your money ready, gentlemen. We shall require payment in full.'

He turned his horse and rode away. Brus, Vidal and Zajíc followed him. Hainault waited until they were out of earshot. 'You must make no mistake this time,' he said.

'We shall not,' said the man from the north.

'Things happen in war. I understand this, but my friends are less tolerant. Alençon in particular will lose patience quickly. Are you certain you can find the White Road?'

'I am.'

'Good.' Hainault mounted his horse and sat for a moment in the saddle, looking down at them. 'Good luck, my friends. And remember, no more mistakes.' Hainault rode away. The man from the north stood looking after him for a moment, and then suddenly, uncharacteristically, he spat hard on the ground.

'He always was an arrogant bastard,' he said.

Airaines, four miles south of the Somme, 22nd of August, 1346
Evening

'We have tried every bridge,' said Warwick. The marshal looked exhausted, his armour covered with dust and his surcoat dark with

313

dried blood. 'Pont-Remy, Longpré, Hangest, Picquigny, every time with the same result. Our archers cut the Bohemians to pieces, but they stood their ground and replied with crossbows and stone shot. We could gain no ground.'

Another sunset flamed and died in the west, the end of the hardest day of the campaign so far. A few miles away to the south, the rearguard under Arundel, reinforced by the Red Company, had spent the entire day fighting off a relentless series of French attacks.

'We left the causeway at Pont-Remy paved with blood,' said Godefroi d'Harcourt. 'Their losses were terrible, but so were ours. God curse King Jean. Even blind, he can read a battlefield better than most men.'

'What about Amiens?' the king demanded.

'Heavily fortified, and now most of the adversary's army are inside the walls. It is even more impregnable than Paris.'

'Abbeville? That is the last bridge downstream.'

'Fortified too, with a garrison of local troops and a contingent of Bohemians to stiffen them.' Warwick paused. 'There is still the Blanchetaque. The White Road.'

'The ford west of Abbeville,' said the king. 'I've heard of it, of course. Does anyone know where it is?'

'The Blanchetaque? It is a myth, sire,' said Lord Rowton. 'The country people talk about a white road under the water where ghosts of Roman soldiers march when the moon is full.'

'Perhaps it is a myth, and perhaps it isn't,' the king said. 'But if the ford is there, and we can't force the bridges, then it may be the answer to our prayers.'

Rowton looked sceptical. 'Even if there is a ford, it is fifteen miles from Abbeville to the sea. Finding it will not be easy.'

The king turned on him. 'God damn it, Eustace, what else are we supposed to do? We've food for only three more days and no other way across the river. What do you suggest?'

Rowton said nothing. 'Find that ford,' the king said. 'Either that, or find someone who knows where it is. That is an order, Eustace. I am holding you personally responsible for this.'

Rowton bowed, his face stony. 'Yes, sire.'

'Good, make it so.' The king turned again, shading his eyes in the sunset light. 'Who are these people, and what do they want?'

Three horsemen were riding down from the north, pulling up as they neared the camp. Their leader held a large white flag on a staff over his head. 'It is Montjoie Herald, sire,' said Andrew Clarenceux. 'The adversary's ambassador. It seems he wishes to parley.'

'What in Christ's name for? He already has us exactly where he wants us.' The king nodded. 'Very well, Clarenceux, go and see him. Merrivale, go with him. But if they are offering another proposal for peace, tell them to go to hell.'

'What do you suppose they do want?' Clarenceux asked as they trotted their horses towards the waiting men.

'I don't know,' said Merrivale, watching them with narrowed eyes. 'Andrew, I suggest you talk directly with Montjoie. I will deal with the other two.'

They reined in their horses a few yards from the waiting men and bowed from the saddle. 'Montjoie,' said Clarenceux. 'What brings you here?'

'I am glad to see you well, Andrew,' the French herald said, smiling. 'I heard you were running low on food. I can send for some bread, if you wish, or perhaps some fruit? The quinces have ripened early this year.'

'Ah, you remember my fondness for quinces,' said Clarenceux, bowing again. 'It is kind of you to think of me, but the hour is growing late and I think we should get down to business.'

'Very well. We took some of your men-at-arms prisoner today, and I believe you took some of ours a few days ago. Would your king be willing to consider an exchange, with prisoners on both sides to go free provided they give their parole?'

'Certainly we can discuss it,' said Clarenceux. 'Whom have you taken?'

Merrivale listened a moment while Montjoie began to list the prisoners, and then turned his mount and rode a few yards away. The other two horsemen followed.

'Simon, my friend,' said Vidal, the brown-robed Franciscan. 'A pleasure to see you again. And you remember Vilém Zajíc, of course.'

'Good evening, sir,' said Zajíc smiling. He wore a tabard with a distinctive badge, a white lion rampant with two tails on a field of red. 'I see you survived your dip in the river.'

'It was kind of your master to arrange for me to have a bath,' said Merrivale. 'What do you two want?'

'I will be honest with you,' said Vidal.

'That would be a novelty.'

'There is a first time for everything,' he agreed. 'You know about the plots, of course, the conspiracies in England and in France. But you do not yet know who is behind them.'

'Are you going to tell me?'

'Here and now? No. But there is a way you can gratify your curiosity.'

'What do you mean?'

'You can join us,' said Zajíc.

'Ah,' said Merrivale after a moment. 'Why would I wish to do that?'

'Because we are going to win,' Vidal said. 'What you said in Lisieux was right. The French plot centres around Alençon and Cardinal Aubert. The Italians are involved too, Cardinal Ceccano and Doria and Grimaldi. But there are others too.'

Merrivale looked at Zajíc. 'The King of Bohemia?'

The other herald nodded. 'Count Rožmberk his chamberlain is one of us.'

'And the Knights of Saint John,' said Vidal. He paused for a moment. 'And an old friend of yours. Louis of Vaud, the regent of Savoy.'

Merrivale turned his head for a moment, staring out at the livid red glow of the sunset, full of smoky brilliance like the entrance to a furnace, or the gates of hell. 'Why do you mention him?'

'As a lure, of course,' said Vidal. 'We know you trust Louis. With him on our side, you can be sure that our intention is genuine and that our actions will be honourable. We are doing this to bring about the end of the war, Simon. The fighting has already lasted for too long.

We all need peace. Removing both Edward and Philippe is the only way to reconcile the two nations.'

Merrivale shook his head. 'This is not about the war. This conspiracy has longer roots than that, Raimon. Is John of Hainault involved?'

The two men glanced at each other. 'Yes,' said Vidal. 'He is.'

'King Philip's councillor and friend. Formerly, councillor and friend to the young King Edward. And before that, he was Roger Mortimer's right hand. This conspiracy has been twenty years in the making, has it not, Raimon?'

'I cannot answer that,' Vidal said. 'But Louis of Vaud can.'

Silence fell. 'We have told you who the actors are,' said Zajíc. 'If you want to know the rest, how the plot began and who is pulling the strings, all you have to do is join us. But of course you will never be able to go back.'

'You will not want to,' Vidal said. 'This time you will be on the winning side.'

'I wish to speak to Louis of Vaud,' Merrivale said. 'And to Doria and Grimaldi. All three of them.'

Again the two men glanced at each other. 'Perhaps it can be arranged,' said Zajíc.

'Where and when?'

'That depends on whether they are willing to meet you,' Vidal said. 'We will let you know.'

—

Clarenceux and Montjoie finished their business, parting with professional courtesy. Silently Merrivale rejoined his colleague and rode back towards the camp around Airaines. Vidal and Zajíc watched him go. 'He is an unusual man,' said Vidal.

'Why do you say so?'

'Well, for one thing, he didn't even ask how much we were going to pay him.'

Inquisition into the death of Edmund Bray, knight, near the village of Quettehou in Normandy on the XIIth day of July, in the nineteenth year of the reign of King Edward III. This report was composed on the XXIInd day of August, at the town of Airaines.

Item, one of the leaders of the conspiracy can now be identified as John of Hainault, Lord of Beaumont, a member of the adversary's council.

Item, John of Hainault was also a lieutenant of Roger Mortimer, Earl of March, and was present at Berkeley Castle the night the king's late father was assassinated. Hainault was also privy to a plot by Mortimer to remove his Grace the king and to rule England in the name of the King of France.

Item, some of Hainault's late co-conspirators are still working with him, and are attempting to complete the plot they began at Berkeley Castle. Their aim is the overthrow of both England and France. They have powerful allies, including the King of Bohemia, the Count of Alençon, Cardinals Aubert and Ceccano, the Knights of Saint John, the captains of the Genoese mercenaries, and possibly the regent of Savoy, Count Louis of Vaud.

Item, the conspirators attempted to destroy the English army at Poissy. They are now attempting to complete their work, and are undermining our foundations even as I write these words.

Simon Merrivale, heraldus

Airaines, four miles south of the Somme, 22nd of August, 1346
Night

'What in hell's name is this?' The king, in his night robe, waved the piece of parchment at the herald. 'You were appointed to enquire into

Bray's death, not go raking up old events. For Christ's sake, Merrivale, what did you think you were doing?'

'There is something else I did not put in the report, sire,' said Merrivale. 'Edmund Bray's father was also present at Berkeley Castle that night. He fell out with the others when he learned of your father's death, and never spoke to them again.'

The king stared at him. 'Bray's father? How do you know this?'

'Does your Grace really wish me to answer that question?'

The king paused for a moment. 'No,' he said. 'No, God damn it, I don't. I want this entire business to disappear. Do you understand me? If my father really did die at Berkeley, it was twenty years ago. There is nothing to be gained by bringing it up again now. Understood?'

'Yes, sire. What about John of Hainault?'

'Even if he is plotting against the King of France, so what? Let the bastard plot. Have you any direct evidence that he is plotting against me also?'

'No, sire. Just rumours and suspicion.'

'Rumours and suspicion,' the king repeated. 'The usual stock-in-trade of you spies.'

'Yet someone tried to poison you and your entire court at Poissy, sire.'

'The poisoners are both dead. Can you connect them with Hainault?'

'No, sire. But men wearing his badges also raided our camp several days before Poissy. It is possible that they were attempting to assassinate you and the prince.'

The king waved the parchment again. 'Of course they were. We are at war, and Hainault is on the enemy's side. He always was a ruthless bastard. Well, so am I, Merrivale. This army *will* cross the Somme, and we *will* reach Flanders and safety, and Hainault is damned well not going to stand in our way. Right now, that is the only thing that matters.'

'Yes, sire.'

'Dragging up the past is not going to help. Twenty years ago, we were a nation divided and riven by strife. I have spent two decades

319

reuniting us and giving us a sense of purpose. I will not see that undone now. Do you understand me?'

'Yes, sire.'

'Good. Now, make an end to your enquiry and resume your usual duties. Let Edmund Bray rest easy in his grave.' The king paused for a moment, staring into space. 'His father, you say. Is he still alive?'

'Yes, sire.'

'Hmm, well... a matter for another time, perhaps.' The king dropped the parchment onto a side table. 'That is all, Merrivale. You may go.'

23

Airaines, four miles south of the Somme, 23rd of August, 1346
Morning

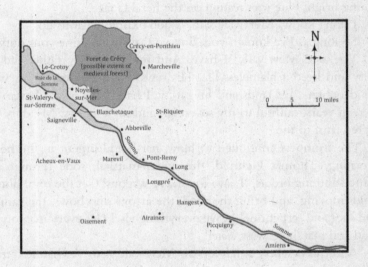

'The Bohemians are on the move,' the scout said breathlessly. 'I saw their banner, the lion with two tails. The blind king is coming.'

Dawn was still breaking when word began to run through the camp. Trumpets sounded the alarm. 'It is not just the Bohemians,' Sir John Sully's esquire reported as he buckled on his master's armour. 'It's the whole French army. The adversary himself is on the way.'

'Well, we can't fight him here,' Sully said, looking around at the flat open fields around the camp. 'So we'll have to keep running.' He glanced at Merrivale. 'But I reckon we can't run for much longer, boy. My archers have worn through the soles of their boots, and they're thin as rakes. Sooner or later we're going to have to fight.' He picked up his painted shield and stood while his esquire strapped it to his forearm. 'What are you going to do now?'

'What can I do? The king has ordered me to drop the inquisition. We have more important things to worry about, he says.'

'*He* has, there's no doubt about that. But what about you?'

Merrivale glanced at the esquire. Sully nodded. 'See to the horses, Baker,' he said.

The esquire bowed and departed. Sully waited, those ridiculously young bright blue eyes resting on the herald's face.

'I don't know,' Merrivale said. 'I don't know what to do.'

'So long as I've known you, boy, you've always done your duty.'

'Yes,' said Merrivale. 'I have. And for what? My father did his duty and lived a blameless life. His reward was the loss of his wife, his daughters, his lands and his sanity. I have been a king's man for sixteen years, faithful to my sovereign and my country. My duty is a sacred trust to me.'

The trumpets continued to blow, harsh and urgent in the heavy morning. Thomas Ughtred, the under-marshal, rode through the camp shouting orders. 'Leave the heavy wagons! Get the royal households moving, and bring the food, the arrows and bows, the cannon and shot and serpentine! Leave everything else! Get every man on the road and marching west, *now*!'

'And this is where it has led us,' Merrivale said. 'A chaotic retreat, a day of disaster, and most likely our deaths. And for what?'

'God alone knows,' said Sully. He smiled. 'But let's make sure we ask Him, shall we, when we reach the gate of pearls.'

Oisemont, four miles south of the Somme, 23rd of August, 1346
Late morning

It was very hot now, the air thick with dust and humidity, and the stink of fresh blood was so strong that the herald could almost taste it in his mouth. The bodies of men and horses lay in a thick trail across the fields towards the open gates of Oisemont half a mile away. Smoke boiled above the town, rising in furious clouds into the sky. Even at a distance the screaming could be heard as the English, ruthless as terriers, ran through the streets exterminating the last defenders. As at Caen and Gaillon, the defenders had failed to surrender; therefore, according to the laws of war, they could expect no mercy.

The laws of war, thought the herald. Of all the falsehoods that had been perpetrated by humanity, the notion that wars had laws that must be obeyed was surely one of the most cynical.

Roger Mortimer raised his visor and wiped the sweat from his face. 'Stupid bastards. There were only a few hundred of them, they never had a chance. Why did they come out to fight us?'

'Orders, of course,' said Warwick. 'They were sacrificed to slow us down so the main French army could keep up with us. Is there any news of the adversary? Is he still moving?'

'His men halted at Airaines to plunder our baggage, as we knew they would,' said Thomas Holland. 'That won't distract them for long, though. They will be marching again soon.'

'And the king? Any word from him?'

The king had ridden north with a strong party to reconnoitre the walls of Abbeville, in the faint hope that a coup might be possible. The Earl of Salisbury shook his head. 'A messenger came back a few minutes ago. The walls are high and thick and the ramparts are full of troops. His Grace is retiring to join the main body.'

Warwick turned to John Grey. 'A night attack? You pulled it off at La Roche-Guyon.'

Grey shook his head. 'The defenders of La Roche-Guyon were few, and they were not expecting an assault. Abbeville sounds like the exact opposite. Is there any word about this ford?'

'Lord Rowton is searching for it now,' Warwick said.

The smoke from Oisemont continued to rise, choking off the sun. One of Warwick's esquires rode up, flipping up the visor of his bascinet. 'Flag of truce approaching, my lord.'

'Again? Who is it? Montjoie, come to gloat?'

'No, my lord. It is Bohemia's herald.'

Warwick looked at Merrivale. 'Go and see what he wants.'

Vilém Zajíc sat on his horse in the middle of a field of stubble, looking at the smoke and the corpses with disapproval. 'Such a waste,' he said as Merrivale rode up. 'There is no honour in slaughtering peasants.'

'Oh? Would your master agree with you?'

'His Grace has slaughtered many peasants in his day, but always for expediency. Never for honour.'

'It is the same with us. These men were trying to slow us down and prevent us from reaching our destination.'

Zajíc raised his eyebrows. 'And what is your destination? The sea? Are you planning to swim back to England?'

'Perhaps. Do you have a message for my king?'

'I do. It comes from his Grace the most serene and puissant Jean, King of Bohemia and Count of Luxembourg. He challenges your King Edward to single combat. The outcome will determine who is victorious in this campaign, and who is the loser.'

Merrivale raised his eyebrows. 'King Jean is challenging King Edward to a joust?'

'Exactly so. His Grace bids me add also that he knows he is the older man, and blind in both eyes, but even so he is a more noble warrior and skilled master of arms than Edward Plantagenet will ever be. Therefore, if Edward Plantagenet refuses to meet him, King Jean will know that he is afraid and wishes to avoid defeat. His fear will be understandable, although of course,' Zajíc added, 'it will also show that he is a dishonourable man and not fit to wear his crown.'

'I see,' said Merrivale. 'You realise that my king will be greatly offended by these words.'

Zajíc smiled. 'That is my lord's intention,' he said. 'Now, to more important business. The Count of Vaud and Signor Doria have agreed to meet you. Signor Grimaldi also.'

'Where and when?'

'In two days' time, at compline. They will be in the cloister of Saint-Pierre, outside the walls of Abbeville. You will be expected. Your herald's tabard will identify you, but the count sends you a *laissez-passer* in case there are difficulties.' Zajíc reached inside his own tabard and brought out a small parchment roll tied with a blue ribbon.

'It seems a long time to wait,' Merrivale said.

'Count Louis is here, but his troops are a long way behind, still marching up from the south. He has four thousand men, and he wants them at his back before he makes his next move.' Zajíc paused for a moment. 'I am curious. Aren't you going to ask what we are offering you?'

'Does it matter?' asked Merrivale. 'Clearly you want my services. If the conspiracy is successful, I can name my price. And if it fails, it will not matter.'

Acheux, five miles south of the Somme, 23rd of August, 1346
Evening

'We might be able to take Abbeville,' the king said. Like most of the men around him, he was still in full armour, the gold leopards on his surcoat angry in the firelight. 'But it would cost too many men and take too much time. The adversary is close at hand. Long before we could storm the town and get our men and the remaining wagons over the bridge, the whole French army would be upon us.'

He looked at the circle of men who had gathered on the side of a low hill above the village of Acheux. 'I had considered trying to capture one of the seaports, Saint-Valery perhaps, in hopes of finding enough ships to take us home. But Godefroi reconnoitred the place this morning and saw no ships there.'

'The adversary will have ordered all ships dispersed elsewhere, to prevent us from seizing them,' said Warwick.

'Doubtless,' said the king. 'And to save you saying it, Thomas, yes, it is a damned pity we ordered the fleet home earlier this summer. Huntingdon and his ships would have been quite useful right now. However, there it is.'

He turned to Rowton. 'The Blanchetaque. Have you found it?'

Rowton looked down at his feet for a moment, then back up at the king. 'No, sire,' he said steadily. 'I have not. I have failed you.'

Another monarch might have been furious, Merrivale thought, but Edward merely nodded. 'Never mind, Eustace. You did your best.'

Rowton shook his head without speaking, the pain of disappointment plain in his face. The king turned to the others. 'Well, gentlemen? What about the rest of you? I gather there was some wholesale butchery at Oisemont this morning. I don't suppose any of you managed to take any prisoners?'

The captains looked at each other. 'I did, sire,' said Edward de Tracey. 'We caught a party outside the west gate trying to escape towards Saint-Valery. We have them under guard now.'

'Who are they? Anyone of quality?'

'No, sire. Peasants mostly, called up under the *arrière-ban*.' Tracey hesitated. 'I was thinking of sending them home. They're worthless in terms of ransoms, and we can't afford to feed them.'

'Bring them here,' the king commanded.

The prisoners were paraded a few minutes later. There were about twenty of them, guarded by a quartet of Tracey's archers, and they knelt in a row with their hands resting on the ground. Some of them were shaking with fear.

'You know who I am,' the king said.

The man at the end of the row looked up. 'Yes, sire,' he said.

'Do any of you know about the ford over the Somme? The one called the Blanchetaque?'

The same man looked at his comrades, who continued to stare at the ground. Finally he nodded. 'Yes, sire, I do.'

'Where is it?' the king demanded. 'Where is the ford?'

The man said nothing. 'Give him some money, Northburgh,' said the king.

Northburgh tossed a leather pouch onto the ground in front of the man. It landed with a heavy metallic clunk. 'Tell me where the Blanchetaque is,' the king said.

The man made no move. The king motioned with his hand. 'Very well. Take them away and hang them.'

The man sat upright. 'Spare our lives, sire, all of us, and I will tell you,' he said.

Silence fell. 'I am waiting,' the king said, his voice growling in the back of his throat.

'The southern end of the ford is at the village of Saigneville, six miles from Abbeville. At low tide you will see it clearly, a road of white stones beneath the water. Then you can cross.'

'When is low tide?' the king demanded.

'About now, sire.'

Rowton shook his head. 'We will never get there in time. By the time we reach the river the tide will becoming in.'

'No, but it will be low tide again at terce,' Northampton said. 'If we march at first light, sire, we can reach the ford by then.' He looked at the prisoner. 'I assume the French also know about the Blanchetaque. Is the ford guarded?'

'Yes, my lord. I saw men-at-arms riding down the north bank yesterday.'

'How many?'

The prisoner shrugged. 'A few hundred, perhaps.'

A sigh of relief went up from the circle of men. The Prince of Wales clapped his hands. 'They might have received reinforcements,' Warwick warned.

'They might,' said the king, 'but we'll have to take the chance. Well done in securing these men, Sir Edward. You have given a very great service to your crown and country today. It will not be forgotten.'

Tracey bowed. 'I am honoured to be of service, sire.'

The king turned to the prisoners. 'You asked for your lives to be spared, and they will be. Go now, and return to your homes. And remember my generosity,' he added, pointing to the pouch on the ground.

The prisoner who had given the information tucked the pouch into his tunic and bowed. 'Thank you, sire,' he said. 'Your liberality does you great honour. Hopefully one day France can repay the debt it owes you.'

'Speak with respect to the king who showed you mercy,' Tracey said sharply, resting his hand on the hilt of his sword. The prisoners bolted into the darkness.

John Sully looked at Merrivale. 'What do you suppose he meant by that?'

'I don't know,' Merrivale said. 'But I rather fear I can guess.'

–

The other captains dispersed. The herald and Sully walked down the slope towards the little stream at the bottom of the hill, Matt and Pip following them discreetly as ever. 'The conspirators have made me an offer,' Merrivale said.

'I see.' Sully considered this for a moment. 'A good one?'

'Terms are still to be negotiated, but I have no doubt they will be favourable. They are arranging for me to meet some of the conspirators. Louis of Vaud is one of them.'

'The Regent of Savoy? I recall I met him some years ago, back when Aymon the Peaceful was still on the throne.'

'So did I. Even though we were on opposite sides, I trusted him. More than I trusted some of our friends, come to that.'

'Will you meet them?'

Merrivale shrugged. 'You see the situation we are in. What do I have to lose?'

'Your head,' Sully pointed out. 'If things go wrong.'

'Things have already gone wrong,' Merrivale said. 'This is the last chance to put them right.'

Saigneville, south bank of the Somme, 24th of August, 1346
Morning

The sun rose in colours of carnelian and gold, flaming off the green fields and the rippling waters of the river. The towers and spires of Abbeville were silhouettes against the light. Looking west, Merrivale saw a dark fog bank hovering above the sea five miles away.

The ford was clearly visible, a pale ribbon beneath the water: the Blanchetaque, the White Road, just where the Frenchman had promised it would be. Grey and Percy and their men were already down at the river's edge, testing the depth of the water. Everyone else was gazing at the north bank a mile and a half away, where a solid mass of men stood on the slope above the estuary. Some were mounted and some were on foot, lances and spears tipped with the bright flecks of coloured pennons. Armour flashed like sparks in the sunlight, and they saw the unmistakable white coats of crossbowmen.

'Holy Mary, Mother of God,' said Nicholas Courcy quietly. 'That fellow told us there were only a few hundred of them. By Christ, there's four thousand if there's one.'

'At least five hundred men-at-arms,' said Thomas Holland, shading his good eye with his hand. They had seen little of Holland on the march north; the wound he had taken at Gaillon had begun to fester. He had spent much of the journey from Poissy consumed with fever, but he was here now, thin and wasted with illness and pain, his knuckles white on the hilt of his sword.

'And another five hundred Genoese,' said young Salisbury. 'And we can only ride about ten abreast across that ford. They will pick us off as we come, and if we do get a foothold on the north shore, the men-at-arms will charge downhill and drive us back into the river.'

'Aye,' said John Sully. He had taken off his bascinet, resting it on the pommel of his saddle, and his white hair shone in the sunlight. 'It will be just like Stirling Bridge all over again.'

Mortimer turned his head. 'What happened at Stirling Bridge?'

'William Wallace held his men back until about a third of our army had crossed the bridge. Then he charged home. Once the Scots seized the bridgehead, it was all over. Every Englishman who crossed the bridge died, apart from a few that could swim. I was one of them.'

Courcy grinned at Mortimer. 'I'll bet you're glad you asked,' he said.

'Anyone who wants to survive should stick close to Sir John,' Matthew Gurney said. 'Clearly he has a knack for it.'

'And the rest of us should pray for a miracle,' said Salisbury. 'Because we will need one to get across that river.'

Holland shook his head. 'Save your breath,' he said. 'We already had one miracle, at Poissy, and we threw it away. I doubt if God is in the mood to grant another.'

Horsemen came riding up from behind, the Prince of Wales with Warwick and Northampton. 'We have just seen his Grace,' the constable said. 'Bohemian horsemen are advancing down the south bank from Abbeville, with the rest of the French army behind them. The king and Arundel will hold them off as long as they can, while we seize the ford.'

The prince stared across the river at the massed French troops. 'How many of them are there?'

'Sir Nicholas Courcy reckons four thousand,' said Salisbury. 'With men-at-arms and crossbows.'

'Four thousand.' The prince looked at Warwick and Northampton. Suddenly he grinned. 'Then we're fucked, aren't we?' he said.

'Hardly the language to use to encourage the men, Highness,' murmured Burghersh, his tutor. But he was wrong; the men around them were smiling, some of the archers sniggering behind their hands.

'Ah now,' said Courcy. 'I seem to recall old Caesar saying something very similar when he crossed the Rubicon. And that turned out pretty well.'

'What Caesar actually said was "the die is cast",' Burghersh said.

'Translate it into Irish and it comes out the same thing,' said Lady Gráinne.

The prince laughed out loud. 'Very good,' he said. 'The die is cast indeed. Well, Lord Marshal, Lord Constable? Shall we decide the order of march?'

'The Red Company goes first,' said Warwick, pointing to the men down by the river.

'No,' said Hugh Despenser.

In the silence, every eye turned on Despenser. 'No,' he repeated. 'I have spent this entire campaign waiting for a chance to prove myself, to wipe out the sins of my father and grandfather. This is my hour.'

'And I am coming with you,' said Mortimer.

'So am I,' said Matthew Gurney, riding up alongside them and halting. 'Sir Hugh is right, Highness. We deserve our chance.'

Despenser looked at Gurney. 'You said that anyone who wanted to survive should stick with Sir John.'

'I did. I didn't say I was one of them.'

'So be it,' said the prince. 'Sir Hugh's men will lead and the Red Company will follow. Sir Thomas Holland's company is third, and I will come after them.'

'Highness,' said Burghersh. 'Think of your safety.'

The prince did not turn his head. 'Once we are in that river, there is no safety for any of us. Very well, Lord Marshal. Make it so.'

Warwick nodded. 'We cross as soon as the water is low enough.' He rode a few paces forward and shouted down to the men on the bank. 'John! Richard! Are we ready?'

'Not yet,' Grey called back. 'The water is still too deep. We must wait.'

—

They waited. The sun climbed higher into the sky. Dust clouds boiled in the east as the Bohemians drew closer and closer. More companies came crowding down onto the riverbank, followed by the royal servants and some of the remaining carts and wagons. Merrivale spotted Tiphaine on the back of a pony and motioned to her to join him. 'Stay close to me,' he said. 'On my left side. You will be downriver, and I can shield you from the current.'

He looked around again and saw another familiar figure, the little cowherd. My God, he thought, water that is chest height on a man will be over her head. He beckoned to her quickly. 'Mistress Driver! Come here, girl. Up on the saddle in front of me, quickly now.'

She scrambled up, holding onto the mane of his horse. Michael Northburgh rode past and grinned at him. 'Adding to your collection of *demoiselles*, I see.'

The dust clouds were very close now. Some of the Red Company men were venturing out into the river, linked by ropes. They called something to the shore, and John Grey nodded. Turning towards Warwick, he cupped his hands and shouted, 'The water is deep, but we can cross.'

331

High and clear, cutting across all other sounds like an angel announcing that the gates of heaven had opened, a trumpet called.

The water was cold, despite the summer's heat, and it deepened quickly. Despenser's archers, leading the way, were soon up to their chests, holding their bows over their heads to keep the strings dry. The Red Company followed, their ponies half walking and half swimming, and then Holland's Lancashire men and the prince and his household, Warwick and Northampton riding with them. Courcy and Gráinne and the gallowglasses had moved up to join them. Merrivale felt his boots fill with water, and Nell's kirtle was quickly wet to the waist. She leant forward, twining her fingers into the horse's mane.

Progress was painfully slow. Men and horses, struggling against the weight of the water, seemed to move only inches at a time. As they left the shelter of the shore, the current increased, the flow of the river amplified by the receding tide. The water eddied and boiled around them. The bed of the ford was uneven, and both men and horses stumbled. Tiphaine's pony tripped, nearly pitching her into the river, but Merrivale grabbed her arm, dragging her back into the saddle.

Up ahead, a mounted man-at-arms veered off the road into the deeps, and he and his horse were both quickly sucked under. They saw the horse rise again, whinnying with fright, kicking and thrashing against the tide that swept it away towards the sea. The man-at-arms did not resurface.

It seemed to take an eternity to reach the middle of the river. Merrivale glanced back briefly, seeing the long, glittering column following them across the ford. The ominous dust cloud was no more than a mile from Saigneville. Up ahead, the figures of the enemy were becoming more distinct, the coats of arms on surcoats visible now, men-at-arms resting on their horses with lances raised, Genoese winding their crossbows, foot soldiers armed with gleaming swords and spears, waiting.

Another horse slipped and fell, pitching its rider into the river; Gráinne. Even as she went under, Courcy was already diving from the saddle after her. They saw him struggling to lift her, burdened by her antique armour, and Merrivale tried to urge his horse towards them, but the pressure of the water held him back. It was Donnchad, surging past them in a shower of spray, who lifted Gráinne and slung her over the back of Courcy's horse, while Courcy himself grabbed the pommel and dragged himself back into the saddle, shedding water. 'Are you all right there, my lady?' he asked.

'Shut up and get us out of this goddamned river,' she gasped.

Silence fell, the only sound the rushing water around them. Merrivale fancied he could hear his own heart beating. In front of him Nell was trembling a little with nerves and cold. 'When the shooting begins, stay low,' he said quietly to Tiphaine. 'If your horse is hit, get out of the saddle as soon as you can and swim for the shore.' She nodded, face pale under her sunburn.

The north bank was a quarter of a mile away. Despenser's men were still in deep water, bows over their heads. Up on the bank, the Genoese were in motion, moving down to the foreshore, kneeling and taking aim. Wading slowly, unable to shoot back, Despenser and his archers were vulnerable as fish in a barrel.

At a range of three hundred yards, the Genoese began to shoot.

–

One by one Despenser's men went down, floating away on the current, some struggling to pull the bolts from their bodies, others already inert. Other bolts flew high, whistling past the Red Company and Holland's men to land among the prince's household. One bolt passed between Merrivale and Tiphaine; another splashed into the river alongside him. Up ahead, the Red Company's archers and crossbowmen were shooting from the saddle, and some of the Genoese fell too, white coats littering the foreshore. The rest of them dodged for cover, their fire slackening as they raised their heavy wooden shields, and in that brief respite the first of Despenser's men reached the shallows, plucked arrows from their quivers and began to shoot back.

The shields provided some protection, but not enough. More Genoese fell, and the rest sagged back. Merrivale saw Despenser come ashore, Mortimer and Gurney behind him, all three with drawn swords in their hands. Despenser shouted something and the three of them launched themselves at the enemy, the remainder of the company running after them, screaming like maniacs. The Genoese turned and fled, scrambling up the bank.

A trumpet sounded, and the French men-at-arms lowered their lances and launched themselves down the slope, crashing into Despenser's men, spearing some of them and driving the rest back into the water. Merrivale saw Despenser go down, bludgeoned by the butt end of a lance. Mortimer stood over him, sword sweeping in steel arcs as he slashed at the horsemen milling around. Gurney fought his way towards them, dragging a French man-at-arms off his horse and stabbing him, and then the Red Company were roaring ashore, horns blowing, jumping from their saddles and breaking left and right to allow passage for the troops behind them, spearmen driving solid wedges into the French, archers following and shooting down any who resisted, and that howling war cry he had heard at La Roche-Guyon went up again, *'Rouge! Rooooouge! Roooooouge!'*

The French hesitated, their momentum checked by the Red Company's counter-attack, and the fighting in the shallows turned into a vicious mêlée full of stabbing spears and hissing arrows. Holland's men came up the middle, slamming into the fray, and then the prince and his household reached shore. Merrivale urged his horse out of the water across a foreshore churned to red mud and carpeted with bodies. Courcy rode across in front of him, yelling and dodging the lance thrust of a French man-at-arms and then slashing at the man's head. Gráinne jumped down from the back of the horse and ran after him, followed by the gallowglasses. Another Frenchman rode towards Merrivale, lance lowered, but at the last moment he saw the herald's tabard and checked, pulling up his horse; as he halted, Donnchad ripped him out of the saddle and hurled him to the ground, pulled open the visor of his bascinet and stabbed him. Northampton and Warwick were already in the middle of the fray, swords swinging.

The prince rode forward, yelling to his companions to follow him, making for the spot where Mortimer and Gurney were still defending the fallen Despenser.

The French men-at-arms wavered and broke. The survivors fled up the bank with the English racing after them, screaming and shooting. The French foot soldiers, wilting under the showers of arrows, turned and ran too. More companies of English troops surged up out of the river, yelling with exultation and relief. The miracle they had not dared pray for had happened. The Blanchetaque was taken, and the way across the Somme was clear.

–

Hugh Despenser was on his feet, his bascinet off and wiping blood from his face. The bascinet was badly dented and there were more dents on his breastplate and arm guards. Mortimer stood beside him, leaning heavily on his sword; Gurney was down on one knee, recovering his breath.

'Well,' Mortimer said. 'At least I didn't shit myself.'

'No,' said Despenser. 'Not this time.' He grinned suddenly and slapped Mortimer on his shoulder guard, and after a moment Mortimer smiled back at him.

The Prince of Wales dismounted and walked towards them, pulling up his visor. Despenser and Gurney knelt in front of him, and after a moment Mortimer did the same. The younger knight saw Merrivale watching him and smiled again, both remembering Saint-Vaast. *The day will come when I bow the knee to no one*, Mortimer had said. But those words had been spoken a lifetime ago.

'There is no need to kneel, my friends,' the prince said. 'Rise, I pray you.'

Startled, the three men rose to their feet. The prince embraced each of them, and Merrivale saw there were tears in the young man's eyes. 'This is why I asked you to serve under my command,' he said. 'This has been my great hope, right from the beginning: that we could forget the past and fight together, side by side like brothers. I rejoice that this day has come.'

He stepped back a little and held out one hand. 'Give me your hands,' he said. They did so, Mortimer's gauntlet still dripping blood. 'Swear this to me,' said the prince. 'Swear that we will be brothers, and that discord will never come between us. Swear that this bond will last all our lives, and will be sundered only by death.'

'We swear it,' the three men said in unison.

'So do we all,' said the Earl of Salisbury, and Thomas Holland nodded.

A murmur ran around the watching men. Merrivale turned and met Bartholomew Burghersh's eyes, and the tutor nodded in silent satisfaction. The boy who had landed at Saint-Vaast had won his spurs.

24

Forêt de Crécy, 24th of August, 1346
Evening

'The man who told the king about the Blanchetaque,' said Nicholas Courcy. 'He was remarkably willing to talk, don't you think?'

'Yes,' the herald said. 'He had been paid to do so.'

Around them the exhausted army was making camp on the edge of the forest, the last of the battered rearguard slowly straggling in. There had been hard fighting on the south bank; the Bohemian *panzerati* in particular were vicious opponents, and despite the best efforts of the king and Arundel, a number of baggage wagons had been lost, including most of the remaining food. Fortunately the vanguard had captured stores of bread and peas and salt meat in Noyelles and Le Crotoy. Both these small towns were now burning fiercely in the distance.

'Who paid him?' demanded Gráinne.

Tiphaine stirred. Her tunic was in rags, her hose worn through at the knees. 'The conspirators,' she said. 'It was another trap.'

'It was,' the herald agreed. 'And planned with care. They drove us deliberately towards the ford, paid that man to tell us where it was and lied about the number of men guarding it so we would be encouraged to make the attempt. Their intention was to bottle us up in the river until the tide turned and the water rose and drowned us all.'

He remembered the prince's words. 'Like rats in a sack,' he said.

'Just so,' said Courcy. 'Only they didn't reckon with Hugh Despenser and his men, or the Red Company, our latter-day Myrmidons. Come to that, neither did I.'

'We are not out of danger,' Merrivale said. 'As John Sully said, the time will come when we can run no longer.'

Courcy nodded. 'Warwick told me that the king is determined to fight. Northampton has gone out to look for a battlefield where we can meet the French. I have been ordered to make the cannon ready.'

Tiphaine shivered. 'I saw their army at Rouen. It is more powerful than you can imagine.'

The four of them, Merrivale, Tiphaine, Courcy and Gráinne, were seated on wooden benches outside the herald's tent, smoke drifting around them in the falling dusk. As part of the Prince of Wales's household, the herald's baggage had not been abandoned at Airaines, and Mauro had somehow managed to get the cart across the Blanchetaque before the Bohemians closed in. He and Warin stood behind the herald; Matt and Pip leaned on their bows a few yards away, chewing on rinds of bacon.

'Tell us about this conspiracy,' Courcy said.

'It has two parts,' Merrivale said. 'The first is the destruction of the English army and the death of the king and the Prince of Wales. Then I imagine the conspirators would attempt to gain control of Queen Philippa and the next heir to the throne, Prince Lionel. He is only eight years old, so they might push the queen aside and attempt to rule as regents.'

'The queen would not give up without a fight,' said Courcy. 'Which could mean another civil war. What is the second part?'

Merrivale told him about the plot to overthrow Philip of France. 'I am not desperately interested in what happens to him, but I prefer not to see England torn apart. I remember the violence of the 1320s all too well. I have no desire to see those days return.'

'What do you have in mind?' Courcy asked.

'The conspirators have asked me to join them,' Merrivale said.

The silence that followed lasted for quite some time. 'And how did you respond?' Tiphaine asked.

'I asked to meet some of their leaders, and they agreed. The meeting is in Abbeville, tomorrow night.'

Gráinne snorted. 'This is a trap.'

'Not necessarily. I know some of these men.'

Courcy raised his eyebrows. 'How?'

'When the war began, I was sent to Savoy to support our envoy there, Brother Geoffrey of Maldon. Both England and France were trying to woo Savoy to their side, but the French had the upper hand. They had enlisted the help of Cardinal Aubert and also of Jean de Nanteuil, the Grand Prior of the Knights of Saint John, two of the most powerful men in Europe. Count Aymon was promised a kingdom. With support from France and the Knights, Savoy would annex all of its neighbours, Geneva, Dauphiné, Montferrat, Provence, Monaco, even Genoa, and form them into a single state under Aymon's rule.'

'Wait a moment. Wasn't he the fellow known as Aymon the Peaceful? He doesn't sound like a builder of empires.'

Merrivale nodded. 'Aymon was not particularly enthusiastic about the idea, but his chief councillor, Louis of Vaud, was very much in favour. But then we discovered Aubert's real aim. Once this new kingdom had been created, France would depose Aymon and take control, annexing Savoy directly to the French crown. Just like Normandy.'

'And what did you and Brother Geoffrey do?'

'We made a counter-move. We persuaded Aymon that he could remain independent by joining forces with Genoa and the other states, forming a confederation of allies rather like the Swiss cantons. We then bought the loyalty of the other states, including Genoa and Monaco. Our master stroke, or so we thought, was to recruit the Count of Rožmberk, Jean of Bohemia's chamberlain. Bohemia was trying to establish its own empire in Italy at the time, and would have made a useful friend. With all the other pieces in place, we then bribed Cardinal Aubert and the Grand Prior to abandon their own plot and walk away. But the one man we could not corrupt was Louis of Vaud.'

'An honest man,' said Courcy. 'How rare and refreshing.'

'It was unexpected, yes, and it was the rock on which we foundered. When Vaud refused our offer, Aubert and Jean de Nanteuil reneged on the deal and turned the Bohemians against us. The entire scheme fell apart, and Geoffrey and I were very lucky to escape with our lives.'

'And now, you will be betrayed again,' Tiphaine said. She rose to her feet. 'The entire French army is camped around Abbeville. Lady Gráinne is right. This is a trap.'

'I must take that chance,' the herald said. 'I know I can talk to Louis of Vaud, and to Doria and Grimaldi. They can tell me what I need to know.'

'Which is?'

'The names of the Englishmen who are part of the conspiracy. The men who worked with John of Hainault twenty years ago to use Mortimer and Isabella to bring down the crown of England. They came within a hair's breadth of destroying the country then. I believe they are about to try again.'

Courcy wrinkled his brow. 'Where does Hainault fit into all this?'

'Back in the '20s, he and his friends controlled Mortimer, not the other way around. When the king launched his coup and arrested and executed Mortimer, that knocked the bottom out of Hainault's plan. He tried to curry favour with the king, with some success, but his Grace already had his own friends, Salisbury, Northampton, Rowton and the others. The king liked Hainault and admired him, but the young men always had more influence. Hainault couldn't break into that circle.'

'Didn't Hainault go back home and try to dispossess his brother?'

'He did, but that also failed. Now he is in France, where he is influential, but once again he has risen as far as he can. My guess is that the coup they are now planning is aimed at giving him power in both England and France, far beyond what he already has.'

'So you are going to meet these men in Abbeville tomorrow night,' Gráinne said.

'I am.'

'Well, you're not going alone,' said Courcy. He glanced at Gráinne. 'We're coming with you.'

'So am I,' said Tiphaine.

'You know what will happen if the French capture you again.'

She shivered. 'I know. But I am coming all the same.'

Pip flicked the last of the bacon rind over her shoulder. 'Our orders are to go wherever you go, sir,' she said.

'And you cannot expect Warin and me to remain behind, *señor*,' said Mauro.

Merrivale sighed. 'I am quite capable of going to Abbeville on my own,' he said. 'I am going openly, as a herald and ambassador. I will be perfectly safe.'

Courcy nodded. 'As I said once before, I'm sure you can get there quite easily. But you might need a little help getting back again.'

Forêt de Crécy, 24th of August, 1346
Night

It was late when the herald returned from the prince's table. Tiphaine was waiting for him in the tent. 'Where are the servants?' he asked.

'I told them to sleep outside. The night is warm, and they will not be uncomfortable.'

'Why did you do that?'

'Can you not guess?'

They looked at each other in the shadows. Merrivale tried to read her face. 'Tiphaine,' he said. 'It has been a very long time.'

'You are not the only one. I have been in prison for two years, remember.' She paused for a moment, 'You wear that tabard like a suit of armour, but I know that underneath it you have a soul. I was hoping there might be a place for me within it.'

She stepped towards him, and before he could move, took his hand in hers. 'I am not Iseult,' she said. 'I am not Morgana or Blanchefleur, and I am not the lady you lost.'

'No,' Merrivale said gently. 'Be yourself, Tiphaine, as you have always done. That is more than enough.'

Forêt de Crécy, 25th of August, 1346
Afternoon

'There'll be a fight tomorrow,' said an archer, sitting on the ground and carefully tying thread around the fletching of an arrow.

Clouds had rolled in from the west overnight, trapping heat and humidity under the canopy of the trees. The entire army was camped inside the forest now, protected from the prying eyes of enemy scouts. Mauro looked at the archer. His russet tunic was stained and faded, and his boots had worn thin. 'You think so?' the manservant asked.

'Old Northampton's found a field he likes. Crest of a hill just the other side of the forest. We'll make a stand there and wait for the French to come to us.'

The archer held up the arrow, squinting along the line of the cock feather and checking the fixing of the broad barbed head. Satisfied, he laid it aside and reached for another arrow, this one with a long needle-like point.

'Why the different heads?' Mauro asked.

'That one's a broadhead. We use them at long range, to cripple or kill the horses. This here is a bodkin point.' The archer touched the long needle. 'That goes through the rings on a mail coat. We use them next, and when the enemy are good and close, we turn to these.' He held up another arrow, this one with a cylindrical head ending in a sharp point like an awl. 'At thirty yards, that will punch through armour,' he said. 'Nothing'll stop it.'

'Can we hold the French?' Mauro asked.

'Nah. Forty thousand men coming at us all at once? They'll wrap around our flanks and roll over us.' The archer looked down the shaft of the arrow, rotating it in his fingers. 'Don't reckon I'll be seeing Wigan again.'

He looked up at Mauro. 'I remember you. Spanish fellow, the one that gave us water at Sainte-Mère-Église. Don't suppose you have a drink now, do you?'

Mauro tossed over the waterskin, and the archer drank deeply. 'Thanks, mate. Fair parched, I was.'

'I wasn't sure you would still be talking to me,' Mauro said.

'Why not?'

'Because I am the herald's servant.'

'You mean because of Bate? Don't worry about that. Batey wasn't thinking straight, hadn't been for a long time. That knock on the head he took in Prussia scrambled his wits, I reckon.'

The archer took another long drink, stoppered the waterskin and threw it back to Mauro. 'Tell your master not to worry,' he said. 'We don't hold a grudge. Nicodemus, now, that's a different story. If we catch him, we're going to cut his balls off.'

'Have you seen him?' Mauro asked.

'No, but it's said he's still around. I knew he was trouble right from the first day, when we spotted him and Slade waiting by that road.'

A cold finger crawled down Mauro's spine. 'Jack Slade, the Somerset man? What road was this?'

'The road from Quettehou to Valognes, the day we landed. He and Slade were crouched down behind a hedgerow beside the road. They had their backs to us, so they didn't see us, but we saw them all right.'

'The other man you mentioned, Macio Chauffin. When did you see him?'

The archer thought. 'A little later, I guess. A bit further up the road too, towards Valognes.' He frowned. 'We thought Nicodemus and Slade were out looting, just like us. Do you suppose they were waiting for Chauffin?'

'They were waiting for someone,' Mauro said, 'but it was not Chauffin. Thank you, *señor*. You have been most helpful.'

—

'I think Nicodemus and Slade killed Sir Edmund Bray,' he reported a few minutes later. 'They were guarding the road, with orders to kill anyone who disturbed Señor Chauffin's meeting with Señor de Fierville. When Sir Edmund appeared, they followed him and shot him.'

'Come with me,' the herald said grimly. 'I may need a witness.'

They found Edward de Tracey talking with one of his vintenars, the rest of his archers scattered among the trees waxing bowstrings and checking arrows. 'I need a word with you,' Merrivale said.

Tracey motioned to the vintenar and the man walked away. He glanced at Mauro and the two archers waiting a few yards away, but the herald shook his head. 'They stay.'

'What do you want now?' Tracey asked, his voice level.

343

'When you landed, was Nicodemus with the rest of the company on the beach at Saint-Vaast?'

Tracey thought for a moment. 'Yes. He went up to Quettehou with the rest of us, after the alarm had sounded.'

The herald shook his head. 'But that is not true, is it?'

Tracey's hand rested on the hilt of his sword. 'Are you challenging my word, herald?'

'I have witnesses who saw Nicodemus and Jack Slade near the Valognes road at almost exactly the same time as Edmund Bray was killed. Why did you tell me Nicodemus was with your company on the beach?'

'I thought he was. I didn't keep an eye on him the whole time, I had other things on my mind, like organising my company and making sure they were armed and ready. Clearly I was mistaken when I spoke earlier. Don't you ever make mistakes, herald?'

'Frequently. But Nicodemus was no ordinary retainer, was he? You relied on him, and he had worked for your father, too. He was practically a family retainer. And yet on the day of the landing, you had no notion of where he was?'

'None whatever.'

'Take care, Sir Edward,' the herald warned. 'You know what Nicodemus stands accused of. It is more than just Bray's murder, much more. The selling of innocent children into slavery at Southampton. The murder of Jake Madford at Pont-Hébert. The attempted poisoning of several members of the Prince of Wales's retinue at the Lammas feast, and the much more ambitious attempt to poison the king and all his captains at Poissy.'

Tracey said nothing. 'The king looks on you favourably,' Merrivale continued, 'and your banker brother has great influence. But if it is found that you have any connection with Nicodemus and his crimes, neither favour nor influence will save you. Hanging will be the kindest death you could face.'

'I swear to God,' Tracey said. His face had gone pale. 'I swear on the bones of all the saints, I had nothing do with this. I employed Nicodemus because I thought he was reliable and had a good head for numbers. I had no knowledge of or interest in his other activities, so long as he served me faithfully.'

'Oaths are easy to swear,' the herald said. 'Why should I believe you?'

'For God's sake, man! Why would I risk throwing my lands and wealth away for some insane plot to kill the king?'

'I was wondering the same thing.'

'Very well. If you think I am guilty, provide some evidence. I challenge you to do so. Prove a case against me if you can.'

'I cannot,' said Merrivale. 'But you had better start making your peace with God, Sir Edward. Because if there is evidence, I will find it.'

—

'Do you believe him?' asked Courcy.

'He lied to me about Nicodemus's whereabouts, that is certain,' Merrivale said. 'And I find his claim of ignorance about Nicodemus's activities unconvincing at best. But at the same time, I also find it hard to believe that he is capable of organising a conspiracy of this size and scope.'

'And he is right about one thing,' Courcy said. 'He already has power and wealth. What motive would he have for getting involved in a plot like this?'

Gráinne was sitting on a bench beneath an oak tree, honing the blade of her sword to a glittering edge. She snorted. 'Men who have power and wealth want only one thing. More of both.'

'That's two things,' Courcy said.

'Exactly.' Gráinne stood up and tossed a feather in the air. She watched it flutter towards the ground for a moment, and swung her sword. The blade was a flash of light, faster than the eye could see, and the feather, cut cleanly in two, landed on the dead leaves at her feet.

'Sharp enough,' Gráinne said. She sheathed the sword and planted her hands on her hips. 'Nicodemus could be threatening Tracey, or forcing him to pay blackmail. Perhaps he knows something about

Tracey's past to his discredit. Tracey does know what is going on, but Nicodemus is forcing him to keep silent.'

'Possibly,' the herald said.

'You don't think Tracey has the wit or ambition to be the kingpost of this conspiracy,' Gráinne continued. 'But your instinct tells you that he is involved somehow, or at least he knows what is going on.'

'Yes. But I haven't enough evidence to arrest him or question him further. He has already persuaded the king to order me to abandon the inquisition once again. I doubt I can persuade him to reopen it.'

'And tomorrow, his Grace will have other things to worry about,' said Courcy. 'So this is our last chance. We go to Abbeville tonight.'

'Yes,' the herald said. 'Are you still determined to come with me?'

'Try stopping us,' said Lady Gráinne.

25

Abbeville, 25th of August, 1346
Night

They halted in the shade of a coppice wood a mile from Abbeville. The last flames of sunset were fading from the sky. The smell of a charcoal burner's fire drifted on the wind. 'Wait here with the horses,' Merrivale instructed Mauro and Warin. 'Be ready. When we return, we may be in a hurry.'

The two servants nodded. Merrivale looked at the others. Gráinne had abandoned her heavy armour and wore a stiff leather jerkin like her husband; a red stag, the badge of the MacCarthaigh Riabhachs of Carbery, shone in the dim moonlight on one shoulder. Both she and Tiphaine had tucked their hair under felt caps. Matt and Pip leaned on their bows, waiting.

'Let us go,' Merrivale said.

Quietly the six of them slipped away through the lambent shadows. Campfires burned in the fields around Abbeville, the vast French army waiting to resume its march in the morning. Lights flickered on the walls of the town, and glowed nearer at hand in the abbey of Saint-Pierre, outside the walls and surrounded by fields and gardens. To the left of the abbey was a dark patch of marshland where a minor stream ran down to join the Somme. Waiting in the coppice wood, Mauro and Warin listened to the distant murmur of the camp and the nearer, softer sounds of the horses stirring behind them.

Another noise, the soft pad of a horse's hooves. They both whirled around, Mauro reaching for his knife and Warin gripping a heavy wooden staff. A pony came trotting out of the darkness, and the girl riding it pulled up and slid down from the saddle.

'Who are you?' Warin demanded in a whisper.

'My name is Nell Driver. I am a friend of the herald,' she hissed.

'A friend?' said Mauro. 'Ah, yes. You are the cowherd.'

'And his friend!' she insisted.

Mauro was briefly amused. 'What are you doing here, *señorita*?'

'I followed you from the camp. Where is the herald?'

'None of your business,' said Warin.

'He is going into Abbeville, isn't he?' Without waiting for an answer, she handed him the reins of the pony. 'Watch the beast for me,' she said, 'I need to return him to his owner in the morning.' Without waiting for a reply, she hitched up the hem of her kirtle and ran into the darkness.

–

The torches and fires of the camp were close at hand, but the marshes were still dark; for obvious reasons, no one had camped there. 'If we have to leave quickly, we will come out through these marshes,' the herald said. 'Matt, Pip, I suggest you conceal yourselves here and wait.'

'We were told to follow you everywhere, sir,' Matt said.

'I know. But if we must make a rapid retreat, we will need you to cover us. Remain here.'

The two archers looked unhappy, but they obeyed. Followed by Tiphaine, Courcy and Gráinne, Merrivale walked towards the camp. Sentries around the nearest fire stepped forward, presenting their spears. A man-at-arms, clanking in armour plate and mail, opened his visor and stared at them. 'Who are you?'

'I am Simon Merrivale, herald to the Prince of Wales,' the herald said calmly. 'Here is my *laissez-passer* from the Count of Vaud.'

He presented the roll of parchment. The man-at-arms read it quickly and looked at the other three. 'Who are these?'

'My escort.'

'Escort? Two of them are women!'

'You are observant, *messire*. The Count of Vaud is waiting for me at the abbey. Take us there immediately, if you please. My business with him will not wait.'

The man-at-arms hesitated. Merrivale touched his glittering tabard. 'My business here is official, *messire*. You have no right to impede or delay me.'

The man motioned with his hand. 'Very well. Come with me.'

Sometimes the laws of war were useful after all, Merrivale thought wryly. They followed the man through the camp towards the abbey gates, where more sentries admitted them. A messenger was sent to inform the count. They waited, listening to the sound of singing in the chapel; the monks, chanting the service at compline.

A man in a brown Franciscan habit walked across the courtyard, putting his hands together and smiling as he bowed. 'My dear Simon,' said Raimon Vidal. 'As always, it is a pleasure to see you.'

'Are they here?'

'They are waiting for us in the scriptorium. Come.'

An arched gateway led into the double-columned cloister. On the far side the chapter house blazed with lamplight and they could hear men's voices raised in argument. Several did not sound particularly sober. One voice in particular was insistent, shouting over and over. Vidal wrinkled his nose. 'The king is giving a banquet,' he said. 'Today is the feast day of Saint Louis of France. They have been at the board since this afternoon. I cannot begin to tell you how much wine has been consumed.'

'The feast of Saint Louis? The canonised French king who managed to lead not one but two armies into disaster in the space of twenty years?'

'The very same. Perhaps it is a portent, who knows? The king is attempting to use the feast to persuade his nobles to unite and follow him.' Vidal nodded towards the chapter house. 'You can hear for yourself how much luck he is having.'

'Your friends are at work already, it seems.'

'They are. The French army is rotten from within. They will triumph tomorrow; given their advantage of numbers, they can hardly help but do so. But the king's enemies are already waiting to pounce.' Vidal opened a heavy wooden door and motioned them inside. 'This way.'

The scriptorium was lit dimly by candles in iron sconces around the walls. Rows of wooden desks stretched across the floor, each with a bench and writing set. The walls were covered in frescos of the Italian style, showing the temptations of Christ in the wilderness. Angels hovered overhead, looking down with dark, judgemental eyes.

Five men stood on the far side of the scriptorium, watching them without expression. Merrivale had not seen some of them for eight years, but he recognised them without difficulty. Louis of Vaud, tall, distinguished, grey-haired, in a surcoat with a white cross on red. Doria, big and muscular, wearing the Saint George cross of Genoa. Carlo Grimaldi of Monaco, his hard, brutal face bearing some scars the herald did not remember, wearing a coat decorated with red and silver lozenges. Zajíc the Bohemian herald, in the familiar tabard blazoned with the lion with two tails, stood next to the bearded Count Rožmberk.

Merrivale's scalp tingled with apprehension. I wish Geoffrey was here, he thought. 'Wait here,' he said quietly to his companions, and he followed Vidal across the room. Stopping in front of Louis of Vaud, he bowed. 'My lord count. It has been a long time since last we met.'

'Some might say it has not been long enough,' said Vaud. 'Why are you here?'

'Your associates made me an offer,' Merrivale said. 'I have come to name my price.'

Ottone Doria raised his eyebrows. 'Surely we should know what we are buying first.'

'You intend to overthrow King Philip of France. You need my assistance.'

Rožmberk looked sceptical. 'We already have heralds of our own. I doubt we need another.'

Merrivale smiled. 'As you well know, my lord, I was not always a herald.'

'Very well. What can you offer us?'

'Normandy,' said Merrivale.

There was a pause of a couple of heartbeats. 'Explain,' said Grimaldi.

'I control Normandy,' Merrivale said. 'I own the western half of the province already. And Jeanne of Navarre, who has the east in her hands, is ready to do my bidding.'

Vidal stepped forward. 'What?' he said sharply. 'How is this?'

'I have been in correspondence with Queen Jeanne for more than five years,' Merrivale said. 'We have been laying our plans for nearly as long. Last winter, she wrote to say that she had doubts about the loyalty of the Count of Eu. I went to Caen to persuade Eu to honour the pledge he had made us, but I was too late. King Edward's agents had already bribed him to turn his coat. So, I told Jeanne to withdraw from any arrangement she had made with you until I could negotiate a new agreement.'

The others looked at each other. 'You said you own western Normandy,' Vaud said. 'What do you mean by that?'

Merrivale turned towards the group by the door and beckoned with his finger. '*Demoiselle*,' he said in a voice of command. 'Come here. At once, if you please.'

Ragged and pale, Tiphaine walked across the scriptorium to stand beside him. 'This is the Demoiselle de Tesson,' Merrivale said, 'the heir of Jean de la Roche Tesson. When I learned she had been imprisoned at La Roche-Guyon, I raided the place and took her into my hands. She is now my prisoner.' He paused. 'Or my hostage? Hmm. Perhaps a little of both.'

Rožmberk looked at the young woman. 'This?' he said with disdain. 'This is the instrument through which you claim to control Lower Normandy?'

'Certainly. The Norman rebels are bruised, but they are not beaten. When Godefroi d'Harcourt's conspiracy failed, they transferred their loyalty to the *demoiselle*, the daughter of their former leader. Her loyalty in turn is to me. She follows my orders.'

Rožmberk looked sceptical, but Grimaldi was thoughtful. 'What force can you command?'

'I can raise five thousand men-at-arms in Lower Normandy, and Queen Jeanne can raise another five thousand from her lands and those of her allies. Once the size of our army becomes known, I strongly suspect that those Normans currently loyal to King Philip will come over to us. They will want to be on the winning side.'

Rožmberk snorted. 'This is a tissue of lies.'

'I am not so sure,' said Louis of Vaud slowly. 'We all know this man, remember?' He looked at Vidal. 'What do you think, Brother Raimon?'

Vidal scratched his tonsured scalp. 'It would explain certain things about the behaviour of the Queen of Navarre,' he said finally. 'Including her sudden withdrawal from our coalition. Reports say she has gone into seclusion at Évreux, but she is clearly waiting for something. A signal, perhaps?'

'Suppose you are telling the truth,' Doria said to Merrivale. 'You mentioned a price. What is it?'

'Affirmation of the agreement Queen Jeanne and I have already made,' Merrivale said. 'We will divide Normandy between us. She will take Rouen and the east and add them to her lands, and I will take Caen and the west to rule as my own independent duchy.'

'You?' demanded Grimaldi. 'An upstart English adventurer, ruling a duchy?'

'We all have to start somewhere,' Merrivale said mildly. 'Like your father, Signor Grimaldi. *He* was an upstart Italian adventurer, was he not, when he seized Monaco and declared his independence?'

Grimaldi growled in his throat. 'I will also take the *demoiselle* as my wife,' Merrivale continued. 'She is nubile, and I have found her biddable, but more importantly, through her I can command the loyalty of the Norman nobles. She can bring me five thousand men-at-arms. That is a dowry worth having.'

Tiphaine turned and stared at him. 'You bastard,' she said slowly.

Merrivale slapped her, hard enough to knock her to her knees. 'Speak only when you are spoken to. When you are my wife, you will know your place.'

In the silence that followed, Zajíc the herald cleared his throat. 'Will Queen Jeanne confirm that this arrangement has been made?'

'Of course.' Merrivale gestured around the scriptorium. 'Write to her yourself, if you wish.'

'Why delay until this moment to come forward?' asked Rožmberk, his face still suspicious.

'I decided to wait and see if you could carry out your promises. I am glad I did so.'

'What do you mean?' asked Vaud.

'So far, your conspiracy has not been very successful, has it? The incompetence of King Philip hasn't helped, of course, but the English should have been trapped at Poissy, and they *really* should have been annihilated at the Blanchetaque. Frankly, I am a little worried. If Edward escapes again tomorrow, what then?'

He shook his head. 'I fear, gentlemen, that you chose the wrong Englishman for your partner. Sir Edward de Tracey is wealthy and has influence, but he has no experience of this sort of business. You needed a man who was adept at intrigue. Someone like me.'

'How did you know Tracey was involved?' demanded Vaud.

'I wasn't certain, until now. But thank you, my lord, for confirming it.'

The silence was broken by Vidal clapping his hands. 'Very good,' he said. 'Very, very good, my friend. You have not lost your touch. So, you want to take Tracey's place. Would you like an English duchy to add to your French one?'

'If I can ensure that Edward's army is defeated tomorrow, will you give me one?' Merrivale asked.

The wooden door to the scriptorium slammed open, bouncing off the walls. A tall man with a coronet on his head and wearing a blue robe studded with the lilies of France stood in the doorway. 'Treason!' shouted the Count of Alençon. 'By God, I can smell its stink a mile away!'

Unsteadily, the count stalked forward across the room. Another man followed him, cloaked in red with the white cross of the Knights of Saint John. Courcy and Gráinne stood silently by the door, unnoticed, waiting to see what would happen.

Alençon glared at Merrivale. His eyes were red and he smelled strongly of wine. 'English spy!'

'I am no spy,' said Merrivale. 'I am a herald.'

'And what is this whore doing here?' Alençon seized Tiphaine's arm and jerked her violently to her feet. 'I ordered her to be burned!'

'And I pulled her out of the fire. She belongs to me, my lord. She is protected, and so am I.'

The Knight of Saint John spoke in a cold voice. 'You claim immunity as an ambassador? Then what is your embassy?'

'He came at my invitation, Nanteuil,' Louis of Vaud said sharply. 'If you ask whose protection he is under, it is mine.'

Alençon exploded. 'Negotiating with the English behind my back! What about the oath we swore at Poissy, hey? Hey? What about the pledges you made, sworn on the hilt of a sword? And now you invite an English spy and a Norman traitor into our house to conspire against me!'

'No one is conspiring against you—'

'God damn it, Vaud, don't interrupt me! I will be king, do you hear, *king*! And I will be emperor too one day, by God, and the world will kneel at my feet, and I will not tolerate any insolence from *you*, you treacherous upstart!'

He really was very drunk indeed, Merrivale thought. Vaud's lips tightened.

'Have a care for your language!' Doria said sharply.

'Fuck you, Doria, you Genoese maggot! And you, Grimaldi, you pox-ridden pirate! By God, I ought to hang every last one of you right now!'

Jean de Nanteuil moved forward. 'Let us not be too hasty,' he said. 'If these men are traitors, then of course they will be dealt with. But we must make certain of our facts.'

He turned to Merrivale. 'I will ask my question again. What is your mission here?'

'The Count of Vaud spoke truly,' Merrivale said. 'I came at his invitation to negotiate with him and the *signores* Doria and Grimaldi and the Count of Rožmberk. You see, I know about your conspiracy.'

The Grand Prior's eyes narrowed. 'What conspiracy?'

Merrivale said nothing. 'He knows everything,' Rožmberk said. 'Or nearly everything. He even knows about Edward de Tracey.'

354

'Tracey!' Alençon exploded. 'Jesus Christ! You told him about *Tracey*?'

'No, of course not,' Vaud said coldly. 'He already knew.'

'How?' asked Nanteuil.

Vaud hesitated. 'I don't know.'

'I begin to think his Imperial Majesty is right,' Nanteuil said. 'This looks very much like treason.'

Grimaldi slammed his hand down on the hilt of his sword. 'Enough. I will not be insulted, and I will not be called a traitor. I withdraw. I shall take my troops and my ships and return to Monaco. And do not ever call on me for aid again, Alençon. If you do, I will return your messenger's head in a sack.'

He strode out of the room. Doria followed him. Vaud glared at Nanteuil and Alençon. 'You damned fools! What have you done?'

'What have *we* done?' demanded the Grand Prior. 'It is you who have questions to answer, my lords.' He turned to Alençon. 'Call the guards. Arrest them all.'

'No,' said another voice from the door. 'Wait.'

—

John of Hainault was in his late fifties now, but he still moved like the champion swordsman and jouster he had once been. Ignoring Courcy and Gráinne, silent spectators in the game, he walked forward and stopped a few paces from the herald, crossing his arms over his chest.

'He knows about Tracey,' Nanteuil said.

'So it would seem,' said Hainault. 'Something needs to be done about that.'

'For Christ's sake!' Vidal said sharply. 'Merrivale is not the problem that needs dealing with! The Count of Alençon's drunken outburst has ruined everything. We have lost the Genoese!'

'We shall get them back,' said Hainault, his eyes still resting on Merrivale.

'We don't need them!' Alençon snapped. 'We are better off without them. They're mercenary bastards who will work for the highest bidder.'

'As do you,' Hainault said. 'Your price, I seem to recall, was a hundred thousand écus.'

Alençon checked, swaying a little, and lapsed into sullen silence. Hainault continued to stare at Merrivale. 'Why are you here?'

Again, Merrivale said nothing. 'He has promised us the support of Normandy,' said Louis of Vaud.

'Has he now? How interesting. But I think proof of his loyalty is required before we believe him.' Hainault paused for a moment. 'Tell me where the English army is.'

'At this moment, they are concealed in the Forêt de Crécy.'

Alençon started to speak, but Hainault silenced him with a sharp motion. 'What are Edward's intentions? Will he stand, or will he retreat to the north?'

'He will stand. He has chosen a position on a ridge east of the forest. He will meet you there.'

'Liar!' Alençon shouted. 'The English would not dare to stand against us! They are retreating towards Flanders! I told everyone this, but you fools will not listen!'

'Perhaps that is because our scouts have found no sign of them,' said Louis of Vaud. 'If they have marched away north, they have left no trace behind them. Not so much as a hoof print on the ground.'

'Why are you not listening to me? Edward of England has duped you, all of you! And now he has sent his spy to pour poison into your ears. God rot you all for blundering idiots!'

Hainault rounded on him. 'Shut up,' he said.

'How dare you—'

Hainault's fist did not travel far, but it thudded into Alençon's midriff like a tree trunk, knocking the wind out of the count and doubling him over in pain. 'Enough!' he commanded. 'You damned puppy! I have spent nearly half my life on this project, and I will not see it fail now. You will keep a civil tongue in your head and obey orders, Alençon, or by God I will find another king!'

'Or queen,' said Merrivale. 'Jeanne of Navarre has as good a claim to the throne as this man.' He eyed Alençon with open insolence. 'And more balls,' he added.

Vidal laughed. Alençon glared at them, his face almost purple with rage, his mouth opening and shutting silently. Still clutching his midriff, he staggered out into the cloister. A moment later, they heard the sound of retching.

Hainault stood for a moment, his own eyes calculating. 'Your idea is not without merit,' he said.

'Of course, there is a problem,' Merrivale said. 'The law says that a woman cannot inherit the throne of France.'

Hainault waved a dismissive hand. 'We invented that law, and we can abolish it just as easily. So. Edward intends to fight. How strong is his army?'

'With the losses he took at the Blanchetaque, fewer than ten thousand. They are tired and hungry, and desertions are increasing. But I give you fair warning, my lord. They are still formidable, and the position at Crécy is a good one; Northampton himself has chosen it. You are likely to take heavy losses.'

Hainault shrugged. 'Sometimes one must sacrifice pieces to win the game.' He looked at Vaud. 'Have you reached an agreement?'

'We have,' said Merrivale before Vaud could answer.

'Then this is your test. If Edward is where you say he is and we win the victory tomorrow, we will pay whatever price you have agreed. But if you have played us false, I will put every assassin in Europe on your trail. As surely as night follows day, you will die. Have I made myself clear?'

'Yes, my lord,' Merrivale said.

Hainault nodded. 'Go,' he said. 'And let us see what tomorrow brings.'

—

Merrivale turned and strode across the scriptorium towards the door, Tiphaine hurrying behind him like a dog. 'Quickly,' he whispered to Courcy and Gráinne. 'Before they change their minds.'

Outside, there was no sign of Alençon. They hurried through the cloister and into the courtyard, and nearly collided with a man running in the opposite direction. Tiphaine gasped. The man looked at her, and his eyes opened wide.

'*You!* What the devil?'

Tiphaine turned to run, but the man grabbed her arm and spun her around, drawing his dagger from his belt. 'You treacherous bitch! I'm going to finish you, here and now!'

Courcy hit him on the point of the chin with an audible crack, and they saw his eyes roll back in his head before he slumped to the ground. Merrivale looked around, but no one seemed to have noticed the brief commotion in the shadows. Restraining the impulse to run, he walked calmly to the gatehouse. 'Where is the man who brought us here?'

'Gone,' said the captain of the gate. 'He said he wasn't going to wait around all night. Do you need an escort, Sir Herald?'

Merrivale smiled and touched his tabard. 'This will do.'

'Then I bid you good night, sir.'

They walked away from the gatehouse towards the camp, quickly veering towards the darker patch of the marshes. 'Who was that fellow?' demanded Courcy.

'Rollond de Brus,' said Tiphaine. 'My former lover, and the man who betrayed me in Rouen.'

'He was your lover?' said Gráinne. '*Máthair Dé*, girl, but you have terrible taste in men.'

'I should have hit him harder,' said Courcy. 'Either he has woken up, or someone has found him. There goes the alarm.'

A trumpet sounded from the abbey, harsh and urgent. Another joined the call. 'This way,' Merrivale said, and they hurried towards the marshes.

The moon was down behind the trees; they had only the reflected glow of the campfires to guide their way. Water squelched around their boots. Smells of rotting vegetation rose to their nostrils, along with other things more foul; the men in the camp had clearly been using the marshes as a latrine. They followed the winding course of the little stream, guided by the faint glimmer of light off water, hearing the commotion behind them growing louder. 'They'll be sending out search parties,' Courcy predicted.

'I know. Hurry.'

Somewhere up ahead Matt and Pip would be waiting. They too would have heard the trumpets and be ready… on the heels of the thought, Merrivale saw someone coming out of the shadows ahead, an archer with a longbow in hand. 'Is that you, Matt?' he whispered.

The archer said nothing. He stopped, pulling an arrow from his quiver and nocking it. Then he turned his head, and Merrivale saw his face.

It was Nicodemus.

–

The four of them halted and stood very still. The range was no more than twenty yards. Even in the dim light the archer could hardly miss. Merrivale waited, watching the barbed arrowhead glinting in the light; the same kind of arrow that had killed Edmund Bray.

Nicodemus smiled. 'I am going to enjoy this.'

'Then get on with it,' said Merrivale.

'What's the hurry? You have caused me more trouble than you can imagine. You owe me a little suffering.'

'Like the suffering of the slaves you sold at Southampton?'

'Don't be so fastidious, king's messenger. You've done dirty deeds yourself in your day.'

'I have made mistakes, Nicodemus, but you are human filth. The mud of this sewer is pure and noble compared to you.'

Nicodemus raised his bow. 'I know just where to plant this arrow, herald. It's going to take you a long time to die.'

A figure hurtled out of the gloom and crashed into Nicodemus, hitting him in the small of the back. He stumbled and fell to his knees in the mud, dropping the bow and arrow. Nell Driver jumped on him, climbing onto his back and pummelling him with her fists. Raging, Nicodemus shook her off, picking her up by the shoulders and throwing her hard into the mud. Gráinne and Courcy were already running forward; Nicodemus saw them coming and reached for his bow. He was too late. Courcy slipped in the treacherous mud and fell, but Gráinne's sword flashed like lightning in the gloom, slashing

Nicodemus across his side. The archer yelped with pain, but he raised the bow and clubbed Gráinne's arm, knocking the sword from her hand. Before she could pick it up again, he had bolted into the darkness.

Nell stood up, mud dripping from her tunic. 'Are you all right?' Merrivale asked her.

'Yes, sir.'

He wanted to ask what she was doing here, but that would have to wait; from behind he could hear Brus's voice, perilously close, urging the pursuers on. Matt and Pip were running towards him, splashing through the water. 'Go on, sir,' Matt said, low-voiced. 'We'll cover your retreat.'

They ran, hearing behind them the venomous hiss of arrows and shouts of pain. They were beyond the perimeter of the camp now, and they came up out of the water and sprinted towards the copse of trees where Mauro and Warin waited with the horses, expecting at any moment to be spotted and the French to come yelling after them. But the darkness hid them well, and they reached the trees without incident. Matt and Pip followed a few minutes later, breathing hard.

'We let the air out of a few of them, sir,' Matt said. 'But there's more coming after us. Horsemen too. That fellow who leads them isn't giving up.'

'Time we were gone,' Merrivale said. 'Ride for the forest, and ride fast.'

They heard the drumming of hooves behind them, but they reached the dense forest before the pursuit could catch them. Once there, Matt and Pip led them deep into the woods, where they dismounted and stood in silence, holding the muzzles of their horses to keep them silent and listening to the sounds of their pursuers crashing through the undergrowth trying to flush them out. The sky was pale with dawn by the time Brus shouted angrily to his men and they rode away towards Abbeville.

In the wan light, Merrivale turned to Tiphaine and took her hands gently in his. 'I am so very sorry,' he said softly.

'Don't be. I know you had to do it, to convince them. There is no better way for a man to prove himself to other men than to treat a woman like a dog.'

They rode in silence back to the English camp.

The sentries recognised them at once and let them pass. Merrivale rode to the cluster of tents around the king's pavilion, dismounting outside Northburgh's tent and going inside to shake the secretary awake. 'We must arrest Edward de Tracey. Immediately.'

Northburgh sat up, rubbing his eyes. 'It's him?'

Doubt still nagged the herald, but he pushed it aside. Vaud, Zajíc, Rožmberk, Alençon; they had all named Tracey. 'It is,' he said.

'I will call the serjeants at once.'

But Tracey was not in his tent, and his bewildered esquire and servants had no idea where their master had gone. The serjeants scoured the waking camp, but Sir Edward de Tracey had vanished.

26

Alençon's head hurt, and the inside of his mouth tasted like a slurry pit. He had no idea how much wine he had drunk last night, most of it unwatered. There were significant gaps in his memory of the evening's events, but he could recall some things; arguing with his brother the king, for example, then going outside to get away from that gloomy, horse-faced idiot and clear his head. He remembered also the confrontation with Vaud and the Genoese, and Hainault's intervention, and the taste in his mouth became more bitter still.

Around him, the men-at-arms of the vanguard were mustering in the fields outside Abbeville, brilliant with gleaming metal and the shimmering colours of heraldry, lances raised like the quills of porcupines. He watched them gathering in their thousands, and his headache receded a little. To hell with Hainault, he thought, to hell with all of them. I don't need those treacherous bastards. I can do it alone, without anyone's help. This will be *my* day, *my* victory. And then, who will dare to stop me?

Rollond de Brus rode alongside him, raising his visor. 'What are the orders, your Imperial Majesty?'

'The English have retreated north,' Alençon said. 'We shall follow the river and pick up the trail after they crossed the ford. Their men are tired and hungry. They won't have got far.'

Brus raised his eyebrows. 'Hainault says they are waiting for us at Crécy. The herald told him as much.'

'The herald was lying, and so probably is Hainault. For Christ's sake, Brus, they are trying to throw us off the scent! If we ride hard, we can overtake the English by sundown.'

'But sire—'

'God damn it, Brus, are you challenging my authority?'

Angry and sullen, Brus bit back his retort. He was still smarting from last night, when John of Hainault had reprimanded him for sending pursuit after Tiphaine and the herald. 'But my lord, she is a traitor,' he had protested.

'She is also useful,' Hainault had said. 'And in future, Brus, mind your own goddamned business.'

'No, sire,' he said now.

'Good.' Alençon slammed his visor down, wincing at the pain in his head. 'Find Marshal de Montmorency,' he said. 'Tell him to order the advance.'

—

'You may congratulate me on my cleverness,' said Jean de Nanteuil, smiling.

Like the others, he was fully armoured, wearing the bright red surcoat and white eight-pointed cross of the Knights of Saint John. John of Hainault looked at him. 'What have you done?'

'I have acquired Tracey,' Nanteuil said.

'What do you mean, *acquired* him?'

'He realised last night that his secret was out, and escaped from the English camp just before they came to arrest him. He approached me for sanctuary, and I gave it on condition that he join my Order. The Knights of Saint John will protect him and ensure his safety.'

'So what? He is of no use to us now,' said the Count of Rožmberk.

'Oh yes, he is. Like everyone who joins the Order, he swore a vow of poverty. He has agreed to hand over all of his wealth to us. I have already written to the Grand Prior of England asking him to take Tracey's estates into his hands. That will preserve them from confiscation by the English.'

'Excellent,' said Zajíc. 'We now have Tracey's money and can divide it among ourselves, without waiting for him to act as paymaster. But my lord is right. We have no further need of him.'

Nanteuil shook his head. 'The financial transactions are not yet complete. Records and deeds must be signed and sealed. Once that is done, and the money is safely in our bank, *then* we will have no need of him.'

'What will you do with him?' Hainault asked.

'Send him out to one of the eastern garrisons. Smyrna, perhaps. Once there, he will soon disappear. If the Turkish arrows don't get him, the dysentery will.'

Zajíc laughed. 'And if those fail, there is always a knife in the back.'

Nanteuil's smile broadened. 'Precisely.'

Hainault nodded. 'You have done well. That fool Alençon nearly ruined everything last night, but I think we have recovered. I spoke to Doria, and he has agreed to remain with us. Vaud and Grimaldi have withdrawn, but we can go ahead without them. Now that we have Tracey's money, we are strong enough to proceed.'

Rožmberk shook his head. 'I am not happy about Alençon. He has exposed himself as an arrogant fool. Have we no better candidate for king?'

Hainault paused, thinking. 'There is Jeanne of Navarre,' he said. 'Or if the nobles will not accept her, then her son Charles. He is fourteen now; we could make something of him.'

Grooms arrived with their horses. Hainault stepped easily into the saddle, armour clattering. 'But first we must dispose of the English,' he said.

'Do you think the herald told the truth?' asked Rožmberk. 'They are waiting for us at Crécy?'

'We will know soon enough. I am riding out with the scouts to see for myself.' Hainault picked up the reins. 'And I meant what I said. If Merrivale has played us false, he will die.'

'It is a good position,' Sir John Sully said. 'Northampton has chosen well.'

The ridge where the English would make their stand was high and steep, but not too high or too steep to deter the French from attacking. Anchoring the position on the right was the village of Crécy, a huddle of deserted houses next to the forest; the left flank was protected by another village and the marshes of a small river.

A windmill stood on the highest point of the ridge, its sails unmoving in the hot, still air. Even though it was not yet midday, Merrivale could feel sweat trickling down his back, and his shirt was soaked beneath his thick tabard. Sully's dog lay on the grass behind his master, panting in the heat.

Around them the army flowed out of the forest, men-at-arms on horseback shining with metal and colour, long columns of archers in faded russet and green, the remaining baggage wagons pulled by their tired teams. Thomas Ughtred sat on his horse at the crest of the ridge, guiding each company into position. The wagons went to the rear; Mauro would be there, with the cart, and Merrivale had made sure that Nell went with him.

Courcy had taken command of the guns and was siting them on the forward slope of the ridge a little east of the windmill, while men carried barrels of serpentine down from the wagon park. Gráinne and the gallowglasses were there too, protecting the gunners. Only Tiphaine and Warin remained with Merrivale.

Michael Northburgh rode up beside them, mopping his brow in the heat. 'You are a herald,' he said to Merrivale. 'You should stay out of the fighting.'

Merrivale shook his head. 'My place is with the prince.'

'You have done enough already. You exposed Tracey.'

Merrivale shook his head. 'Too late. I did what I could, and tried to sow dissension amongst them. But I doubt it will be enough.'

Northburgh nodded. 'Then send the *demoiselle* with me. I will see she is kept safe.'

Tiphaine looked at Merrivale, the bruise plain on her face. 'You are not a fighter,' the herald said gently. 'Go with him. He will be near the king, and well protected.'

She stared at him for a long time, and then suddenly, surprisingly, she smiled. 'It seems we have another river to cross,' she said. 'I will see you on the further shore.' She turned her horse and rode away, trotting beside Northburgh. Merrivale dismounted, handing over the reins to Warin. 'Find Mauro and Mistress Driver. Stay with them.'

'Yes, sir.'

'A moment, young man.' Sully slipped a lead onto his dog's collar and handed it to Warin. 'Take him with you, and keep him safe.' He grinned at Merrivale. 'I may be too old for *demoiselles*, but he is still precious to me.'

'You will never be too old for *demoiselles*,' said Merrivale. 'Remember Algeciras?'

'Every day,' said Sully.

The prince and his men-at-arms were dismounting too. Warwick and Ughtred were among them, giving quick, terse directions. The vanguard deployed across the forward slope, the dismounted men-at-arms and Welsh spearmen forming a dense hedge with the archers in wedges on each flank. Northampton and the second division were off to the left, covering that flank; the king's division were in reserve, deployed around the windmill.

It was a strong formation, the herald thought, and one that had given England victory before; but never against odds of four to one.

The sun climbed higher in the sky. Flies buzzed around them in the heat, feasting off men's sweat. Men-at-arms broke off the butts of their long lances to make them easier to handle on foot. Some of the Welshmen dug potholes in the ground in front of their position, hoping to trip up the enemy's horses. Beyond them, archers sat on the ground, checking and rechecking the fletchings of their arrows and the stringing of their bows. The king arrived, accompanied by Northampton and Rowton, inspected the position and was gone. The Bishop of Durham followed, raising his pectoral cross and blessing the troops. Then he too departed.

They waited.

—

Most of the Red Company were behind the front line, where Warwick had posted them as a tactical reserve, but their sixty longbowmen had been sent to join the other archers. They were waiting now at the tip of one of the wedges, closest to the enemy. 'God's bones, I'm hungry,' said one of them, rubbing his stomach. Last night's dinner had been pease pottage with onions; this morning there had been no food at all.

'Where do you think the French will come from?' Pip asked.

Robert Fletcher, the master bowman, pointed to a road in the distance, running out from behind the forest and across the fields. 'That's the road from Abbeville. That's where they'll come.'

'No sign of 'em yet,' said Matt.

Fletcher bent his bow and strung it, testing the string. 'They'll come.'

'Aye,' said Pip, looking at the sky. 'That's not the only thing coming. See those clouds?' Bulbous white clouds were billowing up on the horizon. The air was thick and heavy, and the drone of the flies was a constant nagging song. 'There's rain on its way,' Pip said.

Fletcher squinted at the clouds for a moment, and then came to a decision. 'Unstring your bows,' he said to his men. 'Put the strings under your caps.'

They obeyed, and the other archers around them began doing the same. The bowstrings were waxed to keep them dry, but the rain that accompanied thunderstorms could be torrential; it was better to be safe than sorry.

Thunder growled distant in the air. Matt pointed suddenly. 'There,' she said quietly.

Bright specks of colour in the distance, four horsemen came riding up the road from Abbeville.

Near Abbeville, 26th of August, 1346
Early afternoon

'We have found them, sire,' John of Hainault said an hour later. 'They are just where I said they would be, on the ridge above Crécy.'

'What strength have they?' King Philippe demanded.

'Perhaps ten thousand, sire, no more. They have dismounted and are drawn up for battle. Now is the time, sire. You must order every man to march towards Crécy.'

'Of course, of course.' The king looked around, nervous and irritable as always. 'What has happened to my brother? Where is Alençon?'

'He and the vanguard rode away towards the north-west, sire,' said another man.

'The north-west? For Christ's sake, what for? Find him at once and tell him to march towards Crécy as quickly as possible. And tell him I don't want any goddamned arguments this time. For once in his life, he is to obey orders. He is to march to Crécy and wait for me there before deploying his men.'

'Yes, sire.'

'Find Doria too, and tell him to get his men up there, now. I want him on the field before the rest of the army arrives, so his crossbowmen can cover us while we deploy for battle. Tell him I want him at the head of the column of march, in front of Alençon. Quickly now!'

Hainault waved a hand and the messengers sped away, their horses kicking up clouds of dust in the heat. 'Tell me this will work,' Philippe demanded. 'Tell me that bastard Edward won't escape again.'

'He cannot escape,' Hainault said. 'His army is all but finished. They are exhausted, footsore and out of food. But remember, a wounded lion is still dangerous. Be calm, sire, act with deliberation and remember the principles of war. If you do, you will prevail.'

The king said nothing for a moment, biting his lip. 'Very well,' he said finally. 'Our destiny awaits us at Crécy, it seems.'

-

The messengers found the Count of Alençon and the vanguard five miles north-west of Abbeville. 'The scouts have located the enemy, Majesty. They are at Crécy, just as the reports said. They are drawn up and waiting for us.'

'At Crécy?' Alençon glared at them. 'Have you taken leave of your senses? Of course the English aren't at Crécy. God damn it, I tell you, they are marching north!'

'Sire,' said Rollond de Brus. 'The scouts have seen the enemy with their own eyes. They are at Crécy.'

'Christ's blood, Brus, you too? Are you as incompetent as the rest?' Brus looked at him, tight-lipped. 'First you let the enemy snatch that treacherous little bitch from La Roche-Guyon before you could burn her,' Alençon said. 'Then you let her and that damned herald walk straight into our camp, and even worse, let them get away again. You failed me, Brus. I don't like people who fail.'

'I apologise if I have given offence, your Imperial Majesty. Meanwhile, the English are at Crécy, and every minute that passes increases the chance that they will escape once more. Is that your desire?'

'Shut up,' Alençon told him. 'Where is this place Crécy, anyway? Does anyone know?'

Brus said nothing. 'Eight miles to the north-east, Majesty,' said one of the messengers.

'Then what does the king want me to do?'

'You are to march to Crécy with all possible speed, Majesty. Once you reach the field, you are to wait until the king arrives.'

'Wait? Why wait, for Christ's sake? Very well, find my captains and tell them to turn the column. But by God, my brother had better be right about this.'

—

Ponderously the vast column of men-at-arms turned and began riding north-east across the open fields towards Crécy, the dark shape of the forest ahead on the left. To the right, boiling clouds of dust showed where other columns were also marching hard towards the battlefield. Alençon seethed behind his visor, furious at being made to look like a fool in front of his own men. He needed someone to blame for this, someone he could punish in order to restore his esteem. He considered taking it out on Brus again, but Brus was useful. A different scapegoat was needed.

An hour later, he found one. The vanguard reached the road running north-east from Abbeville and swung into column, but almost immediately their progress stalled. Couriers came galloping back from the leading companies. 'There are men on the road ahead of us, sire. It's Doria and his Genoese.'

'By Christ!' Alençon exploded. He turned to Brus. 'I shall deal with these bastards myself.'

Clouds were building up over the forest, the unmistakable anvil heads of thunder clouds. Tired from the heat and marching, the white-coated Genoese plodded wearily up the road. Alençon galloped through them, scattering them and lashing out with his riding whip at any who were slow to respond. 'Doria!' he shouted. 'Get these men off the road! At once, do you hear me?'

Ottone Doria turned his horse. 'Why?' he asked coldly.

'Your peasants are blocking the way. Move them and allow my men through.'

Doria shook his head. 'I have orders from the king. I am to lead the line of march and cover the rest of the army while it deploys.'

'Lead the line of march? Christ's blood, Doria! *I* command the vanguard, not you! Now get these men off the road!'

'No,' said Doria. 'I do not take orders from you.'

Another horseman came galloping up; Brus, his face red with heat under his bascinet. 'Blois and Lorraine are close behind us. They are demanding that we move forward so they can get to grips with the enemy.'

Doria slapped his thigh in anger. 'Do they teach you nothing about war in this country?' He pointed towards a distant huddle of houses. 'That village is called Marchemont. When we reach it, we will be able to see Crécy and the enemy. I will deploy my men there and move forward, and you will follow me. Those are the king's orders. Is that clear?'

'It will be done,' Brus said curtly, and he turned his horse.

Alençon lingered for a moment, eyeing Doria. 'There will be a reckoning between us,' he said.

Out on the far horizon, thunder growled. 'I look forward to it,' Doria said. 'Now, if there is nothing else, your Imperial Majesty, we shall resume our march.'

—

The clouds towered over them now, dark bellies pregnant with lightning. Couriers rode in, all telling the same story. 'We have forty thousand men crammed in on half a dozen roads,' Hainault said. 'The captains are not following the order of march. The men-at-arms are riding ahead too quickly and apart from the Genoese the rest of the foot soldiers are lagging behind.'

King Philippe bit his lip again. 'What do you suggest we do?'

'Halt and make camp. We can use the rest of the day to restore order to the army and make certain each company is in position. At the moment, everything is darkness on the face of the deep.'

The king looked at him. 'Do you think if I ordered the captains to halt now, they would obey me?'

Hainault said nothing. 'I know what is happening,' the king said. 'I know there is a conspiracy against me. Isn't there? Are you part of it, by any chance?'

'No, sire,' Hainault said steadily.

'Are you telling the truth? I wonder. If I order a halt now, my brother will disobey me. He will attack and very likely defeat the English without me. This will be Alençon's victory, not mine. His prestige will increase, and mine will decline. Men will murmur against me, more than they do already. But perhaps that is what you want.'

'I want what is best for you, sire,' Hainault said. 'And for France.'

'Of course you do,' the king said ironically. 'Therefore, the march to Crécy will continue as planned. Make it so.'

First came the thunder, booming in the air and reverberating off the wall of the forest. Hailstones followed, quickly turning to pelting rain, soaking the tired and hungry men standing waiting on the slope above Crécy. For a while the valley below them was blotted out entirely, but after a few minutes the rain began to ease and the archers saw the fields and the distant road again.

But something had changed. The road was moving now, crawling with motion. As the curtain of rain lifted a little further, they saw the white coats of Genoese crossbowmen marching steadily forward. They waited, holding their breath, as more and more of the enemy came spilling out from behind the forest. 'Christ,' breathed a Red Company archer. 'How many of them are there?'

'Thousands,' said Pip.

'Five thousand at least,' Fletcher said quietly. 'They must have emptied half of Genoa.'

Matt touched her cap. 'Do we string up?' she asked.

'Not yet,' said Fletcher. 'Not until the rain stops.'

'What if it don't stop?' someone asked.

'It'll stop,' Pip said. She pointed at the sky. 'Storm's clearing. There's blue sky in the west.'

'Aye. But will it clear before the Genoese come within range?'

Silence fell. The archers waited, listening to the patter of the rain and the sound of their own fast-beating hearts. The Genoese were swinging off the road now and moving into battle formation, long dense lines marching steadily towards them, crossbows at the ready. Behind them, bright colours blurry in the rain, came the first men-at-arms, hundreds of them pouring down the road after the Genoese.

The rain continued. The Genoese tramped steadily forward. They were a quarter of a mile away now, with a huge mass of mounted men, several thousand of them now, pressing eagerly behind. 'They're getting close,' Matt said.

'Wait,' said Fletcher.

Down the hill a trumpet called, and the Genoese began to shout, five thousand voices roaring in the rain. '*Morte!*' they bellowed. '*Morte! Morte!*' Their voices echoed like thunder around the valley.

'What does that mean?' asked Pip.

'Death,' another archer said.

'Christ,' someone else whispered. 'They're getting awful near, Rob.'

'Wait,' Fletcher said again.

Pip looked up. The blue sky was over their heads now, and there came a sudden dazzle of sun. A few final raindrops flashed golden in the light and the storm was gone, grumbling away into the east. A rainbow danced against the clouds. Three hundred yards away, the Genoese halted and presented their bows. 'Christ,' a voice whispered again.

A black storm of crossbow bolts filled the air. The English archers tensed, bodies waiting for the impact, but the bolts fell short, plunging into the rain-softened earth in front of them and kicking up little spurts of mud. One landed almost at Matt's feet; the others were yards away.

'String your bows,' Fletcher said.

–

'For God's sake!' Doria snapped. 'Why can't we hit them at three hundred yards?'

'We're shooting uphill, my lord,' one of his captains said. 'And the bows are wet. The strings are losing their tension.'

'Advance fifty yards and try again.'

A trumpet sounded. Chanting once more, the Genoese marched forward. Doria watched the enemy ranks ripple into motion, the archers stringing their bows and reaching for arrows. 'They are preparing to shoot, my lord,' the captain said.

Doria frowned. 'Do they think they can hit us at this range?'

'We're about to find out...'

The air whispered, and then was torn apart by the passage of a thousand arrows. One hit the captain in the neck, two more piercing his body, and he fell to the ground. Doria's horse was hit in the same instant, and the animal collapsed and pitched him out of the saddle.

He fell heavily, rising with his white surcoat stained with mud, and stared in disbelief. The air was full of whistling death, arrows falling from the sky in clouds; all around him men were going down in heaps, their coats stained with blood.

'Retreat!' he shouted to the trumpeter, but the trumpeter was already dead.

The rest of the Genoese had not waited for the signal; they were running, desperate to get away from that hideous rain of arrows. Doria followed them, gasping as he laboured on foot. The French horsemen crowded forward, and he heard Alençon's voice raging at the Genoese. 'Stand firm! Stand firm, you bastards!'

'For Christ's sake!' Doria screamed. 'Can't you see what is happening? They are slaughtering us!'

'Cowards!' Alençon spat. 'Cowards and traitors, all of you! *Come on!*' he shouted to his men. 'Ride the bastards down!'

'No!' Doria yelled, but it was too late. Lowering their lances, Alençon's men charged straight into the packed mass of crossbowmen, and the killing began.

–

The Genoese had betrayed them; that much was clear. They had taken English bribes and were refusing to fight. Alençon rammed his lance through the body of one crossbowman, felt the lance shatter, dropped the butt and drew his sword, slashing at the heads and shoulders of others. Up ahead, he saw Doria seize a crossbow, fit a bolt to the stock and shoot one of the French men-at-arms; the bolt punched through the man's breastplate, and he slumped and fell from the saddle. Other Genoese were fighting back too, but Alençon ignored them. He rode straight towards Doria, bloody sword in hand. Rollond de Brus was beside him, yelling and waving the rest of his men forward.

Doria had reloaded. He raised the crossbow again, aiming at Alençon, and squeezed the trigger. The bolt hit the count's shield, splitting it in two. Ignoring the splintered shards hanging from his arm, Alençon raised his sword. Doria lifted the crossbow to ward off the blow, but Alençon smashed it out of his hands and raised the blade again. The second blow tore Doria's face open and he fell to the ground, his head gouting blood.

Hailstones rattled off the armoured men around him; had the storm returned? No, by Christ, those were arrows; the English were shooting again. A horse fell, throwing its rider; another went down kicking and thrashing. Furious that mere peasants should be shooting at his men, Alençon rose in the saddle, waving his sword. 'Come on!' he shouted. 'Kill the bastards! Montjoie Saint-Denis! Come on, come on!'

Shouting and screaming, the men-at-arms of the vanguard raced up the slope after him. The arrows lashed at them like furies, hundreds falling every second. Further up the slope came a blast of white smoke, and stone shot whirred in the air. Alençon's horse screamed as an arrow scored across its neck, and he felt the repeated hammer blows on his armour, then a stab of pain as one found the gap between his cuisse and his knee guard. He tried to pull the shaft out of his leg, but was encumbered by his broken shield. Another arrow rammed into his shoulder, splitting his armour, and his arm went numb; he realised he had dropped his sword. He was disarmed, with the enemy only a hundred yards away. A wave of panic washed over him. He turned his head and yelled to Brus. 'Christ, I'm hit! Get me out of here!'

Three arrows protruded from Brus's shield. 'You led us into this hell,' the Norman said violently. 'You get yourself out of it.' He turned in the saddle, waving his sword. 'Montjoie!' he shouted to his men, '*Montjoie!*' and he spurred his horse up the slope, the rest of the French swarming after him.

'Halt, God damn you!' Alençon shouted through a haze of pain. 'Obey my orders!' No one heard him. His horse was hit again, and came to a halt. He tried to spur the animal into motion but it would not budge, and then an arrow shot by an eighteen-year-old woman from Warwickshire smashed through his visor and the front of his skull and drove into his brain. By the time his body hit the ground, he was already dead.

–

Standing by the windmill, Tiphaine could see everything clearly in the rain-washed air: the blizzard of arrows, the clouds of pale smoke belching from Courcy's cannon, the charging mass of French men-at-arms disintegrating steadily, men and horses going down every second. She saw too with dismay that there were too many of the enemy; even shooting fifteen arrows a minute, the archers could not kill enough to stop them. She saw the blue and gold colours of Alençon fall, and then another coat surged into the lead as the French raced up the slope, and she felt suddenly sick. It was the red saltire of Rollond de Brus.

She had to admit he had courage, not a virtue she had ever ascribed to him. The archers had marked him out; the air around him was thick with arrows, and she saw him hit twice, then again, but he never wavered. Behind him the arrows took their deadly toll, whittling his men away, but the rest forged on, dragged up the hill by his unflinching will. They were thirty yards from the English line when his horse was shot and foundered, throwing him to the ground. She had a brief glimpse of the red saltire moving feebly before the wave of armoured horsemen rolled over it. Then he was gone.

The rest of the French did not pause. Lowering their lances, they crashed up the slope and slammed into the English line like a battering ram.

–

The Welsh spearmen held the first line of French attackers, but as more and more of the enemy charged home, they began to give way. The line of battle disintegrated, French horsemen surging forward, the Welsh and English men-at-arms trying desperately to stop them. Merrivale saw Despenser and Mortimer fighting back-to-back, saw Gurney wrestling on the ground with an armoured French knight, Thomas Holland duelling desperately with two mounted men circling around him swiping at his head. Shouts and screams and the hammer of metal filled the air.

'Come on!' yelled the Prince of Wales, and he ran forward into the fray, followed by Fitz-Simon the standard-bearer. The French spotted his coat of arms at once, and Merrivale heard men shouting behind their bascinets, 'Le Prince de Galles! Take him, take him!' The prince paid no heed, slashing one of Holland's assailants hard across the leg, plunging through to help Mortimer and Despenser, fighting with desperate enthusiasm.

'Ware your back!' Merrivale shouted, but he was too late. Another French man-at-arms rode up behind the prince and raised his sword. The blow crashed down onto the prince's helm with a shower of sparks, and he fell hard to the ground. Fitz-Simon stood over his body, standard in one hand and sword in the other, slashing at the French who circled around him like hawks over a kill. The sword rose and fell again, and Fitz-Simon collapsed beside his master.

Merrivale ran forward and picked up the standard, ripping the fabric away from the wooden pole and gripping it like a quarterstaff. The horseman who had knocked the prince down rode up to him, armour dented, surcoat shredded by arrows, and pointed the tip of his bloody sword at Merrivale's throat. 'Do you yield?' he asked.

Merrivale looked at him (*three gold boules on a red fess*, his herald's mind told him; *the Count of Aumale*). 'I am a herald,' he said. 'I am protected.'

He could hear the sneer behind the bascinet. 'Then you should have stayed away from the battlefield, herald. I have killed the Prince of Wales. Now I will kill you, unless you yield.'

The first blow of the staff smashed the sword out of Aumale's hand. Reversing his grip, Merrivale aimed the second at his head, knocking his bascinet off; before it had hit the ground, the third blow fractured Aumale's skull and he reeled out of the saddle. Sensing rather than seeing the men behind him, Merrivale whirled around, ducked under the belly of an onrushing horse and clubbed another man to the ground. Standing over the prince's body, he fended off the blows aimed at him, splinters flying from the staff. A detached corner of his mind said, *I cannot hold them for long. Not alone.*

And then, he was no longer alone. Holland was beside him, and Salisbury and Despenser and Mortimer, and Gurney guarding their backs, and they fought with a desperate fury that stunned the French and drove them back. For a few moments the enemy circled them, probing with sword and mace, looking for an opening. 'Christ,' said Holland through his teeth. 'We're outnumbered.'

'Nothing new,' said Mortimer. His arm was dripping blood.

'Let us make a good death, gentlemen,' said Despenser, and the French turned again and closed for the kill.

But even as the first blows fell, the wolves began to howl, '*Rouge! Roooooouge! Rooooooouge!*' and the Red Company were there, smashing bodily into the French and shoving them back. Warwick and Sully followed with a phalanx of men-at-arms behind them. Three of the French went down in a moment, and the bloody spears rose and fell as they lay on the ground. The rest, bleeding and battered, broke and fled down the hill, desperately trying to escape the arrow storm and return to their own lines.

Merrivale leaned on his broken staff, gasping for breath. Thomas Holland knelt over the body of the prince, unfastening his bascinet and feeling his neck. 'Praise God,' he said, and when he looked up, there were tears on his face. 'He is alive.'

–

'They're running out of arrows on the front line,' said the messenger. He was panting with effort, having run all the way from the prince's division to the baggage train. 'We need volunteers to carry them down to the archers.'

Mauro and Warin were on their feet at once, other men crowding forward. 'Me too,' said Nell.

'All right, lass. We'll strap them to your back, like so.'

The arrows were in bundles of four dozen; they were not heavy, but they were bulky to carry. They strapped five bundles across her back, loading her like a donkey, and she tucked two more under her arms and ran after the others down towards the prince's division, passing the guns on the way and smelling hot metal and the strange brimstone stink of the burnt serpentine. The last of the French were galloping down the slope, still pursued by arrows. The men down at the far tip of the wedge would have been shooting longest, she reasoned; they would be most in need of arrows. She ran along the ranks of the archers until she came to the men in the red iron caps.

'I brought arrows,' she said breathlessly.

'Good girl,' said the master bowman. He unfastened the bundles and began handing round the arrows. Other archers came in from the field where the dead men and horses lay thickly on the slope, carrying more arrows with bloody points that they had pulled out of the corpses. Pip was one of them, holding an arrow that still had a string of flesh hanging from the barbs. 'Did you bring any water?' she asked.

'No. I'll bring a waterskin next time.'

'Do it, and I'll light a candle for your soul.' The ground vibrated to sudden thunder, and she looked around sharply. 'Here they come again. Get down, girl, and stay behind me.'

Another French company was launching itself up the hill, bright banners flowing, lances levelled, men shouting 'Montjoie! Montjoie Saint-Denis!' The archers waited, tense and still, arrows embedded point first in the ground in front of them. Crouched behind Pip's legs, Nell heard someone murmuring a prayer.

'Steady,' the master bowman said quietly. 'Wait till they're in range...'

There were fewer horsemen than before, only a few hundred this time, but the drumming of their hooves was deafening and the ground shivered. Sudden panic seized Nell, and she looked around for somewhere to run.

'Now,' said the master bowman.

Pip nocked an arrow, drew back the string to her ear and released. The first arrow was still in flight when she shot the second, and then she and all the archers around her became machines, nock-draw-release, nock-draw-release, nock-draw-release, over and over without pause. The grey-feathered shafts rose and fell, descending on the French like hail. Looking between Pip's legs, Nell saw men falling and dying, some pierced with arrows, some trampled under the hooves of horses running mad with pain, more arrows sticking out of their bodies like pins in a cushion. She heard the shouting and screaming, the cries for help, the hoarse exhortations to charge on, charge on, until the French battle cries of *Montjoie!* were finally drowned out by the sounds of death.

The enemy almost made it to the English line; the last horseman was shot down so close that his mount rolled kicking and thrashing in among the archers, knocking several down. Its rider lay on the ground a few feet from Nell, and she watched with fearful fascination as blood poured from the breathing holes in his bascinet. Then he gave a long groan of pain as his soul left his body, and lay still.

'That's the last of them for now,' Pip said. She looked down at Nell. 'Go on, girl, we need more arrows. And don't forget that waterskin.'

–

The second attack had been led by the Count of Blois (white bend on blue, the herald's mind recorded with detachment) and his brother-in-law the Duke of Lorraine (three white eagles on red). Both men were shot down within a few yards of the English line and their followers recoiled back down the bloody slope. 'They attacked without support!' Warwick said sharply. 'What in hell were they thinking?'

No one answered. The prince was on his feet, groggy, bleeding from a head wound; Fitz-Simon was up too, tying the standard to its battered staff. 'You are wounded, Highness,' said Burghersh. 'You should retire.'

The prince looked at him. 'Retire, and leave my friends to fight? No, Sir Bartholomew. While there is a drop of blood left in my body, I shall remain here.'

'By the looks of you, that won't be long,' said Roger Mortimer.

The prince glanced at the bloody cut on Mortimer's arm and grinned at him. 'You're one to talk.'

In front of them, another French company launched its attack, and then another. Each time the arrow storm hit them and shattered them, driving any survivors back down the slope. Along the face of the ridge the bodies piled up, and the air stank of blood. 'This is carnage,'

Holland said softly. 'The fools. They had us in the palm of their hand, and now they are throwing it away.'

Everyone knew the usual French tactics; form up in three divisions one after the other and attack in waves, the first division punching a hole in the enemy line, the second following to exploit the advantage and the third moving up to complete the rout. The French vanguard, after inexplicably massacring its own crossbowmen, had attacked according to plan, but there was no support. Now, a collective madness seemed to have overtaken the rest of the French army. Company after company came off the Abbeville road and attacked without thought or tactics, barely pausing to form up before launching up the hill towards the enemy. In companies of two or three hundred at most, they stood no chance. The archers slaughtered them like deer at a driven shoot.

Afternoon turned to evening, and still the French came, and still they died. A larger corps of horsemen rode into view, and a murmur ran through the English ranks. Even at a distance, the lilies of France could be seen plainly. 'The adversary is here,' said Sir John Sully, leaning on his sword. 'Now let us see what he will do. Will he call off the attack?'

'I think it is too late for that,' Merrivale said.

—

'Mary, Mother of God,' John of Hainault said quietly.

Men wandered dazed and wounded and bleeding, or simply sat on the ground in a stupor with arrows embedded in their bodies. Riderless horses galloped in confusion and pain, sometimes knocking men over. Beyond them were the dead Genoese, and then the slope of the ridge carpeted with dead horses and the bright motionless figures of men. Above them the English waited, the setting sun haloing their position with light.

Beside him the king sat motionless, staring at the scene. 'What in Christ's name has happened?' he said finally. 'Where is my brother?'

'I don't know,' Hainault said. He called to a man-at-arms, his surcoat and armour stained with blood, leading a limping horse. 'Montmorency! Where is the Count of Alençon?'

'Dead,' said the marshal. 'They're all dead. Alençon, Blois, Lorraine, Aumale, all of them.' He shook his head wearily. 'We were lambs to the slaughter.'

Hainault nodded. 'Go and get your wounds seen to,' he said. He sat for a moment, thinking. This was a disaster, but it could still be salvaged. It had been a mistake to rely on Alençon, but a replacement could be found. 'Your Grace, we must halt the attack. Withdraw, make camp, give the men time to recover and then resume in the morning.'

'Withdraw?' The king stared at him. 'Are you mad?'

'Sire, we have suffered heavy losses, but most of the army is intact. It is jammed together on the roads behind us, unable to get near the battlefield. Give the men tonight to rest, and then tomorrow form them up and attack in orderly fashion. Do you remember what I said? The principles of war?'

'To hell with your principles,' the king said violently. 'If I withdraw now, I may as well abdicate. The nobles will spit me out like gristle and feed me to the dogs. No, Hainault. We are going to attack, and if we die, at least we will have died with honour.'

'And let Edward win the victory?' Hainault said steadily. 'And perhaps seize your throne?'

'If he can take my throne and hold it, he is welcome to it.' The king shook his reins. 'Trumpeter! Sound the attack!'

There was nothing to do but ride forward, surrounded by the royal bodyguard, horses tripping and stumbling over the bodies underfoot, watching the grim lines of steel and the dark wedges of archers facing them. Hainault saw the bows come up and braced himself for the shock. Then the arrows fell in clouds, so thickly that they darkened the red sun, and the air was filled with the dreadful tintinnabulation of arrows striking armour and the screams and shouts of horses and men. The standard-bearer, the target of the storm, was shot half a dozen times in as many seconds and fell from his saddle. The king tried to snatch the standard before it too fell, and yelped in pain as an arrow slammed into his arm, piercing his vambrace and spouting blood. Another hit him high on the shoulder, wedging itself between breastplate and gorget. One after another the royal bodyguard went down, and the enemy were still two hundred yards away. The English cannon thundered once more, stone shot slamming into the French ranks and completing the wreck.

'Sire!' Hainault shouted. 'You must withdraw! Now!'

Transfixed by pain, the king said nothing. Hainault seized his bridle and turned his horse, yelling at the rest of the men to follow. The arrows pursued them for a moment longer, and then faltered. In near silence they rode back towards Marchemont.

'Damn you, Hainault,' the king said finally, his voice hoarse with pain. 'This is all your fault.'

'Yes,' Hainault said. 'I think it probably is.'

–

The sun had set and twilight was drifting in when the Bohemians arrived at Crécy. 'I smell blood,' said the blind king. 'Tell me what you see, Rožmberk.'

'It is over,' Rožmberk said. 'How, I do not know, but we are defeated. The French army has been wrecked. I can see no sign of King Philippe.'

'And our plan? Wrecked too, I imagine. Edward wins the victory. He is unassailable now. And our friends have lost.'

'I fear so,' said Rožmberk. 'France will have to rally behind its king if it is to survive. Civil war now would be equivalent to handing the country over to the English.'

'And so it ends,' Jean of Bohemia said. 'All my life, I dreamed of empire. Twice before I have been thwarted. This time, I thought it was within my grasp.' He shook his head, staring towards the enemy with unseeing eyes. 'It was the last gamble,' he said. 'And now, it is time.'

Two of his knights looped their reins through the king's, so that his horse should not stray. Slowly, for the rain-wet ground had been churned to mud and the bodies in places were piled high as breast-works, the Bohemians rode up the hill. In the final few minutes of his life, Rožmberk wondered what had gone wrong. Nanteuil and Hainault were inclined to blame Tracey, but that was wrong; Tracey was only the money man. It was the other Englishman, the arrogant bastard who treated them all, even Alençon, as if they were pieces on a gaming table; he was the one who had overreached himself, and it was his blunders that had sent them to their deaths.

In the falling shadows they heard the twang of hundreds of bowstrings and saw the flashes of light as the cannon fired, and then the steel rain began, arrows sweeping through the Bohemian ranks and scything men and horses down. King Jean and the men who guided him went down at once, horses and men all riddled with arrows. Rožmberk saw them fall, just before two arrows hit him in the neck. He tugged at them, seeing his hands covered in blood, feeling his strength draining away, and then the world went dark.

The Bohemian attack failed in blood and wreckage, and its survivors retreated into the gathering shadows. Night fell on Crécy-en-Ponthieu.

27

As darkness fell, the English army lit torches and set them around the perimeter of their position, in part in case the French should mount a night attack, but mostly, Merrivale thought, to ward off the ghosts of the thousands who lay dead on the slopes below. He found Tiphaine near the windmill, staring into the darkness with enormous eyes. 'You are unhurt,' she said. 'Thank God.'

'Give thanks instead to Thomas Holland,' the herald said. 'You are shivering.'

'I watched him die. Rollond. He went down, and the others rode over him.'

The herald watched her for a moment. 'Are you sorry?'

'No. The world is better without him.' She looked down at her hands. 'But all the same, it was hard to watch a lover die.'

Someone came out of the shadows, the big spearman from the Red Company, the one called Jacques. 'Sir Herald? We apprehended a man just now, a Franciscan friar. He says he has a message for you.'

Raimon Vidal was waiting by the wagon train, guarded by two more spearmen from the Red Company. 'Simon, my friend! I am glad to see you alive.'

'And you also,' said Merrivale.

'Ah, I was nowhere near the battlefield. Cardinal Aubert believes that men of God should also be men of peace and stay as far from the fighting as possible. Do you wish to know where Sir Edward de Tracey is?'

Merrivale paused. 'Where?'

'He has taken refuge with the Knights of Saint John, and has joined their order. He is with them now, at their camp near Saint-Riquier, between here and Abbeville.'

'Should I believe this?'

'My dear friend, I have absolutely no reason to lie. You have won. The conspiracy is smashed. Alençon is dead, Rožmberk is dead, Doria is gravely wounded, Grimaldi and Louis of Vaud have withdrawn and Tracey has been exposed and forced to flee. Hainault must abandon his plan, or at least postpone it. The day is yours.'

'But why betray Tracey to me?'

'So that you will owe me a favour. I may wish to call it in one day. And also, my master will appreciate the service you are about to do for him.'

Merrivale raised his eyebrows. 'Service?'

'Think about it,' said Vidal.

Merrivale thought. 'One game has ended, another begins. Cardinal Aubert wishes to attack the Knights.'

Vidal smiled. 'The destruction of their sister order, the Knights Templar, was a great success. The confiscated lands of the Templars added greatly to the wealth of the papacy, and of many kingdoms including France. Seizing the lands of the Knights of Saint John in France would add greatly to his Eminence's power, and he would be one step closer to the throne of Saint Peter.'

'There is little loyalty amongst your confederates,' Merrivale said.

'None whatever. If you expose the Grand Prior of France for accepting a convicted traitor into his ranks, you will be assisting Cardinal Aubert's cause. He will thank you for it.'

'I am sure he will,' Merrivale said. 'Tracey was not the only Englishman involved in the conspiracy. Who was the other?'

'Cardinal Aubert prefers I do not tell you. He might have need of this man in future.'

'And if I discover who it is anyway?'

Vidal shrugged. 'Then it is in God's hands.'

Merrivale bowed his head. 'So it is. Thank you, Raimon. Journey safely.'

'You too, my friend.'

–

'We faced less than a quarter of the French army today,' Northampton said. 'There are thirty thousand men at least still in the field. We must assume that in the morning they will resume their attack.'

Skeins of mist swirled around the ridge, hiding the corpses from view. 'But they have been decapitated,' Warwick said. 'The adversary left the field wounded. Alençon and Bohemia are dead, and so are Blois and Lorraine and most of the others who could have taken command. Their army is leaderless now.'

'What do you have in mind?' asked the king.

'A counter-attack,' said Lord Rowton. 'At dawn tomorrow, before they have time to muster. The scouts tell us they are spread out, camped all across the country between here and Abbeville. We can exploit this before they have a chance to re-form. Sire, we destroyed part of the French army today. Tomorrow we can complete the work.'

'I won't risk the whole force,' the king said. 'Take five hundred men-at-arms and two thousand archers, and do as much damage as you can.' He looked at Northampton. 'William, you are in command. Thomas, Eustace, go with him.' The three men nodded.

The king turned to the herald, waiting to one side. 'You wish to speak with me?'

'I know where Edmund de Tracey is, sire. He is with the enemy at Saint-Riquier.'

'Is he, by God?' The king turned to Rowton, then paused and looked instead at Warwick. 'Order the Red Company to go to Saint-Riquier tomorrow morning. Herald, you'll go with them. Bring back Tracey, or bring back his head. I don't care which.'

The mist had risen in the night and turned into a cold, clinging fog that draped like a blanket over the fields and forests. Drops of water hung from the leaves and branches of the trees, and dew glittered on the grass. Visibility in the dawn light was not much more than a quarter of a mile.

The Red Company had stuffed wadding around the bridles and bits of their horses to reduce the noise, and they moved almost soundlessly through the fog. 'It's an old Border trick,' Sir John Grey said. 'Both sides do this when they are out stealing cattle.'

'An interesting example to follow,' the herald said drily.

'We learn where we can. Who knows? We may need to take up cattle-stealing ourselves one day.'

Shapes in the fog ahead, the pavilions and tents of a French encampment; they had already passed two of these. Northampton and Warwick, following behind, would deal with them. Grey raised a finger for silence and then motioned left, and the column slipped away through the fog.

Leaving the camp behind, they passed over broad open fields. The light grew a little stronger, the fog swirling around them. More silhouettes loomed up, houses this time, and beyond them the tower of an abbey church, dark and indistinct. Grey held up his hand again and the column came to a halt. Richard Percy, who had been scouting ahead, rode back to join them. 'The Knights are there,' he said. 'Some in the houses, some in tents in the meadow beyond. The Grand Prior's banner flies over the gateway of the abbey.'

'Then that is where Tracey will be,' Merrivale said. 'Nanteuil will keep him close, I think.'

'The Knights are supposed to be neutral, under the protection of the pope,' Percy said. 'Are we certain we want to do this?'

'The Prior of France is not neutral,' Merrivale said. 'Nanteuil has mustered his men and is serving in the adversary's army. As one makes one's bed, so one finds it.'

'The Grand Master will be angry,' Grey said.

'The Grand Master is far away on Rhodes, killing dragons,' Percy pointed out. 'He has other things on his mind.'

Sudden commotion in the fog, the distant sound of shouting as Northampton and Warwick began to overrun the sleeping camps. 'Let's go,' said Grey. 'Quickly, before they are alert.'

The Red Company exploded out of the fog, surrounding Saint-Riquier on three sides and riding hard into the town, men jumping down from the saddle and shooting or stabbing the startled knights and their retainers who came running out of the houses. Grey, Percy and their esquires, followed by twenty archers and Merrivale, rode straight to the abbey gates, ignoring the fighting around them. Two of the red-cloaked Knights of Saint John who tried to bar their way were shot down in pools of blood; the rest fled. 'These fellows really aren't as tough as I thought they would be,' Richard Percy said.

'I agree,' said Grey. 'My money is on the dragons.'

Behind them, the brief carnage in the streets was already over, the surviving knights fleeing across the fields into the safety of the fog. More red-capped men ran up to the gatehouse, pushing an empty wagon. 'Battering ram,' Grey explained. 'All right, Jacques, break it open.'

Rammed by the wagon, the abbey gates opened with a splintering crash and the archers raced inside. Two more knights were shot down in the courtyard almost before they could move. Grey, Percy and Merrivale rode through the gates and dismounted. 'Where is Nanteuil?' Grey asked.

'I am here.'

Jean de Nanteuil walked out of the abbey church, his cloak with its white cross swirling around him. He held a loaded crossbow in his hands. 'In the name of Christ,' he said sharply. 'You are committing blasphemy! Those men you killed were crusaders, sworn to the service of God. And you have stained this holy place with their blood.'

'Where is Edward de Tracey?' Merrivale asked.

Nanteuil's eyes narrowed. 'What do you want with him?'

'To see justice done to a traitor.'

'Justice done to a traitor,' Nanteuil repeated slowly. 'How ironic.' He raised the crossbow, aiming at Merrivale. Bowstrings twanged in unison, and Nanteuil fell down the steps of the abbey, arrows protruding from his chest and neck. His body twitched once and lay still. Blood pooled on the worn stone, shining in the dim light.

Percy stepped over the body and walked inside the church. He returned a moment later. 'Tracey is there,' he said. 'He is at the altar, claiming sanctuary.'

'Sanctuary be damned,' said John Grey. 'Bring him out. Use whatever force is necessary.'

Two archers dragged Tracey outside. He wore the same red cloak as Nanteuil, over a simple robe, the habit of the Knights; he was neither armed nor armoured. Blood ran down his face from a cut on his forehead. The archers held him upright, arms pinioned behind him, and Merrivale walked slowly forward to face him.

'So this is how it ends,' Tracey said.

'Yes,' said the herald. 'But you knew the risks.'

'I did.'

'Then there we are.' Merrivale turned his head. 'Sir John, Sir Richard, ask your men to fetch a rope, if you please.'

Tracey stared at him. Blood dripped down onto his cloak, staining the white cross of Saint John. 'You're not going to hang me,' he said.

There was a long silence. 'No,' Merrivale said finally. 'Tempting though it is, I shall instead do something rather worse. I intend to bind you and take you to face the king whom you betrayed.'

Tracey's hands were tied tightly behind his back. The archers dragged him into the saddle and more ropes secured him to the horse. 'Take him out,' Merrivale said.

Around them the Red Company were mounting and riding though the gateway. Out of the gloom came a single arrow, hissing a little in the wind, and Tracey sagged sideways, the feathered shaft protruding from his chest. The herald froze in shock, looking around to see a lone archer throw himself onto the back of a horse and ride hard away. There was just time to see his face before the mist swallowed him.

It was Nicodemus.

28

Eight miles north of Crécy stood the abbey of Valloire, its gardens bathed in mellow sunlight. Bees buzzed around the last summer flowers, and a heron stood fishing in the pools of the nearby river. The air was tranquil and calm.

Wagons rolled up outside the abbey church and gentle hands lifted the dead men and carried them inside. The commoners, including the Genoese, had already been laid to rest in pits dug at the battlefield. It had taken four hundred men all day to bury them.

'What will happen to the bodies?' Tiphaine asked.

'The remains of the French army are regrouping around Amiens. We have sent messengers with a list of the dead, telling their families to come and collect them if they wish. Those not claimed will be buried here.'

He looked at the young woman. 'What about Brus? Will his family come for him, do you think?'

'No. He is not one of the dead.'

'But you saw him go down.'

'I did,' said Tiphaine. Her face was very still. 'I was certain he had been killed. But I asked Master Northburgh. No knight bearing a red saltire was found on the field.'

'Then he may have survived,' Merrivale said. 'Perhaps his friends discovered him once darkness fell, and carried him away.' He paused. 'I am sorry.'

'For what?'

'That this might somehow cause you distress.'

'I am not distressed. Mostly I am angry, because I wanted the bastard dead. But a little piece of me still feels the sentiment. He really was beautiful to look at.'

They watched the wagons roll slowly forward. The heron continued to fish, undisturbed. 'But that was in the past,' said Tiphaine. 'For the first time since I escaped from prison, I am beginning to realise that I am free.'

'What will you do with your freedom?' Merrivale asked.

'I do not know.' She looked up, the bruise on her face dark in the sunlight, and smiled her sudden smile. 'But when I decide, I promise I will tell you.'

'In Saint-Lô you spoke of needing to avenge your father. Have you done so?'

The smile faded. 'Perhaps. I don't yet know. I have learned that vengeance does not change the past.'

'No,' Merrivale said. 'It does not.'

'And you? Have you found justice for Sir Edmund Bray?'

'Yes.' Merrivale gazed out over the river. 'But it has come at a high price.'

Roger Mortimer had been pale but composed when the herald told him what had happened. 'Edmund did not die in vain,' Merrivale said. 'He was the first to expose the traitors. Thanks to him, the plot is ended for the moment.'

'I suppose that will be some consolation to his family,' Mortimer had said quietly.

'What will you do now?' Tiphaine asked.

'Continue with my duties,' the herald said.

'That is not what I meant. Tracey, the man from the West Country, is dead, but what about the other? The man from the north. Will you try to find him?'

Three men had ridden to Berkeley Castle that dark night in 1327. One was Sir Robert Holland, and he was dead. The second was John of Hainault. The third was the one he must find.

Tiphaine studied him. 'Why does this matter so much to you? The king, the prince, the knights and archers, the little girl who drives the cows; why do you care what happens to them?'

Merrivale looked at the river again. The heron gazed back at him with round dark eyes. 'Because if I don't, I have nothing,' he said.

–

'Farewell, Sir Herald,' said Nell Driver. She dipped a little curtsey. 'I wanted to thank you for all your kindness. And the cheese.'

'It is I who should thank you,' the herald said. 'Where will you go?'

'Back to England. Master Coloyne says we have captured some ships at a village over on the coast. One of them is going to England with letters for the court. I am no longer needed here. It is time I returned home.'

'Then I wish you fair winds and a safe journey,' Merrivale said. 'You said once that you wanted to see what the rest of the world looked like. What do you think now that you have seen it?'

'I think it is beautiful and terrible all at the same time. I have seen things that filled me with horror and things that made my blood sing. But I'm not denying I'll be glad to see Southwick again, and feel its grass under my feet.'

'You have had your fill of adventure?'

'I think so. At least for the moment.' She smiled up at him. 'But perhaps when I am fully grown, I shall learn to shoot a longbow.'

'You will need to be very strong.'

'Try milking a dozen cows every morning and evening. That makes you strong.' She glanced up at the sun. 'I must go.'

'Farewell, Mistress Driver,' the herald said.

He stood by the side of the road and watched her small figure walk away, her back straight with confidence. When she reached a bend in the road, she turned and waved, and he saw the gleam of her teeth as she smiled. Then she was gone.

Acknowledgements

Many thanks to our excellent Editor, Kit Nevile for all his help and encouragement. It is such a joy to have a dedicated editor to work with. As ever our map-maker *extraordinaire*, Gary Beaumont, (and how wonderful to have him in the same very small Devon village) has come up with the goods and he coped with last minute changes with his usual good humour and grace. Thanks too to our careful and talented copy-editor Jane Selley, and to Michael Bhaskar at Canelo for showing such enthusiasm about archers and medieval spying when we first floated the idea past him at a drinks party. And finally thanks to Nick Venables for designing such a great cover.

We have, perhaps unusually, to thank two different agents for helping to bring this book to fruition. Its concept and early stages were helped on its way by our wonderful first agents, Heather Adams and Mike Bryan; a delicious lunch in Bruton not long before lockdown was crucial to the development of the book. Thanks are due to them for passing us on so smoothly to Jon Wood of RCW Literary Agency. It has been a delight to work with Jon on the book and we look forward to meeting him in person one day...

A Flight of Arrows has in some way been a long time in development as it draws on our work on the battle of Crécy which has been ongoing for over 40 years. It also, of course has drawn on our non-fiction book *The Road to Crécy* published in 2004. Some of the characters in the book (both real and fictional) have been floating around in our heads for decades and are old friends. So, perhaps thanks to all these "old friends" for being so persistent and hanging around while we found the right fictional vehicle for you.